The
Bookseller

ALSO BY TIM SULLIVAN

The Dentist
The Cyclist
The Patient
The Politician
The Monk
The Teacher

SHORT STORIES
The Lost Boys
The Ex-Wife
The Hunter

The
Bookseller

A **DS GEORGE CROSS** THRILLER

TIM
SULLIVAN

HEAD
of ZEUS

An Aries Book

9 7 5 3 1 2 4 6 8

A catalogue record for this book is available from the British Library.

ISBN (HB): 9781035910427
ISBN (XTPB): 9781035910434
ISBN (E): 9781035910441

Cover design: Matt Bray | Head of Zeus

Typeset by Siliconchips Services Ltd UK

Printed and bound in Great Britain by
CPI Group (UK) Ltd, Croydon CR0 4YY

MIX
Paper | Supporting
responsible forestry
FSC® C171272
FSC
www.fsc.org

Head of Zeus
First Floor East
5–8 Hardwick Street
London EC1R 4RG

WWW.HEADOFZEUS.COM

*For Steve Hawes, with thanks for all the encouragement
early in my career and a year-long tutorial in Simenon's
Jules Maigret, whose presence, I hope, haunts these pages
occasionally, looking over George's shoulder,
and whispering cogent words of advice.*

Prologue

'I have cancer, George.'

Raymond and his son George Cross were sitting in the presbytery kitchen of their friend Stephen, who also happened to be a Catholic parish priest.

George didn't react at all to this information, initially.

Then, 'I see. Where?' asked George.

'It's in my lung.'

'Has it spread?'

'Not as far as we know,' replied his father.

'What's the prognosis?' George continued, flatly.

'Difficult to say. But they're fairly optimistic. It's the kind of cancer that is operable and can normally be got out cleanly. A carcinoid. If that happens, then I should be clear,' Raymond said as positively as he could frame it.

George made a note of this. He then glanced around Stephen's kitchen.

'Why have we come here for you to tell me this?' he asked.

'In case you want to talk,' Stephen replied.

'With whom?' George asked.

'Me,' the priest replied.

'You're not an oncologist,' Cross pointed out.

Stephen smiled. 'I am not,' he agreed.

'Then I don't know exactly what we would talk about in this situation.'

'Your feelings, perhaps?' replied the priest.

Cross ignored this and turned back to his father.

'What are the next steps in your treatment?' he asked.

'Surgery.'

'Nothing else?'

'No, I'm very lucky. Like I said, it's a carcinoid and completely operable. I'll be cancer free afterwards, with no need for chemo, hopefully.'

'But not definitely.'

'No.'

'When is your next appointment with the oncologist?'

'The week before the op.'

'Which is when?'

'Six weeks.'

'No, that won't do. We'll need an appointment this week,' Cross insisted.

'What for?'

'Because I have some questions, and I think speaking to a consultant oncologist will be of more value to me than a Catholic priest.'

'Now you're just being rude, son,' replied Raymond.

George knew that his father only referred to him as 'son' when he was upset with him.

'It's not my intention to be rude. Just practical. Is that everything?' he asked.

'I'll call the surgeon,' said Raymond.

'What's his name?' asked George.

'Mr Moseby.'

George made a note of this, got up and left. Partly because he didn't want to cause any further inadvertent offence to anyone. But also because he wanted to get home and start researching carcinoids, together with this Mr Moseby. He needed to be armed with as much information as possible, before he met his father's consultant.

'I'm sorry, Father,' Raymond said as the kitchen door closed behind his son.

'Nonsense. He's upset. He just doesn't know it yet,' replied the priest, causing Raymond to smile at how well Stephen knew his son.

As George cycled away from the church he wasn't feeling at all upset. Concerned, yes. Surprised, no. His father had as much as told him something was amiss the week before. His father never lied to him. So, he was certain that if the diagnosis was terminal his father would have just come out and said so. He thought he was right about this or, if not, that he wasn't as au fait with how most parents function when it came to protecting their children from unpleasant news. George had to meet the surgeon, because if it came to his father's having to make any choices of a medical nature, he wanted to be involved. He was also aware that this was something one should do for a parent of advancing years. He would attempt to be helpful, rather than overbearing. But even as he thought of this, he knew the likelihood of it happening wasn't perhaps as great as it ideally should've been.

When he arrived home, he got straight onto his computer with the enthusiasm of an amateur genealogist who had just received an alert from ancestry.com that a distant relative from some far-flung, distant continent wanted to get in touch. He began researching carcinoid tumours for much longer than

he intended. It was only the sound of the urban dawn chorus –
bin men doing their weekly collection and the build-up of traffic
– that alerted him to the fact that he had just disappeared down
an internet wormhole of research that was eight hours deep.

I

Torquil Squire walked nimbly down New Bond Street. As nimbly as a well-preserved ninety-year-old can, that is. But there was also a sense of purpose about him that day. This wasn't conveyed solely by his determined perambulation, but also by the way he was attired. He was wearing a three-piece tweed suit, shirt and bow tie, topped off with his favourite fedora from Locks of St James's. He looked like a background artist from a period movie; something from a bygone age, which of course, at his age, he was. He'd worn this very suit sixty years before, walking down this same famous London street, heading for the exact same destination as this morning – Sotheby's. Sixty years on and the same size waist. How many people could lay claim to that? he thought. He nodded occasionally, acknowledging smiles from passing pedestrians, admiring his sartorial style. Perhaps it was the hat. He reflected how things had changed in the decades since he traipsed these streets as a book runner, particularly when it came to wearing hats. No one wore hats these days, unless you counted baseball caps, which he didn't. The wearing of a homburg or trilby often elicited curious looks nowadays. The city also smelled different. Gone, the soot and diesel fumes of the past. He missed them, even though he knew what damage they'd done to the atmosphere. Nowadays it was more like walking past a candy floss stall at an old funfair, with raspberry, strawberry and other fruit-scented clouds swirling over the shoulders of vapers and engulfing you as you walked behind them.

But nothing was going to dampen his spirits this day. He was in a determinedly good mood. Everything seemed perfect and positive in central London that morning. Even a couple having a heated argument on a street corner just made him reflect, wistfully, on the intemperate nature of young love.

He walked into the famous white building of Sotheby's with the familiarity of an Edwardian gentleman entering his favourite London club. He checked his pocket watch, suspended by a brass chain from his waistcoat, and made his way through to the auction room. He'd registered for this morning's sale and so picked up his numbered paddle. This, despite the fact that he had no intention of buying anything and everyone knew it. He'd travelled all the way from Bristol that morning, just to keep his hand in. To make early bids and then withdraw, so as not to influence the final price. Torquil Squire was a well-known and well-liked bookseller from the south-west. The proprietor of Squire's Rare Books in Bristol, where he lived quite comfortably in the attic above the shop, in panelled rooms, like a post-war Oxford don. He joked that climbing the stairs every day was what had got him to such an ancient age.

Ed Squire, now in his mid-fifties, lived nearby in Henleaze with his wife Victoria. Ed walked down to the shop in Berkeley Square early every morning, taking him just under an hour on a good day, to have a pot of tea with his father before opening up. When he arrived on this particular morning, he called up the stairs as usual, took off his coat and hung it up. There was no reply. His father was normally up a good couple of hours before Ed arrived. So, this was odd. Ed called up again. Still no answer. A knot of apprehension, familiar to anyone with nonagenarian parents, gripped his stomach. He ascended the stairs slowly, wondering whether the inevitable day, when he came to wake his father only to discover he'd died peacefully in his sleep, had finally arrived. But when he went into his father's bedroom, he found the bed had been neatly made and contained no paternal corpse.

The answer to his father's whereabouts was waiting for him on the kitchen table. A note in his father's glorious, Gothic, italic handwriting – always written in turquoise fountain pen – informing him that he'd gone on a day trip to London. Next to the note lay his mobile phone, unhelpfully. This meant there was no means by which Ed could get in touch with his frustratingly independent father. Today's trip could only mean one thing. He'd gone up to a sale. Ed had initially been worried by these trips, concerned that his father might go out on a limb and buy some egregiously expensive text, which he then expected his son to offload at a good profit. But as Torquil had explained to him, these trips were just a way of making him feel alive. He missed the buzz of the auction room. So revered and fondly was he thought of in the trade, he was always greeted by former colleagues with great affection, which was wonderful for his mental well-being. To his delight he would also occasionally be described to a younger bookseller as 'a legend of our trade'.

Ed made himself a cup of coffee and sat in front of his computer in the second-floor office, which looked out over the square. He didn't think it would take him long to figure out where Torquil had gone. There was normally only one sale a day in London, with all the big houses careful not to compete with each other and thereby dilute the buying pool. Sotheby's had a sale that day. He was happy just to know where his father was.

There were some tantalising books in the Sotheby's catalogue. In Torquil's buying heyday he would've been fully occupied. Buying books at auction was a bit like gambling, to his mind. It had the same associated highs and lows, just in an auction room rather than at a racecourse, or in a bookie's. He still felt a frisson of excitement when in the presence of a rare book. It was difficult to explain, but it had never left him. Even though not really bidding, he always got there early enough to get a seat at the front. This was so he could be as close as possible to the porters as they held up that day's treasures. The highlight of this particular morning was a third folio Shakespeare – extremely rare as the majority of copies were destroyed in the Great Fire of 1666 – and he was swept away by the vertiginous ascent of the bids which culminated in an unprecedented, record-breaking price of £1.2 million.

He rounded the morning off in what was becoming something of a ritual on these London trips, a self-indulgent treat. Lunch at Sotheby's Restaurant, with a glass of claret. He sat there, at his usual corner table, with a perfect view of the entire dining room, content to watch the comings and goings of many people he knew and, increasingly, a lot he didn't. Some people came over to pay their respects. Others settled for a wave of greeting from their table. There was only one fly in the ointment. Patrick Gibb of Carnegie Books, who seemed not only surprised to see Torquil there, but not at all pleased. He paused to make sure that Torquil had seen his displeasure. Then as he went to sit with his lunch companions, he changed seats so that he wouldn't be looking in Torquil's direction. In light of the last two years' events, this was unsurprising. Had Torquil been thirty years younger he would've gone over and punched Gibb's lights out. However, he wasn't going to let the wretched man spoil his day. The morning had been perfect in every way, he reflected. The effort of getting smartly togged up, walking to Temple Meads train station – weather permitting – and reading that day's auction catalogue on the train, filled him with a sense of purpose. With the feeling that, as ancient as he was, there were still things he could look forward to in life. There was nothing wrong in wanting to be part of a world he'd been at the centre of for over fifty years. Today's lunch had an unexpected highlight when the auctioneer came over to Torquil's table with that morning's extraordinary sale in his gloved hands, inviting the old man to have a closer look at it, before it left for the United States. He handed Torquil a pair of gloves so that he could examine the folio more closely. It was a delightful gesture by the auction house, which was both respectful and redolent of the, at times, familial nature of the book trade.

Feeling refreshed and invigorated, he decided to extend his stay in London through the afternoon. He walked over to Cecil Court, the former historic home of booksellers in London. He used to work as a runner here in the nineteen fifties. There weren't as many shops now as there used to be, and the old names had moved out, to be replaced by a new generation. But it was a nice stroll down memory lane. He walked past Goldsboro Books and turned right, up Charing Cross Road, past Any Amount of Books, one of the last surviving used bookshops on a road once world famous for them. He'd actually known Frank Doel, the head buyer of Marks & Co, whose correspondence with Helene

Hanff was later immortalised in the novel 84 *Charing Cross Road*, and the film and play thereof.

He took the underground back to Paddington station and reflected on what a charmed life he'd led, doing what he'd always wanted to do. How different it could have been, had a friend not asked him to run a book from a shop in Cecil Court to Bernard Quaritch's when he was seventeen.

Ed Squire was starting to get a little worried about his father's whereabouts as the sun started to set over the west side of the square. A golden hue warmed the limestone of the buildings and a couple of windows in the building opposite reflected the waning sun in a blindingly bright, bowling ball of an orb. He phoned a fellow bookseller in London, who he knew would have been at Sotheby's that day, and was assured that his father was in fine fettle. He then called his wife Victoria and told her he'd be a little late as he was going to wait for his father to get back.

Torquil slept on the train back to Bristol after a satisfying and tiring day, ignorant of his son's concern about him and safe in the knowledge that Bristol Temple Meads was the last stop and he therefore wouldn't miss it. Then he treated himself to a taxi home. The front door hadn't been double locked, which meant that Persephone had forgotten to do it, as was her wont. The irresponsibility of youth. He'd have to talk to her about it again. But as he opened the door to the book-lined hall he felt that something was amiss. Several books were on the floor, which was unusual. He called out 'Hello?' before ascending the stairs slowly and a little fearfully.

2

George Cross was having dinner with his father and mother when he received a call from Josie Ottey. Christine now ate with them every other Wednesday. It was a compromise, giving George ample time alone with his father on the other Wednesday, which she knew he cherished – inasmuch as George cherished anything, that is. Although she'd been slightly confused when she'd asked Raymond what they talked about, when it was just the two of them, to be told, 'Oh, nothing. We generally just watch *Countdown*.' She concluded it must just be the regular physical contact with his father that George needed. He was able to relax and be himself with him. Raymond was perhaps the only one in his life that he could do this with. He certainly didn't feel that way about her. Yet.

She hoped with time that might change, but wasn't overly optimistic. It had been agreed that Christine would move into Raymond's flat for a time after the operation, to aid with his recuperation. She was in the process of selling her house in Gloucester and moving down to Bristol. So it made a lot of sense. George was initially resistant to the idea. He felt it was yet another incursion of his mother into his life. But he saw the sense in what was, after all, only a temporary measure.

During dinner they were debating the merits of renting a hospital bed for the sitting room. It was George's idea, but

Raymond was having none of it and had become quite vexed by the very notion of it. He wanted to come *home* from hospital, not just to another hospital room, which was what his sitting room would feel like with that kind of bed in it. It was the refuge of the old and infirm, he told George.

'Which, I would suggest, describes your current state perfectly,' George replied.

Raymond was about to object when George's phone vibrated. It was unusual for it to ring in the evening. It could only mean one thing. Ottey and a new case.

'We have a body,' she said when he answered the call.

'Okay, send me the address,' he replied.

'No need. I'm outside,' she said.

'How did you know I was here?'

'I'm a detective. It's Wednesday, so it wasn't exactly a stretch.'

Ottey's car pulled up just along the road from Squire's Rare Books. There were a couple of police cars and a forensic van already there. Cross had actually been to the bookshop many times when he was young. It was based in a listed Georgian building in Berkeley Square, Bristol, just off the top of Park Street near the university's Wills Memorial Tower. The square itself was well preserved. Damaged during the Bristol blitz, the new buildings had been thoughtfully designed in the same Georgian style and stone. There was also a hotel now. Several buildings were owned by the university. A few other businesses occupied various buildings, with only a few still used as residences.

Ottey and Cross, now suited up, walked past the constable on the door, through the book-lined entrance hall and took note of the books on the floor. The building smelled musty, of old books – leather and sun-dried parchment. Cross liked bookshops and libraries. The latter in particular. He found it a comfort to know that if you were looking for something, the answer could probably be found within a library's walls. The books in Squire's seemed to occupy every available bit of space. They were absolutely everywhere. It was almost as if the ones in the hall had, of their own volition, moved down from the crowded upstairs to find a bit more elbow room for themselves below.

The ground-floor room had large sash windows overlooking the square. There was a desk near the door, which had an office telephone system on it, presumably for a receptionist. There was a long table in the centre of the room. A couple of leather armchairs flanked the fireplace in the centre of the wall opposite the door. A warm invitation for browsers to be comfortable and take their time as they decided whether to make a purchase or not. The front half of the room contained new books and looked much like a small independent bookshop. It seemed a little out of place to Cross. He didn't remember it being there before.

They walked up the staircase to the first floor. The stairs creaked suitably as they did so. The first floor was made up of two rooms, both lined from floor to ceiling with books. These seemed to be of a different nature altogether. The ground floor was filled with paperbacks of all genres and in all conditions. The books on the floor above were collections of leather-bound tomes with some old texts displayed in glass cabinets. In the room towards the rear of the building, also lined floor to ceiling with old books, there was a large antique desk in front of the window. It had a dark green leather inlay. The room looked like it hadn't changed in years. The desk was piled with books, all of which seemed to have scraps of paper protruding from them, with handwritten notes scrawled on them in tiny writing.

The body lay to the side of the desk. The surrounding rug and bare floorboards were stained dark red with blood. There were several narrow puncture wounds to the bookseller's chest.

'Do we know who it is?' Ottey asked one of the uniformed police officers.

'It's Edward Squire,' answered Cross. 'Son of Torquil Squire, whose establishment this is.'

'Did you know him?'

'Not really. Met him a few times when we were both adolescents. Raymond was a regular client of the old man. What time was the body found?'

'Eight thirty or thereabouts,' replied the constable.

'Where is Mr Squire senior now?'

'In the hotel on the corner, with the deceased's wife and a WPC.'

'I'll go and speak to them,' said Ottey. Cross said nothing. 'You okay with that?'

'Yes.'

He continued to examine the room. He looked around for a murder weapon but couldn't see one on first inspection. Maybe the forensic team would when they conducted a thorough search. He'd also get a team to search the surrounding area, the square and the adjacent Brandon Hill. This was a park area overseen by the Cabot Tower and a possible place for the disposal of a weapon.

Dr Michael Swift, the forensic investigator, arrived. Something of a George Cross fan boy, he was always happy to work on a case with him. Part-time goth who was also unusually tall, Ottey had once described him as 'Noel Fielding with six-inch lifts'. He admired Cross's methods and thoroughness, not least his success rate.

'Wow,' he said, coming into the room and looking around. 'What a place. I love it. I could so easily live here.'

Cross didn't understand why the young man would think a bookshop was such an ideal place for him to live but decided not to enquire. Swift's appreciation of the way Cross worked was fully reciprocated. He admired the way the young investigator plied his trade. Immensely thorough, he believed every crime scene had a story to tell. It was his job to find it. Cross liked the way, as he was doing now, Swift never rushed straight over to the victim, but stood and took in the whole scene first. Only then did he move. He remained in the door initially, without going anywhere near Ed Squire. One of the things Cross had learned over the years was that when you came across someone exceptional in their field, delegation was highly effective. Let them get on with what they did so well, and then interpret their results.

'I'll leave you to it,' said Cross and left the room.

'Alice sends her best,' Swift replied.

Alice Mackenzie was Swift's girlfriend. A former police staff officer in the Major Crime Unit, she had recently started a course to qualify as a detective. The decision had come after she was assaulted sexually by a superior officer and decided she wasn't going to live her life as a victim. She was in the first few months of a two-year course at the University of the West of England and the police HQ in Portishead.

Cross simply nodded acknowledgement of this, then remembered what Ottey had told him about conversational cues. He was fairly sure this was one. He also remembered he'd thought about Mackenzie himself only the previous week and wondered how she was getting on. Now was his opportunity to find out.

'How's she faring?' he asked.

'She's loving it, but then again, she is in the comfort of a classroom. It'll soon be a different kettle of fish when the reality of the job hits her.'

'Indeed,' replied Cross, satisfied that he'd fulfilled the current conversational requirement. He would tell Ottey this nugget of information about their colleague. In truth, not because it might interest her, but to prove that he did listen to her advice on social interaction. He left without saying anything further.

'I'll make sure to give her your best,' Swift ended by saying to the departing detective's back.

Cross walked up the stairs. The next floor was one large room. It was similarly replete with books but also large wooden sets of thin drawers which, upon investigation, seemed to contain various old prints and technical drawings. The rear of the room also housed a desk and appeared to be perhaps the administrative part of the operation. There were cardboard boxes filled with books everywhere, possibly recent acquisitions to be sorted out. Also, books with post-it notes with names and addresses on them and piles of folded cardboard containers to pack them in. The room was fairly chaotic, but it was an ordered chaos. Again, there were books everywhere, piled high on the floor. The books continued in piles up the side of the staircase to the top floor. Here he found a small bedroom with a double bed covered in an old-fashioned counterpane and blankets rather than a ubiquitous duvet. On the bedside table there was a framed black and white wedding photograph. It looked like it might date from the sixties. Opposite the bed was a large dark wood wardrobe. Next to it a full-length tilting mirror and a Corby trouser press. There was also a small kitchen with a gas cooker, a fridge and a larder cupboard. Cross felt the kettle, out of habit, as he left the room. It was warm. There was a cafetière with a bed of fresh coffee grounds at the base of it, a carton of milk and three mugs.

An airing cupboard was filled with towels and sheets and the hot water tank. There was one further door off the landing. He tried to open it but couldn't. He tried again. It was definitely locked. He looked through the keyhole and could see the rounded end of a key. It had been locked from the inside. Someone was in there. He went over to the stairs and called for another officer to join him. When he arrived, Cross knocked on the door.

'Hello? This is the Avon and Somerset Police. I am Detective Sergeant George Cross. Can you open the door?'

There was a pause followed by the sound of the key being turned and the lock clicking. The door opened slowly to reveal a young woman, probably in her late twenties, early thirties, Cross estimated, and clearly terrified. She had long, dark, curly hair and was dressed mostly in black with red tights. She looked like a librarian. She was as pale as a ghost and shaking involuntarily. Her forearms were covered with a huge number of bracelets which jangled as she shook. He thought she might be in shock.

Torquil Squire was sitting in the living room of the Berkeley Square Hotel with his daughter-in-law Victoria. Ottey was struck by how protective she was towards the old man, despite her own devastating loss. She looked up at Ottey with red-rimmed eyes.

'Was it theft? There are many, quite valuable, books in there,' she asked.

'It's too early to say,' replied Ottey. 'When was the last time either of you spoke to Edward?'

'Ed,' Victoria corrected her. 'He called me at around six to tell me he'd be home late as he was waiting for Pa to get back from London.'

At this the old man lowered his head into his hands and started to weep.

'If I'd come home after lunch as I intended to, this would never have happened,' he said.

'Stop it, Pa. It's not your fault. Let me check my phone,' Victoria continued, in quite a businesslike manner, Ottey thought. 'It was 6.07 when he called. The call lasted just under a minute.' Now she faltered. Ottey wondered whether it was because she had just realised this was the last time she would ever speak to her husband. Sixty seconds seemed such a cruelly short time for a last call.

'What made you delay your return to Bristol, Mr Squire?' Ottey asked.

'I was just having such a lovely day, I wanted to make the most of it,' he replied.

'Does anyone else work in the bookshop?' Ottey went on.

'Percy,' replied Victoria.

'Percy!' Torquil exclaimed, suddenly alarmed. 'We must tell her.'

'Her?' Ottey asked.

'Yes, Persephone. She works with me and Ed. She'll be distraught. Vicky, you must call her,' Torquil insisted.

'I think maybe in the morning. No point in calling her now. There's nothing she can do, and she won't get any sleep if I do,' Victoria replied.

'How long has she worked for you?'

'Just under four years. She's my great-niece,' Torquil explained.

'By marriage, not blood. She's my brother's daughter,' Victoria clarified.

Ottey found this distinction unnecessary and a little strange. Why did it matter? Victoria did seem in complete control of herself and the situation, though. This despite the fact that her husband had just been brutally murdered.

'Persephone!' Torquil proclaimed, looking over to the door.

Ottey turned and saw Cross leading a young woman into the sitting room of the hotel.

'Percy, what are you doing here?' asked Victoria.

Cross turned to Ottey.

'I found her locked in the bathroom. I think she's in a state of shock and possibly needs medical attention.'

'The bathroom? What were you doing in there?' asked Victoria.

The girl didn't answer. Couldn't answer. She just stood there, still shaking, her eyes in a catatonic-like stare.

'Why was she there?' Victoria asked Cross.

'I'm unable to tell you,' he replied.

'This is DS Cross, my partner,' explained Ottey.

Cross held up his warrant card to back this statement up. Torquil looked at him for a second. His face was now grey and the lines in it deeply engraved with sadness.

'George Cross? I know your father,' the old man said.

'Raymond. That's correct,' replied Cross.

'You came here with him when you were younger.'

'Again, correct. My father is very interested in Brunel and as you are an acknowledged expert we often visited,' replied Cross, impressed by the bookseller's knowledge of his clients.

'How is he?'

'He has cancer.'

'I am sorry to hear that. He'd often pop in for a chat. He loved looking at Brunel's books, particularly the inscribed ones,' the old man reminisced.

'He did. I remember one particular occasion, you were selling some of Brunel's drafting instruments. You let my father handle them. He was quite overcome, I seem to remember. That the great man had drawn with them and he was now holding them in his hands,' replied Cross.

'He never bought anything, mind you,' Squire remarked with a cackle.

'Also true,' Cross conceded.

'But he was always welcome. Very knowledgeable about Brunel. Please give him my best.'

'I will.'

'Do you remember Ed? My son. He was always in the shop when he was a child,' Torquil reminisced.

'I do,' Cross replied, adding nothing further.

He became aware that Ottey was possibly sending him a cue. He thought for a moment, then realised what it was.

'I'm very sorry for your loss.'

'Thank you.'

'Does anyone else work in the shop other than Persephone?' asked Cross.

'Yes, Sam. But he was off today.'

'You should let him know what's happened. That the shop will be closed for a period while we investigate,' said Ottey.

'I'm not at all sure it would be right to open anyway, in the circumstances. In fact, if ever,' muttered Torquil.

'That's a conversation for another day, Pa. Not tonight,' replied Victoria. She then lost her composure and started to cry. Cross turned to Persephone.

'What were you doing locked in the bathroom, Persephone?' he asked her. She said nothing and just stared at the floor.

'Did you see anything, anyone, Percy?' asked Ottey. The young woman suddenly let out a loud howl.

Victoria, still sobbing, moved over and took Persephone to a small sofa. They sat and she put her arm round her niece.

'We need to get her to a doctor,' suggested Ottey.

Cross surveyed the emotional turmoil in front of him. 'Agreed. Maybe we should reconvene tomorrow,' he suggested.

'Am I allowed to stay at home?' Torquil asked.

'Unfortunately, not. It's a crime scene,' said Ottey.

'They can both come and stay with me. I'll call my GP. He's a friend. I'll get him to come round and have a look at Percy,' said Victoria.

3

Raymond's operation had finally been scheduled on Mr Moseby's list, for the morning after Ed Squire's murder, as it transpired. It had been pushed back after weeks of discussion. That is to say, George's discussion and research. Raymond knew the path to the operating table was not going to be an easy one with George involved, and so it had proved, right from the first meeting with Moseby and George. But Raymond, always positive by nature, was actually looking forward to it. When he discovered it would be laparoscopic, he secretly hoped it might be performed by a robot. His only regret, if that was indeed the case, was that he would be asleep for the entire procedure.

George had done extensive research into carcinoid tumours of the lung. So much so, that this first meeting with the consultant oncologist became more like a police interview with a suspect than a medical consultation. George repetitively pressed the poor doctor on various aspects of the surgery, until he felt he'd received a comprehensive answer. The surgeon was charmingly unfazed, commenting that Dr Google had a lot to answer for these days. This confused George as he didn't know a Dr Google and certainly hadn't spoken to him.

'How many times have you yourself performed this procedure?' Cross asked the consultant.

'Over five hundred,' the surgeon replied calmly.

'George, please...' uttered his father in an attempt to bring the inquisition to an end.

'Raymond, these are completely normal and valid questions. Your son is quite right to ask them,' the consultant assured him.

'What is your success rate?' George asked, as if completely unaware that his father had said anything.

'Over ninety per cent.'

'How do you account for the other ten per cent?' Cross pressed.

'Every operation has its risks. Complications can arise. In this case, there is an added risk with your father being the age he is.'

'A risk of what exactly?' asked Cross.

'Death,' replied the surgeon candidly. 'Which is why I've advised your father to think very carefully about going ahead.'

'But he has a tumour. Surely it's imperative it's removed?' Cross pointed out.

'A slow-growing carcinoid. At his age there is an argument to be made, which indeed I have made, for leaving it where it is,' continued the surgeon.

Raymond looked uncomfortable. He hadn't shared this with his son.

'Because something else might kill him first?' asked George.

'Precisely,' said the surgeon, who was actually beginning to wish all of his conversations with patients' relatives were this frank and honest.

'I need to discuss this with my father.'

'I'm a little surprised you haven't done so, prior to this appointment.'

'We haven't discussed it, because my father neglected to mention it,' replied Cross.

'I understand. Perfectly natural.'

'Not to inform his son of all the pertinent facts?' asked Cross.

'I see it all the time. What you have to remember here is that it's your father's decision whether to proceed with the surgery.'

'I want it out, George. It's as simple as that,' Raymond began on the bus home.

'In the light of what Mr Moseby has just told us, I would question the idea of its being simple,' replied George.

'I don't want to spend the rest of my time worrying about Arthur growing inside me,' said his father.

Cross didn't say anything for quite a long time, checking he'd heard right.

'Arthur?' he repeated slowly.

'My tumour. Note the possessive determiner. Christine thought giving it a name would take away some of the fear,' his father replied, with as much dignity as someone relaying an idea they themselves think is absurd can. He was clearly unconvinced of the worth of this psychological trick.

'I see, and how is that working for you?' George asked.

'George, look at me,' Raymond replied. George turned to face his father. 'I am going to have this operation. It's what I want to do, and I'd like you, as I know you will, to respect that and help me.'

George thought about this for a moment and realised that it was a perfectly reasonable point of view.

'Very well,' he said finally.

'Thank you, George,' replied his father, relieved until—

'But we'll need to get a second opinion,' insisted George. Raymond sighed at the inevitability of this.

Having sought one, George finally concluded that Moseby was indeed the right choice to conduct the procedure and so the operation was now due to take place.

4

Ottey was determined to get hold of Cross that morning, the second he got into work. Her need to head him off had nothing to do with the case, but something altogether more significant for her fellow detective. She wasn't sure, although she had a pretty good idea, how he was going to take it. Carson had called a meeting at nine, ostensibly about the Squire murder, but also about her. This was why she needed to get hold of Cross urgently and speak to him. He arrived bang on nine, just as Carson was calling the assembled troops to order.

'George, could I have a quick word?' said Ottey, trying to usher him into his office.

'There's a meeting,' he replied.

'I know, but it's important I speak with you.'

'Josie? George?' Carson called over. 'Could I have you over here, please?'

Cross grabbed a seat and, as usual, placed it by the door at the back of the room – his escape route, if needed. Ottey sighed and walked over to her desk. This could now only go one way. The wrong way.

'So, Edward Squire, a well-known rare and antiquarian bookseller, was killed last night. DS Ottey and DS Cross were first on the scene. They will coordinate the investigation. All of you are here because you have been assigned to this case.

George will put together a plan of action and actions. We are still waiting on path reports and the results of the preliminary forensic investigation. I don't have much to say at this point. We don't have a murder weapon, so there will be a grid search of the surrounding area, which includes Brandon Hill.' At the mention of this large area of parkland, there was a collective groan around the room. 'I know, I know. I couldn't put a number on the amount of times I've been on my hands and knees on that hill.' This of course instigated a ripple of laughter across the room. 'Ha, ha. We'll reconvene in twenty-four hours for a progress report. Let's see if we can get this one wrapped up quickly and efficiently.'

People seemed to take this as a cue that the meeting was over, so started to get up and chat.

'One more thing,' Carson said. 'A piece of good news for a change, I think. Josie, would you like to do the honours or shall I?'

Ottey looked over at Cross nervously.

'Perhaps now is not the right time, sir,' she suggested hopefully.

'Detective Inspector Ottey is being modest, methinks,' said Carson, beaming from ear to ear. There was a moment where people thought he'd mis-ranked her. Nothing was said as no one wanted to make a fool of themselves. 'Congratulations, DI Ottey. This was well overdue. I'm so glad you put in for promotion and, needless to say, you passed with flying colours.'

The place duly erupted with whoops of congratulation and scattered applause. Ottey looked over at Cross. He was staring at her completely impassively. Then the noise became too much for him and he left. Ottey was surrounded and so unable to follow him. She'd known about the promotion for some time and had meant to discuss it, or rather, tell George about it. But the time never seemed right. Then Carson had sprung the idea of this morning's announcement on her when she got into work. She knew how resistant Cross was to change and, with this being a big change, wasn't at all sure how he'd take it.

Cross sat on the stairs in the quiet back staircase, overlooking the car park, where he often sought sanctuary. He had been taken aback by Carson's announcement. Thoroughly discombobulated. Affronted, even. Why had Josie not seen fit to give him a little warning? Such a promotion had an implicit and fundamental effect on him at work. It meant working with another detective sergeant – a new partner. Experience had taught him that this was a far from straightforward prospect. Ottey had once commented he'd gone through more partners than Zsa Zsa Gabor, which had confused him as he had no idea who she was. People found him difficult to work with. He didn't deny this and had tried to counter this statement in the past by saying that he found it much more difficult to work with these people than they did with him. Unsurprisingly, this argument, if indeed that was what it was, held little sway.

But Josie Ottey had proved to be different. He hadn't held out much hope for them at the beginning of their working partnership. He was well aware of the fact that she had no desire to be partnered with him either. This had changed over time. On both their parts. He hadn't spent any time reflecting on this before, as he wasn't given much to pondering over personal relationships. Indeed, he didn't have that many. But he'd realised, as he left the open area that morning, that his working relationship with Ottey was the most successful he'd ever had. He may not have said as much to her – in fact he was pretty sure he hadn't – but they made a great team. What was more, he now realised and appreciated that she was the first person he had ever worked with who had made any attempt to understand him and try to help him. She tolerated things he did, said and how he behaved on occasion, in a way that others simply wouldn't have done. It wasn't until this very moment that he realised how much she had done for him and how grateful he was. This was quite some realisation. He was also aware that it was something he should impart to her, as it might be important to her. He resolved to do just this the minute he saw her. Rather than think of how he was feeling and the effect this would have on him, he would tell her how grateful he was, in a selfless gesture.

Then she arrived on the stairs.

'George...' she began.

'Ma'am,' he replied.

From anyone else this would have been laden with either sarcasm or irony, depending on how they got on with her. She knew it was neither of these with George.

'I'll have none of that crap, thank you very much,' she replied.

'You're my senior officer. It's a requirement.'

'Not in my world, George.'

He said nothing further. His recent resolution to inform her of his gratitude apparently completely forgotten.

'I'm sorry I didn't get a chance to tell you, but Carson sprang it upon me,' she said.

'I see,' replied George, knowing full well she must've known about it for weeks but for some reason hadn't seen fit to tell him.

'I know it must have come as a shock to you, but I just felt the timing was right for me. If I didn't do it now, I'd end up still a DS in my bloody mid-fifties,' she said, realising immediately that she was looking straight at a DS in his bloody mid-fifties.

'What a terrible thought,' he said.

'I didn't mean that. I'm sorry.'

'Why didn't you discuss it with me? You've had ample opportunity,' George pointed out.

'Um…' To anyone else her reply might have been, *Because it was none of your bloody business.* But this was George Cross. 'Because I wasn't a hundred per cent sure and I thought you might succeed in talking me out of it.'

'Why would I have done that?' he asked.

'Because you're very persuasive.'

'No, *why* would I have done that? What makes you think I'd want to talk you out of it?'

'Oh, I don't know.'

George knew from experience that people often said this when they didn't want to discuss something any further. So he changed the subject.

'Who will I be working with now?' he asked.

'Oh, we're not breaking up the band,' Ottey said, laughing. He looked at her blankly. 'There's nowhere else for me to be assigned to currently. So, we'll just carry on as normal.'

'Except that it won't be. Normal.'

'Nothing's going to change, George.'

'Everything's changed already. You're the senior investigating officer.'

'If it ain't broke, don't fix it,' she continued, earning her another look of incomprehension. 'Like I said, we'll just carry on as normal.'

'And like I said. It is no longer normal.'

'It's a new normal, George. Surely even you can work with that?'

He then remembered what it was he wanted to say to her

about how thankful he was for their time working together. How grateful he was for her help. He looked at her and tried, but nothing came out of his mouth. He froze. He simply couldn't work out how to say what he was feeling. So he said nothing.

'How's Raymond?' she asked, filling the interminable pause.

'He's fine.' Cross looked at his watch. 'He's having his operation at eleven.'

'He's *what?*'

'Having his operation at eleven,' Cross repeated.

'Then what on earth are you doing here?' she exclaimed.

'It's where I work.'

'You should be at the hospital.'

'Why?'

'Because he needs you.'

'To do what? Christine's with him,' Cross replied.

'But you should be there as well.'

'We have a case. Which is something I can usefully contribute to. There's nothing I can contribute to my father's surgery.'

'Fine, but we're going there at the end of the day.'

'Stephen's going and you're only allowed two visitors at a time.'

'Well, we'll figure it out. Did you tell him about Ed Squire?'

'No, I haven't spoken to him,' replied Cross.

'What? Since last night?'

'No.'

'You didn't even call this morning?' she asked, getting more exasperated, despite herself.

'He'd have been preoccupied.'

'Of course he'd've been preoccupied. He's having bloody major surgery. Which is why you should've called him to take his mind off it. You should call him now,' she went on.

'Why?'

'To wish him luck.'

'He'd find that odd and possibly alarming.'

'Why?'

'Because he knows I don't believe in luck in such situations. It's all down to the skill of Mr Moseby and how my father's body withstands the surgery. He also might intuit that I thought he was going to die.'

'Why would he think that?'

'Because he knows there's every chance, thanks to his age, that he will. It's something we have discussed.'

'What? Then why aren't you there?'

'I think we've already covered that, ma'am.'

'Well, I'm going to call him,' she said.

'Fine, if you think you should,' he said in such a way that, as he left, she genuinely didn't know whether to or not.

5

Victoria Squire and her husband lived in a modest post-war house in a road of similar dwellings in Henleaze, north of the city centre. Cross and Ottey parked in the road outside the house. They had driven there in silence, which wasn't unusual for them, although Carson's announcement may have had something to do with the current dearth of conversation. It was difficult to know. They rang the doorbell. The blurred shape of Victoria appeared behind the glass of the door. The house had the feeling of somewhere well lived, somewhere a family had been raised. The skirtings and walls still bore the scars of careless children's heels and prohibited games of indoor football. Cross reflected how different it was to the Georgian grandeur and interior proportions of Torquil's place in Berkeley Square. They did have one thing in common though. The house was filled with books. Wherever you looked, in bookshelves and piled up on the floor, against any available wall space. The general state of the house and furniture gave the impression that there wasn't necessarily a lot of money to be made in the second-hand book trade.

Charlotte and Sebastian, the Squire children, had driven down the night before. They seemed very protective of their grandfather, with Charlotte sitting on the arm of his chair. Less so with their mother, perhaps because she seemed to be coping with the situation by bossing everyone around and organising them. The two police officers declined her offer of refreshment and sat on chairs opposite the family, who had instinctively gathered themselves together. Persephone hadn't stayed the night. Victoria had provided her with a sleeping pill before she went back to her flat.

Ottey began the interview. She looked at Torquil, who seemed to have shrunk into himself a little since the night before.

'Mr Squire, can you tell us exactly what happened when you got home last night?' she began.

'The first thing I noticed was that the door wasn't locked. I thought for a moment Percy had forgotten to double lock it. She's always doing that. I've had a word with her. But she's young,' Torquil began. 'When I opened the door, I saw that a number of books had been knocked off the shelf by the front door.'

'Why didn't you pick them up?' asked Cross.

'Because I knew something was wrong. If Percy, Ed or Sam had knocked them over, they would've put them back. I called out, but there was no answer. I looked in on the ground floor room but no one was in there. That's when I noticed the smell.' Torquil faltered at this.

'What smell?' asked Ottey.

'When you've lived in the same place for decades and worked there, you know everything so well. Intimately. It's like a part of you,' the old man ruminated. 'The smell, it's so familiar. But you're never really aware of it until you've gone out and returned. Then you can sense it. As with all bookshops of its ilk, Squire's smells of learning, scholarship, creativity. But last night there was an unfamiliar smell. Metallic, like the inside of a metal container.'

This was, of course, the smell of blood, but neither Ottey nor Cross mentioned it.

'I went upstairs and found him. My boy. All that blood on the carpet. I knew he was dead before I touched him. He had these beautiful blue eyes, piercing, inquisitive, and they were quite dull.'

Victoria and Charlotte both sobbed as this image flashed before them.

'I checked for a pulse.' Torquil stopped, not needing to go on.

'Was the body cold or cool?' asked Cross.

'What? I don't know,' Torquil snapped for the first time, at Cross's indelicacy. 'Not normal. He was dead, for God's sake!'

'Has anything out of the usual happened in the last few months?' asked Ottey. The question seemed to be aimed at the room as a whole.

'In what sense?' asked Victoria.

'In Ed's personal life, or to do with the business? Any arguments or disputes with anyone?' Ottey expanded.

'No, not really. I mean, certainly not in our life. Not on the verge of divorce or anything like that. We're pretty boring, to be honest,' replied Victoria.

'Business is fine, isn't it, Pa?' Charlotte asked.

'As far as I know, yes,' he replied, then turned to Ottey. 'I'm a little more hands-off these days. I mostly write the catalogues for our collections…'

'He has quite the reputation in the books world for his catalogues,' said Charlotte. 'Some of the early ones are collector's items now, aren't they, Pa?'

'For the misguided few,' Torquil chuckled. 'I also sort out libraries we've acquired.'

'What are those exactly?' asked Cross.

'We often get families who want to sell their late parents', or maybe more distant relatives', libraries,' explained Victoria.

'And what happens then? What is the process involved in acquiring them?' asked Cross.

'Well, if it's an attractive proposition, Ed would go and examine them,' Torquil said.

'Just in the local area?' asked Cross.

'Good heavens, no. All over the country and even in the States on occasion,' Torquil replied with some pride.

'Did Ed always make these trips on his own?' asked Cross.

'If it was a large collection, he might take Sam with him, or Percy. He was trying to teach her the ropes until he realised her interest seemed to be solely in selling new books. Examining a library can be quite time consuming. Particularly if it's a sizeable one.'

'Had you come into possession of any significant libraries recently?' Cross went on.

'One or two.' Ottey noticed the bookseller's brow furrow a little. As if he was wondering where this line of questioning was going.

'Any issues?' Cross pushed.

'I'm not sure I know what you mean,' came the confused answer.

'Were the sellers all happy with Ed's valuations?'

Torquil paused slightly before answering. 'Yes, as far as I know.'

'But you're not certain. Which is understandable. As you say, you are much more hands-off these days,' Cross pointed out.

'Yes, but I still know what's going on. It's my name above the door,' he replied with noticeable irritation.

'Speaking of names, Torquil is fantastic,' added Ottey, trying to ease the situation slightly.

'Thank you. It seems to be one people remember.'

'Any financial problems?' Cross persisted, oblivious of Ottey's intention.

'With the business?' asked Victoria.

'Either with the business or you personally,' Cross replied.

'A few years ago, we had to remortgage the house to help with cash flow. It was after the pandemic. Lots of businesses obviously had problems then,' she said defensively.

'Which house?'

'This one.'

'Why not Berkeley Square?' asked Cross.

'It just seemed easier this way with Torquil's age,' she said.

'I don't understand.'

'It was just easier, is all I can tell you. Anyway, the business has paid it back. So we're all square,' she said.

'Marriage okay?' Ottey pried.

'Yes. I mean, we've had our ups and downs. What marriage doesn't? But we were perfectly content,' Victoria replied.

'Not happy?' Cross qualified.

'Yes. Happy. Everything was fine.'

'If you're asking in a roundabout way whether we know anyone who would want to kill Dad, the answer is no. He was a bookseller, not a member of the bloody mafia,' said Sebastian, speaking for the first time.

'Could we have a list of recent acquisitions made by your son?' asked Cross.

'All of them?' asked Torquil.

'Why not begin with any libraries at the higher end, value-wise.'

'I won't be able to do anything until I can get back into the shop,' Torquil pointed out.

'Of course,' replied Ottey. 'We'll let you know as soon as it's possible.'

As they were leaving, a taxi arrived. A man in his fifties got out of the back door. He had a cabin-sized wheel-along trolley case. He was tanned, as if just back from holiday.

'Ian!' Victoria exclaimed from the front door. She walked over and they hugged, the long, wordless, but fully loaded kind of hug you give your sister after her husband has just been murdered.

'This is my brother, Ian,' she explained to Cross and Ottey. 'I didn't think you'd be this early.'

'I got the first flight out of Malaga this morning. Oh, sis, I don't know what to say,' he said.

At this she started weeping and they hugged again. Sebastian and Charlotte appeared and joined their mother and uncle in a group hug of grief. Suddenly the road seemed a very private space. Not the place for a couple of murder detectives. Ottey indicated for Cross to get in the car, and they left, the bereaved huddle receding in her rear-view mirror.

6

Victoria had got hold of Persephone Hartwell, who'd then put in a call into Ottey as requested. She didn't want to meet them in her flat – 'it's a tip,' she'd said on the phone. But she was happy to come into the MCU and talk to Cross and Ottey, which she did after lunch that day.

'Are you not going to call the hospital and check on Raymond?' Ottey asked Cross just before the meeting.

Cross looked at his watch. 'He's still in surgery. Christine is going to call me when he comes round.'

Persephone was clearly still in shock from the previous evening's events. She was shaking visibly, her face unnaturally pale.

'Have you seen your doctor, or any doctor for that matter?' Ottey began by asking.

'No. I don't want to be medicated. I'll be okay. I imagine I'm just feeling what everyone else feels in these situations,' she replied.

'Can you talk us through exactly what happened last night, as best you can remember?' Ottey went on.

'I'd gone up to the kitchen to make Ed some coffee. He was waiting for Torquil,' she began.

'This is the kitchen on the top floor?' asked Cross.

'In Torquil's flat, yes,' she replied.

'What time was this?' Cross went on.

'Around seven, I think. I was putting the kettle on when I heard the door buzzer go. Then the front door closing.'

'So, someone came into the building? Ed let them in,' asked Cross.

'Yes, Ed has a door release next to his desk, as do I. I assumed it was Torquil, so thought nothing of it,' she said.

'Doesn't he have his own key?' asked Cross.

'Yes, but he's ninety years old. He does tend to forget things now and then,' she replied.

'So, Ed had let someone in?' asked Ottey.

'Yes. Then I heard shouting.'

'Straight away?' asked Ottey.

The young woman thought for a moment.

'Yes, I think so. I was filling the cafetière. One cup of coffee was never enough for Ed.' She smiled, then looked like she was about to lose her composure. 'He likes a cafetière.'

'There were three mugs,' Cross commented.

'I'm sorry?' she said.

'Three cups with the cafetière,' he clarified.

'Yes, one for Ed, one for me and one for Torquil, who I thought I heard come in,' she explained.

'What happened then?' Cross asked.

'I called down. There was more shouting. A commotion. Then Ed yelled like he was in pain. I went to the top of the stairs and saw a man run down and into the front room. I didn't know what to do. I went down as quietly as I could. I think I cried out as soon as I saw Ed. I knew he was dead. His eyes. There was so much blood...' She broke down. They let her compose herself, then she continued. 'The man was still there. So, I ran back upstairs and locked myself in the bathroom.'

'Which means you were there for almost two hours,' Cross commented.

'Was that all? It felt much longer than that. I tried to listen for the front door, but couldn't hear anything.' She started to cry again.

'Why didn't you call the police?' asked Ottey.

'I didn't have my phone. I'd left it downstairs. How did he die?' she asked.

'He was stabbed multiple times in the chest. Death would have been swift,' replied Cross. 'This man you saw. Can you describe him?'

'Not really. I mean, I was above him. He was walking away, and I was scared, to be honest.'

'Try,' Ottey encouraged her.

'I'd just seen my uncle pretty much dying, for God's sake,' she said, suddenly animated and sounding just like her great-uncle earlier.

'Was he big, small, average size?' Cross continued.

'Average.'

'What was he wearing?'

'He had a grey woollen hat. A beanie. Jeans, I think.' She began weeping. They waited till she gathered herself.

'Colour?' asked Ottey.

'Blue. But I'm not sure.'

'Coat?' asked Cross.

'A bomber jacket. The kind bouncers wear,' she replied.

'Why do you describe it like that?' asked Cross, wondering if some detail had led her there. She thought for a moment.

'Because it had a transparent, plastic pocket on one of the upper arms. You know, the ones they have their ID or licence, whatever it is, in.'

'Do you go to clubs much?' Cross asked.

'Gosh, no,' she laughed through her tears. 'But I've walked past them. I mean, some pubs even have them now.'

The detectives made no comment.

'There was one other thing. I mean, it may not be important. But when they were arguing I thought I heard an accent,' Persephone said.

'An accent?' asked Ottey.

'The man shouting had an accent. I think it may have been Russian.'

Cross made a note of this.

'Had anything unusual happened in recent months?' he asked.

'How do you mean?' she asked.

'Any problems with customers? People coming into the shop?' Cross went on.

'No. I don't think so.'

'Did Ed seem normal?'

'Yes. I mean, he was a bookseller. We don't, as a rule, have problems with customers. Our customers don't tend to be those kinds of people,' she said proudly.

'Well, thanks for coming in,' said Ottey, bringing the interview to an end.

'When will we be able to reopen the shop?' Persephone asked.

'In the next few days, hopefully. It depends on the forensic investigators,' said Ottey, who was left to reply as Cross had already exited the room.

Sam Taylor turned up to work that morning to find the normal oasis of quiet and calm cordoned off with police tape, police cars, a forensic investigator's van, as well as Michael Swift's SUV. No one had thought to call him the previous night to tell him what had happened. His resigned attitude seemed to imply there was nothing unusual in his being the last to know anything at Squire's Rare Books. He sat on the kerb, just outside the tape, his feet in the cobbled gutter. A police officer went to a nearby café and bought him a cup of coffee laced with sugar. The same officer took him home when he had regained a modicum of composure. Ottey and Cross decided to go and see him the next day.

7

Josie could sense from Christine's posture and expression that something was wrong the moment they entered the Intensive Care Unit of the Bristol Royal Infirmary early that evening. George didn't pick up on any such signals. Possibly because his attention was fixed on the figure in the bed. The fact that Raymond was in the ICU and not on the ward was obviously immediately concerning. Something must've gone wrong. He was also on a ventilator, which was breathing for him. Tubes and wires were attached to his father. Machines beeped incessantly. To George, this man, so capable, so quietly in charge, so innately understanding of him, looked stricken, diminished. His face was grey, like many corpses George had seen in his work. How could someone who, only hours before, had been a picture of health for his age – this despite the tumour in his lung – look so close to death? It was then that George turned to Christine, now being comforted in Josie's arms, and saw from her shrunken expression that things definitely weren't as they should be.

'He looks awful,' he said to her. 'Is he supposed to look like that? Is it normal?'

'DS Cross?' a voice enquired behind him. George looked and saw Mr Moseby walking towards him. 'Could I have a word?'

'Is he all right?' asked George who felt a wave of concern, possibly panic, pass through his body.

'Please follow me,' replied the surgeon, giving nothing away and leading him to a side office behind the nurses' station. It was similar to the way George and Josie often spoke to the relatives of victims. If George hadn't noticed the tone of voice, he definitely noticed the familiar expression on the doctor's face. It was the one he saw on Josie's face when breaking bad news to people. It was an expression he'd tried to emulate in such circumstances, without success. Josie had actually asked him to stop after a couple of attempts, telling him he looked like he was in pain. Surely that was the effect he was trying to convey, he responded. She then informed him it looked like the pain of someone constipated trying to evacuate their bowels. Not someone trying to express empathy. She followed George and Moseby into the side office.

'The removal of the tumour was completely successful. As we expected we were able to remove it in its entirety. It was actually in a very uncomplicated location,' the surgeon continued.

'But...' George interjected.

'But, as I told you and your father, this operation was not without its risks in a man of his age.'

'You did,' George agreed.

'We think your father may have suffered a stroke during the course of the operation,' the surgeon informed them.

'You think?' asked George.

'When he came round, he was unable to speak and there was no movement in his left side.'

'Why is he on a ventilator?' George went on. 'Is that a result of the stroke?'

'He began losing consciousness and the ability to protect his airway. That was why we intubated him and he was moved here, into the ICU.'

'How long will he be in this condition for?'

'It's hard to predict. A few days, perhaps.'

'What will the effects of this stroke be?' asked George. 'Will he be able to speak? Walk?'

'Tomorrow we'll scan his brain. Then we'll know more,' Moseby informed him.

'I knew Arthur was best left alone,' said George, getting up abruptly and leaving the room.

'Who is Arthur?' Moseby asked Josie after George was gone.

'I have absolutely no idea,' replied Josie. 'Can I give you my number if you need to get in touch with George? It's probably quicker and easier that way.' She gave him her business card.

'Yes, of course.' Moseby fumbled in his jacket pocket and brought out a business card of his own, which he then wrote on the back of. 'This is my personal mobile. Do call if he has any questions or concerns, which I imagine he will.'

She found George standing at the end of his father's bed. Josie thought he looked confused, possibly frightened.

'George?' Josie said quietly.

'Yes,' he replied and, taking this as a cue to leave, did just that. Without a word.

Josie turned to Christine and took her into her arms once more.

'Don't stay here too long. You'll need your strength for when Raymond wakes up,' she advised her.

'I know,' Christine replied.

'George…' Josie began, excusing her friend.

'You don't have to explain, dear. He's my son,' Christine replied warmly.

'Yes. He is,' said Josie, smiling.

Josie left the hospital and found George standing next to her car.

'I'd like to go back to my flat,' he informed her.

When he got out of her car some ten minutes later, without a word, and walked up to his front door, fumbling for his keys in his trouser pocket, Josie felt a huge pang in her stomach. He seemed so alone in that moment. If only he would let people into what he was thinking, what he felt, surely he'd feel so much better. Then she realised that the one person George let do that was lying unconscious in a hospital bed.

8

When Sam Taylor opened the door to his flat, he looked like a ruffled academic who had just been rudely woken from a nap between tutorials. He was in his late thirties, early forties, Cross calculated, with long, dark, frizzy hair sprouting bountifully from the sides of his head but not from the top. Together with his goatee beard, there was something of Hergé's Professor Calculus about him. He wore denim dungarees, a Viyella checked shirt and a pair of vibrantly yellow Crocs.

He was expecting the two police officers and let them in with a resigned, mournful gesture. His flat reflected his obvious bibliophilia. Cross looked around and saw there were books simply everywhere. Bookshelves sprouted up at all sorts of angles to the walls, often into the centre of the room. They filled the surround of all the door architraves. But he thought that even if it appeared a little cluttered, there was an odd sense of order about it all. It wasn't in the least bit chaotic. Sam obviously organised his collection with great care. They were shelved alphabetically by author and into genres; biography, history, fiction, first editions: something Cross was appreciative, almost admiring of. The top-floor flat, off Whiteladies Road, was also filled with a large collection of houseplants, all well-watered and in good condition. Not a brown-tinged leaf to be seen anywhere. Cross had often considered having houseplants in his flat and made a mental note to ask Sam about his maintenance routine, if a more appropriate opportunity presented itself.

He observed that Sam didn't look at either Ottey or himself for the entire time they were with him and wondered why this was. He made a note of it.

'How long have you worked at Squire's?' Ottey began.

'Over fifteen years now. Most of my adult life,' he replied.

'Is it a good place to work?' she went on.

'If you like books, it's perfect.'

'I can see that you do,' she replied, looking around the book-lined room.

He made no reply to this.

'What does your job entail?' she continued.

'Helping with acquisitions, cataloguing, that sort of thing, and running the shop. Well, helping to run the shop these days,' he replied.

'Could you explain?' Ottey asked.

'I was shop manager. Promoted ten years ago. I was only twenty-nine. It was a sign of faith by the old man, which is why I've stayed there so long.'

'Why might you have left?' enquired Cross.

'I've always dreamed of running my own business. What bookseller hasn't? But I felt I owed it to Torquil to repay his faith.'

'Torquil, not Ed?' asked Cross.

'Well, it was Torquil who promoted me. Not Ed,' came the reply.

'Could you please go back and tell us what you meant by "these days"? Has something changed?' asked Ottey.

'Not officially, but Persephone's arrival changed things

somewhat. She started to get more involved. Ed encouraged her to do so.'

'Was it Ed who brought her into the business?' asked Cross.

'Yes. Neither of his children are interested, which is fair enough. It's not for everyone and it's not exactly surprising that he would want to keep it in the family.'

'So, her arrival changed things?' Ottey went on.

'Not initially, but once she got her feet under the table, as it were. Yes,' he said a little testily.

'In what way?'

'You may have noticed that the front section of the ground floor is now populated with new books. It started with fiction but now includes non-fiction. This is Persephone's project,' he informed them.

'I get a sense you don't agree with it,' Ottey suggested.

'We're a rare and second-hand bookshop. It's what we're known for.'

'Were Ed and Torquil both agreeable to this change of direction?' asked Cross.

'Ed was, definitely. Torquil was less sure.'

'Why?' asked Cross.

'Because it was a significant financial outlay just for stock alone and there are major competitors already out there, who are well established. Torquil knows what his trade is, what his market is and has made a great success out of it,' Sam said, again answering the question without looking directly at Cross.

'Victoria told us that they'd had to remortgage their house, at one point,' Ottey said.

'Which was all part and parcel of funding this nonsense. Percy bought a vast amount of stock and couldn't shift it. She didn't know her readership yet. What they wanted to read. Did no market research at all. What they were looking for. Then she was remarkably inefficient at returning stock. You have a year to return to the wholesalers and she kept missing those deadlines. It was a nightmare. The wholesalers had Ed over a barrel. Her answer was to hijack part of the website and sell the stock at ludicrously discounted prices "to get a foothold in the market", she said. But you can't do that when Amazon and Waterstones have got their size twelve hobnail boots all over it. Everyone knows that. Ed gave her far too much power and to be honest with you it was a mistake.'

'Just financially, or in other ways?' asked Cross.

'Percy said new books would attract new, younger customers. But there are two problems with that. The location of the shop for a start. Shops selling new books rely on passing footfall. Our shop is off the beaten track, which is fine, because people with an interest in second-hand books know where it is and make a beeline for it. It doesn't have to be on a high street. It's part of its charm, if you like. They know they can come and browse, sit and read before they buy. It's a club of sorts. But there was no footfall, we're too far off Park Street. Customer numbers dropped off. Our traditional customers didn't like the changes to the shop. Her stock took up space for the second-hand stock. The new customers didn't turn up,' he told them, as if it was all so sadly predictable.

'Were you responsible for the traditional stock?' asked Cross.

'Absolutely. Then Ed had the nerve, during one meeting, to ask why my numbers were down. Well, you can't sell stock that isn't on display any more. It stands to reason, doesn't it?' he seemed to be asking them, in a genuine attempt to ascertain that he wasn't being unreasonable. 'I was furious,' he added and then looked like he instantly regretted it.

'It must be doubly upsetting seeing these changes knowing they're not going to work and then being proved right,' Cross observed.

'Of course. I mean, the notion that her books would attract a younger clientele was just nonsense. Even if it had worked, I doubt they'd've been interested in the second-hand stock.'

'People do love a bargain, though. Don't they?' asked Ottey.

'Sure, but a lot of that generation use Kindles and their phones these days. They don't buy books and if they do their first port of call is the internet to find the cheapest price,' he argued.

'Do you have regular management meetings with Torquil and Ed about the running of the business?' asked Cross.

'Of course,' he answered defensively, as if this question had implied a certain amateurishness about the business.

'And did you make your views known?' Cross went on.

'I tried, but Ed would have none of it. He was convinced it was the right direction for the survival of the business. Persephone's answer to my objections was that we should sell more of the used stock on the internet. As if we weren't already doing that,' he said, still addressing the carpeted floor.

'That must've made things quite difficult for you,' said Cross. 'What is your relationship with her like?'

'Professional. We tolerate each other. I've moved to the first floor with Ed now, which makes things a little easier,' he replied.

'How did you feel about that? Wasn't the ground floor something of your domain?' asked Cross.

'It was. For over a decade,' he said wistfully. 'I remember Persephone being brought in as a child by her mother and here she was, with no experience, usurping someone who had shown the Squires nothing but loyalty. Someone well-read with experience and taste.' He seemed to stop himself at this point.

Like someone who felt they had, or were in danger of, giving too much away.

'How have things been recently in the shop?' asked Ottey.

'Tense.'

'Any particular reason?'

'You have to work hard in the book trade. Get to know your customer base. Get on first-name terms with some of them, even. Curate your stock for them. Not just obtain what they want but be a source of knowledge for authors they don't know yet, but you know they will enjoy. Change your stock enough so they come back. Percy lets it go stagnant. Week on week it's the same books on the central table. They need to be refreshed regularly, otherwise people don't have a reason to return. To be fair to her she does try, in her own way. It's just that her ideas are so cart before the horse. Her latest idea was to introduce a coffee shop on the ground floor. This was too much for Torquil. He said he wouldn't have cups of coffee sploshing all over the place with all the rare books in the building. It caused quite a ruckus with Ed, which wasn't unusual, it has to be said. Then she wanted to start a book club. That never happened, of course. She has enthusiasm in spades. The ability to deliver, not so much.'

'In what way was the ruckus not unusual?' asked Cross who wished people would be more specific in these kinds of situations and not allude to things so vaguely.

'A father and son working together is often going to lead to different sorts of tensions, isn't it? Particularly when the old man has set it up from scratch. I mean, they have to try and develop a new relationship at work and move away from the personal,' he pointed out.

'And that was proving difficult?' asked Ottey.

'The truth of the matter is that everything was fine until Torquil gave control of the company to Ed.'

'When was this?'

'Just before Covid. Twenty nineteen, I think. Then things got a lot more difficult. Disagreements about libraries and collections to buy. The direction of the business. The internet. Torquil had always been resistant, but even he knew he had to move with the times.'

'What was the problem with the internet?' asked Cross.

'It's been a blessing and a curse for the second-hand bookseller, to be honest. On an esoteric level it's taken a lot of romance away from the book-collecting world. In the old days you had to do masses of research and even travel to get hold of a particular book for a customer. Torquil was particularly good at that and he loved doing it. Travelled to all parts of the world in order to acquire books. He was known as the Indiana Jones of the book world at his peak. But that might have had more to do with the hat, if I'm honest,' he explained affectionately.

'And that's all gone?' asked Ottey.

'A few clicks on a keyboard and you can find almost anything, wherever in the world it might be,' Sam replied.

'It's taken the fun out of it,' Ottey suggested.

'The fun and the adventure. But the main issue is the pricing. That's where Ed came a cropper, in my opinion. We'd be selling a book at a certain price then someone would come along and say they could get it somewhere else, on AbeBooks, for half the price. But they had no idea of the condition of the book or the authenticity of the edition. There were reasons it was priced as low as it was,' he told them.

'Such as?' asked Cross.

'The dust cover is a prime example. Pristine dust covers can add immeasurably to the price, especially with a first edition. But Ed would concede almost immediately on the price, just to get the sale. He was quite impatient in that way. Torquil got more and more frustrated that books he'd acquired, sometimes years before, and had valued properly, were being constantly undersold.' He stopped as something occurred to him. 'I should go and see Torquil.'

'I have one more question. What will happen to the bookshop now? The two children don't want it. Do you have any idea?' asked Cross.

'I don't know. It really depends on Torquil. I mean, this obviously wasn't the plan. I would imagine that Torquil still owns the shop. I just don't know. You'd have to ask Victoria.'

'Perhaps it might be left to Persephone to run it?' suggested Cross innocently. 'That would keep it in the family.'

'That would be insane and will never happen, despite her delusions,' scoffed Sam.

'What delusions?' Cross pushed.

'She talks, at times, as if the place will be hers one day. But to be honest with you, she lives in a parallel universe most of the time,' he replied.

9

'It's a real mystery,' began Carson. 'Thoughts, Josie?' He knew better than to ask Cross, and currently had nothing more to offer himself.

'Too early, but the number of stab wounds implies an angry attack,' she replied.

'So, someone he knew, you think?' asked Carson.

'Or someone he'd had dealings with. It doesn't feel random,' she went on.

'What do you suggest, George? Plan-of-action-wise?' Carson asked.

'I'm the junior officer here, sir. You should be asking DI Ottey that question,' replied Cross. Carson and Ottey exchanged a look. Cross couldn't help but go on, though. 'As always when nothing is presenting itself as an obvious line of enquiry, we should look at the victimology. Build up a picture of Ed Squire's life, both professional and personal. It's the only starting point we have.'

'Murder weapon?' asked Carson hopefully.

'None,' replied Ottey. 'We're still searching Brandon Hill, the surrounding streets, but nothing's turned up thus far.'

Clare Hawkins the pathologist didn't have much to help them with either.

'Death was fairly instantaneous. The weapon was about six inches long with a sharp tip and fairly blunt sides,' she said when they visited the mortuary.

'How can you ascertain that?' asked Cross out of genuine interest.

'From the shape of the wound. A knife with sharp edges would have left a different entry shape. I also found a fragment of something in one of the wounds, which I've sent on to Dr Swift,' she went on.

'Any idea what it was?' asked Ottey.

'Why don't we wait until Dr Swift has had time to conduct his tests?' Cross asserted. While he had no time for speculative ideas and she knew that, Ottey felt there was a slight irritation in his response, but said nothing. They hadn't had a chance to discuss her promotion and she thought he might still feel a little betrayed by her not giving him a heads-up.

Cross's phone vibrated. He would normally ignore this, but he checked, in case it was the hospital. It was. He answered it.

'Mr Moseby,' he said and left the room. Ottey stood up and followed.

'We've done the scan and I'm afraid it's not good news. There is a bleed on your father's brain. I have Dr Khan with me who's a consultant neurologist and is now in charge of your father's care. Obviously, I will be consulting with him, but this is his field of expertise.'

'Good morning, DS Cross. As Mr Moseby says there is a small, but not insignificant bleed on your father's brain and a certain amount of swelling. It's not uncommon in these circumstances but it does mean we'll have to keep him on a ventilator for the next few days,' began Khan.

'Is there any treatment for this?' asked Cross.

'Unfortunately, we can't give him blood thinners, which we would normally do at this point, as he's only just had surgery. But it's something we'll look at again in a couple of weeks,' Khan explained.

'What about a hemicraniectomy?' asked Cross.

'I see you've been doing your research, DS Cross,' said Khan.

'A little,' admitted Cross, although the truth was he'd spent most of the previous night researching strokes, brain bleeds and swelling.

'A hemicraniectomy is a massive procedure involving, as you doubtless know, removing a large part of the patient's skull to alleviate the pressure. But I wouldn't recommend it for a man of your father's age. The risk is far, far too great,' replied Khan.

'So, what do you propose?' asked Cross.

'We'll monitor him over the next couple of days, then do another scan. But it's really up to your father, and how much he is able to recover from this. As I'm sure Mr Moseby has told you, the prognosis is still uncertain. I'm so sorry.'

With the other member of their unofficial 'team', Alice Mackenzie, away, studying in her new ambition to become a detective, a new police staff officer was assigned to them. This was Prianka Patel. She seemed perfectly likeable to Ottey, even though she seemed to have a preternatural shyness about her. Possibly this was something to do with her diminutive stature. She was barely over five feet tall. Cross had been impressed by the way she'd helped them on a recent case and had requested her for this one. This was mainly because she was very methodical and adhered fastidiously to his instructions. She'd been tasked with looking into Ed Squire and the bookshop. They met with her for a catch-up, on their return from the mortuary.

'Anything of interest?' asked Ottey.

'Well, I'm not sure if it's of any interest, but I have found something, yes,' she replied.

Cross liked the modest clarity of this answer. Implicit in it was that it was not for her to determine whether something was pertinent to the case, but the two detectives.

'As I was looking into the victim, I discovered the circumstances in which Torquil Squire came into possession of the building in Berkeley Square. It was left to him by a wealthy, childless widow in the nineteen eighties. She was a frequent customer of his,' Prianka started.

'Bloody hell, that's a nice customer to have,' Ottey commented.

'At the time he co-owned a bookshop with Denholm Simpson, down near the BRI,' Prianka commented.

'It's still there, isn't it?' asked Cross who thought he'd noticed it on one of his recent visits to the hospital.

'Yes. It was called Squire Simpson, but now it's just Simpson's.'

'What else do you know?' asked Cross.

'Nothing. Simpson is still alive and working, he's a decade younger than Squire, so around eighty.'

Ottey thought Cross might be annoyed at the paucity of this information, but he didn't seem to be.

'Look further into Ed, rather than Squire senior. We'll pay Denholm Simpson a visit,' he said.

'I love these names – first Torquil and now Denholm,' said Ottey. Cross looked puzzled by this for a moment, then got up and started putting on his coat. Prianka took this as a cue that the meeting was over and also got up.

'Thanks, Prianka,' said Ottey as the young woman left. Ottey looked at Cross and thought, why can he not understand the need for the occasional expression of gratitude?

'Where are you off to?' she asked him instead.

'Are you not coming?' he replied.

'That's an odd question, as I have no idea where you're going. So, what makes you think I'd be coming with you?' she asked.

'Good point,' he answered. But instead of furnishing her with that information, he simply left. She, in turn, just sighed and followed.

10

As they drove past the Bristol Royal Infirmary, Ottey turned to Cross.

'Do you want to pop in as we're passing?' she asked.

'No. I'll go in after work.'

'Would you like me to come with you?' she asked.

'No,' he replied.

She smiled and made a mental note to text her mother and tell her she'd be late that evening.

Simpson's bookshop was on a sloping street near the hospital. The downhill nature of the street gave the impression that perhaps the shop was falling over, as it appeared to tilt down the hill. What was also instantly noticeable was the difference between this establishment and Squire's in Berkeley Square. This was a much humbler, less grand, establishment. More of an emporium of second-hand books. The inside of the shop was fairly chaotic. As if the owner had neither the time nor the energy to organise things in an orderly manner. It seemed predominantly a second-hand and used bookshop, rather than a rare and antiquarian dealer, like Squire's. There wasn't a leather-bound spine in sight. At the front of the shop was a small detached bookshelf with a scrawled sign saying, 'Everything under a pound'.

It gave Cross the impression that it might be run as more of a hobby than an actual business. There was no one in evidence.

'Hello?' Ottey called out.

Cross noticed a once white, now grubby, piece of string hanging from a bookshelf with another scrawled sign which said, 'Pull for service'. He managed to find a clean section of the string and did so. A small bell tinkled high above them. A few moments later a door with a reeded glass panel opened and a ball of white hair, in the middle of which could be two small black eyes, appeared. Denholm Simpson, for it was he, had a resplendently thick mop of hair on his head and a vast white beard almost covering his entire face, ending just below his eyes. His mouth was completely hidden somewhere in this hirsute undergrowth, its location indicated only by a brown nicotine stain. He looked like an out-of-control muppet on a windy day.

'I was just making tea. Would you like some?' he enquired politely.

'No thank you,' replied Ottey. Cross produced his warrant card.

'Detective Sergeants Cross and Ottey, Avon and Somerset Police,' he announced out of habit. Then he remembered. He held up his card again. 'Correction. Detective Sergeant George Cross and Detective *Inspector* Josie Ottey,' he said.

'Oh,' replied Simpson. The disappointment was palpable. 'And there was me thinking you might be my first customers,' he cackled with a modicum of self-reproach.

'You haven't had any customers today?' asked Ottey looking at her watch and seeing it was nearly three.

'Today? I haven't had any customers all bloody week,' he guffawed again. 'The police? What's happened? Someone stolen some books and you think I'm some kind of literary fence?

Come to think of it, chances are I've handled some hot tomes in my time. Almost inevitable. How can I help?'

'Edward Squire,' Cross began.

'Little shit bastard, son of a bigger shit bastard,' the bookseller said vituperatively. 'What about him?'

'Have you not heard?' Ottey asked, a little surprised as it had made the local news.

'What?'

'The little shit bastard was murdered a couple of nights ago,' Cross informed him.

'What?' This seemed to knock the wind out of the old man.

'Perhaps you'd like to sit down?' Ottey suggested. He did so, disappearing behind a mound of books, underneath which presumably there was a desk, behind which presumably was a chair. 'Can I get you some water?' Ottey continued.

'He was my godson,' Simpson began, ignoring her. 'I was a terrible godfather.'

Cross reflected that this was something of a modern refrain. One he heard frequently. So often, he wondered why people bothered with the concept of godparents any more. After all, did young people really believe they were renouncing the devil, when the chances were they didn't even believe in the existence of such a thing anyway? The only explanation he could come up with was that it satisfied a need to belong. That it was a badge of honour, which marked your membership of an elevated echelon of friendship. Something that went beyond normal, run-of-the-mill friendship, as it involved your friends' child. A fundamentally serious undertaking that, before long, wouldn't be taken in the least bit seriously. This was an instance in which Cross was quite grateful his life was without such friendships, and that being asked to be a godparent wasn't something he'd ever had to deal with.

'You were the business partner of his father, Torquil, for some time,' Cross observed.

'That's right. Is he okay? I should give him a call, I suppose, but...'

'But what?' asked Cross.

'We haven't spoken in over twenty years.'

'Why?' Cross pushed, even though they knew the answer.

'We used to be partners,' Simpson replied wistfully. 'Before he dumped me as soon as the opportunity presented itself.'

'What happened?' asked Ottey. 'Did it end badly?'

'Well, if I say I don't think this business ever recovered, what would you think?' he asked her. The two detectives said nothing. 'Do you see a rare or antiquarian book on these shelves? I can't even remember what a first edition looks like. I've just become a recycling centre for books that no one has any further use or room for. The council should be paying me a fee for the service.'

'How did you come to be in business with Torquil Squire in the first place?' asked Cross.

'That man owed me everything and what did he do? Left me high and dry. Then tried every trick in the book to force me out of business. It's one of the only reasons I haven't retired – to stick it to him.'

'Could you elaborate?' asked Cross.

'I won't give him the pleasure. Do you know he even tried to buy me out once? Early on. He had no real interest in it. He just wanted to close me down. Get rid of the competition and put me in my place, as he saw it.'

'You don't look much of a competitor to me,' said Cross.

Simpson laughed at this. 'Talk about getting straight to the point. I like you. You're quite right, of course. I have no idea why I keep going. A mixture of pride, I suppose, and the need to have something to do. It's a struggle, I admit. But it'd be more of a struggle if I gave it all up and just sat staring at the walls. I don't make any real money, but then again, I don't lose any. So why stop?'

'How did the two of you meet? You and Squire?' asked Ottey.

'Farringdon Road book market, London. He had a barrow. I used to buy books from him. I've always been interested in books. But I was a signwriter at the time. Something I didn't really enjoy, to be honest. Anyway, my father died unexpectedly and left me some money. Long and short of it, Torquil knew about a bookshop that was up for sale in Bristol. You're standing in it. We went into business together. It was terrific, until it wasn't. Happiest days of my working life,' he said ruefully.

'So you used the money from your dad?' asked Ottey.

'Correct. We couldn't have done it otherwise.'

'What were the terms of the agreement?' asked Cross.

The owlish man sighed a long sigh of regret.

'In many ways I was so naive. I owned, still own, the freehold of the building. But he supplied all the additional stock and bought half of the stock that came with the shop. So we were equal partners, pretty much, until Cynthia Sumner died and he left.'

'Were you upset?' asked Ottey.

'Of course I was. He wouldn't have been in a position to inherit from her if it hadn't been for our business, and our business wouldn't have existed at all without my finance.'

'Did he consider taking you with him?' asked Cross.

'You don't know him. Once a barrow boy, always a barrow boy. Look for the upside in any given situation. Take opportunities when and where they present themselves. He was used to always thinking on his feet, looking out for number one.

I tried to persuade him we'd be better off together. Use this as a second-hand shop and the Berkeley Square building as a rare and antiquarian establishment. We could become the south-west equivalent of Bernard Quaritch. But he was having none of it,' he said, with an ache which longed for what might have been.

'Bernard Quaritch?' asked Ottey.

'A leading rare booksellers, established in the mid-nineteenth century, still in business,' replied Cross, jumping in before Simpson had a chance to answer, relishing the opportunity to display his knowledge, as usual.

'It obviously hurt. Still does,' commented Ottey.

'That was just the beginning of it. First off, he tried to make me buy him out of half of the business, which I was in no position to do. So he took half of the stock and buggered off,' he complained.

'Why didn't you stop him?' asked Ottey.

'He did it overnight, didn't he? It was like a declaration of war. As I said, he seemed to make it his purpose in life, from then on, to put me out of business.'

'Why?' asked Cross who, from experience, knew there was always more to these kinds of stories than people let on.

'You'd have to ask him that,' Simpson replied tersely.

Cross would do exactly that when he got the chance.

'What was his background?' Cross asked.

'He started as a runner,' he replied.

'What's that?' asked Ottey.

'Someone who trawled around bookshops in the country and found things they knew a certain bigger London bookshop might be interested in. They bought it and then sold it for a profit. They also worked between the London bookshops themselves. If they couldn't afford a book and were well enough known by the bookshop, they might take it on approval and if they sold it, give the original bookshop a commission,' he explained.

'And he went from there to barrows?' asked Cross.

'Yeah, he wanted to work for himself, rather than just being an agent, or a go-between. A lot of them did it. Big business, the barrows in those days. There were several markets where you could find book barrows all over London. Farringdon, Shoreditch, Portobello Road. All pretty much gone now.'

'There's still one on the South Bank,' Cross commented.

'True, but it's very different. You don't get the quality of books you could unearth on the barrows.'

'Why?' asked Cross.

'Death duties played a big part back then in the availability of good books. People with country houses they could no longer hold onto sold their libraries. Believe it or not, just after the First World War, books were still filtering down from the French Revolution. There were so many around at one time that the big bookshops couldn't cope, so they found their way to the barrows. Those boys were ahead of their time in many ways. Far more entrepreneurial. Seeking out libraries for sale, rather than just waiting for them to land on their doorstep,' he told them.

'Was Torquil much of a success?' asked Ottey.

'Terence he was then. Tel. He changed his name when we set up the shop,' the old man scoffed.

'Really?' asked Ottey, a little disappointed.

'He thought it sounded more like a bookseller. But frankly Terence Squire sounds just as credible to me,' Simpson said.

'So he had the expertise, you had the cash and a desire to leave the graphic arts?' Cross put to him.

'Yes, pretty much. He had great taste. A terrific eye for a book, it has to be said. He also had this way of finding where the great collections were and persuading people to sell them even if they hadn't planned to. He was spot on when it came to valuing and pricing books. Absolutely nailed it every time,' he informed them.

'Was he a popular figure in the book trade?' asked Cross.

'Depends who you ask. He was very outspoken about certain things and had a tendency to rub people up the wrong way.'

'How?'

'Like I said. By getting access to private libraries before the London bookshops.'

'How did he manage that?'

'The man had spies everywhere. In all the great houses. That man had the contact details of more butlers and servants than an employment bureau for domestic staff. He was like a detective, following leads. Nothing made him happier.' He laughed. Ottey noticed an element of affection in the old man when he recollected this. It made it all the sadder, really. 'And then there was the whole ring debacle,' Simpson continued.

'The ring?' asked Ottey.

'It was a mechanism whereby big bookshops would go to auctions around the country and agree amongst themselves not to bid against each other, thereby preventing a proper auction taking place,' said Cross, jumping in again. 'This would keep the price low. They would then meet in a nearby hotel and hold another private auction. The prices would remain much cheaper than they would have been, had an uncontrolled open auction taken place. The difference between the auction price and the price paid in the ring would then be shared out among the members. A dealer who was a member of the ring could actually go to an auction, not make a bid or buy anything and walk away with cash in his pocket. All completely illegal, of course.'

'The detective knows his stuff,' declared Simpson, obviously impressed. The truth was, in this instance, that Cross had steeped himself in researching the world of bookselling in the days since the murder. But he was happy to take the compliment.

'As DS Cross says, it was illegal and completely unfair. Torquil didn't like it and said so. They tried to shut him up by inviting him to join. But he wasn't having any of it. Spoke out even more. He made quite a few enemies that way. Got him into a lot of unpleasantness.'

'Such as?' asked Cross.

'Threats of arson here at the shop. Physical threats. At one auction the bigger bookshops even employed a gang of thugs to surround Torquil and prevent him from bidding. It was quite outrageous.'

'Do you know who these threats came from?' asked Ottey.

'No. I mean, we had a pretty good idea. But this was decades ago. The ring petered out well before the millennium. I can't believe it had anything to do with this week's tragic events.'

'That's true,' Cross observed. 'But it shows that Mr Squire wasn't frightened of making enemies.'

'Was Ed a good bookseller?' Ottey asked.

'I think so. But as I said we haven't been in touch much.'

'Why's that?'

'The fallout from Torquil's leaving the business, and me in the lurch, has been long term. Ed became part of that problem, part of the opposition.'

George spent most of the weekend sitting at his father's side. He would normally work the weekends during an investigation, but he was instructed by none other than DCI Ben Carson he was to do no such thing while his father's health was in such a parlous state. There had been no change in his condition and another scan was scheduled for the beginning of the week. He and Christine mostly took it in turns to sit by the bed, giving the other a break. Stephen brought her back from mass on Sunday morning and stopped by to say hello to George, briefly.

George used the time at Raymond's bedside to think about the case. He may have been told to stay out of the office but that didn't mean he couldn't spend the time usefully reviewing where they were up to. Then a nurse suggested that Raymond might actually be able to hear George, so he began to run through the case quietly, out loud. This was useful in so far as it made him feel he was making good use of his time, but it also confirmed that they really had very little to go on, currently.

I I

Cross and Ottey met Michael Swift at the crime scene on Monday morning. Cross wanted to have another look.

'Detective *Inspector* Ottey!' declared the forensic investigator enthusiastically in the first-floor room where Ed Squire had been murdered. 'How cool is that! Well-deserved and not before time.'

Ottey smiled, before immediately looking over at Cross, who if he had heard and was in the least put out, didn't show it.

'Thank you. So what have you got?' she asked.

'Not a whole lot, truth be told. As you know, the victim was killed here, in front of his desk, indicated by the blood on the floor,' he replied.

The floor was bare floorboards except for a couple of rugs under the table in the middle of the room and Ed's desk. The blood had seeped into the wood and was congealed in a sticky black mess in the cracks between the boards.

'From what we've been told the victim answered the door from his desk. There's a release mechanism on the wall. No video, alas, just an intercom. Obviously he got up from the desk. There was an altercation and he was stabbed.'

Cross noticed various papers and books on the floor near the bloodstain. He looked around the room and saw that it was well ordered and organised. As was the desk. But there was a gap on top of it where the objects on the floor had fallen.

'I think those might've fallen off the desk during some kind of altercation,' Swift suggested.

'But there are no defence wounds on the victim,' Cross pointed out. 'Which would indicate he wasn't expecting the attack. It took him completely by surprise.'

'Which means he probably knew his killer,' added Ottey.

'I think the fact that we believe he let the killer in would suggest as much,' Cross pointed out.

'This is a difficult scene forensically, being a shop, which is why I'm still here. Added to the fact that there was no overtime available for the team over the weekend. *Plus ça change*. So there are multiple traces of DNA, probably fibres, from dozens of customers. All in all, I really don't think I'm going to be much use on this one,' Swift said a little mournfully. He liked to work as closely with Cross as he could, such was his admiration for the detective. But it had become rapidly obvious to him that this case wasn't going to furnish him with such an opportunity. 'It's a bugger,' he concluded. Cross left the room.

'How's Alice?' asked Ottey.

'Good, good,' replied Swift, the mention of his girlfriend bringing a smile to his lips. 'Really enjoying herself, while at the same time hating the idea of being a student again. Her time at uni still doesn't feel that far away.'

'We must catch up some time,' Ottey said.

'She'd like that.'

'Maybe a Sunday lunch. It's the only time I seem to be at home these days,' Ottey suggested, thinking adult company other than just her mother – who managed to imply disapproval of her daughter even when she simply said, 'Good morning' – might be a relief.

'I'll let her know. She's always asking about you and DS Cross. "The team", as she calls it.'

'I suspect it's mainly George she asks about,' she replied.

'True. Oh, I haven't told her about your promotion. She'll be thrilled. One thing though – does that mean the team will be split up?' he asked.

'It's quite possible I'll be transferred,' she said.

'I don't think you'll be going anywhere, now I think about it,' the forensic scientist speculated.

'Oh yes, and why's that?' she asked.

'You've got a secret weapon,' he reliably informed her.

'Which is?' she asked, playing along.

'No one can deal with George like you. No way Carson's going to give that up in a hurry.'

She hadn't thought of this before. The truth was, leaving the department was a possible, unwelcome, price to pay for her elevation. Unwelcome, because she wasn't a great one for change, and to her surprise, Swift's theory seemed to give her a moment's warm solace. It was in that same moment that she knew for the first time how the idea of not working with George was what was really gnawing away at her insides. Like the annoying mouse she'd found, by dint of her children's screams, chewing through all the cables leading to their TV.

Carson wanted to talk through what they had come up with, this despite the fact that Ottey had told him there was nothing to discuss. But this kind of inconvenience was always irrelevant to a man who was preoccupied by trying to show that he is in charge and on top of things. Ottey found these meetings intensely frustrating and time-wasting, with Carson's posturing almost a personal insult aimed fairly and squarely at her. There was nothing to discuss. What were they doing? Cross, on the other hand, quite enjoyed hearing where they weren't at and what they didn't have. Although he never indulged in it, he listened to the speculation of others with interest, as occasionally it prompted a line of thought he might not have considered otherwise. This was, admittedly, rare, but when it did occur, it made all the other hours of pointless hypothesis in the incident room seem a price worth paying.

'Do we have any CCTV from the neighbouring buildings?' Carson asked, as if this might not have occurred to any of them to check.

'We do not,' Ottey replied. 'But Catherine's looking at cameras on streets that lead into the square from Park Street, to see who, if anyone, entered the square at the pertinent times.'

'That was my next question,' he assured them all.

'He could've come from Brandon Hill,' Cross pointed out.

'Indeed. Which, I'm assuming, has no CCTV coverage,' Carson said confidently, having read a preliminary report. 'Our victim let his killer in,' he continued.

'Correct,' replied Ottey. 'He operated the door catch next to his desk. It was an old-style intercom release.'

'So, he knew the killer?'

'Most likely,' sighed Ottey.

'What time does the shop normally close?' asked Cross from the back of the room by the door.

'Six p.m.,' replied Prianka.

'According to Persephone, the visitor rang the doorbell around seven,' said Cross.

'So are you suggesting it was a prearranged meeting?' asked Carson.

'I wasn't aware I was suggesting anything,' replied Cross. 'We've been told by the victim's wife that he was still at work because he was waiting for his father to return from London. So unless the meeting was organised at short notice, that idea seems unlikely.'

'It's not unusual for people to work on after shop hours. Administration, answering emails, etc,' Ottey pointed out.

'Unless it was a regular occurrence, how could the killer be sure Ed Squire would be there?' asked Cross.

'Maybe the killer was observing the building. Knew Squire hadn't left,' replied Carson.

'Or perhaps he wasn't the target. What if it was the old man? I mean, he does live there,' another detective suggested.

'Too many questions, not enough answers,' declared Carson. His usual mantra in such situations. 'Answers, people. Let's find some answers. That'll be all.'

'Helpful as ever,' muttered Ottey as she turned back to her desk. 'George, plan of action after that stirring speech?'

'What stirring speech?' replied Cross, fairly sure he hadn't missed anything. 'We should go back to Torquil Squire.'

12

Victoria Squire was out supermarket shopping when the two detectives arrived. This gave Ottey an immediate feeling of guilt as she remembered she hadn't emailed Cherish, her mother, with the supermarket shop for the week, as she'd promised. Charlotte opened the door and let them into the front room, to speak to Torquil. She then disappeared into the kitchen to make them all tea; 'If there's any milk, that is. Sebastian always finishes it and not only doesn't replace it, but neglects to tell anyone there isn't any left. It's so bloody annoying.'

Torquil was sitting in the front room. He didn't seem to be doing anything. Neither the Roberts radio nor the television were on. There was a copy of *The Times* unopened on a side table next to his chair. He looked like he was simply existing, for no other reason than that his breathing made it so. There was no will, no purpose.

'Hello, Torquil, DS Ottey and Cross,' she began, out of habit.

'D*I* Ottey,' Cross quickly corrected her.

The old man conjured up an empty smile.

'We went to see Denholm Simpson,' Cross informed him. Torquil seemed taken aback by this.

'Really? Why?'

'We're talking to anyone with any connection to you and Ed,' explained Ottey.

'But he didn't have any,' Torquil objected.

'Well, not any more, admittedly. But he very much did in the past,' she went on.

'That was so long ago,' he pointed out.

'You certainly don't get that impression when you talk to him,' she replied.

'Still bitter?' he asked unnecessarily.

'Why didn't you bring him and the business as a whole over to Berkeley Square?' asked Cross.

'The partnership, such as it was, well, more like a marriage of convenience to be honest, had run its course by then,' the old man answered.

'Mr Simpson doesn't seem to think so,' replied Cross.

Torquil thought about this for a moment and then seemed to answer a question he hadn't been asked but had thought about a lot.

'He's not a bookseller. Never was. He's an opportunist. Buying the bookshop was just an opportunity to get out of a life he'd already started to regret. Yes, he'd been interested in books, but not really. It wasn't his calling.'

'Was it yours?' asked Cross.

'Not at the beginning. But it became so, yes. It's the only way you can be a success at it.'

'Denholm Simpson is still pretty resentful about you and the way things ended. Angry even,' said Ottey.

'Really?' he said. 'I suppose I could've handled it a little better. But I've never been one for confrontation.'

'Is that why you took away half of the stock overnight?' asked Cross.

'Not my finest moment. We'd always been quite close until that point.'

'He was Ed's godfather,' Cross observed.

'That's right, and I'm Nigel's godfather. Not that either of us has been much use. Hardly surprising, I suppose, in the circumstances.'

'Nigel?' asked Ottey.

'Denholm and Eliza's boy. Only child. Used to be best friends with Ed. They went to nursery together,' he said.

'And school?' asked Ottey.

'No, they went to separate schools when they were older. They're almost identical in age. We both met our wives when we came to Bristol,' he said with a glint of warm nostalgia in his eyes. As if thinking of better, easier times.

'Is Eliza still alive?' asked Ottey.

'No, neither of them are. They were sisters.' He laughed as if that fact still amused him.

'Really?' asked Ottey.

'Yes, my Sylvie and Eliza. Bristol girls born and bred.' He smiled again.

'Did that make the dissolution of the business even more difficult?' asked Cross.

'Well, what do you think? It's the one thing, the main thing, I regret about the whole affair,' he said ruefully.

'What?' asked Cross.

'Us, driving those two apart. They were so close before we appeared on the scene. Inseparable even. Sylvie was much younger than me. Denny used to joke that I'd only got to go out with her because of him and Eliza. That it happened only because the four of us always went out to the pictures or dinner together. I think he was probably right.'

'How did they die?' asked Ottey.

'Breast cancer. Both of them. Within a couple of years of

each other. Eliza first, she was the younger of the two as well. Sylvie went to her funeral…' At this the old man started to weep quietly. Ottey gave him time to recover, then started again.

'What drove them apart?' she asked.

'We did. Denny and I. He and Eliza came to resent our life,' he said.

'A life given to you by Cynthia Sumner,' Cross suggested.

'Yes and no. I mean, I've worked really hard to get the shop where it is. And Ed did too. But our success wasn't automatic. That wasn't given to us. We can stand shoulder to shoulder with some of the big establishments in London,' he said. 'She wanted me to have the house and expand the business. She didn't want Denny involved. I told him that.'

'Was it a condition of the will?' asked Cross.

'No,' came the quiet reply.

'So you didn't have to abide by it.'

'I didn't, no. But Cynthia was my client, not Denny's. He had nothing to do with her. Only met her when she came into the shop to see me. I cultivated her as a client. We even went on purchasing trips together over in Ireland and Europe,' he pointed out.

'Just the two of you?' asked Ottey.

'She was in her late seventies, Sergeant, before you leap to any conclusions. There was nothing going on there, if you know what I mean,' he said defensively.

'I don't,' replied Cross.

'Romantically.' Torquil spelled it out.

'So, you saw an opportunity and took it?' suggested Ottey.

'There was more to it than that.'

'Did you know she was going to leave you the house and her library?' asked Cross.

'I did not. She'd often asked my opinion of what she should do with it. I offered no opinion on the house, obviously, but said I would be happy to catalogue and sell the library at auction and divest the proceeds to a charity, or wherever she wanted her money to go.'

'So it must've come as a shock,' said Ottey.

'It was, yes. I had no idea. Truly,' he replied.

'What made you decide to go it alone?' Ottey asked.

'We'd had a tough patch in the eighties. Very tough. It was really my side of the business, rare and antiquarian, that kept us afloat. My expertise. I'd felt for some time that the partnership had become too one-sided, and I began to resent it a little,' he explained.

'Had you discussed it with Denholm?' asked Cross.

'Oh yes, frequently. The atmosphere at the shop was terrible, for both of us. It seemed an opportune moment when Cynthia's legacy fell into my lap,' he said. Cross noticed him look to the ground. He was holding something back.

'Had something else happened with your business partner to prompt you to go your separate ways?' Cross pushed. The ensuing pause indicated that Cross's observation might have something to it.

'As you probably know, Denny worked as a graphic artist and occasional signwriter before we went into business. No call for the latter these days and demand was wearing thin even then. Then his father died, rather unexpectedly. Well, you know the rest. It's true that his money enabled us to set up the business and I don't deny that. Denny still owned the freehold. I left him with half of the stock, some of which I considered to be mine – rare, modern first editions, that kind of thing...' He faltered.

'What happened to that stock?' Cross asked, suspecting this might pertinent.

'Do you know much about the book trade, Sergeant?'

'I do not,' Cross replied. He'd learned that concealing any knowledge he might have on certain subjects was often more conducive to interviewees not leaving anything out, in case they felt it was too obvious for someone who had knowledge, however paltry. Relevant minutiae that for him was often the unobvious key to a case, might therefore be left unmentioned.

'The price and value of rare books can vary enormously, even if the two books in question are the same edition. Their condition is important, obviously. The presence of a perfect dust cover, for example, can all add to value. A signed edition can also add value. An edition with a personal inscription from one author to another famous figure can make the value rise enormously. As soon as he realised this, Denny started forging inscriptions in some of our stock and sending them out to auction, or selling them privately using my client list. I was furious. These were clients I had cultivated over years. Who trusted me. Some were even friends. I confronted him and he said he'd stopped. He didn't use my stock any more because he knew I'd notice. He started going on trips to London. I found out because I had many more contacts in the London book trade than he did. He was now forging Graham Greene, Virginia Woolf, Dickens.'

'Were you unaware of this? After you confronted him did you think he'd stopped?' asked Cross.

'Absolutely. It was my reputation at stake. Not just his. But after we parted company he started again, forging Auden, T.S. Eliot, Winston Churchill. But he came unstuck. A dealer friend of mine had sold him a first edition of Orwell's *1984*. Good condition, great dust cover, but with a small annotation from the original owner who had come across a typo, a comma in the wrong place, I think it was. This had passed Denny by, and he duly inscribed the book from Orwell to Aldous Huxley. This made it extremely rare as Orwell died shortly after, in January 1950. The interest at auction was understandably huge. But unfortunately for Denny it was bought at auction by the same dealer who had sold it to him only a few months before. When he examined it, he realised it was fake and called the police,' Torquil explained.

'He didn't call you?' asked Cross.

'No. He knew we were no longer in business together. So why would he? We did discuss it sometime later. I told him he'd done the right thing. Honesty and trust are absolute pillars of our trade. Once that has gone, everything has gone.'

'What happened to Denholm?' asked Cross.

'He was arrested. The police found dozens of autographed books ready for sale and several exercise books filled with practice signatures. He was sentenced to two years in prison for eight counts of forgery. His main market had become the US,' he added.

'How did they know that?' asked Cross, always interested in the detail in case he could learn something from it.

'He kept an inventory, for God's sake! I mean, who does that if they're defrauding people?' he sighed.

'What happened to the shop while he was inside?' asked Ottey.

'Eliza ran it. That's when Sylvie encouraged me to try and buy it. To help out in a bad situation.'

'That's not the way he sees it,' added Cross.

'Oh no. The whole thing was a conspiracy on my part to put him out of business. He even went as far as to tell Eliza that it was me who informed on him.'

THE BOOKSELLER

'So that's why you left? The forged inscriptions?' asked Cross, trying to steer the conversation back to the original question.

'Of course. Rumours had started when I first discovered what he was up to and put a stop to it. I was tarred with the same brush. For all people knew, I was involved. I'd worked for years to gain a good reputation. I wasn't going to let him ruin it. In the end he paid the price. When he got out, his career in the rare-book trade was in tatters. He had to make do with being a run-of-the-mill second-hand bookseller.'

'Grandpa, you sound like such a snob when you say that,' said Charlotte who had appeared with a tray of tea and biscuits. Cross was happy to see that there was a strainer next to the teapot. This meant there was every chance of a decent cup of tea.

'I didn't mean to be. I'm sorry, I just find all of this so hard to accept,' he replied. In that instant he shrank further back into the chair as if he'd just remembered why the two people opposite him were there. His son had been murdered. 'It seems so unreal. I just want to go to bed and sleep. But when I do, I can't. I just lie awake wondering how this has happened. If it has happened at all. But it has. It really has.'

'Have you had any dealings with Denholm Simpson recently?' asked Cross.

'No, we haven't spoken since the trial.'

'Did you go?' asked Ottey.

'I was summoned,' he replied.

'As a character witness?' suggested Ottey.

'No.' He paused. 'As a witness for the prosecution. Needless to say Denholm perceived it as the final betrayal,' he said ruefully.

'Understandably,' said Cross.

'I beg your pardon?' Torquil spluttered indignantly.

'He was just observing how it might have seemed from Denholm's point of view,' Ottey interjected.

'He called the house yesterday,' Charlotte commented.

'Did your grandfather speak with him?' asked Ottey.

'I am still here,' exclaimed Squire. 'No, I did not. Victoria put him off. No doubt he'll make an appearance at the funeral.'

'Will that be welcome?' asked Cross.

'I have no opinion on the matter.'

'Mr Squire, as absurd as this might seem, can you think of any reason why your ex-partner might have anything to do with your son's death?' Ottey asked.

'What? No. He was his godfather. Why after all this time and why Ed?' he asked. Two pertinent questions in Cross's opinion.

'Had Ed been in touch with him or vice versa?' asked Ottey.

'Not as far as I know,' he answered.

The arrival of Victoria and her brother Ian was announced by the rustle of carrier bags in the kitchen. They had come through the back door. When they appeared in the living room Victoria looked put out at the police officers' presence. This wasn't, by any means, an unusual reaction for them to experience. But it was normally on the faces of suspects they had come to interview. Not the relative of the deceased, whose killer they were trying to find.

'Everything all right?' she asked, with no interest in the answer. She was simply making a statement that their presence there, without her knowledge, was a surprise, and not a welcome one at that. Cross thought it an odd phrasing. Things were patently not all right. Her husband had been murdered, hence their presence in the house. But he resisted the impulse to say so.

'We've been talking about Denholm Simpson,' Ottey replied.

'Uncle Denny? What's he done now?' she asked. It was odd to hear him referred to as such after what Torquil had said. But of course it was factually correct. 'No, you can't think…'

'We're simply investigating, Mrs Squire. We don't as yet think anything. When we do, I can assure you, you will be among the first to know,' said Cross, before going on, '"Uncle", are you in touch with him?'

'No,' she said, after a momentary glance at Torquil. 'No, of course not. Too much bad blood there, I'm afraid.'

'Was your husband?' asked Cross.

'No. Why would he be?' she asked.

'Well, two booksellers in the same city, less than a mile from each other. It wouldn't be unusual,' Cross pointed out.

'They were hardly the same kinds of bookseller,' she replied. 'Even so, I don't think Ed had been in touch.'

The detectives went to leave. When Cross got to the door of the living room he turned, looked back and asked Torquil, 'What did Mr Simpson mean when he talked about Ed's recent troubles?' he asked.

'I have no idea,' replied Torquil.

'He alluded to them, but when we asked him to elaborate he wouldn't and told us to speak to you,' Cross went on.

'He's just making trouble, Sergeant. Even at a time like this. He always was a mischief maker. Isn't that right, Pa?' Victoria said. But her father-in-law wasn't listening. His mind was somewhere else. Completely.

'She was lying,' said Ottey as they walked to her car parked in the street.

'I was wondering about that,' said Cross. 'Interesting you confirm it.'

The day ended with Ottey driving Cross to the BRI and dropping him off. He hadn't asked her to do this and indeed it wasn't something they ever discussed. It was one of those telepathic understandings close colleagues often have with each other where they are almost on autopilot, doing things without the need to speak. She didn't go in and just left him be. Another, unspoken, tacit agreement.

13

Cross and Ottey decided to visit their sole witness again, Persephone. Cross wanted to know more about the young woman and so they went to her flat, unannounced, to see her in her own environment. She appeared initially shocked at their appearance on her doorstep, rather like Victoria had been when she arrived home to find them there. Again, this was puzzling to Cross. They were investigating a murder. Why the surprise? It was a one-bedroom flat in Totterdown near Temple Meads station. A lot of houses in this particular neighbourhood were painted in a cornucopia of bright colours. This had in time encouraged a kind of almost curated graffiti on some other buildings in the surrounding area.

'It's become quite Instagrammable, Totterdown,' Ottey informed him as they drove into Persephone's street.

'I'm fairly certain that's not a word,' Cross replied.

'Well, I'm fairly sure that in the modern world, a place you only occasionally deign to inhabit, that it is. It's just a matter of time before it finds its way into the Oxford English dictionary,' she pointed out.

Cross sighed at the sad, inevitable truth of this. He'd always had an old-fashioned, puritanical resentment of commercial brands making their way into the everyday lexicon. He used to correct his father when, on the rare occasion, he decided to 'hoover' the flat. 'You are vacuuming the flat,' he would inform him. People endlessly talked about 'googling' things when what they really meant was they were going to research something on the internet. At the MCU people used to 'xerox' documents when they meant photocopy. But he said nothing. The Americans had even come up with a word for it – genericization.

Persephone didn't invite them in immediately. She seemed a little reluctant, half hiding behind the door, like a teenager trying to discourage her parents from entering her bedroom into which she had smuggled her boyfriend.

'Can we come in?' asked Ottey.

'Yes, of course. I'm sorry,' she said, opening the door and ushering them in.

Her flat was tidy and neat, much like her wayward hair, which had been pulled into a bun. She was wearing an animal onesie, possibly a giraffe, Cross thought. Despite the eccentric attire, he could see she was a very attractive young woman. His first impression of the living room was that it had been decorated by an immature teenager. This was reinforced by the sight of her bed in the small bedroom which had dozens of soft toys, bears and other creatures, neatly organised in a pyramid-like menagerie of stuffed animals on her pillows. In the sitting room there was a lot of pink around the place and a few toy animals which had obviously escaped from the bedroom zoo. She indicated a pink sofa for the two police officers to sit on. It was occupied by a large toy donkey and a toy cat with an angry-looking face and crossed eyes.

'Oh, you can move Spike and Tamara. They won't mind,' she reassured them.

'It would be surprising if they did,' Cross observed.

'Ah,' she said with the kind of sympathetic tone people normally use when they've just been told that someone is terminally ill, accompanied by a tilt of the head. 'Not a toy person?'

Before he answered and they entered a conversation which Ottey knew would be both perplexing and upsetting for the young woman, the toilet flushed in her bathroom.

'Oh, I'm sorry, Persephone,' said Ottey, thinking she now understood the young woman's hesitation at the door. 'Do you have company?'

'Yes. Oh, what? No. Not like that. It's my dad, and it's Percy, please,' she said in a tone which implied they were now part of an exclusive club of intimacy.

Her father duly appeared from the bathroom.

'Dad, this is the police,' she told him.

'Yes, Ian Hartwell. We almost met at my sister's,' he said.

'Oh, yes. That's right,' replied Ottey.

'Do you live in Spain, Mr Hartwell? Or were you there on holiday?' asked Cross.

'I live there, yes.'

'He runs a nightclub in Marbella,' Persephone said proudly, putting her arm through his.

'I do. But I mostly manage holiday villa rentals for a company and some private clients,' he said.

'How long are you staying in the country?' asked Cross.

'It really depends on when the funeral is. If there's time I'll go to Spain, then fly back for it. It's not too far. Will you be needing to speak to me? Let me give you my business card. My mobile's on there, so you can always reach me,' he said, giving it to Ottey.

'Thank you,' she said.

'None of this seems at all real. Everything was so normal a few days ago. Good, boring, normal and now everything seems upside down. Do you have any leads?' he asked.

'It's a little early in the investigation for that,' replied Cross.

'How's Victoria?' asked Ottey.

'In bits, obviously. Looking after the old man is a good distraction for the time being. But I worry how she'll cope when he's back at the shop and the kids have gone,' he pondered.

'It's usually after the funeral that it hits hardest,' said Ottey.

'I might take her back to Spain for a bit. And then there's this one,' he said, putting his arm round Persephone's shoulder, which she leaned into. 'I worry about her. I keep telling her she should maybe speak to someone. I mean, she discovered the body. Saw the killer.'

Persephone looked up at her father and smiled bravely.

'We are aware of that,' said Cross.

'Of course you are. I'm sorry. Bit all over the place myself at the moment. This is definitely one of those times I wish I still lived here,' he said.

'Well, as you say, you're not too far away,' said Cross.

'You will let me know if there's anything I can do?'

'Of course,' replied Ottey.

He kissed his daughter on the forehead and left, reminding her that they were meeting later that day for dinner.

'Have your two families always been close?' Ottey asked the young woman.

'Before my parents split up, yes. My father left when I was seven. My mum felt a little left out by the family. She thought Victoria was embarrassed by her brother's behaviour and the best way to deal with it was just to ignore us. Mum was quite angry about it. I think maybe more for me than herself. Dad went off with someone else, so actually maybe Mum wasn't that keen to see Victoria. I don't know.'

'You didn't talk about it?' asked Ottey.

'My mum's very good at avoiding the things in life she doesn't want to talk about. She just shuts down.'

'How does she feel about you working in the bookshop?' asked Cross.

'She's happy, I think. I mean, she still keeps away from them. It's like she blames them for Dad's leaving. But it obviously had nothing to do with them. I think she realises I'm lucky to have the opportunity Ed has given me. Gave me,' she said, correcting herself.

'As in giving you a job?' asked Cross, for clarity.

'Oh, it's so much more than that. More like a future,' she replied with dramatic sincerity. 'But he's given me a lot of freedom to change things up.'

'By selling new books?' asked Cross.

'Exactly!' she said brightly as if he was agreeing that this initiative, hers, was a good one. 'I'm trying to drag the two of them into this century. Being an independent bookstore will bring more customers in. It's good for the business.'

'New customers who want new books,' suggested Cross. 'It doesn't really affect the core business.'

'Well, we'll soon find out,' she continued, refusing to be thrown by his logic.

'Was Torquil on board with this new direction?'

'Well, Pa is very old,' she replied patronisingly. 'He's never been in the new book trade. So his reluctance was understandable.'

'Neither have you,' Cross pointed out.

'What?' she asked.

'Been in the new book trade,' he asserted. This made her visibly twitch. As if stung by a small wasp of truth.

'How long have you been at the shop?' asked Ottey.

'Just over three years,' she said, adjusting herself in her seat so that she favoured Ottey. As if the other police officer was no longer worthy of her attention.

'So, since some time in twenty twenty-one?' asked Ottey.

'That's right.'

'And when did you go up to Oxford?' she continued. This seemed to cause a momentary hesitation in Persephone.

'Twenty sixteen,' she replied.

'What did you read?' asked Cross.

'English, obviously.' She laughed and frowned, confused that this wasn't an obvious conclusion.

'Did you go straight into the shop?' asked Ottey.

'No. I went into publishing for a while,' she replied.

'Why only for a while?' asked Cross.

'I suffer, well, suffered, from anxiety in the office environment. It was too stressful and then the pandemic came along.'

Cross understood this completely. Ottey less so. She found the modern generation's sensitivity to workplaces, or indeed work of any kind, way too self-indulgent. Now the pandemic had made working from home some kind of fundamental human right, there'd be no end to it, she thought. No wonder police recruitment was in such trouble. Kids find working in an office environment stressful? Try working the beat, sweetheart, she found herself thinking. It's fair to say she'd taken against this young woman in the non-prejudicial, impartial way police officers had been trained not to.

'What happened after the pandemic?' asked Cross as Ottey was too busy being judgemental.

'I was let go. Several of us were. For me it was a bit of a relief,' she asserted, as if to show that it had nothing to do with her abilities.

'So, Ed took you in?' asked Ottey.

'Sam had long Covid and couldn't work for a while. It was actually Torquil's idea to bring me in as cover. I answered the phones and helped Torquil with the cataloguing,' she replied.

'That must've been interesting,' Cross commented.

'Oh, absolutely. Except for the hayfever of course. Had to dose up with antihistamines with all the dust around. Torquil's so gifted at it. The way he curates and presents a collection, and the descriptions are so clever, often very witty.'

'What was Ed's role in the business?' Cross pushed on.

'He's really the business side of it, well, was,' she said and hesitated for a moment. 'He knew his books, mind. Don't get me wrong. He managed to acquire the most amazing libraries. Like Torquil in his heyday, he seemed to be able to search them out before the big boys in London heard about them. He also got them in amazing deals. Sometimes too amazing for Torquil.'

'What exactly do you mean by that?' asked Cross.

'Well, he just managed to get people to part with libraries well below what he might have expected to pay for them.'

'Were the customers happy with that?'

'I think so. It's one more tick on the inheritance to-do list. Some of them have no idea, nor any interest sometimes, in what the collection contains,' she said in mock amazement.

'Presumably Ed informed them if he found something unexpected and rare hidden in the collection,' Cross suggested.

She laughed at this.

'What's so amusing?' Cross asked.

'Oh, I don't know. It's just that it was a constant source of friction between Torquil and Ed. If Ed found a really valuable edition of something in a library or collection he'd bought, he felt it was his right to profit from it. The sellers hadn't bothered to find out what was in the collection, so it was their fault.

Torquil was different. He'd call the seller with the news and suggest a fair adjusted value which still meant he made a good profit. He says it's all about trust. I think Ed's attitude was more like those people on *Storage Wars*. You buy a storage locker at auction and it's like a lucky dip. If you find something really valuable, it's yours to sell.'

'Did this happen often?' asked Cross.

'Less and less. But the book trade is full of stories like this. People finding original Blake prints worth millions hidden away in a collection,' she said. 'Someone found a letter from C.S. Lewis in a copy of *The Lion, the Witch and the Wardrobe* once, that had been written to the original owner.'

'Had it happened recently?' Cross persisted. Persephone looked awkward.

'Denholm Simpson said that Ed had had a few troubles, recently, with the business. But wouldn't tell us what, exactly,' said Ottey.

'Did he?' she answered vaguely.

'Would you know anything about that?' Cross asked. She thought for a moment.

'Look, I don't want to get anyone in trouble,' she began. 'But the de Sourcey family sold Ed their grandfather's library about a year ago. He then discovered a first edition of *The Lord of the Rings* among all the books. It was worth a load of money anyway, but it was inscribed by Tolkien himself to his "great friend Lolly". This made its value go through the roof. Ed didn't tell anyone, not even Torquil, and sold it at auction in London for hundreds of thousands, like three, I think, a few months ago. The sale made the papers and the grandson, Freddy, came to the shop,' she said.

'What happened? Did Ed give them a share of the profit?' asked Ottey.

'No. It got very unpleasant. Freddy threatened to call the police. When this had no effect, he got quite physical. Then Ed threatened to call the police himself. Torquil was so distressed. Sam and I managed to calm de Sourcey down and get him to leave the shop. We said that Torquil would resolve it. He then pleaded with Ed to pay up. They had a terrible row. The worst I've ever heard.'

'What happened with the de Sourceys?' asked Cross.

'Well, you would've thought being a family of some wealth they would've involved lawyers. But I think they've been crippled by death duties. Whatever, Freddy reappeared a couple of weeks ago and threatened Ed. He said he knew people the like of which Ed would never have encountered in the rarefied world of books. People, he assured him, he didn't want to meet.'

'So, Ed hadn't done the decent thing?' asked Ottey.

'Well, that depends on what view you take,' she said, defensively. 'But no. Partly, I think, because he didn't see why he should. But also, I'm not sure he still had the money. I heard him telling Victoria one night that the Tolkien was exactly the kind of luck they needed right now.'

None of them said anything.

'Do you think de Sourcey made good on his threat?' she asked.

'Well, if he did, he must've reconciled himself to seeing none of the profit from the book. With Ed dead, where would he get recompense?' asked Ottey.

★

95

'Something about her,' said Ottey. 'Strange girl.'

'Yes.'

'Do you want to talk to Freddy de Sourcey?' she asked.

'I don't *want* to, but our investigation requires that we do. The bookseller first, though, I think,' he replied.

'Why didn't you tell us about the de Sourcey family, Mr Squire?' Cross asked Torquil at the family home.

'You didn't ask,' he replied.

'On the contrary, we asked if there had been any issues in the recent past with any customers,' Cross went on.

'I don't know. I should've done, of course. It's just so hard to conceive of the idea that anyone might have killed Ed over a book,' he replied.

'It's more likely to have been about money than a book,' commented Ottey.

'Of course,' he replied. 'It wasn't Ed's finest moment. I only found out about it after the fact. Which goes to show he knew I wouldn't approve.'

'What was your opinion about the way he conducted himself?' asked Cross.

'It wasn't how I would've done it, certainly,' he replied.

'What would you have done differently?' asked Cross.

'Well, as soon as I'd discovered the book and the inscription, I would've been in touch with the family to find out who it was dedicated to. That's where Ed went wrong. Always did, to be honest. Rushed headlong for a sale without taking a moment to reflect, like a good book man should.'

'What difference would that have made?' asked Cross.

'Provenance. But not only that. Book collectors like a good

story. I would've asked the family more detail about Tolkien's friendship with their grandfather. Did he, to their knowledge, ever visit the house? Did the grandfather have a visitors' book which JRR might have signed? Was there any correspondence between them? The story alone would've added value, but if there were any letters or any other artefacts, then the price of the book would have gone up exponentially, as well as the price of the ephemera. It could've increased sufficiently for Ed to have made the same amount of money with the de Sourceys adequately compensated. Then none of this unpleasantness would've occurred.'

'Did you take this up with your son?' asked Cross.

'I did. I'm afraid we had very different views on it and it's not just a generational thing. Many people in the book trade would think Ed had done nothing wrong. Swings and roundabouts and all that. But we're the experts and our expertise isn't a tool to rip people off. It's a skill to inform them and get them value for whatever they're selling. It's important for the firm to have integrity and with that comes customer loyalty, which is worth so much more than Ed's obsession with profit and loss.'

14

That night, as Ottey dropped Cross off at the hospital, she decided to park up and go in. This wasn't for her colleague's benefit but to check up on Christine. Raymond was still in an induced coma, but she had been sitting at his bed all day, every day. Doing it this way, without telling Cross, Ottey also solved the problem of having to deal with his objections to her doing so. As she arrived at Raymond's bedside, she was greeted with George informing her –

'You're only allowed two visitors in ICU.'

Christine got up immediately, obviously pleased to see her. Josie gave her a comforting hug and, ignoring George, asked her, 'Have you eaten anything today, Christine?'

'Not for a while,' she replied.

'Why don't I take you down to the café for a cup of tea and something to eat?' said Josie, guiding her gently away from the bed by her elbow. They left George at his father's bedside.

The two women sat in Costa each with a coffee and Josie insisted on getting a heated-up panini for Christine. She looked exhausted and viewed the food in front of her with the dread of someone who doesn't want to do something but knows it will be good for them if they go through with it. She took a half-hearted bite, as if she were suspicious it might contain poison.

'How are you doing?' asked Josie.

'I'm okay,' came the quiet reply.

'It occurred to me as I saw you sitting next to Raymond's bed that this isn't new territory for you, is it?' Josie observed, referring to Christine's late husband, Duncan, who had died, having suffered from Alzheimer's, the year before.

'It's different.'

'How?'

'Because with Duncan there was no hope. No prospect of any improvement, of him getting any better. It was just a dreadful one-way street. A downhill slope. With Raymond, at least, there's hope.' She saw Josie's sympathetic but doubtful expression which she wasn't quick enough to disguise. 'Not much, I know,' conceded Christine. 'But if he's able to, he'll do his best to get through this. He has to.'

'Because of George?' commented Josie.

'Exactly. He's not ready to leave George.'

'Except for the fact that he knows you're around for him now,' suggested Josie.

'Yes and no. I'm not sure I'll ever fully have George's trust,' replied Christine.

'Why?'

'Because of all the damage I did when I left, I suppose. It's not easy to repair. Particularly with someone like him.'

'But he seems to be coming round to you. Be more accepting of you, in his own way,' said Josie.

'Isn't that a strange thing to say about a son and mother? But it's the situation we find ourselves in,' said Christine.

'It wasn't exactly your fault, from what he's told me,' replied Josie.

'Did he tell you that himself, or is it an inference you're making?'

Josie's silence answered this question for her.

'It was selfish. No question about it. I should've stayed around. But I found it too painful. That is so often the case for a mother, don't you think? He was definitely better off with Raymond and Ron but I should've just sucked it up for the sake of my son and stuck around,' she said with a weary regret.

'Raymond and Ron?' asked Josie. Christine looked at her a moment.

'Ah, he obviously didn't tell you everything. He's always been the soul of discretion, right from when he was a small boy,' she said with an affectionate smile. Josie meanwhile was trying to digest what, for her, was something of a bombshell.

'He told me things weren't as straightforward as he thought, as to why you'd left. Did he know about his father?' asked Josie.

'No.'

'I can understand why you would want to leave,' said Josie.

'Really? You're a mother, Josie. Can you imagine leaving your girls?'

Again, Josie's silence provided the answer.

'I loved George so much. Was he a challenge? Sure. But how could you not love him? We didn't know he was autistic. People didn't know so much about it then. He was fascinating and fascinated by so many things, it was often hard to keep up with him. The situation with Raymond and Ron, particularly then, was too difficult for me. Things were so different then. I felt hurt that I wasn't enough for Raymond as a woman. I felt betrayed in a way that I could not understand. In the end, maybe, I was a little homophobic about it all. I just wish I could go back and change it,' she said.

'Well, you can't and for what it's worth society back then was more than a little homophobic itself, and racist and misogynistic.

Like you said, things were different then and if that affected your thinking, it's perfectly understandable. So don't beat yourself up about it,' Josie assured her.

'Thank you.'

'Having said that, I think life has presented you with a chance of making a relationship with George now,' Josie finished by saying.

'How?' Christine asked.

'George can't look after his father in the way he wants or thinks he can. But you can and, more importantly, you want to. Can you imagine what it would be like for him, for both of them, if you weren't here?' she asked.

'I have a feeling George won't be thinking like that,' replied Christine. She smiled and placed her hand over Josie's, gratefully. 'I should get back,' she said.

15

Alice Mackenzie was enjoying, for the most part, her life as a student again. She had no regrets about the path she'd chosen – to become a police officer – despite the look of abject, speechless shock and betrayal on the faces of her ardently socialist parents. They were so left wing they thought that Jeremy Corbyn was a middle-of-the-road centrist, leaning to the right. They felt the modern Labour party was occupying the territory of the Tories of their youth, who they'd spent their entire lives protesting against. Her dad's campaign beret had been rendered shapeless by the number of demonstrations it had been worn on and the good cause badges weighing it down in different directions. But she would no longer be a victim, she told them, having been the subject of an attempted rape by a senior colleague from another force recently. The case was due in court in the next few weeks. Something she was not looking forward to. But she wouldn't be alone. Another woman who had been raped by the same man a couple of years before had had the courage to go and get a rape kit done at the time but hadn't followed up. As a police officer herself, this woman had seen how rape victims were often treated in court and had no desire to either go through that, or the events of that night. But she'd changed her mind with Alice pressing charges and Warner's subsequent arrest. This encouraged another woman he'd raped to come forward. She had also done a rape kit at the time, before changing her mind about pursuing him through the courts.

As well as training to be a detective, Alice had enrolled in self-defence classes, encouraged by her boyfriend, the forensic investigator, Michael Swift. Their relationship had become quite serious. He was even more protective of her since the attack, if that was possible. She had now moved into his flat on Percival Road and was slowly removing what she called the 'goth' elements of the decor. 'No one wants to sit on a sofa with skulls mounted at the end of the armrests,' she'd told him. Also gone from the bedroom were the crime scene photographs from the nineteen forties and fifties. Things were definitely moving in the right direction. But she had become much more aware of her physical vulnerability, and not in a good way. One night she was approaching her car outside UWE on her way home when she heard someone walking behind her at pace. Whoever it was was getting nearer step by step. She felt her heart rate increase. The steps accelerated behind her. There was no doubting that. She wasn't making it up. Her skin felt on edge. Sweat broke out in a prickle on her brow. As she neared her car she searched in her handbag, not for her car keys which were already in her hand, but for her self-defence spray. It was a small cylinder of comfort.

Then a voice said, 'Alice!'

She turned to see a fellow student, Malcolm, holding out a phone towards her.

'Your phone. You dropped it in the seminar,' he said.

'Oh, thanks.' She held out her hand, which was clearly shaking. Malcolm saw the pallor in her face.

'Are you okay?' he asked.

'Yes, I'm fine. Thanks.'

He nodded, slowly. 'Let me walk you to your car.'

'Sure. Okay. Thank you.'

She sat in the car as Malcolm walked away and realised that she was far from okay. Bugger.

One thing she was definitely missing during her studies, though, was working with Cross and Ottey. She'd realised this could be a permanent consequence, when she made the decision to start the course. But felt it was a price worth paying. However, every night when they sat down to eat together, she interrogated Michael about the current case. The trouble was that he had decided recently their relationship had moved on to the teasing stage. Whenever she asked him something he would tease her with titbits. He'd obviously decided that this kind of mental foreplay had elevated their relationship to another level. It would go along the lines of –

'So, where are you with the case?' she'd begin.

'Which one?' he'd answer vaguely.

'The Bookseller,' she would sigh, knowing full well what he was up to.

'Early days,' he'd reply.

'Michael!' she would retort.

'What? There's nothing to say.'

But that night she decided not to play his game. It was a tactic, as she knew that the unofficial secretary of the George Cross fan club would be bursting to discuss the case with her. It was something he revelled in. So he'd really shot himself in the foot. They enjoyed these conversations about investigations, despite his faux reluctance to engage. So much so that recently she'd toyed with the idea of ending the relationship, as it seemed to revolve around murder, blood spatters and the recently deceased way too much for it to be healthy.

'Okay,' she replied instead. They ate in silence for a while.

Eventually she said, oh so casually, 'What's the name of the victim again?'

'Edward Squire,' he answered way too quickly. She nodded and said nothing further. 'Aren't you going to ask me anything else?' he said a little desperately.

As Michael settled down to sleep with his ear plugs and an eye mask, adding to the perception of him being something of a modern vampire who'd dispensed with the need for a coffin, Alice plumped up her pillows and settled down with her laptop. She looked at the figure next to her and tried to remember when exactly it was that he'd felt secure enough in their relationship to look like such a prat when going to sleep. Whatever. She might not be part of the team any more, but that wasn't going to stop her from working the case.

Over her couple of years as a police staffer at the MCU, she'd become something of an expert at stitching together people's lives from their online presence. She could come up with a complete, detailed picture of them – their family, friends, workplace colleagues, car number plates, doctor's surgeries, even home addresses on occasion. Cross had been horrified to discover what she'd been able to uncover about people associated with their investigations online.

She began to piece together Ed Squire's life. He had a social media presence even in the early days of Facebook. As a new father he'd filled his feed with endless, to other people identical, photographs of blobs which turned out to be his newborn babies. He'd even attempted that social media trend of years ago where he photographed his children every month in the same place and then stitched it together. Either he, or more likely they, got bored of it around the age of five and it stopped. The family holidayed together mostly in the UK – Cornwall seemed a favourite spot. He'd visited several book fairs with his father, and they'd travelled to see clients in the US occasionally. Family life seemed good, but then she noticed a period of time where he stopped posting. It was around 2014 and never really picked up again with the same frequency as before. But for a while he just fell off social media completely. Maybe he'd become one of those Facebook voyeurs who have a profile but don't post. They just stalk others. She hated that. I mean, how would that work if everyone did it? There was a quid pro quo about posting. An unwritten social law which, for her, said: if you're on Facebook you have an obligation to post, not just be a social media parasite.

Victoria, his wife, posted quite a lot. Sharing online petitions, protesting about the closure of local playing fields, or to support someone facing an unjust deportation. Putting up photographs of children's parties way back. Eating out with various female friends. She'd been on the board of governors of her children's junior school before they went off to boarding school. Charlotte went to Cheltenham Ladies' College, Sebastian to Bryanston. But her posts seemed to falter for a number of months. Again in 2014. Her experience with Cross made Alice realise that this had to be of interest. 'The most trivial thing is often the vitally significant fact,' he'd told her once. This being over ten years ago probably had nothing to do with Ed's murder. But such things could often be informative in other ways.

There was nothing of particular interest with the two siblings' digital presence, so she moved onto the two other people whose names she'd heard Michael mention. Sam and Persephone. Sam's presence was nominal. He had a Facebook account but didn't post much. His Instagram profile was a different matter entirely; @booksamwidge had quite the following. He posted about the rare books he came across at work and even made videos extolling the virtues of various books that came through the bookshop, revelling in stories about their provenance and always tagging Squire's. His enthusiasm was infectious, and he'd built up a following of over twenty-five thousand. He then started reviewing new fiction on a blog page.

Persephone was a relentless poster. Hundreds of pouting selfies. Her use of filters was incessant. Every photograph was tinkered with in some sort of way, giving her a perma tan and digital plastic surgery. But it was like looking at a young teenager's profile. Lots of pink and stuffed toys. Cocktails with girlfriends, all pouting. Photographs of group pouts were ridiculous to her mind, grotesque even, at times. It was like looking down at a pond, filled with koi, rising to the surface, lips wide open, to feed. The other thing was that the groups of friends kept changing. They disappeared pretty much as soon as they'd appeared. She went through friendship groups quicker than a fickle fourteen-year-old going through imaginary boyfriends. She also made videos of herself talking to her stuffed toys which was, right out there, disconcerting. But then there were a couple of videos that stood out to Alice. Percy, as she termed herself, or The Purse, looking into camera, with no make-up, her complexion almost grey. She looked drawn. She began talking about her mental health and the videos suddenly stopped. 'I've been in bed all weekend crying…' But she'd posted them anyway. Why? What was that all about?

The only other person who appeared in the photographs with irregular regularity was her mother. They seemed close. There would be a flurry of selfie activity in bars, on holiday by pools and they would suddenly stop. The photos were a little creepy to Alice. In some they were obviously mother and daughter, but others were designed to look more like sisters. One of them even had the caption 'on the pull together', which Alice found nauseatingly inappropriate. The idea of a mother and daughter 'going on the pull' together was a toe-curlingly, sick-in-the-mouth-inducing concept.

The only other thing she noticed about Persephone's Facebook account was that she had stopped posting completely at one point in her life. She'd taken a social media sabbatical, as it were.

In 2014.

16

The days since Raymond's admission to hospital had been very discombobulating for George Cross. This wasn't only because of the prevailing concern about his father's condition, but the fact that his weekly routine had been thrown out of the window. The order of his week was long established and simple. It had been this way for years and he liked it being so. It formed the bedrock of his life, which enabled him to deal with it, week in, week out. It was a self-imposed coping mechanism. Every Wednesday night he and his father ate a Chinese takeaway – recently adapted to his mother joining them every fortnight. On Thursday night, after work, he played the organ, occasionally having a cup of tea and a chat with the priest, Stephen. On Sunday he saw his father again. He breakfasted every day during the week at Tony's café, conveniently located below his flat. On Saturdays he would go for a long bike ride. There was a familiarity, a conformity, a comfort in the sameness of it all. This had been fundamentally disrupted by recent events and he found himself oddly out of kilter. Something he was unused to and hadn't experienced for some time. It meant that he found solace in his work. It seemed the only constant left in his life was murder.

A new development in his domestic life was his recent discovery of cooking. Up until this point his kitchen had been somewhere to heat things up and make tea. But now he was in the process of becoming quite an accomplished home cook. He'd applied himself to this new pastime with his usual, diligent thoroughness. Actual, proper cooking, from scratch, with fresh ingredients, was a relatively new concept for him. He'd given up on reheating ready meals after he'd read an article about how processed foods contained a huge number of hidden sugars and salts. This, together with his father's recent health crisis, had made Cross decide to take things in hand and eat more healthily. So he now cooked for himself every evening. Well, excluding Wednesdays and recently not as frequently as usual because of the time spent with Raymond at the hospital. With the usual obsessive dedication he applied to any new venture, hobby or investigation at work, he'd bought a large number of kitchen implements and saucepans. He was particularly taken with saucepans made by a company called All Clad. He thought the pans had an aesthetically pleasing look, as well as a functionality to them with their thick bases. He'd bought various cookbooks and had been given one by Ottey. It was called *The Barefoot Contessa* by a woman in the Hamptons called Ina Garten. 'I'm obsessed with her,' Ottey had told him.

He was cooking a simple pasta dish with prawns and chilli. He liked to think the amalgamation of a couple of different recipes from two different books made it his own recipe. He had bought some fresh linguine as the pasta. He'd decided recently that he was going to learn how to make his own pasta dough. His first attempts hadn't gone well and any further attempts would have to wait till after the conclusion of the Ed Squire case. He was about to put the pasta on when his doorbell rang. He ignored it as he wasn't expecting anyone. He never was. Only one person had been invited into his flat over the years and that was his father. An experiment that hadn't been repeated. Cross hated the way his father crumpled the cushions on the sofa, even though Raymond had pointed out that surely George did that when he sat there. George couldn't disagree. He just knew he didn't like it when someone else did it.

The doorbell rang again. He hadn't ordered anything on the internet and so wasn't expecting a delivery. It had to be someone from a charity. He would just ignore it. But there it was again. Irritably persistent. It was rung in a way that tried to imply whoever it was wasn't going anywhere simply because they were being ignored. Then his phone vibrated on the work surface, so violently that it began edging its way off it, meaning George had to grab it, to prevent an unwelcome, screen-cracking, acquaintance with the floor. He saw it was Alice Mackenzie. He answered it.

'Cross.'

'Very, by the sound of it,' she replied.

'What?'

'I know you're in.'

'I am.'

'The lights are on,' she told him.

'Of course they are. It'd be dark otherwise,' he pointed out.

'Look, will you just let me in?'

'Why?'

'Because I'm outside your front door.'

'Why?' he repeated.

'Boss, just open the bloody door.'

'What do you want?' he greeted her with, as he opened the door.

'Ooh, something smells good,' she said.

'Yes, I'm cooking and about to eat,' he replied.

'Ah, well this shouldn't take long. It's about the case,' she said.

'What case?'

'The Squire murder. I've done a bit of digging,' she told him.

This put him in an immediate quandary. He was in the middle of cooking, but he was intrigued by what Alice might have to say. Her research was more often than not of use. Ideally, he would have just listened to what she had to say on the doorstep. But he'd put a pan of water on to boil and couldn't leave it unattended.

'You'd better come in, then,' he said reluctantly.

As they came into the flat she looked over at the hob.

'Funny, I didn't have you down as a cook. More of a ready meal sort of man.'

Cross looked at her momentarily, then went over to his backpack, which was on the floor next to his desk. He rummaged around and brought out the black notebook he used to note down Ottey's social bon mots of guidance she would occasionally lob in his direction. He flicked through a few pages until he found what he was looking for. Then he sighed and looked up.

'Are you hungry?' he asked, without much enthusiasm.

'I am, as it happens. But I don't want to impose,' she replied.

'Oh, good,' replied a relieved Cross, satisfied he had fulfilled the requisite social norms, satisfactorily.

'Having said that, I wouldn't say no,' she went on.

'To what?'

'Joining you for supper,' she said brightly. 'And before you ask, no I don't.'

'Don't what?' he asked.

'Have any allergies you should know about,' she replied.

This was uncanny as it was literally what he was about to ask her, having observed it in restaurants and conceded that he was going to have to feed her.

'So, what is it you want to tell me?' he said as he went to the fridge to get some more prawns.

'I've been doing some research into the Squire family.'

She then proceeded to tell him what she'd discovered. He insisted she pause in her narrative while they ate, so he could concentrate on his food. She made no comment on the fact that Cross had his linguine and the accompaniments of prawns, parsley and chilli all on separate plates. He had served hers together on the one dish. Mackenzie was surprised at how tasty the food was.

'You'd've made a great chef,' she said. Cross thought about this for a moment.

'Yes, I would,' he finally agreed.

She finished telling him about Persephone. He said nothing.

'Well?' she asked.

'It is, without question, worth investigating,' he told her.

'Good. I shall now do the washing up and leave you in peace.'

'No,' he said quite urgently. The idea of someone washing his kitchen implements was intolerable. 'Just go,' he insisted.

'Said with your usual politesse,' she remarked as she grabbed her backpack and left. 'Give my love to Raymond,' she said at the door.

'He *cooked* for you?' Michael asked her in jealous disbelief, when she returned home.

'He didn't mean to, but let's be honest, it's not like he had a choice,' she replied.

'What did he cook?'

'Prawn and chilli linguine with some panko breadcrumbs, parsley and lemon juice.'

'Wow, you really paid attention.'

'Only because I knew you'd ask,' she replied.

'I can't believe you went without me,' he said like a disappointed teenager. 'I wish I'd been there.'

'No, there wouldn't've been enough. He's quite precise about his quantities.'

'What was his place like?'

'Um, very tidy.'

'Of course,' he said admiringly.

'Not exactly homely, but very nice. Kind of like if you took a photo from an IKEA brochure and photoshopped it into his room. Separate kitchen. Cleaner than an operating theatre. He was constantly wiping down the surfaces as he cooked. A sofa, a chair, dining table with two chairs – don't suppose he has much need for more. A couple of prints on the wall,' she continued.

'Prints of what?' he asked.

'Um, I can't remember to be honest,' she replied.

'What? How can you not know?' he asked in frustration.

'I'm amazed he doesn't have a cleaner. The whole place was spotless,' she went on, ignoring his howl of disbelieving protest. 'It was like a nice suite in a good four-star hotel,' she said.

'Oh, don't tell him that.'

'What?'

'He won't be happy with four stars. He'll want to know why it wasn't five,' he said, perfectly seriously.

'I won't. I mean, I have no intention of telling him any of my thoughts, such as they are, about his flat. You are so weird. But do you know something? I actually think he enjoyed it. Cooking for someone and eating with them at his place,' she said.

Which was odd, as George Cross was thinking the same thing as he got into bed. That he'd quite enjoyed company when eating. Sharing a meal with someone. What was more, she'd been very complimentary about his cooking. He dallied momentarily with the idea of cooking for his mother and father. But by the time he pulled his duvet over himself, he'd come to the conclusion that such an idea was way too stressful to even think about.

17

'So, I gather you had a dinner guest last night,' Ottey said to Cross as she drove them to the de Sourcey house.

'The word "guest" implies an invitation was extended, which in this situation wasn't the case,' he replied.

'She said you were a surprisingly good cook,' Ottey continued.

'I fail to see why my culinary skills should have been a surprise,' he replied huffily, though secretly delighted with the compliment. His phone vibrated with the arrival of a text. He read it, pondered its contents for a moment, then hastily put it back in his pocket. He did this with such speed that Ottey was immediately suspicious.

'Who was that?' she asked.

'Dr Khan,' he replied quietly.

'What did he want?'

'Why is it surgical consultants call themselves "Mr"? It's Dr Khan bur Mr Moseby. It's almost as if it's some form of inverted social snobbery. They work for years, study hard, endure ridiculously long hours as junior doctors, all to finally attain the title "Doctor". Then, once they've done that, as soon as they've excelled and become consultants, reached the apogee of their chosen career, they revert to the commonplace "Mister".'

'Cack-handed as it was, I have to hand it to you. That was

an excellent piece of diversion, a brazenly executed change of subject. Good for you,' Ottey observed.

'I suppose it's a way of distinguishing themselves from the herd. The rank-and-file doctors. Who'd've thought that the everyday, universally used prefix "mister" would be used as a mark of distinction?' he continued.

'What did he want?' Ottey persisted.

'They're going to extubate my father in an hour,' he replied.

'What?' she said and pulled the car over to the side of the road so violently, Cross had to grab hold of the dashboard.

'I'm fairly sure you didn't check your mirrors before that manoeuvre,' he said.

She looked over her shoulder, then started to indicate. 'What are you doing?' he asked.

'I'm turning round,' she replied.

'Why?'

'Because I'm taking you to the hospital.'

'But we're working,' he protested.

'That is irrelevant,' she retorted.

'Not to me.'

'Look, if this was a day when you weren't working and you got that message, would you go to the hospital?' she asked.

'Yes.'

'Fine. Then we're going.'

'Again, that is irrelevant because we are working, ma'am.'

'Don't do that. You only say that to annoy me,' she said.

'So let us proceed to the de Sourcey residence and conduct our interview,' he replied calmly.

'No. I'm taking you to the hospital.'

'I do not want to go to the hospital!'

He said this with such force, with such uncharacteristic

TIM SULLIVAN

violent volume, it actually shocked her. She'd never heard him speak like this before.

'And if you insist on driving us there, I will simply stay in the car,' he said, like a difficult child refusing to go to the dentist with his parent. It was in this moment that Ottey recognised what she was looking at. Fear. She weighed this up for a few seconds, then pulled back out into the road and without saying a word, drove in the direction of the de Sourcey house.

The truth was, Cross's objection to going to the hospital had nothing at all to do with their working. Cross was using that as an excuse. He just didn't want to be there when his father came round. He was frightened of what condition Raymond might be in when he regained consciousness – the uncertainty of it. If he was in a seriously debilitated, disabled condition as a result of the brain bleed, Cross didn't trust himself to behave in a fitting manner in the moment. He needed to be forewarned. Then he could get himself together, make a plan and deal with the situation properly. But he needed Khan or his mother to brief him first. He would of course look after his father for the rest of his life, whatever the outcome of the stroke was, and be happy to do so. He would be completely satisfied with his role as full-time carer for his father, if need be. He would apply himself to it as thoroughly as he applied himself to everything. But he couldn't face the appalling uncertainty of Raymond's condition when he regained consciousness.

One thing had become abundantly clear to him over the past few days, as he contemplated all kinds of potential outcomes with his father. It was unavoidable. He'd weighed it up in his mind, going through all the pros and cons in his logical and unemotional way, and come to the inevitable conclusion. When this investigation was closed, he would resign from Avon and Somerset Police.

They drove up a short drive to a small country house in about ten acres of grounds. It was just outside Bath and belonged to the de Sourcey family. Or did. It seemed the house had recently been sold. A quick Google dive – how Cross hated that expression, as Prianka had found to her cost, then filed it under 'things that upset George' in her mental file on him – indicated the recent owner had been one John de Sourcey, the father of Freddy and Francesca. He had died the previous year, a widower. The two children were now selling up.

'We're having to,' explained Francesca, as she led them through a crowd of removal men. Paintings were being screwed into protective wooden transport frames, china, candlesticks and lamps were being bubble-wrapped and carefully put into the several tea chests that lined the hall. Men with clipboards were going round putting various small stickers on things to indicate their destinations. 'Death duties, inheritance tax, are a bugger,' she said quite cheerfully. 'This was all inevitable really.'

'You don't resent it?' asked Ottey.

'No, well, maybe a bit. But we're what you'd call nouveau riche. The family money's only a hundred and fifty years old, so it was bound to peter out eventually. Not that we're impoverished by any means. My great-great-grandfather was an early Victorian property developer. Well, no, builder would be more accurate,' she replied.

'Still, it's your family home. It must be a bit of a wrench, no?' Ottey asked.

'Yes and no. Neither Freddy nor I wanted it, so it was always going to be sold. I never really fancied moving back in with my parents, even though it would've been without my parents, if you see what I mean.'

'I don't,' replied the befuddled Cross.

'I didn't want to move back into my parents' house, neither did Freddy,' she explained. 'Daddy knew this and gifted it to us five years ago, but couldn't hold out for another two years, poor thing. You have to live for seven years after the gift for it to be tax free.'

'We are aware of that,' Cross couldn't help but say.

'It sounds so mercenary, doesn't it,' she said.

'Not at all,' replied Cross. 'It makes perfect sense, financially.'

'Having said that, the Inland Revenue are absolute buggers. They want the money within a certain time after probate, whether you've managed to sell or not, otherwise they whack on interest at an obscene rate. It's really not fair. Sure take the tax, but give us a bloody chance, mate,' she laughed again.

'Is your brother here?' Cross asked.

'Yes, he is, with the Bonhams' people. The auctioneers. They're taking away most of the furniture and the art,' she said.

'What's happening to the rest of it?' asked Ottey.

'We've decided to keep some pieces for us. Sentimental value, even though we have to pay for the privilege,' she sighed. 'Oh, here he is. Freddy, this is DS Cross and DI Ottey.'

Freddy de Sourcey was in his mid-thirties. He was dressed in fashionably understated, dark clothes. Not the normal uniform of some country rich types Ottey often came across in her work, with their 'look at me!' salmon-pink trousers, check shirts and tasselled loafers.

'Good morning,' he said cheerfully, extending his hand to the police officers as he came into the room. Ottey shook it and the young man seemed to take no offence when Cross ignored him. 'Has the help offered you any form of refreshment?' he asked.

Cross looked at Francesca. 'I was under the impression you were his sister,' he said, with a hint of reproach for her having misled him.

'Ignore him. I am. He thinks he's oh so funny,' she said warmly. 'I was actually about to make coffee for us. Would you like some, or would you prefer tea?'

'He'll only drink loose leaf,' Ottey informed her.

'Is there any other kind?' she asked with mock surprise.

'So, Edward Squire,' said Freddy, sitting down at the kitchen table and moving various half-filled packing boxes off it. 'How can I help?'

'We understand there was a dispute between you and the victim,' Cross began. 'Over a volume of Tolkien.'

'Not any old volume of Tolkien, it turned out,' Freddy added.

'What happened, exactly?' Cross asked.

'Well, as you can see, we're in the process of selling everything to pay off death duties. Even if one of us had wanted to stay, it probably wouldn't have been possible, unless we'd gone into the wedding business, which we had no desire to do. We're not a rich family. Kind of property wealthy, cash strapped, if you know what I mean. Neither of us live in the area anymore. Grandpa had been, like his father I believe, a big collector of books. So, we sold his library to Squire. Ed came and appraised it and offered what we thought was a reasonable price and that was it. Except of course it wasn't.'

'How much did he pay?'

'Seventy-five thousand for the entire library. Which we were perfectly happy with, until someone pointed out the sale of a Tolkien first edition for over three hundred grand, with an inscription from the great man to his mate "Lolly". Lolly was our grandpa Lawrence's nickname. Then an uncle told us that he had in fact been friends with Tolkien. So it was clear that it had come from our library. We were even more certain when we saw that Squire's Rare Books were the seller. We felt completely ripped off,' Freddy explained.

'Ed claimed he didn't know the book was in the collection,' Ottey pointed out.

'Then he didn't do a good job when he did the initial appraisal and valuation, did he? Either that, or he was a liar. I'm sorry, I know we shouldn't speak ill of the dead, but it's true. Had he not known he should have alerted us to it and changed the valuation. Three hundred thousand, for God's sake. It's theft, basically.'

'It's not, in point of fact,' observed Cross.

'Maybe not technically, but I'm sure you understand my point,' he retorted.

'So you went to the shop?' Ottey interjected before Cross got involved in a pedantic discourse on the definition of crime.

'I phoned first. As you can see, we're quite busy here and I didn't fancy driving over to Bristol. But he wouldn't take my calls. I ended up having to go over there, which wasn't exactly convenient.'

'And what happened?' she persisted.

'I told him I'd been made aware of the sale and the price and felt he should do the decent thing and recompense us.'

'And his response?'

'He had the nerve to say we should've been aware of what was in our library. As I told him – that was what we'd bloody employed him to do and he'd failed to do it properly. Look at this place. It's chaos. We have furniture and art experts here to help negotiate our way through it. I have to rely on them and trust them. It was the same with Ed Squire,' he argued.

'You went back and threatened him,' said Cross.

'I did what?' he laughed.

'You implied you knew people who could cause him harm,' Cross said, referring to his notebook.

Freddy laughed out loud. 'Number one, do I really look like the sort of person to make those threats, let alone know those kinds of people? However desperate I might be. Number two, it's completely untrue.'

'We have an eyewitness who said it got quite physical,' Ottey pointed out.

'Look at me!' he exclaimed. It was true he was as thin as a garden rake and didn't come across as the kind of man to make physical threats, Ottey thought.

'So what happened?' she asked.

'I did threaten him, yes. But with reporting him to the Antiquarian Booksellers' Association in London. I suppose you could argue that was the literary equivalent of breaking his legs,' he joked.

'Where were you on Wednesday night last week, between the hours of six and eight?' asked Cross.

'Where do you think I was?' he asked, looking around at the organised chaos, as if it should be obvious.

'I have no idea,' replied Cross. 'Which is why I'm asking.'

'I was here,' Freddy replied.

'Can anyone verify that?' Cross asked.

Freddy looked at his sister, who was coming over to the table with a teapot and cups. 'You didn't get here till Thursday, did you?' he said.

'No, that's right,' she replied.

'No, no one can verify that. But let me ask you a question. Why would I kill him?'

'People have killed for a lot less than a three hundred thousand pound book,' Cross pointed out.

'But if I killed him there'd be no chance of my getting my hands on any of that, surely?' he argued.

'True,' Ottey reflected.

'So, have you just decided to let the matter be?' asked Cross.

'No, it's a point of principle. I've decided to pursue them in the courts,' he replied.

'On what grounds?' asked Cross.

'I don't know. Maybe start with fraud? I'll have to speak with my lawyers,' he said.

'Will you still be going ahead?' asked Ottey.

'Yes, of course. Why wouldn't I?' he asked.

'Because Ed Squire is dead. Murdered,' offered Ottey.

'Probably another disgruntled customer,' joked de Sourcey. 'I'm sorry, that's in bad taste. But let's be frank, if he's ripped me off in this way, who's to say he hasn't done it to someone else? Maybe for even more money.'

This was certainly a thought which had already occurred to Cross.

'I think you should talk to Squire senior. Have you been through all your grandfather's correspondence and things like visitors' books?' Ottey asked.

'No. They're all in boxes, waiting to be gone through,' he replied.

'Maybe, before you go to court, you should let Torquil have a look. He might find something that he could sell for you and make this all go away,' she said.

'I'm not sure about that. Once bitten...' he replied.

'He's a different character, I think, than his son. Has quite the reputation for digging out hidden treasures that others have overlooked. I would've thought it was worth a shot,' she said.

'Maybe. I did think he was charming when I met him, I have to admit. And knowledgeable,' he said.

'Well, there you go,' she said, smiling. Freddy returned the smile, knowingly.

'Very deftly executed, Inspector, if I may say so,' de Sourcey said.

'I think it sounds like an admirable solution, Freddy,' said his sister. 'Saves you all the bother of going to court and I have a feeling he'd take nothing for his services.'

'Sold! Ganged up on, on two flanks. I concede,' he replied playfully.

18

They drove straight to the hospital after they'd finished with the de Sourcey siblings. Ottey parked up nearby and they walked towards the building. They got within sight of the main entrance of the hospital when Cross suddenly stopped.

'What do I say to him?' he asked.

'Raymond? Tell him you love him,' she replied.

'No, I can't do that.'

'Why ever not?'

'He'll be suspicious,' he told her.

'About what?'

'I don't know… that he's about to die.'

'Why would he think that?' she asked.

'Because I've never, not once in my entire life, expressed my love for him.'

'Well maybe now's a good time to start,' she replied.

Christine was, as usual, sitting next to Raymond's bed in the ICU. She stood up as George approached, and smiled.

'He's just sleeping,' she informed him. 'He wakes up for a bit, then nods off again. How did you get here?'

'I came with DI Ottey.'

'Oh, is she outside? I'll go and say hello.'

Christine left and George approached the bed. He sat in the chair his mother had just vacated and looked intensely at the only true constant in his life. His father. After a few minutes two doctors appeared.

'DS Cross, I am Dr Khan. We've spoken on the phone,' one of them began. 'This is Dr Lizzie Moss. She's a stroke and geriatric specialist. She'll be in charge of your father's post-operative care from now on.'

Dr Moss was an efficient-looking woman in her thirties. Her dark hair was tied back in a bun. George looked at her and waited for her to speak.

'As you are aware, during the course of his tumour resection your father suffered a stroke and a subsequent brain bleed. It would seem from initial observations that he has some loss of movement on his left side and his speech is a little impaired,' Moss told him.

'Will he recover?' George asked, matter-of-factly.

'At this point, I can't really say,' she replied with a directness George found gratifying.

'Will he be able to walk, or will he be in a wheelchair?' George asked.

'Again, I can't really answer that at this moment.'

When the two doctors left a few minutes later, George turned back to his father and sat down. Raymond's eyes were open. Presumably he'd been woken by the conversation with the doctors. He smiled at his son, but George had difficulty in recognising this as the left side of Raymond's mouth remained straight.

'George...' he muttered faintly.

'Hello, Dad.'

The old man held up his hand. The one closest to George.

He looked at it and decided that Raymond wanted the glass of water with a straw in it, which was on the bedside cabinet. He reached for it, but Raymond shook his head slightly. Then he held up his hand again. George looked at it for a moment, then realised his father wanted him to hold it. So he took hold of Raymond's hand for the first time in over forty years. Raymond closed his eyes in what George recognised as a look of contentedness. Josie had appeared quietly behind George but didn't want to interrupt. George was thinking about the last time he'd held his father's hand, which was when he was about six years old. They were on their way to school, hand in hand. When they arrived at the school gates, George turned to his father and announced solemnly that, now he was six, it was no longer appropriate for him to hold his father's hand on the way to school. He was far too old. With this endearingly pompous pronouncement, the child had walked into school without looking back, leaving his father beaming with pride.

Raymond opened his eyes again. George realised that in the circumstances, the onus of initiating the conversation was probably on him. But he had no idea what to say. His father had probably heard the doctors talking about his condition, but even if he hadn't, it was hardly material for a cheerful conversation. Which is what he assumed was required. Then he remembered what Ottey had told him and so said, quite stiffly, 'I love you, Dad.'

This had an unexpected, but immediate effect on Josie. Her eyes filled with tears and she beat a hasty retreat. Not so much because George might see her, but because she was encroaching on a private moment between the two men. It also prompted a single tear from Raymond's left eye, which trickled down his cheek to the pillow. George was instantly annoyed with Josie.

He knew this was the wrong thing to say and he'd been proved right by the fact that Raymond was now in tears. But he was, of course, completely wrong. Raymond knew what a conscious effort it had been for George to utter those words so alien to him, and this was what had moved him so. He also knew that either Josie or Stephen had told him to do it and he also found that profoundly moving.

George sat there for some time. A few hours, in fact. Josie and Christine took it in turns occasionally to sit with him. Finally, he looked at his watch and announced, 'I have to go.'

'Why?' asked his mother.

But before he could reply Raymond tried to speak. She leaned closer to him to hear.

'Org...' he mumbled.

'That is correct. I have organ practice,' George affirmed.

'Can't you just leave it for one week?' asked a perplexed Josie in the waiting room outside, after he'd informed her of his need for a lift to the church.

'No. I have been here for a sufficient amount of time to express both my relief and my concern. There is nothing of further use I can do. What is more he is asleep and I think will be for some time now,' he replied.

'Come on then. Let me say goodbye and I'll give you a lift.'

19

Josie pulled up outside the church. Nothing had been said in the car since they left the hospital. As George reached for the door she said, 'I'd quite like to stay and listen.'

'I wouldn't bother if I were you,' he replied.

'Why not?'

'Because you won't be able to hear anything from in here.'

He left and she burst out laughing. But she stayed where she was.

Stephen sat in the pews as he often did on a Thursday when Cross practised. He felt that George's choice of music on this particular night, and the way in which he played, were somewhat meditative and reflective. Unsurprising, in the circumstances. At the same time, he was aware that this might have been his own emotional interpretation of the situation. Even so, he thought there was an element of truth to it. He'd come to the conclusion that, on occasion, George used his playing to process what was going on at work, which was indeed true. Even though he didn't know as much, George had made several breakthroughs on cases while his mind was preoccupied with a particularly tricky piece of Handel or Bach.

Stephen was still waiting in the nave when George finished

his practice on the dot of eight, his one hour's practice strictly adhered to. It wasn't just George's need for routine that meant he always finished promptly, but his sense that the priest was doing him a favour by letting him play, which he was keen not to exploit.

'How was Raymond?' Stephen asked.

'Groggy. They confirmed he's had a stroke,' George replied.

'I'll say a mass for him.'

'If you wish.'

'Would you let me know when's a good time to visit him?' the priest continued.

'I'm not sure what the visiting hours are.'

'I meant when you think he's up to it,' Stephen explained.

'I see. Yes, I will.'

'Well, I mustn't keep you. Josie is waiting outside for you.'

'No, she's not,' said George.

'I thought I saw her from the presbytery window.'

'She sneaked in at the back just after I started playing,' George told him. They both looked towards the back of the church where Josie was sitting, she thought, unobserved.

20

Cross didn't go into the MCU that weekend, as he normally did in the early stages of a murder enquiry. He worked from home. The first thing he did was draft his resignation letter. This was a little more complicated than he thought. Should he provide reasons for it or not? In the end, for the sake of brevity and clarity, he decided not to. He could explain his reasons to DCI Carson when he gave him the letter first thing Monday morning. But, either way, he would leave the force at the conclusion of the current case.

He had decided to do some research into the esoteric world of rare books. He became familiar with the rare bookshops which still operated in the UK, although somewhat depleted now from the heyday of book buying and selling. The majority of the big ones were all in London. It didn't take him long before he came across a couple of interesting stories. One concerned the theft of over two hundred books from a customs warehouse in Feltham, near Heathrow in 2017. A gang had avoided the alarms by descending from the roof skylights on ropes; a journalist described it as being like a scene from *Mission Impossible*. They had stolen over two hundred books, worth around two and a half million pounds, which had been on their way to a big international book fair in the United States. The books were the property of three big bookselling firms and included works by Sir Isaac Newton,

Leonardo da Vinci and Copernicus. After an international search they were found a few years later in a house in Romania. The journalist had written how thieves were suddenly becoming aware of the value of books, the money to be made from them and so there was an increase in such theft. There was a shift in the paradigm away from works of art to works of literature.

More relevant to the case in hand was the charge of conspiracy in the rare book world. This had gained some traction in the last couple of years. Some of the big book dealers had been accused of attempting to fix the price of certain authors. The rare editions of writers such as Auden, Fleming, Waugh, Graham Greene, Henry James and Charles Dickens were being bought up by certain booksellers whenever they appeared on the market. The accusation was that they had chosen an author or two and would buy everything and anything to do with that author. They could then determine the market price of that author. The reason it attracted Cross's attention was that the main proponent of this accusation, which had made it into something of a campaign, was one Ed Squire. It was of course disputed by all the named traders who also took aim at Ed Squire at any given opportunity. It seemed he had made quite a few enemies along the way.

So, if you wanted a first edition of, say, Evelyn Waugh, there was only one place to go in the UK – Carnegie Books of Bedford Square. The problem had begun, as far as Cross could make out, when Ed wanted to acquire a trade first edition of Evelyn Waugh's *Brideshead Revisited*. He'd been outbid at an auction by Carnegie Books. When he approached them to take the £6,000 book off their hands, they told him he could have it for £7,000. He naturally objected to what he saw as an outrageous mark-up. He then saw a pattern in the trade with various authors being bought up by large booksellers. The prices of all these books were in the low thousands, but when you'd cornered the market in a certain author you could fix the price and so the profit became gradually more substantial for the booksellers involved.

The battle between Squire and Carnegie became something of a cause célèbre in the book world with more and more people taking sides. Portrayed as something of a David v Goliath battle, it gained more notoriety and became increasingly personal and vitriolic. Could it have had something to do with Ed Squire's murder? It was certainly of interest to Cross.

Carson came into Cross's office, first thing Monday morning. Cross had just informed Ottey of his findings at the weekend. She was now digesting it.

'So? Still no murder weapon. No suspects,' Carson announced.

'A fair assessment,' concluded Cross.

'This bloody Tolkien, though. Doesn't reflect well on our victim, does it? Got me wondering whether that kind of behaviour was typical of him. Are there other instances in the past that have maybe come home to roost?' speculated Carson.

'The Tolkien situation could have come out of financial desperation. The victim had to remortgage his house to pay off debts,' said Ottey.

'Could it be some other problem, like drugs or drink? Gambling?' Carson suggested. This gave Cross pause for thought.

'Interestingly, his father said the rare book trade was a lot like gambling. Buying a book in the hope that it will give you a good return. It's a business not without its risks,' he observed.

'Speculative?' suggested Carson.

'Yes, but speculation based on scholarship, a good knowledge of the market and a sound client base.'

'None of which it would appear the victim had in spades,' added Ottey.

'Unlike his father, no,' agreed Cross.

'We know he used the profit from the Tolkien sale to pay off the second mortgage on the house,' said Ottey thinking aloud.

'But what if there were other debts?' asked Cross.

'What's the family like?' asked Carson.

'There's something off there,' said Ottey.

'What makes you think that?' asked Carson.

'I don't know. The wife certainly seemed a little put out that we were at the house,' she said.

'But you're investigating her husband's murder. Where does she expect you to be?' Carson pointed out.

'Indeed. I think the family warrants a look at. We need to find out what happened there a decade or so ago,' said Cross.

'You've lost me now,' said Carson.

'It's just something Mackenzie came up with,' explained Ottey.

'Alice? Is she back?' Carson asked, surprised.

'I think even you would've noticed if she were, sir,' said Cross, before leaving the room and a broad grin on Ottey's face.

Half an hour later, there was a knock on Carson's office door. He looked up to see Cross waiting politely for permission to enter.

'Come in,' Carson instructed. He'd asked Cross several times in the past just to knock and come straight in, but the detective persisted in waiting. He walked in and proffered Carson a white envelope, which Carson took. He was immediately concerned. He couldn't remember a single instance of Cross handing him a letter, during the entire time he'd known him. He opened it, read it quickly, then put it carefully back into the envelope.

'Have you spoken with Josie about this?' he asked.

'I have not.'

'Why now?'

'I need to spend time with my father, helping with his recovery. I need to care for him. This job won't allow for that,' Cross replied.

'Have you discussed this with him?' asked Carson.

'I have not.'

'Don't you think you should?'

'No.'

'Why not?' Carson went on, unsurprised by this answer.

'Because I know what he'll say,' Cross said.

'May I ask what that is?' asked Carson.

'He'll tell me not to.'

'And why would he do that?'

'Because he knows I enjoy my work and because he'll think it an unnecessary gesture,' Cross explained.

'Is that what this is? A gesture?'

'Bad choice of word. Action. I should have said course of action,' replied Cross.

'Don't you think you should talk to him? I mean, he may well have views on the matter which you should take into consideration before going through with this,' Carson reasoned.

'That may be so, but they're irrelevant.'

'How can that possibly be?' asked Carson.

'Because I've decided it's what I'm going to do,' insisted Cross.

'You know, George, life isn't always as simple as that. There are often other things to consider in situations like this.'

'Such as?'

'Your father's wishes.'

'Irrelevant,' insisted Cross.

'With all due respect, George, they very much are relevant,' replied Carson.

'DI Ottey says that when people say, "with all due respect", what they actually mean is "with no respect at all",' said Cross.

'I can assure you that's not the case here. But I'll tell you what I'm going to do. I'm not going to accept this resignation. I'm going to place it here in my drawer, until you've spoken with your father,' said Carson, doing just so.

'Why?'

'Because I have a distinct feeling you might change your mind,' Carson said, smiling.

'I won't,' Cross replied confidently, before leaving the room.

Carson was a worried man. He wasn't at all sure, despite what he'd just said to Cross, that a conversation with his father might indeed change his mind. He was a stubborn bugger at the best of times. It was never easy to predict how Cross might behave in some situations like this, while on the other hand being incredibly easy to predict how he would react in others. This was in part because at times he was enigmatically unpredictable. This was what made him such a brilliant, if indescribably frustrating, detective. Carson knew he would be a huge loss to the department and his, Carson's, burgeoning reputation. If Cross had genuinely made up his mind, there was nothing he would be able to do about it. It would be what it was. His first instinct was to inform Josie, his second was that if he did, it might backfire spectacularly. He decided he'd have to keep this to himself till it sorted itself out, one way or another.

21

'Henleaze?' Ottey asked as she and Cross got into her car.
'No. The shop,' Cross replied.

Squire's Rare Books had reopened for business. But when they got there, they were surprised by two things. Firstly, that the shop seemed incredibly busy and secondly that Sam was there on his own. He was on the ground floor when they got there, ringing up the sale of a new book on the till. He seemed to do this almost reluctantly, as if it were a slight on him.

'Is Persephone not here?' asked Cross.

'No. Just me. Torquil said he can't face coming back just now. Which is understandable, but he still wanted the shop opening. Someone's got to be here,' Sam said.

'That's very loyal of you,' observed Cross.

'Are you always this busy?' asked Ottey.

'No. It's amazing what murder will do for a bookshop, it would seem. Brings out all the ghouls, who have absolutely zero interest in buying books. They're just carrion birds hovering over the scene of death,' he said dramatically. 'I've had to close the first floor.'

'Why?' asked Cross.

'"Where was he killed? Can we see? Oh my god! Is that blood?" I can't manage both floors on my own. Unpaid stock would be flying out of the door. Let me close up for lunch early, once this lot have gone.'

The shop, it seemed, maintained the rather quaint habit of closing for lunch at two o'clock, after everyone else's lunch. Once the customers had left, they sat upstairs in the kitchen.

'It's remarkable how much crime there is in the book world. I had no idea,' Cross began.

'What do you mean?' asked Sam.

'Well, the impression it gives, or maybe we as the general public infer, is of a polite, rarefied, well-mannered, possibly old-fashioned, world. But look a little more closely, under the surface, and it's far from the truth. Fakes and forgeries have been going on for centuries. In modern times you only have to look back at Book Row in New York, theft was rife,' Cross began.

'That's absolutely true,' Sam agreed.

'Do you know...' said Cross, turning to Ottey. This always prefaced a small lecture from him about something which she knew nothing and suspected, at times, that he had only very recently become an expert in. '... that in 1920s Manhattan, Book Row was an enormous concern? Dozens upon dozens of second-hand bookstores were situated almost on top of each other. Cinema was in its infancy, no television, no internet. Books were the main cultural currency of the time. There was nothing else. Books had a virtual monopoly on the exchange of ideas. The market for rare books was developing, like the art market. And, as with all markets that have a financial value, the criminal element found a way to exploit it. The thieves of Book Row made a killing stealing from one store and selling to another. Booksellers were also at it. Prowling each other's stores looking for unidentified, underpriced rare books they knew they could sell at a profit. Or a book they already had a client for. But of course, they became well known to each other and a close eye was kept on them. They could no longer steal from each other for themselves. So, they invented a system where they would walk around a bookstore and pull any books they were interested in slightly out from the shelf, or tilt them at an angle. Shortly after, a professional thief in their employ would follow them and steal the designated books for them.'

'Again, absolutely true,' said Sam, who was enjoying Cross's knowledge.

'And then there were the forgers. The most famous of all was Thomas James Wise, a well-known collector and businessman, later discovered to have been one of the biggest forgers of literary works of all time.'

'Indeed,' agreed Sam.

'It's fascinating stuff,' continued Cross, warming to his theme. 'He was exposed in 1939. He'd sold a volume of Elizabeth Barrett Browning's sonnets, claiming it was a first edition from 1847. Two men called Carter and Pollard became suspicious and began an investigation. A forensic analysis of the paper, even back then, revealed that it was composed of chemical wood with a trace of rag, which could not have been manufactured before 1874. Also, the text was printed in a typeface of which certain letters weren't cut till 1880.' Cross delighted in this literary trivia. 'Then there were thefts from university libraries before security was tightened and technology improved.'

'That still occurs,' said Sam.

'Was Ed, to your knowledge, an honest bookseller?' Cross asked, changing the tone of the conversation in an instant.

'I'm sorry?' Sam replied in shock.

'Did he ever indulge in any, shall we say, shady practices in the rare book world, Sam?' asked Cross.

'Whatever leads you to make such a suggestion?' asked Sam.

'His murder, perhaps,' replied Cross.

'This is a reputable establishment,' Sam retorted.

'What was Ed like as a bookseller?' Cross asked.

'Well, he may have been many things, but he was neither a forger nor a thief, if that's what you're trying to imply,' replied Sam, his outrage still close to the surface.

'What many things?' Cross pressed.

'He was a little lazy, if I'm honest. Didn't put in the hours. Do the work. You have to do hours of research to make this business a success. But it wasn't for him. Too boring, I think. He was someone who wanted instant success. So, in many ways, this was the wrong line of work for him. He wanted things to happen fast, and more often than not it caught up with him,' he replied.

'In what way?' asked Ottey.

'He was very charismatic, Ed. Great salesman. But it was always about the sale, not about the book itself. I don't really think he loved books in the way his father and I do. He rushed into things. When he got into trouble...'

'What kind of trouble?' asked Cross.

'If a sale went wrong, or he lost money on a deal, he'd always think the next acquisition would sort everything out. There was always something coming round the corner. He was like a gambler thinking there was a dead cert in the next race, which would make up for the losses in the previous three.'

'Was he in trouble?' asked Ottey.

'Financially? I'm not sure,' he replied uncomfortably. 'You should really speak with Torquil.'

'He wasn't frightened of confrontation, was he? Taking on people or the bookselling establishment, if such a thing exists,' said Ottey.

'Oh, it very much exists,' he said, half laughing.

'You say that as if it's something you don't necessarily approve of,' she commented.

He said nothing back.

'What was your view on his anti-price-fixing campaign?' asked Cross.

'Ah,' he almost groaned.

'You don't approve?' asked Ottey.

'It's not a question of approving or disapproving,' he replied. 'It's just that it became such an obsession with him, at the cost of everything else.'

'Like what?' asked Cross.

'Well, the business for a start. It became all-consuming for him and wherever he looked he saw this conspiracy lurking.'

'You're making him sound paranoid,' remarked Ottey.

'I don't mean to. I just think it got well and truly out of perspective.'

'Do you think he had a point?' asked Cross.

'Yes and no. I thought, in principle, if it was happening then it was wrong. I mean, there's always been talk of a cartel or a big boys' club, right from the days of the auction ring.'

'Some might say this was just a modern version of it,' Cross remarked.

'That's exactly what Ed did say. And Torquil. But the old man tried to persuade him to back down a little, in the end,' Sam told them.

'Why was that?' asked Cross.

'The wisdom of old age, perhaps? I think he realised from his own battles in the past that there was often little to be won. And even that came at a cost.'

'What kind of cost?' asked Cross.

'A reputation as someone who was difficult. It impacted

Torquil's friendships and relationships in the trade. I think that was why he was always glad to be here in the south-west, away from the hub of booksellers in the capital.'

'Did it lose Ed a lot of friends? Make him a number of enemies?' asked Ottey.

'Again, yes and no. A lot of people thought it was a storm in a teacup and in the end there did seem to be one particular target for his anger,' he said.

'Anger?' Cross picked up on this.

'Yes, I think he was angry. He'd sometimes work himself up into a complete rage in here.'

'Who was this main target?' asked Ottey.

'Carnegie Books of Bedford Square, in London. Patrick Gibb. The latest in a long line of bookselling Gibbs going back a couple of centuries, he's fond of telling almost everyone he meets. He got quite het up about Ed's campaign and threatened legal action, as he thought some of his written accusations were libellous. It felt as if Ed was breaking some kind of bibliophile omertà. But it was like he said. He didn't owe these people any loyalty. Particularly the big firms, who showed little or no loyalty to the minnows.'

'Did Ed consider himself to be a minnow?' asked Cross.

'No, not in the least. Quite the opposite. More of a freshwater shark,' he said, laughing. Then his face turned serious. 'You can't think all of this had anything to do with his murder, surely? This is the world of rare books we're talking about here.'

'People keep saying that,' observed Cross.

'Well maybe because the idea of it is absurd,' suggested Sam.

'Except for the fact of one murdered bookseller,' Cross reminded him.

22

Cross decided to have a closer look at Ed Squire's financial accounts, before they paid his father Torquil another visit. He did a lengthy examination of both the business and the personal accounts. Normally this would be outsourced to a freelance forensic accountant, but Cross enjoyed this kind of detailed, slightly monotonous work. He would often come across small anomalies that seemed innocuous initially but turned out to be significant to an investigation. He had also told Ottey when she asked him why he bothered with such a tedious task, that he was much better than any forensic accountant he'd come across.

Before Cross was able to make a start there was a knock on his door. It was Prianka. She waited patiently outside, until he beckoned her. Ottey got up from her desk and followed her in. Presumably she had some information. She then presented it in the way a pupil in school might read out to class in front of their favourite teacher, with nerves but a suspicion that she had done well.

'I've been looking into all the addresses associated with the case, as you asked me to. So, the shop, the Squires' house in Henleaze, Persephone's flat, Sam's flat and Denholm Simpson's bookshop. Something's cropped up. Just over a decade ago the police were called to a disturbance at the Squires' house.

Ed Squire had been assaulted and was hospitalised with facial injuries caused by a broken bottle.'

Cross recalled that there were faint, old scars on the victim's forehead, leading into his scalp, but said nothing.

'Was someone arrested for it?' asked Ottey.

'Yes. A Sarah Hartwell. Ed Squire didn't want to press charges, but the police went ahead anyway. She got a two-year suspended sentence.'

'Hartwell?' repeated Cross, familiar with the name.

'That seems light. Who was this woman?' asked Ottey.

'Persephone's mother,' replied Prianka.

'When was this?' Cross asked.

'Twenty fourteen. But here's what might be interesting. There was another disturbance at the same address earlier this year. The police were called again but she was just moved on,' Prianka told them.

'Who?'

'Sarah Hartwell, of course,' proclaimed a voice in the doorway. It was Carson, who had managed, as he so often did, to sneak up on the conversation unobserved. Ottey had once said she thought he was probably really good at paintball – the kind of thing, she humoured herself in situations like this, she imagined he occupied his weekends with. 'At last.'

'What?' asked Cross.

'We have our first suspect. Bring her in,' he instructed.

'I don't think…' Cross began.

'Make it happen, George. Let me know when she's in custody,' Carson said over his shoulder, retreating before Cross had a chance to further elaborate his objection.

'Why does he always do that?' Cross asked Ottey as they went to her car. He was genuinely interested.

'Because it makes him feel as if he's in charge,' she replied.

'But he *is* in charge,' Cross replied.

'Of course he is. He just needs to remind everyone now and then.'

Sarah Hartwell had the look of someone who felt that life was out to get her at any given opportunity. She was in her mid-fifties. Thin vertical lines around her mouth indicated she was a smoker. Life had added a good decade to her looks. She had short grey hair that almost shouted 'what are you looking at?' to anyone whose eyes strayed north of her forehead. They didn't arrest her. Cross didn't want to, because he felt taking her into the Voluntary Assistance suite would be more conducive to a productive interview, and Ottey simply because it was the precise opposite of what Carson had instructed them to do.

'Mrs Hartwell, you're aware of why we've asked you in here today,' began Ottey.

'I am.'

'Could we begin by asking you where you were on the evening of Wednesday the twenty-fourth of April this year? Between the hours of six and eight?'

'Where I always am,' she sighed.

'And where is that?' Ottey asked.

'At home.'

'What were you doing?'

'What I always do.'

'Which is?'

'Playing mah-jong with my close circle of female friends,' she replied.

Cross wrote this down with interest. He hadn't been expecting that. But then Ottey followed up with, 'I'm assuming that was a joke. What were you really doing?'

'Drinking, eating and watching the TV,' she replied.

Cross looked up, then drew a line through his notes.

'On your own?'

'Correct.'

'Tell us about Ed Squire,' Cross began. 'What was your relationship with him like?'

'You know the answer to that question. It's why you've asked me in here,' she said.

'I'd like to hear it from you,' Cross said.

She paused for a moment.

'I don't have a relationship with any of the Squires.'

'But they're your family,' Cross pointed out.

'I married Victoria's brother, yes. Then he left me, as I'm sure you know. I'm divorced from him, and the rest of them it would seem.'

'You have a daughter, Persephone,' Cross said.

'I do.'

'Interesting choice of name,' he commented.

'Oh, nothing to do with me. She changed it when she went up to Oxford. Her real name, her birth name, is Anne,' she answered, sounding like she was still hurt by this.

'What had happened when you were arrested at the Squires' house?' asked Cross.

'It's all in the police report,' she said unhelpfully.

'What happened is in the police report. Not why it happened,' Cross replied.

'I'm sure if you do a little digging, you'll find out soon enough,' she said.

'It'd be quicker if you just told us,' Cross pointed out.

'And why should I bother with that?'

'Because if you don't, I'll arrest you. Then we can see if a couple of hours in a cell doesn't make you a little more helpful,' said Ottey who was losing patience with this woman. Hartwell weighed up this threat for a moment.

'Persephone has had several mental-health issues over the years. Well, ever since the divorce really. She didn't take it well and her relationship with her father, such as it is, is still a problem for her,' she replied.

'She seemed quite close when we saw them together at her flat,' asked Ottey.

'Yes, well, I'm afraid a lot of that is for show – on his part.'

'Why?' Ottey continued.

'He has another family now. Much younger than her. For a long time it was as if she didn't exist. At least that's how she felt about it. It was as if she was no longer his child. It has got a little better recently. I don't know why. But he's come to understand, finally, that just because she's in her twenties doesn't mean she doesn't need a father. Anyway, she found it really difficult around the age of fifteen, sixteen. I was having problems of my own. She went to live with Vicky and Ed for a while. Well, a couple of years on and off. It seemed a good idea at the time.'

'What made you change your mind about that?' asked Cross.

'She loves Charlie and Seb and to be fair, they were very good to her. I thought it was good for her to be in a secure family environment. She's always been quite bookish. When her dad left she disappeared into them. It was a way out for her. She lived in other worlds thanks to her reading. She's quite academic and Vicky and Ed seemed to offer her something I couldn't.' She seemed to be wandering around the question. Cross ignored the fact that she hadn't answered him.

'Which was?' he asked.

'I don't know. A family life, a semblance of family life maybe. Whatever, more of a family life than I could give her. I was working as a secretary at a small industrial firm. Hardly fulfilling or worthwhile. So I worked, then came home and drank, pretty much. I was that miserable. At least with them she'd get fed properly.'

'Why did you assault Ed Squire? With a bottle,' asked Cross returning to the unanswered question.

'Percy got into Oxford. Everyone was so thrilled. Vicky especially. You could be forgiven for thinking she was her kid. Neither of hers got into Oxbridge. She was obsessed with it. Won't admit it. But she was. They were very good, though. Paid for a tutor for Percy, when it seemed she might have a chance of getting in,' she said, avoiding the question.

'Again. Why did you assault Ed Squire?' Cross repeated.

'Have you spoken to my daughter?' she asked.

'We have,' replied Ottey.

'Did you talk to her about Oxford?' Sarah asked.

'We did not.'

'First time round, she only lasted half a term,' she told them.

'What happened?' asked Cross.

'She couldn't cope,' Sarah answered quietly. 'It was a nightmare. I think in many ways she was too young. Not in numbers, I mean she was eighteen, but maturity-wise. But then again that isn't surprising. She should've taken a year out, particularly in the circumstances. She ended up taking one and travelled with me in tow for a bit. It was wonderful,' she reminisced.

'What circumstances?' asked Cross.

'She became pregnant when she was sixteen.'

'Did she have the baby?' asked Ottey.

'She didn't, no,' she said shaking her head in disbelief.

'What happened?' asked Ottey.

'She had a termination.'

'Why didn't she have the baby?' asked Cross.

'Vicky was completely against it. Said it would ruin Percy's life. What I found completely unforgiveable was that they made her promise not to tell me, but of course she did. And that's why I had a go at him with a bottle,' she said, still smarting at the betrayal.

'You're still angry,' Ottey suggested.

'Do you have children?' Sarah asked her.

'Two. Two girls,' Ottey replied.

'How would you feel about it?'

'I'd want to kill them,' Ottey replied. Sarah said nothing.

'Is that why you attacked Ed?' asked Cross.

'When?' she asked.

'That's an interesting question. Have you attacked him more than once?' asked Cross.

'No. Just the once.'

'Then why ask?' said Ottey.

'Because I wanted to make sure you weren't accusing me of attacking him the night he died,' she replied.

'I was referring to 2014,' Cross clarified.

'I wanted to talk to them. To find out how they thought it was okay. He was so arrogant. As if it was none of my business. They had my grandchild aborted. Made my daughter have an abortion without even discussing it with her mother. They just went ahead. They had no right to do that. When he told me someone had to take control of the situation, because I certainly wasn't in control, I completely lost it. My baby had had an abortion without my knowledge. I'm not proud of attacking him, I was drunk. But it is what it is,' she said. Almost defiantly.

'Persephone works at the bookshop now. How do you feel about that?' asked Ottey.

'She's a grown woman. She loves working with the old man. He and Ed couldn't be more different. It's a good job. She seems happy. What am I supposed to do? I lost her once. I'm not going to lose her again.'

'The police were called to a disturbance at their house, involving you, earlier this year. What was that about?' asked Cross.

'Ian was there. He owed me money. It was nothing to do with Ed,' she replied. Cross made a note of this before looking up.

'Did you kill Ed Squire, Mrs Hartwell?' he asked.

'Why would I? What would I gain from it? And why now?' Cross closed his file and got up.

'Please don't leave Bristol without letting us know,' said Ottey, following his cue by getting up and giving her a card. She read the card. Cross often wondered why people did that. It was obvious what it was. Was it some form of social protocol he failed to understand?

'Were you surprised when you heard about it?' asked Cross.

'Of course. The man's a rare bookseller, for God's sake,' she laughed.

'What was he like as a character?' asked Cross.

'Ed? An absolute charmer,' she said witheringly. 'He had those blue eyes. They were a lethal weapon. His superpower. A complete charmer, but like all charmers he was completely unreliable. If you could monetise broken promises, that man would've been a millionaire. Should've been a car salesman, or a salesman of some sort.'

'He was,' Cross pointed out.

'That's true. But he was a crap bookseller, unlike Torquil. He never had a love of books. He just went into it because it was handed to him on a plate and was the easiest thing to do at the time.'

'So, all was not as it seems in the Squire household,' pronounced Carson.

'Apparently not,' Ottey answered.

'And you've let her go because...?' he asked, not really wanting an answer so much as, if it turned out to be a mistake further down the line, he could point to his having had doubts.

'Aside from the fact that we have no evidence linking her to the crime?' asked Cross.

'Yet,' Carson pointed out.

'Why kill Ed Squire now? Why kill the provider of her daughter's pay cheque at all?' said Cross.

'Our only witness, Persephone, is also convinced it was a man,' Ottey pointed out.

'From the angle she saw the individual, it could be argued it might well have been a woman,' Cross contradicted her.

'So, what next?' asked Carson.

'We should be getting the report on his phone activity in the next couple of days. Hopefully that might lead us somewhere,' Ottey told him.

'I need to complete the accounts audit,' added Cross.

'Any trailers?' Carson asked. Cross didn't have a clue what he was talking about. 'You know, George. Forthcoming attractions? Any teasers you want to impart to whet our appetite?'

'I have no idea what you're talking about, sir. I can tell you that as it's likely he knew his killer, the answer lies either in his personal life—'

'Like Sarah Hartwell,' interrupted Carson.

'—or his business life,' Cross continued, ignoring his boss.

As they left, Carson stopped Ottey.

'Josie, got a moment for a couple of photographs?' he asked eagerly. He'd become a father the previous year and was still in a post-natal state of Dad-euphoria. He got out his phone and showed her probably the fiftieth photograph of his baby he'd shown her in the last fortnight. She made suitably appreciative cooing comments.

23

Frustratingly, not much progress was made over the next few weeks. This was often the case in murder investigations. There would be lulls when detectives just sat at their desks, rereading witness statements, reviewing CCTV footage endlessly and generally scratching their heads, trying to find a breakthrough. The people who found this lack of developments most upsetting were, understandably, the families of the victims. If they couldn't see any progress, arrests, suspects, the discovery of murder weapons, then it seemed as though nothing was happening at all. Cross often took advantage of these periods to visit the families again, ostensibly to inform them of the paucity of leads. But in reality, it was an attempt to uncover anything relevant they might be keeping to themselves. Either because they thought it was unimportant, or because they were worried it might reflect badly on the victim.

So, he decided they should pay Victoria Squire another visit. Both his and Prianka's research had brought a couple more interesting, not necessarily leads, questions for her. DI Ottey had, by virtue of her new rank, been deployed by Carson to oversee a couple of other investigations and outstanding cases at the MCU. So their journey in the car was her first opportunity to catch up with Cross's research. They'd called in advance as Cross wanted Victoria to have notice of their visit so she could consider, if she was holding onto something, whether to reveal it or not.

'This is all very disappointing,' she began, as they sat down in her living room. Cross noticed immediately that there were several new framed photographs of Ed around the room. Cards of condolence, which had adorned the room in the past few weeks, were piled up on the table neatly. She seemed to be in the process of replying to them. 'But I suppose it's often the case in a killing as strange as this one.'

'What do you mean by strange?' asked Cross.

'Well, I don't know. Surprising. Inexplicable. I mean, he sold books for a living,' she replied.

'Murder investigations can take time. It's not like you see on the TV,' replied Ottey.

'I don't watch much television, to be honest with you. So, I wouldn't know,' she replied with that unspoken pride people often had when claiming to avoid what they obviously saw as a rather common, modern vice. They sat there for a moment then she said, 'I sense there is more to this visit than simply telling me there is nothing to tell me.'

'Did your husband enjoy his work, Mrs Squire?' asked Cross.

'Yes. I think so. What am I saying? Yes, of course he did. He was doing what he loved, after all,' she replied.

'Not just doing what his father loved?' asked Cross.

'Well both, obviously.'

'How did he find the book world?' Cross continued.

'Much the same as anyone else, I suppose. Interesting. Challenging. He often said he would've loved to have been a bookseller a hundred years ago, rather than now.'

'Why?'

'Books were such a different phenomenon then. More

important, in a sense, than now. The book trade was different. He loved Walter Spencer's book *Forty Years in My Bookshop*. He marvelled at how literary giants of that age would regularly go into the shop, like Thomas Hardy and Oscar Wilde. Ed thought the whole thing was very romantic,' she told them.

'I can understand that. I've been doing a little research into the world of rare books myself, since working on this case. It is fascinating and I think, had I not become a police officer, it would have suited me very well,' Cross mused.

'Really?' Victoria asked.

'Yes. I like the idea of collecting. I've resisted it myself as I know I'm prone to become a little obsessive. The nearest thing I come to collecting is convictions.'

Victoria Squire laughed at this.

'Oh, I'm being perfectly serious,' replied Cross, surprised by her reaction. 'I have a summation of all of my successful convictions in ledgers. I find it comforting to know they're there. Also encouraging when things aren't going particularly well, as with this case. I'm reminded of when things seemed hopeless in past cases, then something happens and everything falls into place. I like the idea of expertise, and detecting has become my expertise. I think I would have found an area in the rare book world to dedicate myself to, and become an expert in. I like the specificity of specialism. Like Torquil's expertise in Brunel.'

Ottey found herself intrigued by this. It was the closest she'd ever come to hearing Cross talk about himself and it made such sense to her, knowing him as she did.

'Torquil is a world expert,' Victoria stated proudly.

'He is.'

'And what would you have specialised in, do you think, Sergeant?' she asked, warming to the conversation.

'Oh, that's easy. Organ music. Scores. Manuscripts,' he replied.

'DS Cross plays the church organ extremely well,' Ottey said, like a proud parent.

'Really?' Victoria replied, unable to disguise her surprise.

'I think research and cataloguing would have been my main strength though,' Cross continued.

'Well, it's never too late.'

'Oh, I think we both know it is. Did your husband have a speciality at all?' Cross asked.

'His first love was modern fiction, first editions. English authors. That became his speciality. He also had a predilection for the old explorers. But that was a very crowded field. Although...' She faltered, as if she'd changed her mind about what she was about to say. 'But mainly first editions.'

'I've been examining your husband's correspondence on his computer,' said Cross, suddenly changing the subject.

'Oh yes,' she replied nervously.

'He had a great turn of phrase,' Cross commented.

'He did,' she agreed with a smile. 'I always said there was a novel lurking in there somewhere. It was actually something he talked about doing in his retirement.'

'Was he planning to retire?' asked Cross.

'No. It's just something people say, don't they? I think he would've gone on selling books till he...' She stopped and had to compose herself.

'Perhaps he might've written something about the rare book world,' Cross suggested. 'A novel set among the dusty shelves of literary London.'

'Or Bristol,' she corrected him.

'He wasn't shy in taking on things he didn't like professionally, was he?' asked Cross.

'What do you mean?'

'Well, I'm sure you're aware of his latest hobby horse. You can't feel that passionate about something and not discuss it at home,' Cross said.

'I'm not sure I know what you're talking about,' she replied.

'Surely he talked about it at home. Sam Taylor says it became an all-consuming obsession,' Cross continued.

'I think calling it a hobby horse is a little patronising,' she retorted.

'So, you are aware of what I'm talking about?'

'Ed was quick to take on people who he thought weren't playing fair, or abiding by the rules,' she replied.

'What rules?'

'The unwritten rules of the rare book world.'

'I wasn't aware there were any until, of course, I read Ed's campaigning emails. He was quite preoccupied in the last couple of years about the increasing practice by some booksellers in London cornering the market in the first editions of certain modern authors. Thereby gaining a monopoly and controlling the future price of such writers,' he said.

'It was like a bloody cartel. Yes, he was quite animated by it,' she agreed.

'It's not illegal of course,' Cross pointed out.

'No, but grossly unfair to everyone else. Mainly the small bookseller,' she replied.

'Your husband had a good customer with a particular passion for Evelyn Waugh,' said Cross.

'Geoffrey Hardyman, yes, that's right.'

'And he would source rare editions of Waugh for him?' Cross continued.

'Which became increasingly hard to do,' she said.

'Why?' asked Ottey.

'Carnegie, mainly,' Victoria began to explain. 'They're a rare bookshop in London. A while back they started quietly buying up all the Waugh they could. The internet made it so much easier for them. If there was a good quality first edition... actually what am I talking about – they weren't always bothered about quality. They'd buy inferior ones just to get them off the market. But first editions, proofs, volumes inscribed by the author, they just hoovered them up.'

'How did people figure it out?' asked Ottey.

'Because the prices of various authors suddenly increased in a way that didn't make sense. Way beyond their real value. But they had recalibrated the market by then. It became a pattern people couldn't ignore,' Victoria explained. 'Ed became aware of it because of his own interest in Waugh. But the more he delved into it, the more widespread it appeared to be. So, he decided to do something about it and draw attention to it.'

'That must've made him popular,' said Ottey.

'Oh no, quite the opposite,' replied Cross, surprised at his colleague's lack of understanding. 'It must've made things very difficult for you.'

'It did, particularly at auction. Ed would go to an auction and find he was completely unable to buy anything at a reasonable price. Other bidders would suddenly appear and drive the price up to unmanageable heights,' she said.

'Was this just with Evelyn Waugh?' asked Ottey.

'No! Anything and everything. As soon as it was known Ed was bidding, it happened. It was a nightmare. He stopped going for a while. Something he loved doing. He had to bid more and more on the internet. Which in turn made him all the more determined to expose what he saw as essentially corruption,' she said, now getting noticeably upset.

'So it was something of a conspiracy,' commented Ottey.

'It was.'

'But surely Waugh and all these other authors aren't *that* valuable?' Ottey pointed out.

'If you own every book available on the market you can make them a lot more valuable than they should be,' replied Victoria.

'It reminds me of the old book auction ring,' said Cross.

'That's exactly what Pa said,' replied Victoria.

'Which he, in turn, was very vociferous about,' added Cross.

'To his cost,' replied Victoria. 'It was like history repeating itself.'

'This is all very interesting, but would anyone go as far as killing someone over it? I mean, as you said, we are talking about rare booksellers here,' commented Ottey.

'Well, we are investigating the murder of a rare bookseller, DI Ottey,' Cross reminded her. From anyone else this would've carried an edge which she would've resented. But Cross was just emphasising the situation for the benefit of Victoria. He turned back to her. 'Why did Ed's campaign come to a sudden halt about a year ago?'

'I think he just got fed up with it.'

'Really? After expending all that energy? All that effort? That passion, raging against the injustice of it all?' he asked.

'He decided he wasn't getting anywhere and so devoted his time more usefully to the business,' she replied.

'I sense you didn't approve of the campaign,' said Ottey.

'It wasn't getting anywhere fast, and he was in danger of making himself something of a laughing stock,' she replied.

They went to leave. Then, as they got to the door, Cross turned and asked her, 'Why didn't you tell us about Persephone living with you while she was an adolescent?'

'I don't see how that's relevant. I mean, why would I?'

'Do you see much of Sarah, her mother, these days?'

'I don't, no. She seems to assume I've taken my brother's side in their split.'

'Have you? Taken his side?' Cross asked.

'Absolutely not. He behaved like an absolute pig and I told him so.'

Cross nodded thoughtfully.

'Why? Do you think Sarah killed him?' Victoria suddenly asked.

'We don't know,' replied Cross, wondering what might have given her cause to ask this. He and Ottey left.

24

The offices of Carnegie Books were in Bedford Square, London. They were very well appointed. The company had been there for over two hundred years and there was a sedate confidence about the building, as if it knew that, unlike any of the visitors who came through its doors, it would still be there in another two hundred years. The walls up the staircase were adorned with framed notes from famous authors and signed photographs of them. Bills of sale for books were made out to Charles Dickens, Anthony Trollope and Oscar Wilde. It had the same musty smell as Squire's Rare Books in Bristol. As they walked past the ground floor where various people were working in complete silence, you could be forgiven for thinking you were in an ancient university. Gibb's large office was at the top of the building. His chair backed onto the square behind. The room was filled with bookshelves and mostly ancient-looking leather volumes, some in glass cases. Gibb was a quiet man, bald, with a goatee beard. Probably in his seventies, Cross thought. Quietly spoken too, as if raising one's voice to be heard wasn't something he had to do in the world he operated in. He looked like he would be more comfortable buried in a book rather than engaged in conversation. He had a habit of stroking his hands when speaking, as if he were comforting himself. Their dryness made a strange phasing sound, emphasised by the hollows of his palms, as he did it. He seemed not only dismissive of Ed Squire's campaign, but of the man, his father and their 'provincial' operation. He said the word as if it were a universally understood slight.

'Both my father and I had dealings with Torquil,' he said with some disdain. 'He's a barrow boy.'

'With an acknowledged expertise in Brunel,' Cross pointed out.

'He seemed perfectly affable. Everyone's got to come from somewhere,' added Ottey.

The bookseller looked at her and, to her mind, was possibly verging on the edge of the dangerous, racist, 'and where did you come from, originally?' question. Something she'd become all the more familiar with since she joined the police. But fortunately for him, he refrained. Or was it just that she was becoming oversensitive? No, he was definitely toying with it.

'Don't let that sweet old bookseller act fool you,' he said instead. 'That man was ruthless in his time when it came to pursuing a book.'

'Something, presumably, Carnegie Books is above?' asked Cross.

Gibb ignored him.

'Just look at the way he left his partner,' Gibb continued.

'A partner later jailed for forging inscriptions in first editions. I think it could be argued he showed good judgement in leaving,' Cross reflected.

'If, of course, he was unaware of it,' said Gibb.

'Why such an aggressive attitude? Such a low opinion of the Squires?' asked Cross. 'Is it perhaps because there was more than an element of truth to Ed's accusations levelled against you and others?'

'There was no truth in any of it.'

'Then why did it concern you so much?' asked Cross.

'It didn't.'

'Yet you threatened him with legal action,' Cross pointed out.

'I did.'

'Did you consult lawyers, or begin proceedings?'

'I did not.'

'Why was that?'

'I realised it was just an annoyance and I could more usefully spend my time on other things,' he replied.

'Nothing to do with the fact that, if you went to court, the alleged price fixing might be examined in detail, with results that might not be favourable to you?' asked Cross.

'No,' he replied cagily.

'Not a good look, I imagine,' Cross went on.

'The claims were without merit,' Gibb protested.

'According to you. Perhaps the court might have seen it a different way. Not worth the risk,' said Cross.

'What's your point?' asked Gibb, starting to get tetchy.

'I'm not making a point, merely asking questions. Did Squire's campaign have an adverse effect on your sales, would you say?' said Cross.

'Of course not.'

'What makes you say that so emphatically?' Cross asked.

'Why would it? Because someone makes misguided and unfounded accusations? Would that stop people buying from us? Of course not. I'm afraid it shows how little you know about book buying and selling,' he retorted.

'Just so we're clear, I know nothing of the book world. I may well learn more over the coming days or weeks, maybe months.

But you should treat me as a complete ignoramus when it comes to your world, Mr Gibb.'

This discomforted Gibb, Ottey noticed. It often happened with people when they didn't know how to deal with Cross. The more astute of them often inferred a need to be cautious. As was the case here.

'You're a specialist in Evelyn Waugh,' Cross continued. Gibb sighed, knowing where this was going.

'Among other authors, yes,' he replied. 'I have a particular fondness for Waugh. My father met him on several occasions. He was a regular customer of his.' He then got up and went to a glass cabinet on the other side of the room which he unlocked. He carefully took out a book and brought it over. He sat back down and held it up for them to see. 'A first edition of *A Handful of Dust*, nineteen thirty-four. My favourite of his novels. It ranks alongside *Brideshead Revisited*, in my opinion. Look inside,' he instructed Cross, leaning over his desk to hand it to him. Cross did so.

'"To Patrick on the occasion of his sixteenth birthday, with fondest regards from Evelyn",' Cross read.

'My father had the edition in stock and knew my love for it. Waugh signed it at a memorable lunch the three of us had at Wiltons,' Gibb told them.

'What's it worth?' asked Ottey.

'It's priceless to me. As you can see, I have a personal and emotional attachment to Waugh. I personally own a first edition of all his novels. This, I can assure you, is not out of a determination to corner the market in Evelyn Waugh, but for my own pleasure,' Gibb replied pompously. Cross handed the book back to him. 'Would I be the first to say how unlikely it is that Ed's murder had anything to do with the book trade?

I mean, look around you,' he said referring to his office. 'It's a very reserved, conservative world.'

'You would not,' said Cross. 'This firm has something of a history with the Squires, does it not?'

'We haven't done a huge amount of business with them, I don't think. When Torquil was a runner, he might well have bought and sold from my father. But I wouldn't know,' he answered.

'I didn't mean business. I meant conflict. Torquil and your father,' replied Cross.

'Yes, the ring business. I've often thought recently how history seemed to be repeating itself. But Torquil did single us out as one of the main organisers of the auction ring.'

'Was that true?' asked Cross.

'Oh yes, absolutely. But then again, all the main houses were at it.'

'Does that mean it was a legitimate practice?' asked Cross.

'No, I just meant we weren't the only ones.'

'An excuse I suppose you could use in relation to the price fixing,' Cross observed.

'Except that it didn't exist. It simply wasn't happening. It was the imagination of a fevered mind who sought to attach the blame for his own business's problems to others.'

'Why did Ed's campaign suddenly stop just over twelve months ago?' Cross asked.

'I have no idea. It just seemed to fizzle out,' he replied.

'Nothing to do with you or this firm?' Cross asked.

'No, nothing at all. What is more, that question itself should give you the answer you're looking for.'

'Which is what?'

'That the campaign had indeed stopped over a year ago. Why in that case would it have had anything to do with Ed Squire's murder? Where's the logic, if indeed there was any logic to your question in the first place?' the bookseller asked him with a steely eye.

'You make a good point. It does however ignore the fact that a murder enquiry must investigate all possibilities, however remote, in order to succeed, and that murder more often than not has no sense of logic in its execution. In its solution perhaps. But not in the very act,' Cross finished by saying, got up and left.

25

George was visiting his father in the BRI every night. Raymond's condition was still serious. There was always a danger of his having another stroke. Raymond had been moved into a geriatric ward and one thing had become rapidly clear to George over the past few days. He needed to get him out of there as soon as possible. He wasn't sure that the treatment his father was receiving actually required him to stay in hospital. Raymond was barely getting any sleep as some of the patients who had dementia would constantly call out at night. He felt sure that being surrounded by such old and ill people was no good for Raymond's mental health. Some of these unfortunate people were just shells of their former selves, with their heads arched back and their mouths contorted into a ghastly silent scream which no one heard. What was more, a couple of patients Raymond had struck up conversation and become hospital chums with had subsequently both died.

'It's like death's waiting room,' he'd told Ottey.

Dr Moss had told Christine that they wanted to move Raymond to a stroke rehabilitation and recovery unit outside of the hospital. George thought about this, did some research, and quickly came to the conclusion that it would be more of the same for his father. He therefore grasped the opportunity and formulated a different plan for his father which he wanted to propose to Moss before any action was taken.

'I have some money saved,' he told the geriatric care specialist. George had formed a great respect for this woman who had dedicated her professional life to the least glamorous end of the medical profession. To care for the sick elderly. It surely had to be a thankless task. But she was committed to it. She wanted the best for her patients. This had not only earned her George's respect but also convinced him that the medical woman would hear him out. They both had the same aim in mind. To do the best for Raymond. 'I don't have any family other than my father and I have no dependents,' George continued.

'But there is your mother,' the doctor pointed out.

'I am resigning from the police in order to care for him,' George told her, ignoring what she'd just said.

'Really? Have you discussed this with him?' asked Lizzie Moss, a little surprised. Why was everyone asking him this?

'I have not,' George replied.

'Well, I suggest you talk to him before you do anything drastic,' said Moss.

'Why?'

'Because it affects him, and it might not be what he wants.'

'Why wouldn't it be what he wants?' asked George, a little puzzled.

'From what I understand, he's immensely proud of your career as a detective. I don't think for a minute your resigning would be what he wants and to be honest, might not be the best thing for his recovery. Added to the fact that he might not actually want you involved in his care,' Moss continued.

'Has he said as much to you?' asked Cross, alarmed.

'No, it's not something we've discussed,' Moss admitted.

'Then how can you arrive at such a conclusion?' Cross pressed.

'It's not a conclusion, merely a suggestion.'

'Based on what?' asked Cross, not letting go, like a terrier with a bone.

'Based on the fact that some people are better equipped to care for the ill than others,' said the doctor.

'Are you suggesting I'm not capable of caring for my father?' asked Cross whose admiration of this young doctor was now being sorely tested.

'I just think you should discuss it with him, that's all. And your mother, for that matter, as she is also going to be involved in his care.'

George thought for a moment and realised that what the doctor was saying was coming from the same place everything she did and said at the hospital came from – a desire to do what was in the best interest of her patients.

'I will, of course, heed your advice and speak to my father as soon as the opportunity presents itself. In the meantime, if you are agreeable, I would like to discharge my father tomorrow into my care. I think this would be preferable for him, while also freeing up a bed at the unit for someone else in need,' George continued. 'I will pay for him to have a daily visit from a geriatric specialist nurse – perhaps you could advise me on that. Also carers to get him up in the morning and put him to bed in the evening. I will also engage a private physiotherapist, the frequency of their visits, again, to be determined by you. Please add to this any other specialist care you think he requires. My mother, who you mentioned, will be living with him. So he will not be alone. I will also visit him on a daily basis.'

'What about speech therapy?' asked the consultant.

'I believe the NHS can provide one. I'm assuming that on top of the care I pay for, the NHS will be providing some alongside it?' replied George.

'We will, but I think Raymond will benefit from more than that.'

'As I said, I will be guided by you in terms of any additional help and care my father needs. I should also mention my mother was a teacher and has brought up the idea of helping with his speech. Maybe she could follow the therapist's lead? It's something I feel I can also contribute to and, what is more, would enjoy doing.'

'Raymond is a lucky man,' replied the doctor.

'I don't see how having a stroke while under anaesthetic for an operation to remove a cancerous tumour on his lung can be described as lucky,' replied George.

'I meant having you as a son, DS Cross.'

'I see. I think that's probably the first time my being his son has been described as a lucky happenstance,' George observed.

'Have you put all the necessary arrangements in place? I can't discharge him without that,' Moss told him.

This flummoxed Cross, who felt immediately stupid for failing to see this coming. 'I can see that tomorrow was perhaps overly optimistic,' he said, eventually.

'Perhaps in two or three days?' Moss suggested. 'I can certainly advise on a nursing agency who will provide suitable help, as well as a good physiotherapist.'

'In a few days, then,' said George.

'I should like to see Raymond in a month, just to monitor how things are progressing.'

'Very well.'

'I'll also arrange for a district nurse to come in twice weekly.'

'To check up on us,' said George.

'Not exactly,' she laughed.

'I think that's an excellent idea. I wouldn't want us to get anything wrong,' George said genuinely. 'It'll be reassuring to know that someone is going to come and keep an eye on us.'

But as he left the room without thanking her or saying goodbye, Lizzie Moss was left wondering whether George was being sarcastic.

Raymond was thrilled at the prospect of getting out of hospital while at the same time a little nervous.

'You... sure?' was all he could manage, uncertainly, just as a man wailed horribly from the other end of the ward. George simply raised his eyebrows as if no verbal answer was required.

'You'll have all the support you need.'

'This is very generous of you, George,' commented his mother.

'Not at all. It's what I should do in the circumstances. Will you be able to move into the flat in readiness for his coming home, whenever that is?' he asked her.

'Yes, that should be fine.'

'I'll ask Marina if she can come along and settle you in,' he added.

'Thank you. She's been in to visit a couple of times. Do you know she speaks in Spanish to him?'

'I did. She's been teaching him for a couple of years now.'

Marina was Raymond's delightfully bossy Spanish cleaner. George had found her for him when working the case of a murdered ex-mayor of Bristol. She 'did' for the woman three times a week at her house on Sion Hill. Marina had resigned, as she no longer wanted to work for the husband, who she didn't like. She'd been devoted to the victim, however. George had hired her after Raymond's flat had been cleared out, to keep it firmly in order. After a sticky start, she had now become a permanent fixture in their small, extended family.

Raymond looked up and gave George the lopsided smile that his son had now become familiar with. George nodded and left.

26

Back at the MCU, Catherine, the CCTV officer, came to see Cross and Ottey. The front of Squire's Rare Books wasn't covered by CCTV – 'We have no need of it,' Torquil told them, before remembering the circumstances which had led to him talking to the two police officers. 'Or at least we didn't think so. If only we had,' he'd added regretfully – but she was going through other CCTV from various cameras in the square, adjoining streets and the alley leading to Brandon Hill. It was hours upon hours of video and so took time. Cross admired Catherine's patience when it came to viewing tape. He was also quite jealous of her job in its boring predictability, which in turn meant safety and also no need for dealing with other people. She was content, as he would have been, to go back and forth over footage to ensure nothing had been missed. He'd heard her joke once that, when she slept, she often dreamed in fast forward, reverse and freeze frame.

She'd found footage of someone, male, walking out of the square onto Brandon Hill, just after the time of the murder. It was inconclusive, thought Cross. But if at any point they made an appeal to the public, it could come in useful.

'I have something else though. I noticed a couple of cars seemed to frequent the square in the months leading up to the murder.'

'People who worked in one of the other firms in the square?' suggested Ottey.

'I wondered about that, but then saw that on a few occasions they just sat in the car.'

'Can you make out their faces?' asked Ottey.

'Not really, but I'm sensing a pattern here,' she said, looking at Cross as she knew the 'p' word would get his attention.

'How many people in the vehicles?' he asked.

'Always two. Sometimes they both stay in the car, but if one of them leaves, the other stays put,' she said.

'Two cars, you said?' Cross asked.

'Yes. A BMW and a Mercedes SUV.'

'Number plates?'

'Working on that. Holly's doing her best. But I've saved the best to last. On two occasions a man approaches the car and bends down to speak through the driver's window. I couldn't be sure on the first occasion, but I had a clearer view on a later occasion. It's Ed Squire,' she said.

'Did the driver get out of the car?' asked Ottey.

'No, but then, interestingly, on another occasion, when one of them has left the car then returned, getting into the front passenger seat of the car, Ed Squire appears,' she said.

'That is interesting,' commented Ottey.

'What does he do?' asked Cross.

'Knocks on the driver's window, then tries the door, which is locked.'

'Does he appear angry?' asked Ottey.

'Here, have a look,' replied Catherine, putting her laptop on the desk and playing the footage.

'He knocks and stands back,' commented Cross. 'He's angry, probably shouting.'

'Good work, Catherine,' said Ottey.

'Plates and faces,' was all the encouragement Cross had to offer.

'Like I said. Working on it,' replied Catherine, smiling. Ottey noticed this with some colleagues. It was as if this blunt, graceless kind of instruction from Cross, following on from something he'd been told, or shown, by them, was in its own way some sort of compliment. It seemed to mean that Cross found their efforts both relevant and possibly important. Catherine had definitely left with an additional spring in her step. The beneficiary of DS George Cross's idiosyncratic personnel skills. The existence of which were completely unknown to him.

27

The planned transfer of Raymond from the BRI back to his flat, a few days later, was delayed, thanks to the unavailability of an ambulance. They had to wait for two hours with Raymond now fully dressed, sitting on his bed, looking up expectantly in his wheelchair, as soon as anyone came into the ward. His eagerness assured George that discharging his father was unquestionably the right thing to be doing. A porter finally informed them that the transport for his father was ready.

Raymond's first reaction to the ambulance, which was a transport vehicle rather than an emergency response one, was to swirl his arms round in the air chaotically and make an awful whining noise.

'Is he all right?' asked Christine, who had become immediately alarmed at this bizarre display. She obviously thought he was having some sort of fit.

George seemed completely unconcerned by it, as he'd noted Raymond's lopsided smile. He studied his father for a few moments, then said, 'It's not that kind of ambulance, Dad.'

Raymond let out a long groan. Even in his physical state it was obviously a comical one. At least to George.

'He's asking if the ambulance can put on its lights and sirens,' George explained to Christine, who laughed, probably more out of relief than amusement.

Raymond had an almost childlike fascination with blues and twos. George couldn't understand this. He absolutely hated it when either in a patrol car in pursuit, or with Josie in her car when she decided they needed sirens and lights. This was not only because he couldn't stand the noise, but because the additional adrenalin the situation created, together with the lights and the noise, conspired to make her drive like a maniac. At times she had looked over at her passenger, only to see him curled up against the door, his eyes closed so tight they were just a mass of wrinkles and his fingers in his ears. He looked like a child wilfully making a point of not listening to his parent, while being told off. On one occasion he'd actually insisted on her pulling over, mid-pursuit, to let him out of the car. When she pointed out that he was supposed to be her backup, he argued that he would be of little use in that situation, as she well knew. On several of these occasions she'd asked him why he'd bothered becoming a policeman in the first place, if he couldn't provide backup. He took this question very seriously and after a few moments' consideration replied that his strengths as a police officer lay elsewhere. Something she found she couldn't really argue with.

Then there was the occasion where she'd tipped up on Raymond's birthday one year, announcing that she was taking him out for a spin. George thought nothing of this as he watched them drive away from his father's flat. That was until they'd reached the end of the road and turned onto the main thoroughfare, whereupon the blue lights in her radiator cover and on the back window started flashing and the siren blared out as they disappeared. George couldn't believe that she'd answered a call with his father in the car. When Ottey told him there had been no call, that it was just Raymond's birthday treat, he couldn't work out which he thought was worse. Taking a call with a civilian in the car or taking his father for a joyride complete with lights and sirens. Raymond was, of course, completely thrilled. 'Best birthday ever!' he'd announced when stepping out of the car with all the maturity of a thirteen-year-old.

The transfer of patient to residence went smoothly. Raymond didn't want to go to his bedroom, he'd explained to George on the journey over. George was concerned about this. How would his father be comfortable in the living room? If he sat on the sofa, it would be difficult getting him in and out of it. The answer was waiting for them in the middle of the sitting room. There, in pride of place, like some geriatric velour-covered throne, was a hideous mustard-coloured reclining armchair, complete with remote control.

'What is that?' asked George as the ambulance men got his father into it.

'He bought it off eBay while he was in hospital. It arrived yesterday,' his mother told him.

Raymond was thrilled with his purchase. He grabbed the remote control and the chair launched into action. It moved up and leaned so far upright and forward it was about to tip him out. The two paramedics dived in to stop Raymond being spilled onto the floor. One of them took the remote control and managed to get Raymond back into a sitting position. They then left and Raymond insisted on giving his ex-wife and son a full demonstration of all the chair's features. He demonstrated its massage function, how it would go halfway back in a reclined position to watch TV and then fully back in a completely horizontal position. But then he couldn't get it back up. No matter how hard he or George tried, pushing all of the buttons on the remote, they couldn't get the chair back to a sitting position. He was stuck. At that point both Christine and Raymond burst into uncontrollable, hysterical laughter. She was shrieking with hilarity, tears streaming down her face, as Raymond hit the side of the chair with his good arm to express his amusement. George stood there, completely straight-faced, staring at the pair of them, trying to understand why they were failing to realise the seriousness of the situation.

His phone vibrated. It was Michael Swift. George took the call.

'Is everything all right?' he asked, hearing the chaos in the background. When George explained the situation Swift ended the call by saying, 'I'll be there in twenty minutes.'

Half an hour later the giant frame of Michael Swift picked Raymond up out of the chair. He seemed like a small child in comparison to the six-foot eight frame of the forensic investigator. Swift was wearing one of his long, sweeping black capes and so it was that the district nurse, who was on her first visit, walked into the flat to seemingly witness her patient being gathered up by a giant undertaker and carried into the bedroom.

George made them all a cup of tea as the nurse sat with Christine and Raymond in the bedroom and they talked about various practicalities of looking after Raymond.

Swift had the results of the analysis of the foreign object found in Ed Squire's wound and replayed them to George back in the living room.

'It's paper,' he informed him.

'Can you ascertain what kind of paper?' George asked.

'Nope. But I do have a theory,' he said, bringing out his phone. He brought up a picture of Ed Squire's desk from the crime scene.

'If you remember, the stuff on top of the desk was disturbed with some of it spilled onto the floor,' he said.

George studied the photograph.

'There was no altercation, we've determined. So, I think the weapon was on the desk and the killer grabbed it in the moment they decided to kill Squire.'

George considered this possibility.

'The shape and depth of the wound suggests it was a blade about six inches long with a sharp tip and blunt sides,' Swift went on.

'A letter opener,' George suggested.

'Exactly,' replied Swift, beaming with satisfaction, pleased that Cross had come to the same conclusion as he. Then a realisation hit him. 'Now we have to find the bloody thing.'

'If it was on the desk as you suggest,' George pointed out.

'As the evidence suggests,' Swift countered.

'As your interpretation of the evidence suggests. If correct, it would imply that he was killed on the spur of the moment. That it was not the killer's intention when he or she arrived.'

The district nurse left, happy that everything seemed in place for Raymond's care. The two men finished their tea to discover that after the exertions of the day, Raymond was now sleeping.

'I'll see you tomorrow,' George said to Christine.

'Of course. I'll call you in the morning to let you know how he is,' she replied.

'In the evening. I'll bring takeout.'

'There's no need,' she said.

'It's Wednesday,' he informed her.

'Oh yes. Of course. He'd like that,' she said, remembering their weekly ritual.

'I know,' said George and left.

He got into Swift's SUV. He hadn't asked for a lift but often in these situations felt that his need to be taken home was obvious enough not to require a request. As Swift started the car up he turned to George.

'Thank goodness for Christine,' he said.

'What do you mean?' asked George.

'Well, if she wasn't here, what would you do? Presumably Raymond would still be in hospital. But even then, when he was discharged, who would look after him?' he replied, pulling out from the kerb. George thought for a moment.

'Could you stop the car?' he said. Swift did so and George got out. He walked back to the flat and let himself in. He found his mother sitting next to his father, reading a book. He stopped in the doorway as she looked up.

'Everything all right, George?' she asked.

'Yes,' he said. Then, 'Thank you.' After which he nodded his head as if satisfied that sounded sufficient and left.

28

Catherine came up with clearer images of the men in the two cars. There were three of them in all who seemed to take it in turns to remain in the SUVs. The question was, where had they gone when they got out? The answer, from the topography of the square and where the cars were parked, had to be the shop.

Torquil Squire was back working at the bookshop although he was still sleeping at Victoria's house. Persephone greeted Cross and Ottey as if they were potential customers.

'Hello,' she said brightly. 'Are you looking for anything in particular?'

'We're here to see Mr Squire – Torquil,' answered Ottey.

'Can I let him know what it's about?' the young woman replied.

'Do you really not remember us?' asked Ottey.

'I'm sorry, I get so many customers through the door,' she said, looking at the only customer in the shop, browsing. 'It's hard for me to remember them all.'

'DS Cross and DI Ottey,' said Cross, holding up his warrant card.

'Oh, my goodness. I'm so sorry. I think I'm still in shock. You found me in the bathroom.'

'We've also interviewed you twice. Once at the Major Crime Unit and once in your flat in Totterdown,' Cross reminded her.

'I think I'm kind of blanking things out. People do do that in times of crisis or having experienced a traumatic experience, don't they?' she said, with a light sprinkling of melodrama. 'Torquil's upstairs.'

'Do you recognise any of these men?' Ottey asked Torquil Squire, showing him blow-ups from some screen grabs. As he looked at them, Cross noted a shift in the old man's demeanour, which indicated he did.

'Never seen them before,' he told her. One thing was immediately evident to Cross. Torquil Squire was frightened.

'Are you sure?' Ottey asked.

'Yes,' he replied without looking up at her.

Cross gathered the photographs up and took them downstairs to Sam Taylor.

'Yep. All three of them have been in the shop at one point or another in the past few months. Don't know who they are, though,' he said.

'Did they buy anything?' asked Cross.

'Not from me, no. That one there, he was odd. Look at him. No neck. His head literally just grows out of his shoulders. If he wanted to look around at something, he had to turn his whole body. Wouldn't want to mess with him.'

Cross often wondered why people said this. On the whole, surely people didn't want to mess with anyone.

'What did they do when they came into the shop?' asked Ottey.

'Just wandered about the place. Picked up the odd book. But not in a way that said they were at all interested in buying.

Never put them back, though. That was strange and annoying,' Sam told them.

'Did they speak at all?' asked Cross.

'Only when I asked if I could help,' he replied. 'They just mumbled no. I think they were foreign. Eastern Europe, Russia or something.'

'Weren't you curious?' asked Cross.

'Of course.'

'Did you ask Ed about them?'

'He said he knew nothing about them.'

'Did he speak with them?' asked Cross.

'Not to my knowledge, no.'

'Yes, I remember them,' said Persephone, looking at the pictures. 'Didn't like them one bit. Soon as I saw them. Gave me the chills. One of them had no neck.'

'Yes, your colleague told us that,' replied Cross.

'My colleague?'

'Sam,' Cross replied.

'Oh, yes. Right. Having said that, they did seem to spend most of their time on the first floor.'

'What were they doing?' asked Ottey.

'I don't know. But they weren't buying books. Actually, that's a lie. One of them did buy a book from me. Spy novel. Can't remember which. Maybe Charles Cumming?' she said.

'Did he pay cash or pay by card?' asked Cross.

'Card. No one uses cash these days, do they?'

'I'll need you to track down that transaction,' said Cross.

'You're kidding, aren't you?' she laughed.

'It shouldn't take you long,' he said, looking around the empty shop. 'If this is a typical morning's trade for you.'

'Fine. I'll look into it after you've left,' she said tersely.

'Thank you,' said Ottey as she and Cross turned to leave.

'There was one thing that happened, which was odd. When they'd been here one day, I heard shouting in the road outside. I went to look out the window and Ed was standing next to a car shouting at it. I think it must've been them. But I can't be sure.'

'Did you ask Ed what it was about?' Cross asked.

'Obviously,' she replied, with an emphasis which seemed to imply they had no idea of the closeness of her relationship with him. 'Ed and I talked about everything.'

'What did he tell you?' asked Cross.

'That the man had tried to steal a book from the first floor.'

'I have no recollection of that,' said Sam who had appeared and was leaning on the door jamb into the room.

'Of his attempting to steal the book? Or Ed telling me? Because if it's the latter I have no recollection of you being in the room when he did,' she replied haughtily.

'Of any attempts to steal a book by those blokes. You're such a drama queen, Percy. Did you really hear an argument between Ed and one of them or are you just trying to put yourself centre stage?' he asked angrily.

'Why don't you go back to your own floor and let me speak with the detectives? It wouldn't, after all, be the first time you'd fail to notice someone stealing stock,' she replied. This seemed to irk him somewhat. But he didn't appear to have a suitable riposte and so just left. Cross watched him go, then turned back to Persephone.

'I think he might have been a little jealous of your relationship with Ed and your position here within the company,' he observed disingenuously.

'Tell me about it. It's like he feels threatened or something. Honestly, it's like dealing with an oversensitive ten-year-old sometimes,' she replied.

'Perhaps it's just that he didn't understand your relationship with Ed,' suggested Cross.

'Right?' she said in a way that Cross always found perplexing in these situations. An exclamatory question that was supposed to agree with what he'd just said always threw him.

'We met your mother,' he said.

'She told me,' she replied, less confidently.

'You lived with Ed and Victoria for a while in your teens,' Cross observed.

'Yes.'

Cross looked at Ottey. She took this as a cue for her to take over the conversation at this point. Maybe he thought she'd be more personable. Either that, or because she was a woman, a mother.

'Not a great fan of Ed and Victoria, your mother. Well, Ed in particular,' said Ottey.

Persephone looked mildly alarmed at this suggestion.

'I think maybe she was jealous of them,' she suggested uncertainly.

'It was a bit more complicated than that, surely, Persephone,' Ottey suggested.

'Yes, well, that's all in the past. I'm not entirely sure what it has to do with Ed's murder,' she replied.

'Except that your mother was arrested for assaulting Ed,' said Ottey.

'Sure, and that was terrible. But you can't be suggesting

she went back years later and killed him,' she laughed. 'That's ridiculous.'

'You were very close to Ed,' Ottey went on.

'Very. I'm grateful for what he and Vicky did back then. It was the right thing to do, and I could see that more as I got older. As for my mum, I think it was more about her than me. The fact that she wasn't involved in the situation more than anything else,' she replied.

'Their making you have an abortion?' asked Cross.

'They didn't make me,' she retorted. 'It was something we discussed and I agreed to do.'

'Why did you stop living with them?' Cross asked.

'Mum wanted me back before I went to Oxford.'

'Are you close?' asked Ottey.

'Do you have children?' Persephone asked.

'I do.'

'Daughters?'

'Yes.'

'Then you'll understand. We're very close. Went on holiday together recently. To Mykonos. We had such a great time. She said we were like a pair of teenage sisters more than mother and daughter,' she laughed.

'How's your relationship with your father?' asked Cross.

'Better than it was. Way better,' she answered.

'Why?'

'Well, we were out of touch for a while after he left. Then he had another family, basically,' she said.

'How did you feel about that?' Cross asked.

'Honestly? I hated him. But then later, I realised him not being in touch, not being part of my life, was a lot to do with my mother.'

'In what way?' asked Cross.

'She didn't have a good word to say about him. Then when I met his wife, my stepmum – but don't, please don't,' she said, suddenly worried. 'Whatever you do, don't tell Mum I called her that.'

'Why not?' asked Cross. 'That's what she is, after all.'

'Sure, I know. But she'd be really upset. Anyway, I went to visit them in Spain and met their two boys.'

'When was this?' asked Cross.

'My first year at Oxford. I learned that things weren't quite as black and white as my mother had made out when he left.'

'You could argue he would say that,' Cross put to her.

'Oh, absolutely, and I did,' she agreed with enthusiasm. 'But it didn't feel like he was pushing his version of events down my throat. I think he made a real effort to be objective. About how badly he behaved, but at the same time how it wasn't all him,' she said.

'Do you see him often?' asked Ottey.

'Much more often now and we FaceTime a lot. It's really great having him back in my life. It's like I tried to make Ed, Vicky, Seb and Charlie my family when he wasn't around. But now I realise I have my own. I have two brothers in Spain,' she said with an exaggerated sense of disbelief.

'That must be lovely,' said Ottey.

'It's changed my life.'

'How?' asked Cross.

'I don't know. I'm more confident. In a way I feel less rejected. I know that sounds weird but, all that time, I thought my dad had rejected me. But I was wrong. He'd do anything for me. He's shown me that since everything happened. He's been there for me. I'm so grateful he, they, are in my life.'

Ottey was beginning to think Persephone sounded like a soapy podcast the way she talked about her life. Almost as though she was talking in the third person, about someone else. She also thought it was a different representation of the relationship than her mother had given them.

'Do you think these Russians had anything to do with Ed's murder?' she asked.

'Who said they were Russians?' asked Cross.

'Ed.'

'How? Exactly what was it he said?' asked Cross.

'He just swore about them, something along the lines of, "If I see those bloody Russians again",' she said.

'Did you get the feeling he knew them?' Ottey asked.

'I think he did. I mean, they were around so often and it's not like they were interested in buying books, like I said. They just hung around in Ed's eyeline. I think all that stuff about them stealing, or trying to, was just rubbish. But there were a couple of times I left work and they were sitting outside in their car. It was quite frightening, if I'm honest.'

They walked out to Ottey's car, not entirely sure they were much closer to the truth. Sam appeared behind them. He looked back at the bookshop to make sure no one was watching.

'I just wanted to say, you need to take what Persephone says with a pinch of salt. She's obviously still in shock after all that's happened. But she's a complete fantasist. Lives in a world of her own. Always has done. She actually thinks she's going to run this place, or thought so, after Ed retired,' he said.

'I see. Why are you telling us this? Other than the fact that the two of you clearly don't like each other,' asked Cross.

'Ed never said anything about the Russians, if that's who they were, trying to steal books and I saw nothing like that happening on our floor. I think something else was going on. Ed was worried. Frightened, now I think about it. I don't know what it was about. I asked Torquil and he said he didn't know what was going on. But I'm not sure I believed him,' Sam said.

'Why didn't you tell us about this earlier?' asked Ottey.

'I don't think it occurred to me, to be honest.'

29

Robert Warner's trial had been ongoing for a couple of weeks before Alice Mackenzie was called to the witness stand. Warner had been seconded to the Bristol MCU the year before, to help on a murder case. He'd been partnered, not entirely successfully, with Cross, as Ottey had been in the middle of moving house. What they didn't know was that he was an habitual sex pest at work, but had thus far got away with it. Possibly on account of his success rate in making arrests. But more likely because the women he targeted were invariably young and new to the force. They feared for their careers and so made no formal complaints about his behaviour. Two women who had subsequently left the Kent force had been raped by him. Although they'd had rape kits processed, they hadn't pursued their case in the courts.

He'd seemingly got away with it until he came to Bristol and made the mistake of assaulting Mackenzie in the underground car park before, on another occasion, attempting to rape her at Swift's flat. She wasn't of a mind to let him get away with it. Other victims, including the two rape victims, then came forward when they heard he was being charged. He was now on trial for the two rapes, attempted rape and four counts of sexual assault on vulnerable witnesses on various cases.

By the time this day came round she felt like she'd been

cross-examined by a defence counsel several times already. This was due to the fact that she'd spent many an hour wondering, or imagining, how it would go. This usually followed a worst-case scenario, with an appalling defence barrister tearing her testimony to shreds and portraying her as some kind of wanton slut. She persisted with this, even though she knew full well – she'd done her research – that the guidelines for cross examination in such cases had changed radically to protect victims. In the past, women in rape trials had often been left feeling that it was them in the dock, and not the defendant. Their sexual history, the way they dressed, whether they drank alcohol on a regular basis, was laid out in front of the jury for everyone to pore over. The age-old injustice was the all too frequent accusation levelled at them, that they had been 'asking for it'. It was the go-to egregious weapon of the unscrupulous defence lawyer. The fact that these practices were well and truly in the past did nothing to prevent Alice's imagination running wildly down the dark, winding corridors of potential inquisitorial prosecutorial horrors.

It played over and over in her mind, like a film scene she couldn't forget. She often did this. When she had a problem at work or in life, or even if she didn't have a problem, she'd have endless imaginary conversations with people about situations. Playing out various different outcomes, responses, opposing arguments which often carried real plausibility, justifications for this or that. She'd try and see things from other people's points of view, as if she was doing some sort of impartial due diligence. To prove to herself that even in her own head she was being fair to all parties involved. She would argue extensively against her own profoundly held beliefs in certain situations. It was quite exhausting at times. This went on for so long that on occasion she actually began to believe that certain conversations had actually taken place, when they hadn't. Swift joked she should get help, which only prompted a series of conversations with herself about whether or not it was actually a good idea.

She saw Swift, Cross, Ottey and Carson were all in court that day. Something she imagined might happen. It was a welcome gesture of support. The first thing she did, as she took the stand, was to look Warner squarely in the eye. She wanted him to know she wasn't afraid of him and wasn't about to be intimidated by his presence just a few feet away from her. No screen to protect her from her attacker's gaze. She'd said it was completely unnecessary. He was smartly dressed in suit and tie, having changed out of his prison fatigues in the cells. He hadn't been given bail. He'd lost weight and tried to look confident. But it wasn't altogether convincing. This was probably because the word was that the two rape victims' testimonies, together with the physical evidence, had been pretty devastating. The evidence from the rape kits – which included bruising to the vaginal wall – was almost incontrovertible. What Mackenzie didn't know was that their testimonies had demonstrated a pattern to his behaviour. A consistent modus operandi which fitted with her experience. The oppressive, feigned interest in their career and promises to help. The constant sexual innuendo. With the other victims there had also been evidence of continuous 'sexting' by Warner. Asking for photographs and making inappropriate suggestions. The tone of these had varied enormously, from outright sexual suggestions and demands, to innocuous, but possibly inappropriate, gossipy chit-chat. The prosecuting barrister commented that she was surprised Warner had any time to do any actual police work, considering how much time he seemed to devote to his mobile phone, texting and stalking his victims.

She took Mackenzie through the events leading up to the attack at Swift's flat. This included the constant invitations to go out for a drink after work. Offers to help her with her career, as he understood she had ambitions to become a detective. The attack in the car park where she'd pepper-sprayed him. This attack had been partially caught on the garage CCTV. It wasn't in itself conclusive but seemed to corroborate her version of events. The barrister also, as she'd forewarned her she would, took Mackenzie through the attempted rape in minute detail. Mackenzie didn't find this in the least bit upsetting. Maybe because she'd replayed it in her mind so many times. She saw it almost as her job to maintain her composure and be as dispassionately accurate as she could, to skewer the defence case. But when she described grabbing his engorged penis and digging her nails in, there was a reaction from people in the court. It seemed to be divided straight down the gender line. The women tried to stifle their admiring giggles at the image of it, while the men seemed to squirm uncomfortably in their seats.

She'd been told by various people that it was unlikely the defence barrister would take her through the attack, as he wouldn't want the jury to be exposed to it once more. Nor would he want to alienate them by contradicting a victim's account of the attack. Mackenzie had tried to go to court on previous days to get a look at him in action, but hadn't been able to get away from her course. But she'd checked him out on the internet. This erased the images of various vampiric inquisitors she'd conjured up in the previous months. He was younger in the flesh than he looked on the chambers' website and was disarmingly polite; far more so than she had imagined. She was asked about her opinion of Warner leading up to the attacks.

'Did you feel threatened by him at all?' the brief asked.

'Prior to the car park attack, no,' she replied.

'What was your opinion of him?'

'I had no particular opinion of him, as far as I recall. Although I thought his attitude towards DS Cross was wilfully antagonistic.'

The barrister ignored this.

'You sprayed my client with pepper spray. Is that correct?'

'I've already testified to that,' she replied a little tetchily, immediately checking herself. 'It's not actually pepper spray, that's illegal as I'm sure you know. It was EveAid.'

'Indeed. Do you always carry this spray with you in your handbag as a matter of course? Or was it a recent development?' he asked.

Mackenzie looked a little uncomfortable at this.

'It's relatively recent,' she said.

'And why is that?'

'I have a new boyfriend. He's quite protective of me,' she said awkwardly.

'So, it had nothing to do with my client's arrival at the MCU?' the barrister went on.

'Nothing at all. No.'

'Thank you. On the night of the alleged attack…' he began.

'There's nothing alleged about it. It happened,' she interrupted. This earned her a gentle reprimand from the judge.

'Had you perhaps invited the defendant to your boyfriend's flat, by implication or otherwise?'

'I had not,' she replied, resisting the temptation to ask him if he realised how idiotic that question sounded.

'So, you were surprised by his presence there?'

'I was surprised when he attacked me from behind and shoved me into the flat, yes,' she answered. The barrister now looked at her for a moment, as if recalibrating his approach to her. He turned over several pages in his folder.

'One last question, if I may. After the arrival of your boyfriend, Michael Swift, why did you insist on his bagging your hands?'

'I knew there could be DNA evidence, skin cells, under my fingernails.'

'Because you'd deliberately scratched the defendant's face to achieve that result?'

'I scratched his face because he was lying on top of me, trying to rape me,' she insisted.

'Quite a cool and calculated reaction from someone who's being attacked in the way you've described,' he suggested.

'There was nothing cool and calculated about it. He was about to rape me. It was instinctive self-defence,' she retorted. The barrister looked at her just long enough to imply he didn't entirely believe her. Then smiled.

'That's all I have, your honour,' he said and sat back down.

And that was it. It was over in what seemed like a minute. If she was honest, she felt a little disappointed after all her internal mental debate and mock trials of the past months. It was something of an anticlimax. She left the witness stand with one final, defiant look at Warner, then left the courtroom. She didn't wait for Swift, Ottey and Cross to give evidence about what they'd seen when they arrived at the flat. She just went, hoping she'd done enough to contribute to Warner's incarceration.

30

When George arrived for his nightly visit with his father, he often found that Raymond was fairly exhausted from the exertions of the day. Particularly if it was one which involved a visit from the physio. Christine had thought this might afford her and George an opportunity to talk. But she was mistaken in this regard. George resisted all her attempts to engage in conversation, instead contenting himself with sitting by his slumbering father's bed. This changed one night when he'd arrived later than usual, and Christine was cooking. As he sat with Raymond, going over the Ed Squire case in his mind, he was distracted by the smells emanating from the kitchen. Whatever it was smelled enticing to the hungry murder detective, who had foregone lunch that day. Cross had decided to cook something the moment he got home. He resisted the urge to explore what was going on in the kitchen, until he finally justified leaving his father's bedside by looking at his watch and determining that the requisite attendance had been fulfilled. He generally stayed with Raymond for bang on an hour. This he considered to be sufficient, not only to demonstrate that his filial obligations for the day had been fulfilled, but also to allow Raymond ample opportunity to wake up and enjoy his son's company. He appeared in the kitchen doorway as Christine was taking a dish of shepherd's pie out of the oven. She was surprised to see him because, as a general rule, he didn't bother finding her when he left to say goodbye. He simply called out from the door as he went.

'I'm leaving,' he announced uncharacteristically.

'Oh. Did he wake up?' she asked.

'No.'

'It's been a tough day for him. Dessie was round this morning.'

Dessie was the physiotherapist Cross had employed to give his father extra sessions.

'Yes. He texted me,' Cross replied.

'Oh, I didn't know he did that,' she commented.

'Yes. Just to keep me informed of how Raymond is progressing.'

'Oh, that's good,' she replied. 'He's ever so grateful.'

'Really? I imagine he gets a lot of work,' Cross replied.

'Not Dessie. Your father. He's working ever so hard and can see the benefits already. He knows it's because of the extra physio you're paying for.'

'There's no need to be grateful,' he assured her.

'Well, he is.'

He watched as she dished out a portion of the shepherd's pie onto a plate. It steamed invitingly. She looked up at George.

'Everything all right, George?' she asked.

'Yes.'

She strained some vegetables.

'Is that cabbage?' he asked.

'No, sprout tops. They're delicious.'

'Brussels sprout tops?' he asked.

'Have you never had them?' she asked, surprised.

'I have not,' he replied, without moving.

The penny finally dropped with Christine. She was so unused

to getting anything from George that her expectations were very low.

'Would you like to stay for dinner, George? I think there's enough for both of us and Raymond's lunch tomorrow,' she said finally.

He didn't reply, just pulled a chair out from under the kitchen table and sat down. She smiled and got out an extra three plates for George. One for the pie, one for the runner beans and one for the never-before-tried sprout tops. They sat and ate. She couldn't remember the last time she'd enjoyed eating in absolute silence for a full twenty minutes with someone else. George had been a fussy eater as a child but by the way he tucked in enthusiastically, he'd obviously grown out of it. It was, for her, an enormous step forward in the re-establishment of their relationship. For him, it was also something of a revelation.

The Brussels sprout tops were, indeed, delicious.

31

They now had a licence plate from one of the 'Russian' cars on the CCTV. The vehicle was on lease to a company in Somerset called OD Estates. The director of the company was an individual called Jeremy Perrin. Cross made a call to him. He seemed quite surprised to be hearing from the police.

'I'll come straight to the point,' Cross informed him. 'We want to identify and speak to an individual seen driving a car which is leased to your company.'

'I see. What's his name?' Perrin asked.

'We don't know, which is why I said we wish to identify him,' Cross pointed out. 'I'm going to send a photograph to your phone.'

Cross did so.

'Gosh, it's quite hard to tell anything from this,' said Perrin. Cross found this interesting as the photograph was clear enough to tell who the man was, if he knew him.

'Would you like me to send it across to you again?' offered Cross.

'I'm not sure that will help. Why don't you send me the registration of the vehicle and I'll look into it,' he replied, perfectly affably.

'What does your company do?' Cross asked as he texted the number of the plate over.

'Logistics,' came the reply.

'What does that mean?' asked Cross.

'What it says on the tin, Sergeant. Was there anything else? I have another call waiting.'

'No. Just send me the name when you have it,' replied Cross, ending the call.

The day began in the MCU open area with Carson delivering one of his morale-boosting, supposedly rousing, speeches. These generally occurred when nothing was happening on a case. It was, in fact, just his way of venting his frustration and an attempt to lift what he saw as the torpor which was in danger of suffocating the investigation.

Cross paid no attention to it as he was working through Squire's financial accounts and had seen something which caught his attention. It was in the recent statements, which he hadn't as yet got to examining. He needed to talk to Victoria Squire again.

The house in Henleaze had the oxygen-draining vacuum that death so often left behind. It felt even darker than the last time they'd visited. Victoria was now on her own during the day with Torquil sleeping there at night. Her children had gone back to their own homes, work and lives. Everyone else still had a life, even Torquil was at the shop during the day, but not Victoria. Ottey often found herself conscious of their intrusion as police officers in moments like this. Cross not in the least.

Victoria looked like she was going through the motions of everyday existence, as she opened the door and invited them in. Gone was the woman organising everyone else the day after the murder. The whirlwind of activity so obviously designed to avoid facing the grief that was descending on her, like an invisible, suffocating shroud, was no longer available to her. Gone, even, her suspicion or resentment of the police's presence in her house. It was as if the reality of her situation, now that she was pretty much alone, had finally hit her. A life as a widow lay ahead of her. Ottey was well aware, herself, of the challenges not only of being widowed, but in sudden unexpected circumstances. You wondered what that life was going to be like from then on. Had to come to terms with the endless minutes of each waking hour, having given up trying to fill them with purpose. Because, to what purpose were you doing it, other than to avoid the fact that, right now, you felt your meaningful life was over? In many ways it was incredibly ageing. Ottey felt the woman in front of her had come to terms with her situation in an attitude of complete surrender and she understood it. After all, it was something she had done herself before she realised she had to get herself together for the sake of her two young children. Victoria Squire didn't have that incentive, though. Her children were adults.

Cross was aware of it too. He had seen this scenario all too often at work. For him, though, this was a moment of vulnerability in an investigation that had to be taken advantage of. As callous as this may sound, it was simply an objective view of maximising a situation which could help him conclude the case, which in turn would give them some closure.

'What was your role in the company? Your husband's company?' he began by asking her.

'I don't have a role,' she answered.

Cross turned to Ottey. 'Mrs Squire is being modest. I always think it must be challenging, that period when the children have left home. Fledged. Gone off to university or got a job somewhere. Challenging for a woman who has been a dedicated, selfless mother for all those years. How to occupy the time. Bridge perhaps? Local charity work? Alcohol for some. Adult education classes? Mrs Squire used her time very industriously, though, did you not?'

She said nothing.

'A mathematician as an undergraduate and briefly a teacher of A-level maths. She decided to put her numerical skills to good use and qualified as an accountant,' he continued.

'Correct.'

'And became Squire's Rare Books' accountant.'

'It was interesting and occupied my time,' she said. 'It was also another way of cutting costs.'

'Which was crucial at a point when the firm was struggling somewhat.'

She said nothing.

'As the firm's accountant I'm hoping you can help me with something. I've come across a fairly substantial payment into the business. Two hundred and fifty thousand pounds, to be exact, back in March of last year. Nothing particularly significant in itself, even though it's a sizeable sum. What is significant, to my mind, is the withdrawal of that exact same amount, six months later. In cash. Can you explain that to me?' he asked.

'I can't. I don't recall those transactions,' she sighed.

'I don't believe you, Mrs Squire,' said Cross flatly.

No reply.

'Victoria,' began Ottey, softly. 'You have to help us here.'

She said nothing.

'Mrs Squire, do you know who killed your husband?' asked Cross.

'No,' she replied, shocked by the question.

'Mrs Squire, did you kill your husband?' he went on.

'Has he lost his mind?' she exclaimed, suddenly bursting out of her silent bubble. Ottey was a little thrown herself, but had seen this from him before.

'My point is, if you don't know who did it, and you didn't do it yourself, then you have nothing to hide and should really just answer my questions if you are in possession of the answers. You are, presumably, as keen as we are to discover the identity of your husband's killer,' he said, firmly. 'That is all I'm trying to do here, Mrs Squire. Discover the identity of the killer so that they might be brought to justice. It's my job. What I do for a living. Day in, day out. And when I come across something in the course of that job that I don't understand, or something that strikes me as out of the normal scheme of things, I ask questions of those I think may have answers. In the hope those answers might lead me in the right direction.'

She said nothing.

'You yourself would have facilitated the return of the money. Where had it come from and to whom was it then given?' he asked again.

'I don't know the details. You have to believe me. When the money came in, of course I asked my husband about it. It was an out of the ordinary sum. He told me it was for a sale but the terms of it were so confidential that not even I could have the details,' she explained.

'Why?'

'I don't know. I was upset. It caused a lot of tension between us. Married couples shouldn't keep things from each other, particularly when working together. But he insisted it was better if I just didn't know.'

'What was your reaction six months later when he asked you for the money in cash?'

'Well, you can imagine. Not knowing anything because of some confidentiality was one thing, initially, but now it was going back out of the business I wanted to know why,' she said.

'Did he tell you?' Cross asked.

'No,' she replied quietly.

'But you went through with it,' Cross pointed out.

'Not without a fight. I refused initially,' she replied.

'Couldn't he have just done it himself?' asked Ottey. Victoria looked almost embarrassed by this question.

'After we had to remortgage the house a few years back I lost patience. That's when I stepped in, qualified and became the accountant. It sounds terrible, but when it came to business, I realised I just couldn't trust him. The next "big deal" was always about to come over the hill, was just round the corner. But it never happened. He let the business slide. Torquil was in despair. I think he was glad when I got involved. One thing I insisted on was counter signatures and passwords for all transactions. That way I could stay informed and keep my eye on them.'

'Except for this one,' Cross commented.

'Indeed.'

'How well did that go down with Ed?' asked Ottey.

'Well, he had no choice but to accept it. Especially when Torquil added his voice to the argument. I think Ed found that particularly humiliating. But our bloody house was on the line. The children were still at university and needed financial help,' she said.

'You signed off in the end. Why?' persisted Cross.

'When I refused, he was angry at first. We had a terrible row. A marriage-ending type of row, if I'm honest. But at the end of it he was basically pleading with me, and I realised he was frightened. Terrified, even. It was as if something awful would happen,' she said, realising what she was saying as she heard herself say it. Something terrible had happened.

'What exactly was the money for? Was it commission?' Cross asked.

'Yes.'

'And what was your commission percentage?'

'It depends. But on this one it was twelve and a half per cent,' she replied.

'So, two million,' Cross said, doing a quick mental calculation.

'Yes.'

'The question here is, though, where did it go when it left your business account and why was it withdrawn in cash?' said Cross.

'I asked him the very same question.'

'Six months later…'

'I know. It didn't, doesn't, really make any sense,' she replied.

'Mrs Squire, this could be very important. Do you really know nothing about the sale?' Ottey asked.

'I don't. If I did, I can assure you I'd tell you. But I'm fairly sure Torquil will know.'

32

Cross wanted to hold off from visiting Torquil Squire. He decided to go back over all his notes again, together with Prianka's research, and try to come at it afresh. A picture was presenting itself. Torquil had seemed distinctly alarmed, frightened even, when they'd shown him pictures of the men in the car, despite saying he didn't know who they were. According to Victoria, Ed had been terrified of potential repercussions if they didn't pay back the huge commission. But it had been paid. So what was going on? As he was looking through everything one thing jumped out at him. Ed's campaign against Carnegie had stopped around six weeks before he received the two hundred and fifty thousand. His social media posts about it, which had been frequent to the point of obsessional, had suddenly ceased, as had any email correspondence about it. Was it a payoff? Was there a link?

He went through all the information they'd generated about the price-fixing campaign. It became quite personal over time. More on the side of Carnegie than Squire. Derisive comments were made about his appearance, his business. His knowledge of the book world was brought into question. As if he wasn't one of 'them', whoever 'they' were. Patrick Gibb never cropped up in this spat. It was always a Carnegie spokesperson, or an inside source. Cross decided to delve into the torrid pit, as he called it, of social media. It was on X that he came across a thread about Ed which had been initiated by a man called Nigel Simpson. He wrote as if he was speaking on behalf of Carnegie, and when Cross looked at his X bio it said he was indeed employed at Carnegie Books. But when Cross checked their website and looked at the 'our team' page, there was no evidence of him.

He telephoned Victoria Squire.

'Yes?' she replied, in a tone which really said, *what now?*

'Do you know a Nigel Simpson?' Cross asked.

'Of course I do,' she replied.

'Why should it be so obvious?' asked Cross.

'Because he's Denny's son,' she replied.

'I see. Then I'm assuming you knew he worked at Carnegie Books,' Cross went on.

'Of course. He was the one responsible for spreading all that bile about Ed. He single-handedly took on the job of trying to dismantle Ed's crusade and career,' she said.

'I rather thought it might've been Patrick Gibb,' said Cross. 'But you're saying it was this Simpson.'

'Gibb wouldn't get his hands dirty over something like that. But boy did Nigel enjoy the fight. It was awful, such a betrayal,' she went on.

'Did Ed ever confront him about it?' Cross asked.

'Of course! They were supposed to be friends.'

'You're not thinking what I'm thinking?' asked Ottey.

'I have no idea what you're thinking,' replied Cross.

'That the two are linked?'

'Possibly, but how?' asked Cross.

'Simple. Hush money. They paid him off,' volunteered Carson who was also in Cross's office.

'Was it really worth that amount of money to shut him up though?' asked Prianka, who seemed to be growing in confidence by the day.

'If it was hush money, which I for one doubt, why would he pay it back? How does that make any sense?' asked Cross.

'Good point,' agreed Ottey.

Cross put a call in to Carnegie Books.

'DS Cross, what a pleasure,' intoned Patrick Gibb with wasted sarcasm.

'Nigel Simpson,' announced Cross.

'What about him?'

'He seems to have been the figurehead of Carnegie's rearguard action against Ed Squire,' said Cross. Gibb made no reply. 'Why is he no longer in your employ?'

'He decided it was time to move on. Pursue other ventures.'

'Do you know where?'

'The last I heard he was back in Bristol. His father runs a second-hand bookshop there.'

'Interesting,' said Cross as he made a note of this. 'I wonder if you could help me with something. I've come across a payment to Ed Squire of two hundred and fifty thousand pounds, the year before his death,' said Cross.

'Really? Well, credit where credit's due. He was obviously doing a lot better than we thought. Good for him,' replied Gibb.

'The thing is, the payment was made to him in quite close proximity to the time at which he ceased his campaign against price fixing, with particular reference to you,' Cross said.

'What are you getting at?'

'I'm not getting at anything. I'm trying to get to something, but, as of now, I have no idea what that something might be.'

'I'm not sure how I can help.'

'Did you pay him off?' asked Cross.

At this, Gibb burst out laughing.

'I don't know how you came to that conclusion. Ed may have been an irritant and a deluded bore, but not to the tune of two hundred and fifty thousand pounds,' he scoffed.

'My thoughts, almost exactly. But I still can't get beyond the timing. You can see why, I'm sure.'

Gibb said nothing.

'Can you imagine what a single payment of that magnitude could be for, to a bookseller like Ed Squire?' asked Cross innocently.

'I cannot.'

'Shall I tell you what he told his wife, Victoria? I should rephrase that, really. His widow. What his widow said he told her?' asked Cross.

'I have a feeling that however I answer, you intend on telling me anyway,' replied the bookseller.

'He told her it was commission.'

'I see.'

'Quite the sale if it's true. But here's something I've discovered over my years as a detective. When people tell a lie, it is often close to the truth. But in Ed Squire's case I'm not even sure it was a lie. I think it was easier to tell his wife a partial truth than lie his way out of an awkward situation,' said Cross.

'An interesting theory,' commented Gibb.

'I don't deal in theory, Mr Gibb. A theory won't necessarily convict a killer. But a fact, more often than not, will,' said Cross.

'Is there anything more you wish to ask me?' asked Gibb.

'Yes. I think you know something about that money, Mr Gibb. I think the timing of everything points to that. So, I think it's best you tell me what you do know,' Cross concluded.

Gibb, like many other people in their initial encounters with DS George Cross, had come to the conclusion that there was an annoying persistency about the man that wasn't simply going to go away. So, like many intelligent people before him, he did the smart thing and gave in.

'I can't discuss this on the phone,' he said finally. 'But I'm coming down to the south-west on Friday to view a library. Could we meet then? I could come into your office.'

So, it was agreed. They would meet in two days.

33

'Detectives!' Denholm Simpson greeted them warmly. 'Your visit is most guilt-inducing. No! That sounds horribly wrong. Not guilt in the sense of the dreadful murder of our dear Ed, but a realisation that I still haven't been in touch with Torquil.'

'Did you not go to the funeral?' asked Ottey. Ed Squire's funeral had been the week before. Ottey and Cross didn't attend, but Prianka had. It had been well attended by the extended family, people from the book trade and customers. The only thing of any interest was that Ian Hartwell's Spanish wife had accompanied him, which caused a minor scene with his ex, Sarah, who according to Prianka had only gone to be supportive of her daughter.

'Another shard of guilt pierces my heart, Inspector. I did not. I couldn't face it. Too many funerals at my age and all they do is show you what you have to look forward to in a not very inducing manner. But I also thought my presence might not be welcome.'

'Did Nigel attend?' asked Cross.

'Nigel? No. Why do you ask?'

'Well he's back in Bristol, is he not?'

Simpson paused slightly before answering.

'Yes.'

'Something you neglected to tell us on our last visit,' Cross pointed out.

'Something you neglected to ask,' came the swift reply.

'Is he here?' Cross went on.

'He is. Upstairs in his office.'

Cross started to make for a staircase at the back of the shop.

'That only leads to the upstairs of the bookshop. You'll have to go back outside. It'll be the door on your left.'

'You don't live above the shop yourself?' asked Ottey.

'No, never have. We have— I have,' he corrected himself, 'a house in St Paul's. Same one I bought when I first came to Bristol. If I told you how much I paid for it, well you wouldn't believe,' he said cheerfully.

They rang the doorbell outside the shop, with some difficulty, as it was hanging on to the wall for dear life. Ottey took it in one hand and pressed the button with the other. After a moment they heard someone coming down the stairs inside and opening the door. Before them stood a well-preserved man in his mid-fifties with a short, manicured beard. He was enveloped in a huge, baggy cardigan which threatened to swallow him whole. Having identified themselves, they were invited in. His 'office' appeared to be the living room of a one-bedroomed flat above the two floors occupied by the shop. They sat opposite him on a small sofa which meant Cross was closer to Ottey than he was really comfortable with.

'I assume you're here because of Teddy,' he said.

'Teddy?' asked Cross.

'His childhood name. I think I'm the only one who uses it these days. He grew out of it. I guess I never did.'

'Were you close as children?' asked Ottey.

'Yes. Our families were close. As I'm sure you're aware, our fathers married a pair of sisters.'

'Which actually makes you cousins,' observed Cross as it occurred to him for the first time.

'Yep.'

'But you grew apart,' suggested Ottey.

'Cynthiagate,' he replied.

'You didn't go to the funeral. Why was that?' asked Cross.

'I didn't feel I'd be a welcome presence.'

'Because of Cynthiagate?' asked Cross. 'It was so long ago.'

Nigel Simpson elected not to answer this question.

'Perhaps it was something to do with your work at Carnegie Books?' said Cross.

'What is it you want?' he asked, a little testily.

'When did you and Ed Squire reconnect?' asked Cross.

'About three years ago. He got in touch with me. Let's just be clear about that.'

'Why do we need to be clear about that?' asked Cross.

'Well, I'm sure you'll be wanting to have the pertinent facts in their chronological order and context,' he replied.

'What facts and context?' asked Cross.

Simpson declined to answer this. There was something about Cross's direct manner which warned him to be careful. That if he wasn't, he might soon tie himself in knots and trip up.

'Why did Mr Squire initiate correspondence with you?' asked Cross.

'I'm sure you already know that.'

'I think it would be best you make no assumptions about what I may, or may not, know and just answer the question,' Cross instructed him.

'To be clear, he didn't initiate correspondence with me. It was with the head of the company, Patrick Gibb.'

'What was the purpose of his getting in touch?'

'Ed had a theory that we were cornering the market in certain modern authors, well, authors of the last century, mainly Evelyn Waugh.'

'What made him come to this conclusion and why did he get in touch when he did?' Cross enquired.

'He had a customer who collected Waugh. There was a particular edition of a book, inscribed by Waugh, this gentleman wanted. We actually had it and Ed wanted to buy it from us,' Nigel replied.

'Seems fairly straightforward,' commented Ottey.

'He objected to our price, the value we'd placed on the item.'

'He was negotiating,' Cross said.

'And,' Nigel continued, 'suggested that we were trying to inflate the pricing across the entire Evelyn Waugh market.'

'Did he buy the book?' asked Ottey.

'He did not. We couldn't find a price that was mutually acceptable. So we didn't make a sale.'

'To Ed,' Cross added.

'That is what we're discussing, isn't it?' asked Nigel defensively.

'But you did sell the book,' Cross insisted.

'Yes.'

'To Geoffrey Hardyman, the collector in question. Ed Squire's customer,' Cross continued.

'Correct.'

'Who then became something of a regular customer of yours?'

'Also correct.'

'Which must've irritated the hell out of Ed Squire,' Ottey commented.

'It did. It's partly what prompted his absurd campaign against us and a few other booksellers.'

'Because he thought you were cornering the market in certain authors, buying up all available stock and then dictating the market price,' said Cross. 'Was there any truth in that?'

'Absolutely not. For decades certain bookshops have specialised in selected authors. It makes complete sense. They become experts in their field. Buyers know where to go and that they are getting the genuine article when they do. They appreciate all the research and scholarship that has gone into building up a collection of stock for sale. Look at Ed's father, Torquil. A world-renowned expert in Isambard Kingdom Brunel. Has anyone ever accused him of monopolising the market in Brunel? Of course not.'

'Would it be fair to say that Ed Squire became something of a thorn in your side and several other booksellers'?' asked Ottey.

'I wouldn't go that far. But it was inconvenient at times. Having said that, a lot of people thought he was becoming a bit of a joke. It was damaging for Ed, looking back on it,' Nigel continued.

'Fatally, perhaps?' Cross pondered. Simpson laughed.

'I shouldn't laugh, I'm sorry. The rare book world may be many things, but it is not one where murder occurs on a regular basis,' he said.

'Oh, I'm sure it isn't. But we are only investigating the one murder,' Cross commented.

'Why did you leave Carnegie Books?' asked Ottey.

This caused Simpson to hesitate momentarily.

'That's confidential,' he replied.

'In what respect?'

'I signed an NDA,' he explained.

'An NDA in the bookselling world. Who'd've thought?' said Ottey.

'The implication being that you were sacked,' commented Cross.

'Like I said. I can't discuss it. All I will say is that my association with them ended by mutual agreement,' he said, sounding like he was reading from a pro-forma PR statement.

'So, what's the plan now?' asked Ottey.

'I'm not entirely sure. Taking over this place from Dad is an obvious option. It's always been something we've discussed and now might be the right time. My ambition would be to navigate its way back into the rare book trade.'

'In direct competition with Squire's,'?' observed Ottey.

'I think there's more than enough room for both of us in Bristol. So many bookshops have disappeared now.'

'Had you seen Ed Squire before he was murdered, now you're back in Bristol?' asked Cross.

'I had not, no.'

'Were you angry with him?'

'Why would I be angry with him?' he asked.

'Perhaps because he had something to do with your losing your job?' Cross suggested.

'I haven't said that,' he pointed out.

'No, indeed. Because of your NDA. Possibly Patrick Gibb will be more helpful,' Cross wondered.

'I doubt it,' came the nervous reply.

34

Cross and Ottey went back to Squire's to speak with Torquil. But the old man was out, at a doctor's appointment. Persephone and Sam were there, however. The two detectives sat down with Taylor at his desk on the first floor.

'We've come across something which we hope you might be able to shed some light on,' began Ottey.

'Oh yes,' he said, with the enthusiasm people often have when they think they're going to be let in on something secret or confidential. He sat forward to give them his full attention. Cross reflected this was quite different to his attitude the first time they interviewed him when he seemed reluctant to even look at them.

'A payment of two hundred and fifty thousand was made into the shop's bank account, last year, about twelve months ago. Do you know anything about it?' Ottey asked.

'Two hundred and fifty grand? No. But then again, I don't really know anything about the financial workings of the business,' he replied.

'But if it had been a sale, surely you'd have known about that?' she pushed.

'I don't recall anything like that. That's some sale for us,' he said.

'Actually, we think the sale might've been bigger. Ed told Victoria it was commission on a sale,' Ottey elaborated.

'Commission? Bloody hell. What's that? A two million quid sale? We've never done one of those while I've been here. It can't be a sale,' he said.

'Why not?' asked Cross.

'Because he'd have let everyone know about it. That would've been huge news. He'd've taken us out to celebrate. He always took us out for lunch or a drink if he put together a good deal. Two million pounds? He'd've probably taken us away for a weekend,' he joked.

'So, you know nothing about it?' asked Ottey.

'No, sorry. Couldn't Victoria tell you anything?' he asked.

'Ed wouldn't give her any details,' said Cross.

'The money has subsequently gone out of the account,' said Ottey.

'That's odd. Maybe they had more of the mortgage to pay off than I thought,' he commented.

'No. It was paid out to a third party,' Ottey informed him.

'In cash,' added Cross.

'Cash!' He tried to process this in the moment. 'I assume that's why you want to talk to Torquil,' Sam said.

'Indeed,' began Cross. 'I appreciate you may not know anything about the transaction, specifically. But I'd like to discuss any observations you may have had about Ed over the past year. Did anything strike you as being out of the normal?'

Sam thought for a moment.

'He went to Italy a couple of times. That was strange, now I think about it. He said he was going to appraise a library. But afterwards nothing came through the shop. He implied it had been a wasted trip, which was fine. These things happen. But then he went back and again had nothing to show for it. Or at least nothing I was aware of,' he said.

'Did he go on his own?' asked Cross.

'Yes. Which was also a little strange. He'd normally take me or occasionally Torquil would go. As of late, even Madam downstairs went on a few trips.'

'Maybe he took Victoria with him?' suggested Ottey.

'I don't think so.' He began thinking back. 'I do remember one time, she came in to see the old man – they went out for dinner – Ed was away and she joked that maybe he had an Italian girlfriend. But she always made jokes about that,' he laughed.

'When was this?' asked Cross.

'About a year ago, I'd say.'

So around the time of the money appearing, Cross and Ottey were both thinking.

'Anything else?' asked Ottey.

'I don't think so.'

'You will call us if anything comes to mind?' she said.

'Of course.'

As they turned to leave, he said, 'Actually, now I come to think about it, there was one thing which struck me as odd. There's a coffee shop just off Park Street where we often get coffees. I was in there one lunchtime about a week or so before Ed was killed, and he was in there with the last person I'd ever expect him to be with.'

'Who?' asked Ottey.

'Nigel Simpson. He worked at Carnegie Books, Denholm Simpson's son,' he went on.

'We know who he is,' Ottey assured him.

'I knew they'd been friends when they were kids. Weren't they cousins, in fact? But with all the recent problems with Carnegie it did surprise me. The word was that Nigel was the voice behind all the Carnegie vitriol in the trades. I mean, I thought he was like the devil incarnate to Ed. And here they were having coffee, as if nothing had happened. I was very surprised,' he said.

'Did you ask Ed about it?' asked Cross.

'I did not. It didn't seem to be any of my business.'

It was of interest to the two police officers in the light of Simpson having just told them he hadn't seen Ed Squire in years.

As they left the building, Persephone appeared. It was as if she felt she'd missed out with the police officers not dropping in on her.

'DS Cross,' she called after them. They stopped as she came over. 'I have the receipt for the book.'

'Which book?' asked Ottey.

'The one bought by the Russian?' asked Cross.

'Yes. Shall I email it to you?'

'Yes,' replied Cross getting into the car.

'Thanks, Persephone. You still have my card?'

'I do.'

'Send it to that email then. Thanks.'

Persephone looked a little deflated. Like someone saying a reluctant goodbye to friends leaving after a great weekend and realising they'd actually spent no time with them at all. She watched them drive off with her hands on her hips, as if resigned to having missed an opportunity.

35

An address was found for the credit card details Persephone had sent to them. The cardholder was indeed a Russian, by the name of Alexander Kuznetsov. He lived in Taunton, not too far from the address Jeremy Perrin's company was registered at.

'Are you going to pay him a visit?' asked Carson.

'I think we should,' answered Ottey.

'Be interesting to hear what he has to say,' Carson went on.

'He'll say nothing,' ventured Cross.

'What makes you so sure of that?' asked Carson.

'If Perrin is anything to go by, George could well be right,' said Ottey.

'This man has been intimidating our victim, together with two other men. It's unlikely they're doing it for themselves. They're employed by Perrin, so why don't you start with him? Then if, as you suspect, you get nowhere, go to Kuznetsov's address early doors and follow him. See where he takes you,' suggested Carson.

'Excellent suggestion, sir,' said Cross.

'Thank you,' said Carson, leaving. He turned at the door. Ottey knew exactly what he was doing. Checking if Cross was being sarcastic. Then he remembered it was George and so just left, rather pleased with himself.

★

'Alexander Kuznetsov,' said Cross, to Jeremy Perrin minutes later, on the phone.

'Let me look into it,' Perrin replied.

'You don't recognise the name?' asked Cross.

'I do not. But I have several employees on my payroll, Sergeant.'

'I've seen your company accounts as filed at Companies House, Mr Perrin. Your turnover hardly suggests having such a large workforce that you'd be unable to recognise one of their names,' retorted Cross.

'Was there anything else, DS Cross?'

'No,' he replied, but lost out in the phone-going-down-first competition.

At seven the next morning, Cross walked out of Tony's café beneath his flat, with a china mug of tea, a takeaway cup of coffee and an old-fashioned greaseproof paper bag containing a bacon sarnie for Ottey. She took hold of the bag greedily from Cross, biting into it so quickly that he actually thought she'd bitten through the paper.

'Oh my god, it's worth getting up this early just for one of Tony's bacon sandwiches,' she said. 'Best in Bristol, don't you think?'

What Cross was actually thinking was that he wished she wouldn't speak with her mouth full. He was about to say something when she continued.

'He should have a Michelin star, just for this,' she said as she leaned over him in the passenger seat, which he found most alarming, and motioned her thanks to Tony who was standing in the café window. 'Thank you!' she yelled. Cross was horrified as he saw a piece of toast fly out of her mouth and onto his lap. He was paralysed.

'Oops,' she said, scooping it up and horrifying him even further by popping it straight into her mouth. She saw the look on his face. 'Mother of two,' she said by way of explanation, which just left him even more perplexed.

'He can't possibly hear you,' said Cross, making sure she didn't spill his tea.

'He knows what I'm saying,' she replied.

In truth the generosity and thoughtfulness of this breakfast treat, whenever she picked Cross up from his flat early in the morning, had nothing to do with him. The first time it happened, Tony was making Cross a cup of tea in the café when he noticed Ottey waiting in the car outside.

'Your lift?' he asked Cross.

'My colleague,' he replied.

'What does she want?' asked Tony.

'For me to get into her car.'

'To eat and drink, George.'

'Nothing.'

'You asked her, and she said nothing?'

'I did not.'

'So how do you know?' he asked without waiting for an answer. He made her a coffee and a bacon sandwich, which she loved, Cross had told Tony the next day. From then on, whenever Ottey picked Cross up early for work, she was treated to a coffee and a bacon sandwich. This was made sweeter and all the more rewarding when she discovered that Tony actually charged Cross for it.

Ottey parked a hundred yards or so down the road from Kuznetsov's flat. The Mercedes SUV was parked in the paved front garden. He lived in a flat of a mid-century two-storey, suburban dwelling. A time to Cross's mind when architects seemed to be devoid of either ideas or taste. Universally bland seemed to be the rule of thumb when it came to the suburbs of that era. Almost as if it was your fault you ended up there and this was all you were getting in return. Or maybe it was an architectural brainwashing of the population, telling them that life was dull, so just muddle along and don't have any ideas out of the norm, or make any trouble.

The Russian appeared just after eight, got into his vehicle and drove off. Ottey duly followed. They drove for just under half an hour, ending up deep in rural Somerset. They then found themselves driving alongside a long stretch of beautifully renovated stone wall, at least a mile long. It was typical of many country estates in Somerset, but not all owners had the financial wherewithal to fix their perimeter walls to this extent. Kuznetsov turned off the road and pulled up to a grand set of black and gold iron gates. He pressed a code into an entry post. The gates opened and he drove in. Ottey then pulled up and pressed the buzzer on the entry post. The lens of a camera adjusted its iris as she did so.

'Ashleigh Manor,' said a disembodied voice.

'DI Ottey and DS Cross, Avon and Somerset Police,' Ottey informed him.

'Who do you wish to see?'

'The owner,' she replied.

'Do you have an appointment?'

'We do not.'

'You'll need to make an appointment and come back,' the voice said followed by a click, before Ottey could object. She pressed the buzzer again but this time it wasn't answered. She pulled out of the entrance, irritably.

'There'll be a tradesman's entrance, obviously,' she said after a moment.

'The response will surely be the same,' Cross pointed out.

'Watch and learn,' she replied. He hated it when she said this. Because it inevitably preceded her doing something foolish, reckless and possibly illegal.

She drove away from the gates down a lane still bordered by the discreetly, but at the same time for those who knew about such things, ostentatiously renovated wall. Cross occupied himself by googling Ashleigh Manor on his phone. After half a mile or so, they came across another entrance, which was much more functional than the other. Ottey pulled up on the other side of the road. It wasn't long before a delivery van drove up. The wooden gate to the estate slid silently to one side and Ottey accelerated up to the rear of the van and tailgated it through. She was looking childishly pleased with herself when the van stopped at a barrier and a clipboard with an officious-looking man attached to it appeared out of a nearby stone booth. He spoke to the driver and raised the barrier. He then turned towards Ottey's car, walking in the middle of the drive to prevent her repeating her following-on trick.

'Can I help you?' he asked.

'DI Ottey and DS Cross, Avon and Somerset Police,' she informed him.

He went through the motions of looking at his clipboard, although all three of them knew they wouldn't be on any list, then looked up and said, 'I don't have you down here.'

'That's because we don't have an appointment,' she said.

'Then perhaps—' he began, before being unceremoniously interrupted by Cross.

'Could you just call Mr Perrin and tell him we're here?'

'Mr Perrin?' the man repeated.

'Jeremy Perrin, yes,' Cross informed him.

He disappeared into the small building and made a call.

'Nice one, detective,' Ottey commented.

'Thank you, ma'am,' he replied, annoying her unintentionally.

The jobsworth came back out of the building with an upturned mirror on the end of a long pole. He walked round the car looking underneath it with the mirror. He got to the back of the car and said, 'Open the boot please.'

'You're kidding,' replied Ottey.

'I am not,' came the bored reply. She opened it. He had a quick look, then went back into the small building to put away his mirror. He came back with his clipboard and made a great deal of walking to the front of the car and noting down Ottey's licence plate number. He came over to the driver's window.

'Drive up to the main house. You can't miss it. Someone will see to you there.'

The house was vast and sprawling, with outbuildings off to the back of it. Dating back to the seventeenth century, it was baroque in style and imposing. A beautiful building which had obviously had money spent on it recently. It was set in fifty acres of parkland and backed onto a large lake. There was an orangery to one side of it. The ground floor consisted of several tall windows. The gravel leading up to the house looked like it had been recently raked. Ottey thought it was probably raked on a daily basis and for some reason this irritated her. She pulled up to the front of the building and braked sharply, causing Cross to grab hold of the dashboard.

'What are you doing?' he asked, alarmed.

'I don't know. The gravel annoyed me,' she replied, knowing

how stupid it sounded. To her satisfaction, when they got out of the car, she saw that she had left skid marks, dispersing the gravel and revealing the dark dirt underneath.

They didn't have to knock on the door as a man in a well-tailored suit with an open shirt was waiting for them.

'You want to get those brakes checked,' he said as they approached, walking into an invisible cloud of oud and woody scent as they did so. 'Jeremy Perrin. An appointment might have been more conventional.'

'This is a murder enquiry, Mr Perrin. We don't do conventional,' replied Ottey sounding way more like a run-of-the-mill American cop show than perhaps she meant to.

'Murder? Really. I see. Perhaps you should've led with that at the main gate and there wouldn't have been any need for all this cloak and dagger.'

'Are you the owner of this pile?' asked Ottey.

'I am not. I am the executive director of operations for the owner,' he replied.

'Who is…?' she asked.

'A high-net-worth individual who values his privacy,' he answered with suitable smug superiority.

'Is Mr Dimitriev here?' asked Cross.

Perrin thought for a moment then laughed.

'He is not. He is abroad.'

'Really? Where?' asked Ottey.

'On his yacht in the Mediterranean. I believe they are currently off the coast of Naples.'

'When will he be back?' asked Cross.

'In about a week, I believe. But he is prone to change his mind at the last moment. He might fancy getting in one last slope.'

'Slope?' asked Cross.

'Skiing,' translated Ottey. 'Isn't it a bit late for that?'

'He heli-skis. Gets dropped on the summits where there is still snow,' came the pompous reply.

'We would like to see him on his return,' Cross informed Perrin.

'Of course, and I'm sure he'd be more than happy to help. Though how is beyond me. Whose murder are we talking about?' he asked.

'Ed Squire,' replied Ottey.

Perrin made a shape of non-recognition with his lips. 'Why would Mr Dimitriev be able to help with this?' he asked in his best impression of being genuinely puzzled.

'He could begin by telling us why he had three of his employees intimidating the victim shortly before his murder,' said Cross.

'Firstly, are you sure it was them?'

'One of them, Alexander Kuznetsov, led us here. He works for you.'

'I know that.'

'Oh good. It's just that you didn't recognise the name the last time we spoke. So, yes, we're certain,' replied Cross.

'Well, why don't you just ask *him*?'

'Because I imagine if he says anything it will be to say he was just following the orders of his employer, or perhaps his employer's executive director of operations. And as you've already wasted enough of our time, I'm disinclined to let either you, or the people who work for you, waste any more of it.'

They drove back to the MCU by which time Cross had discovered the name of Dimitriev's super-yacht, the SY *Dacha*, and also confirmed on a yacht position tracking website that it was indeed off the coast of Naples.

36

'The NDA with Nigel Simpson goes both ways, DS Cross. It is not something I can breach.'

'This is a murder investigation, Mr Gibb,' said Cross, as he sat opposite Patrick Gibb in the VA suite of the MCU. 'But if that isn't enough to encourage you out from behind your NDA, we will simply have to go elsewhere in search of answers to our questions.'

'And where do you propose going to find these answers? I'm curious,' Gibb said quietly.

'I'm fairly sure the rare book world is much like any other small, specialised corner of the world. The theatre, for example, the world of barristers' chambers off Grays Inn Road, the world of upscale hospitality,' Cross mused. 'Gossip,' he then pronounced. 'The world is full of gossip, Mr Gibb, especially in small select circles and societies. It's our stock-in-trade, us detectives. Our bread and butter, when it comes to solving murder. Why, even in the intelligence services in London, gossip is a major source of currency. So, if you're unable to furnish us with the requisite information, we'll just pop up to Maggs opposite your office in Bedford Square, then Bernard Quaritch, and Shapero in New Bond Street. They might well wonder, indeed ask, why you wouldn't speak with us.'

'People not directly involved in a murder enquiry just love to speak to the police for some reason,' added Ottey.

'Particularly if it involves a competitor or friendly rival,' said Cross.

Gibb sighed.

'What I'm going to tell you is obviously confidential. I'm telling you because, of course, I want to help you find who did this terrible thing to Ed Squire. But it doesn't reflect well on us as a company and in the book world, reputation is everything. Having said that, I do think that in this case that ship may have sailed. Have you heard of the Christopher Columbus letters?'

'I have. They were sent to Ferdinand II and Isabella of Spain in 1493, when he thought he'd discovered the Americas,' replied Cross, while Ottey employed an expression which she hoped conveyed the fact that she was also in possession of such knowledge, even though she completely wasn't.

'Correct,' replied Gibb. 'Several copies were printed at the time, so that the news of the great discovery could be spread around the world, thereby adding to the glory and splendour of Ferdinand's reign. There are only about thirty in existence. All in institutions around the world, except for a couple which are supposedly in private collections, but no one can be sure.'

'They have been the subject of much theft and forgery, am I correct?' asked Cross.

'You are. You must understand that the original copies are worth in the region of two million pounds each. Several years ago it was discovered that one had been stolen from a library in Barcelona and replaced by a brilliant fake. It wasn't spotted until an American academic, a specialist, saw an online picture of the one in the library and realised it possibly wasn't original. He'd seen one that was for sale months before and it had some random marks on it which were identical to the one in the library. One of them had to be a fake.'

'It was the one in the library,' said Cross.

'Indeed. The original had been stolen and replaced with the fake. The substitution wasn't noticed till the American brought it to their attention. But as I said, there are reputed to be a couple still out there in private collections. Nigel Simpson heard about one being sold from such a collection in Italy. He happened to know that Ed Squire, who was something of a specialist in the works of explorers, had a client, Russian I believe, who was desperate to acquire a Columbus letter if one ever came on the market. Nigel brokered a deal, taking no commission, I may add, between the Italian and Ed, who then sold it to a delighted Russian collector.'

'Why did you and Simpson do that? Why not just make the sale yourselves?' asked Ottey.

'Because Carnegie thought it might encourage Squire to back down,' said Cross.

'We thought it was a gesture of goodwill which, yes, might be reciprocated in the way you suggest,' purred Gibb.

'So, what happened?' asked Ottey.

'It backfired horribly. Ed sold it to the Russian buyer for just over two million,' he went on.

'And it was a fake?' suggested Ottey.

'On the contrary, it was completely genuine. The problem was, it was stolen,' Gibb told them.

'Ah,' Ottey responded.

'The Russian was delighted with his acquisition and it was good for Ed as well. It immediately elevated him into the realm of those booksellers who can get their hands on the rarest of manuscripts. But when a university library in the States heard about it – these things have a habit of getting round – they realised it had been stolen from them some years before. Various markings and characteristics proved it to, indeed, be the case,' said Gibb.

'What did the collector do? He can't have been best pleased,' asked Cross.

'Well, this particular gentleman wants very much to be viewed as a serious collector. A man of integrity. There was only one option. To return it to the library and receive the discreet approbation of the rare book world.'

'Approbation which came at some cost,' reflected Cross.

'A cost of two million. But you can't put a price on reputation,' commented Gibb.

'He must've wanted compensation,' Ottey pointed out.

'Of course. He contacted Ed Squire and asked for his money back. But Ed said, quite rightly, that he'd bought it in good faith. We ourselves went after the Italian seller in an attempt to resolve the situation, but they had, unsurprisingly, disappeared.'

'What happens in a situation like this?' asked Ottey.

'What can happen? Caveat emptor,' he replied.

Cross turned to Ottey and was about to speak when she stopped him.

'I know what it means, thank you, DS Cross,' she said tersely.

'I believe the gentleman concerned talked about legal proceedings but decided against it. Going to court would inevitably open them up to an investigation of their lives. Something most people like him are averse to,' Gibb told them.

'Did anything beyond the legal framework happen? Threats, perhaps?' asked Cross.

'I don't know. You'd have to ask Torquil. There were certainly none made against us.'

'Doubtless because the guilty party, as it were, no longer worked for you,' Cross observed.

'Poor Torquil,' Gibb said, changing tack. 'It would have been a terrible shock to him. Not Ed's murder, which would have been devastating, it goes without saying. But the whole Columbus farrago. He'd spent decades building his reputation only to see it tarnished in a moment.'

'Surely it was Ed who it reflected badly on,' said Ottey.

'It reflected badly on the firm as a whole. It's still seen as Torquil's house, whoever has charge of the keys.'

'And Nigel Simpson's career could well be over,' commented Cross.

'We also have our reputation to maintain,' Gibb stated coldly.

Until the Russian returned, Cross wasn't sure where to look next. But he was fairly confident something would turn up. It invariably did. You just had to keep looking. At the small stuff. At the detail. At all the routines and patterns. There was often a lull in activity before a break on a case. It was like the slow ascent to the top of a roller coaster. Taking an age, with the anticipation building, then at the top a moment's pause, before all hell breaks out in the rapid descent to the end.

37

There was quite a crowd at Raymond's flat that Friday night. It was his birthday and, although George hadn't advertised the fact, word had got around. Josie was present, unsurprisingly, as she'd driven him there. But then Michael Swift arrived with Alice. Josie was thrilled to see her, having not had a chance to talk to her in court, and wrapped her arms round her protégée, as she liked to think of her. Christine disappeared into the kitchen to make tea. George then tried to create some order in the living room by sending everyone else into the kitchen, as he needed to do Raymond's speech therapy exercises with him.

George was taking his duties as speech and acuity therapist very seriously. He had purchased several mental mathematics books designed for ten-year-olds. The idea was to do various sums in your head, not write anything down, and time how long each batch of ten questions took to answer. You then competed against your own times when you returned to the same exercise. Raymond enjoyed this immensely and was enormously competitive with himself. There had, though, between a dispute between father and son as to how the timings should be calculated. This was because, much to his frustration, Raymond often had the answer in his head but was then unable to articulate it. He argued, in vain, that the time should be adjudged at the moment he thought of the answer. But his son turned out to be quite the hard taskmaster. Raymond had to say the answer out loud in an understandable, coherent manner and the timing would be taken from that. That was the whole point of the exercise.

Raymond's other objection to his son's totalitarian recovery regime, which he actually succeeded in getting by his son, was that he didn't want to do speech therapy reading children's books. It was dreary, boring and insulting.

'I'm... not... a bloody... child,' he told George, hesitantly. They settled on reading the *Bristol Post* every evening.

George's attempts to keep his father's unexpected and uninvited birthday guests, essentially his colleagues, out of the living room was finally thwarted by the arrival of Stephen bearing a huge birthday cake he'd baked the previous day. Thursday was his baking day in the parish. The priest was accompanied by one of his latest congregants who treated him like he was a living saint. This was Raymond's cleaner, Marina. A Catholic, she had become besotted with the young priest the first time she met him. The effect of this was to miraculously restore her faith which had lain dormant for several years. She was now a devoted member of Stephen's flock whose monthly highlight was what she called her 'alone time' with the priest in the confessional box. His cakes were enormously popular, and George probably wasn't entirely mistaken in thinking that the large increase in Stephen's congregation numbers had more to do with his salted caramel cupcakes than his wise words from the pulpit. His cake that night was an elaborate chocolate creation, swathed in roughly applied chocolate icing. A number of lit candles were swiftly applied, and Raymond managed to blow them all out. An enthusiastic chorus of 'Happy Birthday' was sung by all, with one obvious exception. Something was bothering George and he couldn't hold back when the cake was being cut and shared out. As Raymond was passed a plate, George swooped and, in one deft motion, confiscated it.

'Too much sugar, cream and butter,' he proclaimed parsimoniously to his crestfallen father, who groaned. Marina immediately took the plate back off George.

'It's vegan,' she told him defiantly, as if she'd baked the cake herself.

'*That* is not vegan,' the detective informed her.

'Of course it is, George. Do you honestly think I would bring a cake laden with saturated fats and dairy products to someone who has recently suffered a stroke?' Stephen asked, offended.

'Seriously? This is vegan?' asked Josie, through a mouthful of cake.

'It most definitely is,' replied Stephen.

'Bloody hell. You'd never know. Any chance of the recipe?' she asked.

'It could be arranged,' replied the priest loftily, as Marina returned the slice of cake to Raymond, under George's suspicious glare.

George answered the door about an hour later to find Xiao Bao, the proprietor of their favourite Chinese takeaway, standing there, holding two large heat protective bags.

'Xiao Bao, what are you doing here?' asked George.

'Birthday dinner,' he replied, holding up the bags.

'But it's not Wednesday,' George informed him.

'No, that was the day before yesterday. Was everything okay?' he asked a little anxiously.

George had to think about this for a moment.

'Yes, it was,' he said finally.

'Today is Friday and Raymond's birthday, Christine called

me,' Xiao Bao informed him, edging past George, who showed no inclination to get out of the way. Once he'd decanted the food, which was bountiful, sufficient for at least eight people, Xiao Bao disappeared. Not before having a slice of cake, though, and adding to the chorus of disbelief that such a luxurious cake could be vegan.

They ate in silence, as if it was an innately understood house rule. Then Christine and Josie got out of their seats to clear up. Alice kicked Michael as discreetly as she could, which resulted in him yelling, 'What are you kicking me for?'

'Let us do this, Christine,' she said, as Michael then realised what the shin-cracking social nudge had been about.

'No!' declared an outraged Marina. 'It is my job.' She said this with such territorial fervour that they all sat down and let her get on with it.

A few minutes later Josie and Alice topped up everyone's wine glasses. The wine, George noticed, had mysteriously appeared shortly after the young couple's arrival. The group sat in complete and awkward silence until Stephen broke the ice.

'So, Raymond, your party – what would you like to talk about?' he asked.

Raymond thought about this for a moment.

'Ed,' he finally muttered.

'Ed?' asked Stephen.

'Squire,' Raymond clarified.

'It's the case we're working on,' Josie explained.

'I'm not sure that's appropriate,' said George, unhelpfully.

'I'm not sure your opinion matters,' replied Josie mischievously.

'Yes! Such a great idea,' exclaimed Alice, perhaps giving away how much she missed working with them all. She took centre stage. 'So, let's look at what we've got,' she began.

'We?' asked George, confused. She didn't work with them any longer.

'A bookseller murdered. Dispatched with the nearest available murder weapon – a letter opener,' she continued, ignoring him with the relish of an amateur Agatha Christie sleuth holding a post-dinner murder mystery game. 'We have a witness, Persephone Hartwell, who saw the likely murderer, a man, running down the stairs. The victim's father, Torquil, then discovers the body. George finds Persephone, who has locked herself in the bathroom upstairs.

'Ed Squire's business wasn't doing particularly well, but the recent sale of a stolen copy of the fifteenth-century Columbus letters has made things only worse and, what is more, has possibly put him in the sights of his buyer, who has done the decent thing and returned the letters to the library it was stolen from. Meaning he possibly has two million reasons to kill Squire. The Russian buyer has subsequently slipped out of the country. Squire's sale of a first edition Tolkien, inscribed by the great man himself, without sharing the proceeds with the family he acquired the book from, is no longer of interest to the enquiry as Torquil Squire then came to an agreeable resolution with them. Correct so far?' she asked George. But didn't wait for an answer.

'The Squire family history is complicated. Going back a while, Torquil and his erstwhile business partner, Denholm Simpson, married a pair of sisters. When Torquil left the business through a bequest from a grateful customer, Simpson was furious. But that was a long time ago and perhaps irrelevant. However, the connection passes onto the next generation as Simpson's son became a bookseller at a big firm in London who our victim was at loggerheads with over an alleged price-fixing scam in the rare book world. He attempted to assuage Ed Squire by securing a rare book for one of his best clients, the aforementioned Russian. This backfired, ended up with Simpson losing his job. Did he, now unemployed as he was, lose his rag and stab him several times in the chest? So Simpson needs another interview. And the murder weapon needs finding. Have I left anything out?' she concluded.

'Oh, I do miss you!' said Josie, as Michael looked on with pride.

George had gone very quiet during Alice's exposition.

'Everything all right, George?' Stephen asked.

'The family,' he replied. Alice had left out the family in her summation. This omission led him to realise that they, also, had ignored the family as potential suspects.

'What makes you think they had anything to do with this?' asked Ottey.

'I didn't say that. I was merely answering her question. Had she left anything out? And the answer is, yes. She left out the family. Victoria, her children, her niece and Sarah, the niece's mother,' he replied thoughtfully.

'Well, for that matter, there is also Sam Taylor,' Swift offered up. He then turned to Raymond. 'He works in the bookshop.'

'Correct,' said Cross, who was beginning to remonstrate with himself silently for becoming too one-tracked and closed off in the investigation; something he always tried to avoid.

'I got the sense that Taylor was a Torquil Squire man – an Ed man, not so much. Taken for granted, resentful of Persephone's arrival and her incursion, as he saw it, of his territory,' Michael continued.

Raymond was writing something down on a piece of paper. He handed it to his son.

'No notes, Dad,' said George, handing it back. 'Say what it is you want to say.'

'A lot... to... go on,' Raymond muttered.

This was true and it was possibly something Cross had lost sight of in recent days. He'd been feeling a little deflated of late. It often happened. Surprisingly, Raymond's impromptu birthday party and his father's response had given him just the encouragement he needed.

They ended with a final rendition of 'Happy Birthday'. Raymond was by now quite fatigued.

'That was fun. I miss you guys,' said Alice as they walked to their respective cars.

'We miss you too,' replied Ottey. 'Particularly George.'

He was about to object.

'Of course he does,' said Alice, in such a way that he decided it was meant to be a joke. 'Let's do this again, soon,' she pleaded. The very thought of which caused George to shudder.

'I thought you did great at the trial,' said Ottey as she and Alice hugged goodbye.

'Thanks.'

'Word is, everything's pretty much stacked up against him,' Ottey went on.

'Sure, but juries are curious creatures at times.'

'True. When are closing statements likely to be, do you know?'

'I hear maybe end of next week,' replied Alice.

'Will you go?'

'No. Probably for the verdict. Maybe. I don't know.'

'Well, I'll be there for sure,' Ottey said.

Stephen drove George home.

'Raymond seems to be doing very well. Vast improvement,' he commented.

'Do you think so?' asked George. 'It's hard to tell, seeing him every day.'

'Oh, definitely. You and Christine are doing marvels. As well as my prayers. Obviously.' He smiled. Another joke, possibly, George thought. He wasn't sure, he just knew he really needed his bed.

38

The forensic digital analysis of Ed Squire's mobile finally came through. Cross sat down with the spreadsheet and began sifting through it. There was the normal, to be expected, text traffic with his wife; reminders, shopping lists, links to the Money Saving Expert website. Not many with his father. Cross imagined this was because, like his own father, Torquil Squire didn't have much time for modern technology. It was the amount of calls and texts to a number that turned out to be Nigel Simpson's which obviously stood out for Cross. They seemed to increase in their frequency. The most pertinent of all being a text confirming their meeting on the day of Ed's death.

'But surely the beef goes in the opposite direction?' commented Carson when told of this development.

'If anyone was angry enough with anyone to kill them it was Ed with Simpson, not the other way round,' agreed Ottey.

'I see. Well, speculation aside, the interaction is interesting, particularly in the light of his having lied about it,' Cross replied.

Simpson seemed disconcerted when the police officers appeared at his father's shop for a second visit and asked him to accompany them to the MCU.

'Can you tell me what this about?' he asked them.

'It's about the murder of Ed Squire,' answered Cross.

'Is he being deliberately obtuse?' asked Simpson.

'Oh, I don't think it's him being obtuse,' responded Ottey, opening the rear door of her car.

They took him into an interview room. No VA sofa and potted plant reassurance for him.

'On our last visit to your father's establishment you informed us that you hadn't seen Ed Squire recently,' Cross began. He observed Simpson as he now did what so many people sitting on the other side of the table did in this situation, and tried to weigh up what he thought Cross might have found out.

'I realise, now, that that was stupid,' he replied.

'What were you doing on the day he was murdered?' asked Cross.

'I don't recollect.'

'Another one to add to the stupid answers file,' commented Ottey.

'Most people in your situation might've made a real effort to remember, after an initial visit from the police,' said Cross.

'What situation?' asked Simpson.

'Being asked in for an interview regarding the murder of not only someone they knew, but also someone they've been at loggerheads with for the last few years, ending in a fiasco where they arranged for the victim to buy a rare manuscript, which they sold on for over two million pounds, only for it to turn out to be stolen,' Cross replied.

'I was working, as I am every day at the moment, on my business plan,' he said.

'What business plan would this be?' asked Ottey.

'To turn around my father's operation. Try and get it back in the rare book trade.'

'And how exactly were you going to do that?' asked Ottey.

'Patrick Gibb was going to help with me with some stock. Stuff I'd had a hand in acquiring. He was also going to let me bring some of my clients with me,' he told them.

'Why were you in contact with Ed Squire?' asked Cross.

'I'm not sure you'll believe me,' he said.

'Try us,' replied Ottey.

'I was in touch with him because I was trying to sort things out.'

'How?' Cross asked.

'By suggesting our going into business together,' he said.

'Oh, pull the other one,' scoffed Ottey.

'And there you go,' said Simpson.

'I think what my colleague is trying to express is our surprise that, having besmirched his reputation in the book trade in the first place, and then practically put him out of business with the sale of a stolen manuscript, the victim would in any way countenance the idea of going into business with you,' explained Cross.

'Which of course is perfectly understandable, at first glance. But what you have to remember is that we both found ourselves in an awkward, difficult position. I was out of a job, with no immediate prospect of any income, and Ed's business was in trouble.'

'In no small part down to you,' commented Cross.

'Yes, you could say that,' he replied, sheepishly.

'Oh, I think everyone would say that,' replied Ottey, surprised at his gall.

'Who initiated this idea, of establishing a partnership?' asked Cross.

'It was me.'

'And how was this approach received?'

'He was shocked, I think. I mean, it must've been the furthest thing from his mind. He wasn't interested. Asked me not to call him again,' he said.

'But you did,' said Cross.

'Yes, like I said. We were both up shit creek. I was out of a job, his business was in trouble. The truth was that he was always sailing close to the wind. He was just not a book man...'

'Something you took countless opportunities to point out in print,' Ottey commented.

He decided to ignore this.

'But I think he was essentially a good businessman, if his enthusiasm for reckless purchases could be curtailed.'

Both Ottey and Cross looked astonished at this last statement.

'I know, I know. Look, could we just move on from the history of this for a moment?' he asked.

'Absolutely not. It is all pertinent to our investigation,' replied Cross.

'Nothing indicated that the Columbus was stolen. But you're right. I did broker that deal and my reputation is tarnished, if not completely trashed. Everyone knows I was let go because of it, just as everyone knows that Ed bought it and his business is wrecked. But that was my pitch to him. What did we have to lose?'

'You tell us,' Ottey commented.

'Look, he was up to his neck in debt. He was in trouble way before I came along,' he insisted.

'Which implies he wasn't a good businessman at all,' said Cross. 'So that doesn't really make a lot of sense, your wanting to go into partnership with him.'

'All right, I was exploiting a situation. I think he needed me as much as I needed him.'

'In essence what you're saying is it was his business, his bricks and mortar, his stock, his father's reputation, you actually wanted,' said Cross.

'Okay, yes. All of that is true. But he could see the benefits of such an arrangement. He may have been many things, but he wasn't stupid.'

'Which were, from his point of view? You'll have to explain because I can't see that many,' explained Cross.

'Here's what was going to happen with that business. Torquil dies and Squire sells the freehold of the building to sort out the debt. Bye-bye, children's inheritance. All Ed's left with is a pile of books and a building owned by the bank. I had a solution. Merge the two businesses. I sell the Simpson's building, invest in the freehold of Squire's thus freeing up cash for Ed and we rebrand. Call it Berkeley Books. A fresh start.'

'What was his response to this?' asked Ottey.

'He was warming to it. I think he actually saw the benefit of a burden shared. But it wasn't a burden for me. It was a dream. We were still talking about it the day the poor bugger died. On the day he died, in answer to your earlier question, I was with him that afternoon.'

'How did he seem to you?' asked Cross.

'About us and the potential partnership? Quite positive, I think. He was amused and concerned about his old man going up to London on one of his ghost book-buying expeditions, as he put it. Looking back on it, though, he did seem a little off. Like something was bugging him. But that's the trouble, isn't it? Looking back on something in these circumstances can lead us into reading more into things than were really there, right?' he asked.

'Why should we believe any of this?' asked Ottey.

'I don't know. Because it's what happened?' he retorted testily.

'I don't dispute you met. We have evidence of that. But going into business together? I have to give it to you. That's quite the spin. Isn't the truth that he was still taking you to task over the Columbus letters?' Ottey asked.

'Nope.'

'That and the dispute about price fixing? That hadn't been resolved,' she went on.

'Not true,' he replied.

'I don't think the Columbus letters were a way of softening him. I think you knew they were stolen. That it wasn't a case of shutting him up, rather shutting him down. Selling a stolen book could be the end of his business,' she hypothesised.

'Not true. Look how it ended up for me. I lost my job, for God's sake.'

'You're still angry about that?' asked Ottey.

'Of course.'

'Is that what happened? You were arguing with him and it reached such a pitch, you killed him?' she went on.

'No!' He almost laughed at the absurdity of this possibility.

'Did you mention the possibility of partnership with your fathers?' asked Cross. Simpson's face lit up at this.

'Yes. If you don't believe me, you can speak to both of them. That'll prove I'm not talking bullshit here,' he replied enthusiastically.

'What was their reaction to the proposition?' asked Cross.

'My father was dead set against it. Torquil, though; that

man's a survivor. He can sense an opportunity, or a way out of a situation when he sees it. I think he felt it was a way forward. He could see more of a future in Berkeley Books than as Squire's with just Ed at the helm.'

'What was your father's objection?' asked Cross.

'It was all emotion with him. All about the sins of the past as he saw them. The betrayal. To be honest with you, I think he would rather have seen both shops go out of business than have any association with Torquil and Ed. He was still very much a work in progress when it came to this.'

39

George had been waiting for the right time to tell his father about his plans to resign. It hadn't been easy as on most nights after their session of mental maths, George had managed to exhaust his father who then nodded off. So, one night he decided to tell him before they did their arithmetical therapy together. George did it in the belief that Raymond would be thrilled at the prospect of having his son around more often to care for him, and also the extent of the sacrifice he was willing to make for him. Namely his career.

'Nnnnaaah!' came the pained, guttural objection from deep within Raymond's stroke-afflicted body. Such an animated response made the left-hand side of him look pitifully deflated. It was so loud, Christine heard it from the kitchen.

'What is it, Raymond? Whatever happened?' she said, appearing. The old man gestured urgently to the newspaper on a nearby table. She moved forward and gave it to him.

'George?' she enquired, hoping he could shed some light on what was going on.

'I simply told him of my intention to resign from the police force.'

Another indecipherable, but clearly appalled, objection from Raymond filled the room.

'Why ever would you do that?' Christine asked.

'So I can spend more time with my father and care for him,' replied Cross in a tone which he hoped implied it should be obvious.

Raymond was now pointing at the newspaper, jabbing it furiously with his finger. Christine leaned over his shoulder and read the words he was pointing to.

'I... do... not... want... that,' she read.

'I think it's for the best,' Cross said.

'I... do... not...' Christine began to read again.

'I can be more available to you. To care for you,' George interrupted. Raymond pointed at Christine.

'He's saying he has me,' she interpreted.

'I know, but I can help. I should help. I want to help,' George said. Raymond started jabbing the paper again.

'No, no, no... please,' Christine read.

'I've already handed in my letter of resignation.' This elicited a long groan from the patient. Christine looked at Raymond and then back to George.

'Don't you think you should've spoken to us first?' Christine asked.

George was instantly startled by this. That 'us' in this context could apply to her and his father took him aback. That collective had always only applied to him and Raymond. No one else. It was a huge intrusion for him. But he managed to put it to one side.

'I'm doing it now,' he pointed out. She looked back at the paper and the word Raymond was now pointing at.

'Unhappy,' she said quietly. George saw that his father's eyes had filled with tears. Was it frustration, sadness perhaps? One thing was certain, though. This hadn't gone as well as he'd hoped, and he had a sneaking suspicion it was all his fault. Experience told him that in these scenarios it generally was.

'I should go.'

'That seems to be your answer to every uncomfortable or complicated situation, George. To leave,' said Christine.

Again, he was completely taken aback. That she should speak to him in this manner. He was at a total loss as to what to say. He wanted to comment but knew it would probably only further upset his already distraught father.

'Why don't you think this over, Dad?' he said calmly. 'We can discuss it next time I come round. I realise now that it has come as a shock and perhaps I could have dealt with it differently. So, let's talk about it more when you've had time to reflect.'

But his father simply closed his eyes and shook his head from side to side, gently. George left.

He was bewildered. He stood outside his father's flat for some time trying to make sense of what had just happened. He was, surely, only trying to do a good thing. When he finally decided to make his way home, he was so unsettled, he had to walk his bike instead of cycling.

40

Cross was beginning to think that getting a meeting with Vladimir Putin himself, in the Kremlin, would be easier than arranging to see the elusive Oleg Dimitriev. They were told he was in London. Met officers were dispatched to his address in Eaton Square, only to be told that he was actually in Somerset. It became a game of residential ping-pong.

A meeting was finally arranged. As Ottey drove them down to Ashleigh House, Cross filled her in on what he knew about the billionaire.

'Dimitriev made his fortune from a gas company in Russia. Common story with a Russian oligarch – bought at a knockdown price in the wake of glasnost, thanks to a generous government loan. When the government insisted on buying it back from him at a price many millions below its true worth, he didn't make the same mistake as others and complain. He'd made billions after all. So he's still alive. Never speaks out publicly against the Kremlin. Got his wealth out of the motherland through various nefarious financial structures which means, despite his silence on politics, he's no longer exactly approved of back home.'

'Probably needs to watch his back then,' commented Ottey.

'Without question,' replied Cross.

★

'Please, follow me,' said Jeremy Perrin as he greeted Cross and Ottey on the front steps. They didn't go into the house but walked round the front past the orangery. It had orange and lemon tree espaliers against the back wall. To the side of the house was a very decorative formal garden, manicured to within an inch of its life. A deep and fulsomely planted herbaceous border ran the length of a red-brick wall, which looked centuries old. On the other side of the gardens was a twenty-foot hedge which had been trimmed and shaped over the years and now looked like a long, flowing Henry Moore sculpture.

'This is all very impressive,' commented Ottey. 'How long has Mr Dimitriev lived here?'

'Over twenty years now. It wasn't like this when he bought it, though. It was owned by some ministry or other. It's become his life's project,' Perrin replied.

'Well, if you have the money,' she commented.

'It's not just the money. He likes a project. Very hands on, as you're about to see.'

They walked through a gap in the red-brick wall to enter a large kitchen garden. It was well ordered with timber encased beds. These beds were immaculately weeded and abundantly prolific. Each bed of plants had a small slate label pushed into the soil with the name of the plant written on it in liquid chalk. A long Victorian greenhouse ran the length of one wall. Perrin led them to a short bald man who looked like the head gardener. Work boots, rough corduroy trousers, a leather apron with a suede tool belt wrapped around his waist. He wore a thick checked shirt which was stubble-worn round the collar. He was talking to a young man with a clipped beard, several facial piercings and tattoo-laden arms who was holding the handles of a barrow filled with produce, as if he was about to leave. The short man turned to greet them.

'Detectives! Oleg Dimitriev. Nice to meet you,' he announced. Ottey shook his hand while Cross just looked away, deliberately not availing himself. The Russian probably thought it was a deliberate gesture to offend, but didn't show it. Ottey couldn't get over the fact that the man was an absolute spit of Putin. Short, stocky, bald with narrow gimlet eyes. It was uncanny. For a moment she fantasised about the possibility of the Russian leader actually holidaying in the UK, living in plain sight of everyone, able to do so because no one would believe it was actually him. He was in his late fifties. He turned to the young man with the barrow.

'This is Joe. He's from Earth, the restaurant in the village. Have you eaten there?' he asked Cross.

'I have not.'

'Probably a bit far from Bristol. But you really should try it some time. We provide all his vegetables as well as meat from the farm. Joe, see you soon.'

'Thanks, Oleg,' the young man replied and walked away with his barrow.

'We're completely organic here,' continued Oleg, as if pitching to a prospective buyer.

'Surely you can't eat all this veg?' asked Ottey.

'I know,' he laughed. 'I started just wanting to be self-sufficient and then got hooked. First the garden and now the farm. I truly love it. Do you have the gardening bug?' he asked Cross, still trying to engage him.

'I do not,' came the short answer.

'In answer to your question,' he said to the more obviously receptive Ottey, 'we supply Joe and another restaurant in Taunton. We also sell through a local farm shop. All profits go to local charities. Any surplus goes to a couple of food banks.'

'Gosh,' replied Ottey.

'Food banks, I know. Anyone would think we were in Russia,' he joked.

'I didn't realise they were needed in rural areas,' replied Ottey.

'Of course they are. Successive shambolic Tory governments don't discriminate when it comes to sharing out poverty. So, you think I had something to do with Ed Squire's murder?' he finished by saying.

'We'd certainly like to talk to you about it,' replied Cross.

'Okay, let's go into the garden kitchen and talk,' he said, walking away towards a small outbuilding at the far end of the garden. As they walked over, Cross observed other gardeners working in the beds. Also, at a discreet distance, two men who had the distinct vigilance of a pair of guards. One of them had virtually no neck. The other wore a black bomber jacket with a transparent plastic pouch on the upper arm.

Inside the small building was a rustic but well-appointed kitchen. A long wooden table occupied the centre of the room. There was a large American-style fridge and a dresser covered in plates and mugs.

'Tea? Coffee?' he asked.

'Tea would be great, thanks,' said Ottey politely, before reminding herself not to fall into this man's web of mellifluous charm.

'Ah!' he exclaimed as he saw a cloth-covered plate in the centre of the table. 'As promised, Mrs Hodge has made us some of her miraculous shortbread. You have to try it. Best shortbread in the county. I do not exaggerate. That is actually factual. I made her enter the county fair a couple of years ago and she won!'

He filled a kettle from the brass tap in the white butler's sink.

'English breakfast, or would you prefer Darjeeling?' he asked, looking at his watch. 'It is late morning, after all.'

'Darjeeling,' pronounced Cross, a little too enthusiastically perhaps.

'Jeremy, are you having tea?' Dimitriev asked the hovering Perrin.

'Yes please, boss.'

'Why don't you start your interrogation, DI Ottey?' he joked. 'No need to wait for me to finish brewing.' She suspected he'd timed his question deliberately at the moment she'd taken a large chunk out of one of the shortbreads, crumbs tumbling off her chin like a small avalanche. Cross saw her problem and so stepped in.

'I would normally ask where you were on the night of Ed's Squire's murder, but I have the feeling that would be irrelevant,' he began.

'And why is that?'

'I think if you were involved in the murder, you'd have employed someone else to do it.'

'What makes you think that? As you can see, I'm not averse to getting my hands dirty,' he said, holding up his dirt-encrusted palms. He noticed Cross transfixed by them. 'You're quite right. I wasn't thinking. Where are my manners and sense of hygiene? I should wash my hands before making you tea.'

He did so.

'So where were you that night?' Cross asked.

'I was here with my girlfriend.'

The mention of a girlfriend reminded Ottey that Dimitriev had been involved in one of the most expensive divorces in British history. It had made his ex-wife one of the richest women in the UK.

'We had some friends over. Jeremy has drawn up a list of all of them, together with their contact details.'

Perrin then produced a sheet of paper, which he gave to Cross. He looked at it very briefly.

'Why have you been sending three of your men to Ed Squire's premises over the last few months?' Cross asked.

'It was four, actually. They did it in shifts, as it were,' Dimitriev responded.

Cross was impressed by the man's English. Not only was it without any accent but he was completely fluent. It was as if he'd made a huge effort to assimilate himself seamlessly into English society.

'What was the purpose of these visits?' asked Cross.

'I would've thought that was obvious. To intimidate the man,' he replied matter-of-factly.

'To what end?'

'I was angry, detective. He had cost me two million pounds.'

'What were you trying to achieve?' Cross went on.

'Again, I would've thought that much was obvious. I wanted paying back.'

'And how was he supposed to achieve this?'

'I don't know. Not my problem. Except, of course, it was,' he said ruefully. 'My men were there to encourage him to find a solution.'

'How?'

'Oh, the usual. An overt presence. Threats of violence. Arson. Do you take milk?' he asked, pouring the tea. Cross was actually more appalled by this suggestion than what Dimitriev had just said.

'Certainly not,' he said.

'Good man. DI Ottey?' he asked.

'Milk and one sugar,' she replied. Cross was unable to suppress a sigh of disapproval.

'Each to their own, Sergeant. Have you tried the shortbread?'

'I have not.'

'You really should. I think you'll find it the perfect accompaniment to the tea.'

Cross wasn't going to play this game, despite the shortbreads looking irresistible with an inviting, light dusting of sugar.

'You seem to have a somewhat glib attitude when it comes to admitting to the issuance of threats and the general intimidation of a murder victim, shortly before his death. Particularly when you're speaking to part of the murder investigation team,' Cross said.

'You've already admitted threatening him. Perhaps it was a case of intimidation gone too far?' Ottey suggested.

'An interesting theory and one I hadn't factored in. Perhaps I should consider my answers to any further questions a little more carefully,' he said.

'That would be more than advisable in the circumstances,' replied Cross.

'You were angry. You wanted your money back and it took a fatal turn,' Ottey offered. Dimitriev thought about this for a moment.

'No. My men are far too professional to make such a mistake,' he said.

'Then perhaps you'd reached the end of your tether and just had him killed. People have been killed for a lot less than two million,' Ottey went on.

'Killing him would not have got my money back, Inspector. I'm afraid you're barking up the wrong tree. In all sincerity I think you should concentrate your efforts elsewhere if you want to have any chance of finding Ed Squire's killer.'

There was something chillingly unsettling about Dimitriev's cold charm. Neither of the detectives were inclined to take him at face value.

It was time to talk to their victim's father again. But only after George Cross had finished drinking what turned out to be an excellently made cup of tea.

41

They found the old bookseller in his sitting room. Cross noticed on the way up that Torquil's desk seemed to have work piling up on it. Ottey took one look at him and said, 'Are you eating properly, Torquil?'

'Why does everyone keep asking me that?' he replied.

'Possibly because you look like you've lost an unhealthy amount of weight,' remarked Cross.

'I have lost my appetite. Has to be said. Not just for food, but for books also. I've lost all my passion for books. Who would've thought?' he said mournfully.

'It's hardly surprising. But you must try and eat,' said Ottey. The old man didn't look up. He was unshaven. The growth on his face looked like an early morning frost had settled on the folds of his jowls.

'I honestly think Ed's death will be the end of me. I have no reason to live any longer,' he moaned.

'I'm not sure either of your grandchildren would agree with you,' said Ottey.

'Well, you say that, but they have their own lives to lead.' He was definitely in the final stages of descent into full-on self-pity, Ottey decided.

'It's time to be honest with us, Torquil,' she began.

'I have been nothing but honest,' he replied.

'All right then, more forthcoming. You've been withholding information which could've been very helpful to us had we known it sooner,' she went on.

'Not to mention saving us valuable time,' added Cross. The old man said nothing. 'Oleg Dimitriev,' Cross went on.

'He killed my son,' replied Torquil, quietly.

'What do you mean by that?' asked Ottey.

'Just that. He killed him.'

'How do you know?' Ottey asked.

'Because the man told me he was going to do it.'

'Why didn't you tell us this earlier?' Ottey asked.

'Because he threatened my entire family. What was I supposed to do?' Torquil asked plaintively.

'When was this?' asked Cross.

'Oh, several times. The latest about a month before he went ahead with it.'

'Let's track back a little, Mr Squire,' said Cross. 'Why did he threaten to kill your son?'

'You must know all of this, surely? I mean, what have you been up to for the past few weeks?'

'We want to hear it from you, Torquil,' said Ottey.

'He was so like me, Ed, and so unlike me at the same time.'

'In what way?' asked Ottey.

'Dear Ed. He wasn't really a book man like me. Don't get me wrong. He enjoyed the business, but it was just the business he enjoyed. I'm sure others have told you the same thing. He wasn't so much interested in the process of rare book buying and selling. The provenance was relevant to him only in so far as it might increase the price. Well, you both know that from the Tolkien episode. So tawdry. We had quite the row about it. Did I tell you the family have reached out to me?'

'Who?' asked Ottey.

'The de Sourceys. I think it was something you must've said to them, DS Cross.' Cross's apparent willingness to take the credit for this, and not correct the old man by telling him it was in fact Ottey, earned him a small look of rebuke from her which he didn't notice. 'I'm meeting with them next week to go through all the family papers. They've held onto them. Not sold them. Something may crop up which might help resolve the situation,' he said hopefully.

'How was he like you, Ed?' said Cross. 'You've told us how he was different. But what did you have in common?'

'He was too ready to take people on. Fight what he saw as the good fight.'

'You mean with the price fixing?' asked Ottey.

'Well, obviously. That's where all of this started. If he hadn't persisted with that, he'd still be alive.'

'What makes you say that?' asked Ottey.

'Because those wretched letters would never have come his way and he would never have sold them to Dimitriev.'

'Had he been a customer of yours before?' asked Cross.

'Only the once. Years ago. But it was a good sale. Complex, but rewarding on both sides. He'd just bought Ashleigh House and was in the process of renovating it. Once he'd completed it he had this beautiful big library. But an empty one, lined with endless, empty shelves.'

'Did you then supply him with one?' asked Cross.

'We did. But it was far from straightforward, which I loved, Ed not so much. When new money buys a stately home they'll often buy a lot of the furnishing, paintings with it, at the same time, and possibly the existing library. As you can imagine, if someone is selling a stately home and downsizing, they're unlikely to have room to house the library elsewhere. We're often talking thousands of books. But if the library has been sold separately, the new owners will want to replace it. So in that instance we might buy an entire library. If that's not possible, then we'll buy parts of collections at auction and build it up from there,' he explained.

'Do they ever read these books?' asked Ottey.

He laughed ruefully at this. 'Of course not. It's more about the number of books. Getting enough to fill the library. And the look of them. I've had buyers more interested in telling me they want a uniform collection of leather-bound volumes across a wall. Uniformly coloured spines, same height. No mention of content. Nothing along the lines of "Oh, I have a passion for natural history or biography". Just the look of the damn things as they sit on a shelf. To be fair, some of them do want what I call "after dinner" items.'

'What are those?' Ottey asked.

'Normally high value. Rare. So that they can say to the guests, "Have you seen my first edition *Paradise Lost?*" Or complete set of Dickens first editions. It's like owning art. The equivalent of people asking if you'd like to see their Chagall,' Torquil continued.

'What was so challenging about Dimitriev's bibliophilic needs?' asked Cross.

'When he looked into the history of the house, which he is obsessed with, by the way – has the original deeds, architect's drawings, garden designs – and discovered that the Denbigh family had lived there for over three hundred years, he wanted to restore their library.'

'Why was that a problem?' asked Ottey.

'Because he wanted to restore *their* library, not *the* library. He wanted us to source and repurchase all the books that had been sold. Well, you can imagine. Over the years certain members of the family had tried to index the entire library, but had never completed the task, which would've made our job much easier,' he continued.

'Was the library not sold as one lot?' asked Cross.

'Yes, but it was then dispersed and sold to several different buyers all over the world.'

'That must've taken forever to sort,' suggested Ottey.

'Just over five years,' he said with the pride of someone who'd done a thorough and successful job. 'I loved it. Tracking down books in all corners of the earth. It was a bit like the old days. I have to admit I was something of an admirer of Dimitriev's passion to restore the library to its original state. To preserve the integrity of its existence in the house. He is a man of discerning tastes. Which I suppose with his money, he can afford to be. But my opinion changed over the course of my time working for him.'

'Why?' asked Ottey.

'Because he's a very determined man, when he sets his mind to something, he doesn't like it when things don't work out or he doesn't get his way. What's strange was that the more difficult something was to acquire, or seemed unattainable, the more fixated he became. It's common with some inordinately rich collectors. If they're told definitively that they can't have something, the more obsessed they become with obtaining it. It's like the ultimate collector's addiction,' he said.

'An extreme version of that is in the art and jewel world,' Cross said to Ottey. 'Certain things won't be stolen because they are so famous. So instantly recognisable that they can't be resold. But there are obsessive, secretive collectors in the world willing to pay a price for such things, knowing they will never see a return on their money. For them it's enough that it will be in their possession for their lifetime. That they can look at it whenever they like and no one else can. It's the ultimate power play. The most extreme of all status symbols.'

'Except that often with status symbols comes the need to make possession public, to fully savour it,' Torquil pointed out. 'With Dimitriev, there were a couple of rare seventeenth-century manuscripts which had been in the possession of the Denbigh family and then sold. We tracked them down. Both in the Middle East, as it happens. The new owners didn't want to part with them, despite offers being made way above their market value. However, when faced with this stumbling block, Dimitriev went from making extravagant offers to other alarming methods of forcing the issue. Threats of violence, arson, beatings. It was awful.'

'You know this how?'

'Because it was either me or Ed who was dispatched to collect the "spoils of war", as he once jokingly described them to me. The seller often seemed really shocked. Rattled by what had happened. Frightened even. Appalled that this kind of behaviour could have entered their world. But they weren't able to tell me much.'

'Why not?' asked Cross.

'Because in those situations we were always accompanied by a couple of Dimitriev's goons. It was most unpleasant.'

'Were any of those men around the shop in the last couple of months?' asked Cross.

'One of them, Nikolai. I didn't recognise the other two. Nasty piece of work, Nikolai. I got the impression he was the one who carried out the threats if necessary. You'd never forget him once you'd met him. The man has no neck.'

'Why didn't Dimitriev just send these men to collect the books? Why bother with you at all?' asked Ottey.

'To verify them. Make sure the real article was being picked up,' said Cross.

'Exactly so.'

'Tell us about the Columbus letters,' said Cross.

The old man sighed.

'It was the equivalent of hush money from Carnegie's. I knew so at the time. But Ed justified it by saying he'd proved his point with the price fixing and it was time to move on. Patrick Gibb had heard about the sale of a genuine set of Columbus letters in Italy and saw an opportunity to appease Ed. I'm assuming you know the history of the letters?'

'We do.'

'In reality the sale was offered to Ed just as a way of shutting him up,' said Squire.

'He'd upset them that much?' asked Ottey.

'It had just gone on too long. There didn't seem to be an end in sight and I'm not sure what Ed thought he was going to achieve any more. What was his objective? An admission of guilt? An undertaking not to do it anymore? I don't think even he knew. A sale like Columbus would not only earn Ed and the business a substantial commission, it was also the kudos such a sale would bring with it. It would have enhanced Ed's reputation as a major dealer in the book world. Or so we thought,' he said ruefully.

'So why wouldn't Gibb want to be at the centre of a deal of that magnitude?' asked Cross.

'That is a very good question, to which, if you think about it, there can only be one answer,' Squire replied.

'He knew they were stolen,' suggested Cross.

'Exactly. How, I don't know. Ed did all the proper checks. It was definitely a legitimate item. What he didn't know was that it was stolen.'

'How would Gibb have known?' asked Ottey.

'He must've had knowledge of the theft from the university, together with the distinguishing marks on the manuscript which made it unique and identifiable,' replied Squire.

'Are you implying he did it deliberately?' asked Cross.

'I'm not implying it. I'm saying it.'

'Do you think Nigel Simpson knew all of this?' asked Ottey.

'You'd have to ask him that.'

'So, what was Gibb's intention?' asked Ottey.

'To ruin Ed and me. Destroy us. He's a vindictive little man, Gibb. Just like his father. I had a long battle with Peregrine Gibb over the auction ring. Part of me thinks this was a settling of old scores. Not that I'm suggesting for a moment that he knew it would end in murder. Why would he?'

'How can you be so sure?' asked Ottey.

'Gibb knew Ed had one customer with the appetite for such a purchase and what's more, the funds,' said Squire.

'Dimitriev?'

'Exactly.'

'So the sale is made. Everyone is happy. The campaign ceases. The commission is banked. How did it all go wrong?' asked Cross.

'The American university heard about the sale and staked a claim,' he said.

'Did they read about it? Even if they did, how would they know it was the one stolen from them?' asked Cross.

'They didn't read about it. Dimitriev had insisted on no publicity. Ever since he moved to the UK, he's liked to keep a low profile. Ed was a little disappointed. But enough people in the trade knew and the commission, two hundred and fifty thousand pounds, was ample compensation. Added to that, he'd just re-established contact with a valuable customer, who was very pleased with him,' Squire said.

'So, how did they find out?' asked Ottey.

'Well, that's just the thing. Patrick Gibb must have told them. It's the only possible answer. Looking back on it, it's easy to see it was always his plan. To ridicule Ed in the business. Ruin his reputation. Put us out of business. Dimitriev was horrified, did the decent thing and returned the letters. But he didn't want it to become news. He didn't want to be made to look a fool. It soon got round that he'd done the decent thing. He's averse to drawing any attention to himself, particularly to people in the Kremlin,' Squire explained.

'But he remains two million out of pocket,' Cross pointed out.

'And he wants recompense. Well, obviously Ed paid him back the commission. It was the least he could do. But that wasn't enough.'

'Surely he knew Ed had acted in good faith?' asked Ottey.

'Of course, but with certain people good faith means nothing.'

'How could he expect Ed to pay him back, though?' asked Cross.

'He knew Ed couldn't, so he came after me. He discovered I owned the freehold of this building. Worth around two million. He gave me a choice. Sell the building or remortgage and pay him back with the proceeds,' he explained.

'Did you consider it at all or try and negotiate with him?' asked Cross.

Squire laughed fearfully. 'You don't negotiate with people like Oleg Dimitriev. It ended with him saying that if I didn't do it, Ed was a dead man.' He shook his head in incredulity. 'He just came right out and said it. It was quite shocking. He also said it wouldn't stop there. He sent me Ed's home address and the addresses of the grandchildren in London and Edinburgh. Which is why I couldn't tell you. Because this isn't over and I know what he's capable of. He even sent flowers to the funeral. Can you believe that?'

'A floral threat,' Ottey commented.

'Was it Dimitriev himself who made these threats?' asked Cross.

'Only the once. After that he made do with his goons.'

42

'A direct death threat? Let's bring him and his heavies in,' announced Carson, clearly thrilled that there was an end in sight for the case.

'We should talk to Nigel Simpson again, first,' suggested Cross.

'Why?' asked Carson, mildly displeased, in the knowledge that Cross's caution often led them down a long and tortuous road.

'I think there's more to his leaving Carnegie's than he let on,' Cross explained.

'Dimitriev threatened to kill Ed Squire if he didn't get his money back, for God's sake. He hasn't been paid the money and Squire is dead. What more do we need?' asked Carson.

'He'll just hide behind a phalanx of highly paid lawyers,' suggested Ottey.

'As with all these things, there is no need to rush,' added Cross.

'Except for the fact that our suspect has, according to the father of our victim, made threats against the entire family,' Carson pointed out.

'You make a good point,' Cross conceded. 'But I think it unlikely, with an ongoing investigation which has already approached him, that he'll be in a rush to go after another family member. There's been no further communication from him to the family...'

'Other than the flowers,' said Carson.

'Dimitriev's men have also not been seen in the vicinity of the shop, Victoria's house, nor either of the children's,' said Cross.

Nigel Simpson turned up at the MCU, as invited, later that day. They took him into an interview room.

'Tell us about the Columbus letters. From your perspective,' Cross began.

'As I've already told you, I have an NDA,' he replied.

'Patrick Gibb has already breached the terms of the NDA with us, while helping with our enquiries,' Cross informed him.

'Really?' Simpson asked in disbelief.

'I'm pretty sure that means you're no longer bound by it. But even if you were, I think the inference is that, with his recent cooperation, he would give full support to your doing the same. However, we can get him on the phone and ask him directly, if you would prefer. But I think we all know what his answer will be,' Cross said.

'What do you want to know?'

'Who was it who discovered the letters were for sale in the first place?' asked Cross.

'Patrick Gibb.'

'And who thought it a way of possibly dealing with the Ed Squire issue?' Cross continued.

'Gibb.'

Cross thought for a minute.

'How was he so sure that he could broker the deal, as it were, for Ed? What about other competitors?' he asked.

'At the time I just thought it was down to him and his persuasive negotiating skills,' came the reply.

'And what do you think now?'

'Looking back, I should've noticed the paucity of other potential buyers,' he said. 'But hindsight's a fine thing. I should've thought something was a bit iffy. I don't know. Maybe I just didn't want to, as it did look like a solution to the Ed problem.'

'Do you think Gibb knew they were stolen?' asked Cross.

The man became noticeably reticent before replying, 'I'm not sure.'

Cross looked at him and made a note. He didn't believe him.

'Why did you lose your job at Carnegie Books?' he asked.

'Someone had to take the fall. The reputation of the firm and its integrity had to be preserved. That someone was me.'

'So, you're saying you were fired because it transpired these letters were stolen,' asked Cross.

'Yes,' he replied.

Cross's phone began to vibrate in his pocket with a call. He decided to ignore it.

'Here's what I don't understand. You've just told us that it was Patrick Gibb who sourced the letters. Found out about the sale. Then encouraged you to persuade Ed it was a good thing,' Cross suggested.

'He didn't take much persuading,' said Simpson.

'But your role in it, the extent of your involvement, was to inform Squire of the possibility. You had nothing to do with identifying the sale, approaching the sellers, brokering any kind of deal. That was all Patrick Gibb,' said Cross.

'Correct.'

'So what I'm having difficulty in understanding is why you lost your job,' Cross told him, puzzled.

'Like I said. Someone had to be seen to take the blame,' Simpson repeated.

'But why you?' asked Cross.

Simpson looked uncomfortable as Cross pushed this simple question. Had he decided he'd painted himself into a corner? Cross thought this was a possibility. His losing his job just didn't seem to make any sense in the narrative he was presenting.

Cross's phone began vibrating in his pocket again. Again, he ignored it.

'What were the terms of your severance that secured your signature on the NDA?' asked Cross.

'Six month's salary. Transfer of my company pension into a fund of my choosing,' he replied, shifting his body weight in his seat, slightly. Cross surveyed him for a moment.

'I don't believe you,' he said finally, in disbelief. 'Twenty years' loyal service. A seat on the board and you take the fall, as you put it, with what can best be described as a rudimentary compensation package, for something you actually had nothing to do with? Why did you really give everything up for that?'

Simpson thought for a moment. Then his body relaxed slightly, as often happened with people when they decide to come clean. It was almost a physical expression of relief.

'Because he knew. He absolutely did know,' he said.

'Who knew what?' asked Cross, knowing the answer full well.

'Gibb. He knew the letters were stolen from the get-go. It was a perfect way of silencing Ed for good.' Then he added hastily, 'And by that I don't mean with his death, obviously.'

'How did you find out?' asked Cross.

'I had a sneaking suspicion. But even I couldn't believe Patrick would be so devious. Then I came across an email which wasn't meant for my eyes,' he said.

'What was your reaction?' asked Cross.

'Disbelief at first. Appalled, obviously. Disappointed. This was long before Ed was killed by Dimitriev,' Simpson told them.

'Who said anything about Dimitriev being involved in Ed Squire's death?' asked Cross.

'Forgive me, I don't mean to be rude, but it doesn't take a detective to work that one out,' Simpson retorted.

'On the contrary, I think you'll find that's exactly what it takes in murder cases,' replied Cross plainly.

He could see this immediately put Simpson off guard. He didn't know if he was joking or not.

'What happened at Carnegie? Did you make your feelings clear to Gibb?' asked Ottey.

'I did. It then became rapidly clear there was no future for me there. From my perspective, anyway. I didn't want to work at a place that dealt with people in such a way. So I struck a deal to leave,' he told them.

'Which was?' asked Cross.

'What I told you. But with the addition of a hundred thousand pounds' worth of stock, which I would repay to them as I sold it. It was just to get me on my feet. Also, a start-up investment in my business of fifty thousand,' he said.

'Did Ed know all of this when you approached him?' asked Cross.

'I couldn't tell him that Gibb knew. Obviously that was covered by the NDA. But I wouldn't have anyway. It would've started a battle that would have made the price fixing war look like a snowball fight. I'm ashamed to admit I did try and use the two million he owed the Russian as leverage. I suggested selling the freehold of Park Street, as I told you before, use some of the proceeds to pay off half of the debt. Then remortgage fifty per cent of Berkeley Square,' he said.

Again, Cross's phone vibrated. He was tempted to look and see who needed him so urgently but felt whoever it was could wait until the interview was concluded.

'But that would have meant you taking on an enormous financial liability that wasn't yours,' Ottey pointed out.

'In part, yes. But in the partnership that money would go against Ed's half. What was more I felt, do feel, and it's so much worse now that he's dead, in some way responsible for the whole mess. I felt we could find a way out to the other side of it. I really did,' he protested.

'What was Ed's reaction to this?' asked Cross.

'He really wasn't sure.'

'What changed his mind?' asked Ottey.

'I came into some information about the identity and whereabouts of the Italian sellers. He could give it to Dimitriev, who could then pursue them and the problem might go away,' he said.

'Why would Dimitriev be willing to do that?' asked Ottey.

'Because there was more chance of his getting back his money from them, than Ed,' he replied. 'Also, people like Dimitriev sometimes have an odd sense of honour. He knew they, and not the Squires, were the right people to go after.'

'How did you come across this information?' asked Ottey.

'Actually, through Patrick Gibb,' he said.

'Why would he tell you that?' asked Cross.

'Torquil Squire. The old man went up to London, marched into the Bedford Square offices and gave him both barrels.

Accused him of knowing all along about the letters. Gibb denied it, of course. But the rare book world is a small one and Torquil is well connected. The idea that Gibb knew hadn't taken long to get back to him,' he told them.

'That made Gibb come clean?' asked Ottey.

'Apparently he was shocked when Torquil told him about the death threats from Dimitriev.'

'A change of heart? I'm not sure I buy that,' said Ottey.

'No, of course not. It was way more selfish than that. He's only interested in one thing – himself, and what he calls his legacy. But the truth is it had nothing to do with that. He's simply terrified of being a fifth-generation bookseller whose family business flounders on his watch. It was when Torquil threatened to tell Dimitriev the identity of the man who initiated the sale, in the full knowledge that the letters were stolen, that Gibb realised he had to do something. If the Russian found out, he would undoubtedly come after him as well. They have a rich stock list, an expensive freehold in Bedford Square and you only have to look at Companies House to see the extent of their cash reserves, despite Gibb constantly denying how rich the company is. He did it out of self-preservation,' Simpson told them.

'What did Gibb propose?'

'That he do some digging and come up with a name.'

'And he gave you that information?' asked Cross.

'He did.'

'Why?'

'Because he knew Ed would believe it coming from me.'

'And possibly because he knew if there were any repercussions, they'd also come back to you and not him,' suggested Cross.

'Who knew the book world could be so devious?' commented Ottey.

'Oh. You don't know the half of it,' he replied.

'What will you do now?' Cross asked him, as the meeting came to an end.

'Um, I think I'll go back to my original plan. Back myself in Park Street. Clear the joint up. Have a jolly launch party, then start buying and selling books,' he said, oddly cheerfully in the circumstances.

'Something tells me you might be the only show in town fairly soon,' commented Ottey.

'You mean when Torquil dies?' asked Simpson.

'I'm not sure you'll have to wait till then,' said Cross. 'I think he may well have come to the conclusion that he's had his fill of the book trade.'

'You think he'll sell up? Really? I suppose with all that's happened, it wouldn't be that surprising,' he said.

'With Ed gone and neither of the grandchildren interested, I'd've thought he may well sell up sooner rather than later,' said Ottey.

'What about that girl Ed had there? His niece?' asked Simpson.

'Persephone? I'm not sure that's a viable proposition, despite what she may think. There's a lot of inheritance for Sebastian and Charlotte tied up in that building,' observed Cross.

'What would you do if he did sell up?' asked Ottey.

He thought about this for a moment.

'Try and buy as much of his stock as possible, obviously. I am first and foremost a bookseller, after all,' he replied, with a little too much opportunism for Ottey's liking.

As they walked to her car Cross took out his phone and saw that he had missed several calls from Christine. He stopped, called his voicemail and listened intently.

'Everything all right?' asked Ottey.

'It's my father. He's been rushed back into hospital. From what my mother says it sounds like he's had another stroke.'

'This is my fault,' he said as they drove to the BRI.

'How could this possibly be your fault?' Ottey asked him.

'I told him I was resigning from the force,' he replied.

'You told him what?' Ottey said, trying to put aside her shock at this being the first she'd heard about it.

'I'm resigning,' he repeated.

'How did he take it?' she asked, not entirely sure how she herself felt about it.

'Not very well. He became quite agitated, in fact. But he'll come to accept it in time,' he said, wondering in the moment if this was perhaps wishful thinking on his part.

'When was this?' she asked.

'When was what?'

'That you told him,' she said.

'Two nights ago,' he replied, quietly. 'Are you implying I may have caused this?'

'No, of course not.'

'It's clearly a possibility though,' he said, sounding worried.

But Ottey was concerned that George's decision to return had simply been a knee jerk reaction to his father's condition. Had he really thought it through? What would he do with himself if he retired? Come to think of it, what would she do?

43

They found Christine in the waiting area of the A&E department of the BRI.

'He started slurring his words again and didn't make any sense. He was all over the place. Quite distressed. I tried calling you. But you didn't answer. So, I called an ambulance,' Christine told them, clearly upset by the whole thing. 'Do you think he's had another stroke?' she asked George.

'I don't know,' he replied. 'Where is he?'

'In a cubicle. He's sleeping. I came out as soon as I knew you were on your way. He has a very young doctor,' she said with a hint of old age suspicion. George looked around at people waiting to be treated. Others for news of those being treated. People stared at their phones half-heartedly. Bored children stared longingly at the forbidden fruit contained in the vending machine next to the stairs. Impatience and fear occupied every available plastic seat.

George was amazed his father could sleep. It was so noisy. After about an hour of Cross pestering anyone he saw in medical scrubs, a young doctor approached them.

'Has he had another stroke?' Cross asked him before he had a chance to introduce himself.

'He has not,' replied the young man.

'Have you alerted Dr Khan?' Cross asked.

'There's no need and anyway, he's in surgery.'

'Are you going to do a brain scan?'

'I'm not, no,' the doctor replied confidently.

'Why not?'

'As I said, your father has not had another stroke,' the doctor continued.

'Then what has happened?' asked Cross.

'Your father has a UTI, a urinary tract infection. Quite common in the elderly, this can often result in confusion, disorientation, slurring and misuse of words. Obviously, after someone has had a stroke like Raymond, when this happens, the immediate reaction from family can be that he's had another. But I can assure you he hasn't. We'll give him some antibiotics and you can take him home. It should clear up in the next twenty-four hours.'

'This situation is precisely why I have to resign,' Cross informed Christine and Josie as they waited for an ambulance to take Raymond home.

'I don't follow,' said Josie.

'So that I can be available for such a crisis,' he said.

'I'd say this situation proves exactly the opposite, George. Christine dealt with the situation admirably,' Josie pointed out.

'She couldn't get hold of me,' he replied, confident this would prove his point.

'Only because you chose not to answer the phone. Maybe answer it next time,' she said. 'Or at least look at who it is. Or, even better, have a second phone which is just for your parents' use. So that if it rings you know to answer it. Actually, now I come to think about it, can't you assign people individual ringtones for when they call?'

'He really doesn't want you to resign, George,' began Christine. 'He's been quite upset about it since you told us. Completely preoccupied with it, in fact.'

'Are you implying this is my fault?' asked George.

'I'm no doctor, but I'm fairly sure being upset doesn't bring on a UTI, George. However, if you really want to help his current state of mind, perhaps you could tell him you've changed your mind?' his mother went on.

'But I haven't,' George pointed out.

'Will you at least consider it?' asked Christine.

'I'll give it some thought,' he replied.

'Did it never occur to you to discuss your resignation with me, or at least inform me of it?' Ottey asked Cross in her car as she drove him home.

'It didn't, no.'

'Why not?' she asked.

'Did it never occur to you to discuss or inform me of your impending promotion?' he replied.

'It did, actually,' she said.

'And yet you failed to do either,' he observed.

'I wanted to. I intended to,' she replied defensively.

'You had ample opportunity to do so.'

'Alright, I'm sorry. I should've but let's not make this conversation about me,' she said.

'It is about you. It's about your being offended that I didn't tell you about my intention to resign from the police,' he pointed out.

'Raymond is obviously upset about it,' she said, ignoring his point.

'So it would seem.'

'Which should have some sort of bearing on your thinking. But also, seriously George, what would you do without your work?' she asked.

'Look after my father,' he replied.

'But he has Christine now.'

'I want to be able to help,' he protested.

'I think you can do both. Help and work at the same time. Have you thought about that?' she asked.

'I haven't, as it happens, no.'

'Well perhaps you should before going through with such a dramatic gesture,' she said.

There it was again, that word, gesture. There was also something in this last sentence which struck a chord with Cross. He had, after all, entertained the, not unpleasant, notion that he was making a great sacrifice on his part, one which he thought might garner universal gratitude and praise. But it hadn't. Was it because it was no more than that – a dramatic gesture? It had to be said, he'd woken up several times in the last few weeks, anxious about what life would be like without his work. So perhaps he wasn't as suited to the role of selfless martyr as he thought he was.

44

The next move was to arrest Dimitriev. This was going to be far from easy. Not your average, run-of-the-mill dawn raid, with the remains of a bacon sandwich hanging off your chin, on a terraced house somewhere in Bristol. So complicated, in fact, that DCI Ben Carson had taken it upon himself to head up the operation. He gave himself the call sign 'Gold commander' for the day, which Ottey found irresistibly hilarious. Then he anointed her 'Silver commander' which made her convinced everyone was now laughing at them both.

'There's a lot of money invested in this op, Josie. So if things go pear-shaped, which I'm confident they won't, that will fall on my shoulders and not those of a newly promoted DI,' he told her magnanimously, explaining why he'd stepped in and taken charge. While she appreciated the thought, she was all too aware of Carson's track record when things went awry. His first action was always to shift the blame elsewhere. The direction that shift would go in this instance would inevitably be wherever she happened to be standing at the time. But, to be fair to him, he came across as quite organised in the planning and not in his usual rush to make an arrest. There were two full days of planning and strategy which both she and Cross attended.

The basic idea was to go in numbers simultaneously. Met officers would knock on Dimitriev's London house. At Ashleigh

House, armed officers from the tactical support unit, snipers and over forty uniformed officers all in riot gear were to be deployed. Armed officers were utilised, because it was widely assumed Dimitriev's men were armed. The riot uniform, well, why not, was the thinking. Better to be prepared, etc. These officers were to position themselves at all the exits from the estate, of which there were four. They would gain access by the most unprotected entrance at the rear of the estate. Carson was going to then make the arrest with his silver commander at his side.

Carson could barely conceal his febrile excitement as he and Ottey were driven to Ashleigh House, first thing on the appointed morning. Cross, never one for these large scale, high octane and noisy raids, had argued successfully that he should stay back at the MCU, to put together his interview script. Carson was happy for him to stay, as he was never of any particular use in these situations. What he didn't know, however, was that Cross's reasons for staying in Bristol weren't quite as straightforward as he'd made out. During one of the briefings he'd spotted something that gave him pause for thought.

When Carson and Ottey pulled up at the assembly point on the outskirts of the neighbouring village, Ottey couldn't believe her eyes at the number of vehicles. All to arrest one man. It looked like a film crew had descended on the village. She wondered jokily whether hair and make-up had arrived. Then, remembering Carson's lust for media exposure, realised she couldn't necessarily put it past him.

All went according to plan. Officers and vehicles were dispatched to their assigned positions around the estate. There was no escape for the Russian. Bang on the dot of eight, Carson barked down the radio.

'GO! GO! GO!'

Ottey thought he must've dreamed of doing this for years. Two officers scaled the low stone wall and found the mechanism to open the electric gates manually behind it. Once they'd achieved this a black, armed tactical van sped through the gates, followed by fully loaded police vans and the car with Carson and Ottey. As the tactical van screamed by, Ottey found herself wondering why it was painted in matt black paint. Was this just to make it look all the more alarming? She told herself to concentrate on the matter at hand, at the same time as realising her heart was beating furiously.

Simultaneously the units at the trade entrance to the side of the estate and the main gates, pressed the buzzers repeatedly and demanded to be granted access. The officers from the Met were also banging noisily on the front door of the Eaton Square house and yelling 'POLICE!' at the top of their voices, much to the consternation, they hoped, of the rich neighbours.

Carson knocked on the front door and waited. After a few moments it was opened by a butler who seemed oblivious to all the noise and commotion around, simply saying, 'Good morning. Can I help?'

'I have a search warrant for this house and an arrest warrant for Oleg Dimitriev,' Carson announced.

'Oh, I'm afraid you just missed him,' he said with an expression of sincere regret, worthy of a RADA graduate.

'I don't think so,' replied Carson confidently. 'We have the place surrounded.' He looked triumphant in the delivery of yet another clichéd and well-worn phrase.

'I can assure you. He's just leaving,' replied the butler with equal confidence.

Carson's superior expression was quickly wiped from his face by the unmistakable whirr of a helicopter's rotor blades starting up somewhere close by.

'You're joking,' he said, almost inaudibly, before running round to the side of the house, just in time to see a black executive helicopter lifting up from the garden. It hovered briefly, then banked and flew off at speed. Dimitriev looked down on Carson with what looked suspiciously, to his mind, like a smirk of victory.

What Carson didn't know was that as soon as the convoy had approached the perimeter wall of the estate, cameras were triggered. The images from the cameras were then relayed to a control room deep in the bowels of Ashleigh House, where a man put in motion a well-rehearsed evacuation plan. This enabled their principal, as he was called, to be off the property and in the air in under six minutes. Such was the wealth and paranoia of the man, that the helicopter was on permanent standby with the pilots living in a cottage on the estate, ready to be scrambled at a moment's notice. Dimitriev had been tucking into his breakfast with his five daily newspapers when the evacuation protocol was put into action. He looked down from the back of the helicopter at the small army enlisted by Carson to come and pick him up. He didn't know whether to be flattered, alarmed or appalled at the profligate waste of public money. He settled back in his seat and began to look forward to an unscheduled break on his yacht. His jet was already fuelled at Bristol airport and a flight plan was being filed as he took off from the house.

Carson looked completely lost. His expression had an air of a schoolboyish 'This isn't fair!' about it. Like a ten-year-old football fan whose team has just lost the Champions League final – his first – on the back of a disputed penalty which should never have been given. He marched back to the butler who was still maintaining his post at the front door.

'Where has he gone?' he demanded.

'I have no idea, sir. It was all very last minute,' he replied sanguinely, the intended humour not lost on Ottey.

'Do you want me to arrest you?' Carson sputtered with as much dignity as he could muster, which wasn't much.

'Well, if you need to arrest someone, as you've gone to all this trouble, then please go ahead,' he said, with a deferential smile.

'Where do you think he might have gone?' Carson asked Ottey, rather pathetically, as he strode back to the car.

'I don't know. The airport perhaps? Should we send units?' she asked.

'What units? They're all bloody here,' he replied.

'I'm sure we could rustle some up somewhere,' she said, sounding more like she was trying to find last-minute guests for a dinner party.

'By the time we do that he'll be long gone, if indeed that's where he's gone,' he said, trying to dismiss her thinking.

As they got to the car to leave, they found their path blocked by the arrival of a TV van.

'How the hell did they know this was happening?' asked Ottey, who in that same moment realised the culprit for leaking the details of the operation was probably sitting right next to her.

'Get out and tell them to move!' he shouted.

'Me?'

'Yes, you!' he yelled, and so the blame game started.

'Did you make the arrest, DCI Carson?' a reporter shouted through the window.

Carson didn't flinch, but just looked straight ahead.

'Or did the bird fly the coop?' the reporter asked mischievously. Ottey got out of the car.

'Move, or you will see an arrest being made, mate,' she growled.

Carson and Ottey arrived back at the MCU, muted and tired. She often found this after something like a raid. As the adrenalin faded from her system, it left her feeling worn out and empty. They walked into the open area. People avoided their gaze. She saw Cross wasn't in his office.

'Do you know where George is?' she asked Prianka.

'Yes,' she replied. 'He's in interview one with the suspect.'

'What suspect?' asked Ottey.

'Oleg Dimitriev,' she replied, matter-of-factly, before going back to her computer screen.

Carson stopped dead in his tracks.

'What?' was all he managed to stutter. For her part Ottey was doing her best to hide the grin which seemed to have taken possession of her entire face.

45

Oleg Dimitriev pretty much knew the aerial route from Ashleigh House to Bristol airport off by heart. It was a short flight. They had landed outside his personal hangar in which his Bombardier Global 7500 was housed. He was thinking how smoothly his extraction from the estate had gone. He would be on his yacht, for an unscheduled break, in under four hours, door to gangplank. The helicopter taxied towards the hangar and once the blades ceased rotating, the door was opened and Dimitriev stepped off. He walked towards the jet. The chief pilot, Mike, gave him a thumbs up from the cockpit window. Yvette the flight attendant waited for him at the bottom of the steps onto the plane. She smiled appreciatively. He was a good employer and had recently paid for her father's hip replacement.

As he neared the steps, a voice beckoned him from behind.

'Oleg Dimitriev?'

He turned to see George Cross approaching, flanked by four uniformed officers.

'I'm arresting you on suspicion of conspiracy to murder Ed Squire. You don't have to say anything...' Cross continued, reciting his rights.

If Dimitriev was surprised by this development, he did well to disguise it.

Cross had noticed, the previous day, when studying one of

the aerial photographs of Ashleigh House, a small grid of lights embedded in the grass to the side of the building. There was a tractor nearby which seemed to be driving in the direction of a newly constructed metal barn. Cross did a little research and discovered that, after a protracted battle with local residents, culminating in several generous donations to a variety of local charities, Dimitriev had been granted permission for a helipad at the estate. This was discreetly hidden in the lawn. He concluded that the helicopter was towed to and from the nearby barn, which functioned as a hangar.

On the basis of this Cross had taken a small gamble by enlisting the four officers and driving to the airport, where he discovered Dimitriev had a hangar for his jet. His logical thought process was proved to be correct when, on the way there, it was confirmed that a new flight plan had just been filed for the plane. Dimitriev was definitely on his way to him.

Carson couldn't believe his eyes as he looked at a monitor feed showing interview room 1. There, as large as life, was indeed Oleg Dimitriev, sitting opposite George Cross and a DC. Ottey walked in and replaced the other officer. Dimitriev was flanked by an expensively attired lawyer. Carson was unsure what his emotions were in this moment. On the one hand he was pleased their suspect was in custody. But there was that familiar, irrational feeling he always got in situations like this. That, somehow, George Cross had done this deliberately. Just to annoy him. But he knew this wasn't true. George just didn't behave like that. Carson went back to his office with a much more pressing matter on his mind. How to spin this to his benefit, not only for the media but, more importantly, for his superiors.

*

'Mr Dimitriev, where were you on the night of the twenty-fourth of April?' asked Cross.

'As I've already stated, my client will not be answering any questions,' the lawyer informed him. Cross ignored this.

'Did you threaten to kill Ed Squire?' he went on.

'No comment.'

'Why did you threaten Torquil Squire that you would kill his son?' Cross asked, as if his previous question had been answered.

'No comment.'

'Was it because he had sold you what he believed to be a genuine, legitimately sourced, historically important document, which turned out to be stolen? Causing you to lose over two million pounds as you did the only thing an honourable man could do in those circumstances, and returned it to its rightful owner?' Cross asked. Dimitriev allowed himself a little smile at Cross's obvious attempt to flatter him and soften him up.

'No comment,' he replied.

'You sent your men to, well I'm not sure how best to describe it, loiter around Squire's Rare Books and the square it's situated in. How did you describe it? "An overt presence." Why was that?' Cross continued.

'No comment.'

'Was it to remind Torquil Squire of your prevailing threat?'

'No comment.'

And so it went on for hours, Cross patiently going through his list of questions, ticking them off one by one, completely indifferent to the fact that none of them gleaned answers; just a constant litany of 'no comments'. He was confident in the knowledge that, now and then, people would lose their patience with this endless, at times deliberately monotonous, questioning, and get bored. It was then that he introduced a topic or question that he knew they might think of as harmless or inconsequential and they would start to talk.

'The SY *Dacha*, a beautiful boat,' he began. Dimitriev smiled at the thought of his favourite sanctuary. 'I admire the fact that you got hold of an old, classic vessel and restored it. It's from the nineteen forties, isn't it?'

'Nineteen thirties,' he replied. His lawyer shifted uneasily in the seat next to him.

'So much more pleasing than these modern five-storey floating apartment blocks you see on the water these days,' Cross continued. 'Did you have much input in the design?'

'I did, yes. We managed to source the original drawings and specs. It's a modern version faithful to the old. It has new engines, of course,' he answered.

'How many guests can you accommodate?' Cross asked.

'Twelve.'

'Quite modest, then,' suggested Cross.

'It meets my needs. I have no need for ostentatious displays of wealth,' he said.

'I think the possession of a classic yacht, in and of itself, qualifies as a somewhat ostentatious display, Mr Dimitriev,' Cross commented.

The Russian made no reply. Cross looked at him. Studying his face.

'Did you have Ed Squire killed?' he then asked, neutrally.

'I did not,' came the calm reply.

'Did one of your men, under your instruction, having threatened Ed Squire, as you've previously alluded to, kill him?' asked Cross.

'No.'

Cross looked at Dimitriev for a length of time most people would've felt uncomfortable doing. Then he proceeded to pick up his notepad and pens. After four long hours and with the suspect finally beginning to speak, Cross had decided this part of the interview was over. He saw that Dimitriev was surprised by this development, little knowing it was a deliberate ploy on the detective's part.

'I would like to speak,' Dimitriev suddenly announced. His lawyer immediately leaned forward and whispered in his client's ear.

'Perhaps you could give me five minutes while I speak with my lawyer,' Dimitriev then said with such authority that it was almost as if he had convened them all for this interview himself.

Cross and Ottey waited in the corridor outside the interview room.

'I feel like I owe you money,' Ottey said.

'I don't think so,' replied Cross. 'I don't as a rule lend people money. It inevitably leads to complications. What is more, if I had, I would undoubtedly have kept an accurate record of it.'

'A huge, stinking, steaming wodge of cash,' she continued.

He looked at her, puzzled.

'For the look on Carson's face when Prianka told him you had Dimitriev in custody. It was priceless,' she gushed.

'Ah,' he said, beginning to understand. Although it hadn't been his intention, his knowledge of Carson meant he understood her immediately.

'How did you know?'

'I didn't. I had no idea he would react like that. But in retrospect I can understand it.'

'Not that, you idiot. Dimitriev heading for the airport?' she asked.

'It was logical. No mention was made of his helipad at the briefing. I felt it was an oversight and that it was the only possible exit from the estate in the circumstances. He wouldn't go to London, as he'd assume the police were also there. He has a private hangar at Bristol airport. So, it seemed the most likely destination.'

'Well, it made my day. What am I talking about? My month.'

'I would enjoy it while you can. It won't be long before Carson finds a way of spinning the entire episode to his credit,' he said.

'You would go and spoil it,' she said, knowing this was true.

The lawyer opened the interview room door behind them and invited them back in. They sat opposite Dimitriev, expectantly.

'I am very grateful for the domicile your country has afforded me,' he began, as if reading from a written statement. 'I now consider it to be my home. As you know, my wealth comes from Russia and there has been a considerable change in the attitude of the Kremlin to those of us who created wealth and then took some of it out of the country. Many of my friends have had sudden, unexplained deaths in this country, which the authorities, the British police included, have been unable to investigate successfully. So, it's every man for himself. I make no complaint. I'm merely trying to explain my situation here and how I have to go to great lengths to protect myself. I try to live under the radar, DS Cross, and my wealth enables me to do that, more or less. I have no desire to attract any attention to myself, adverse or otherwise. So, please, ask yourself this question. Why would I risk all of this by having someone killed?'

'You lost two million pounds,' said Ottey. 'That's got to hurt.'

'Not as much as you might think, despite it being a sizeable sum. I have a beautiful home here in Somerset with extensive grounds where I can be alone. I have another in London. A wonderful house back in Russia which I go back to frequently. Why would I risk all of this?' he asked.

'You lost two million pounds,' Cross repeated.

'If I had to pay money to protect my lifestyle, to be left alone, I would pay ten times that, Sergeant.'

'You've already admitted to threatening Torquil Squire,' Cross pointed out.

'I have,' he agreed.

'What you didn't tell us, though, was that you'd threatened to kill Ed Squire,' Cross pointed out.

'In the circumstances, I'm sure you can understand why. Not exactly a good look in light of the unfortunate man's death,' replied Dimitriev.

'But a threat you made to his father, nonetheless, and his son is dead,' said Cross.

'Not by my hand, nor by any of my people,' he insisted.

They looked into each other's faces, trying to read each other.

'I have two more things for you, detectives. As I've told you, I have a wonderful life here in your great country. But it is a life I live under a cloud. There is the constant, ever present, possibility that the arm of the Kremlin will reach out for my throat successfully at some point and kill me. I accept that,' he continued.

'Have any attempts been made on your life?' asked Ottey.

He laughed quietly at this. 'Too many to mention. It is part of my everyday existence. Now you can call me paranoid, many people do, or besieged by conspiracy theories. But has it occurred to you that this, the murder of Ed Squire, might be the action of a foreign state to get at me?' he asked.

'Now that does sound paranoid,' commented Ottey.

'It may sound absurd to you, DI Ottey. But I can assure you, from where I sit, it is a very real and distinct possibility.'

'How would the Russian authorities even know about the Ed Squire situation?' asked Cross.

'Sadly, my operation is not immune to having people within it who still have one eye glancing back east to the homeland. We've discovered people in my employ who were on the payroll of the FSB. Some have had their families back home threatened; their safety only guaranteed by a steady supply of information about me. My whereabouts, for example. Travel plans. The changes in security at Ashleigh,' he told them.

'It all sounds a little far-fetched to me, I'm afraid,' said Ottey suspiciously.

'That's because you have no idea of how great the anger in the Kremlin these days is, for people like me. Even when, as in my case, I have said nothing negative about Putin or his regime. I consider myself still to be an ally. But the resentment and classification of us as persona non grata has increased year on year. If you think about it, it's the perfect scenario for the FSB to murder a bookseller in his place of work, and put me in the frame for a life in prison, where I can easily be reached and killed. Much simpler than coming after me, not only in full view, but also with all my security in place,' he argued.

'Some people might argue that you opened the door for the Kremlin, if what you say is true,' suggested Cross.

'And sadly, they would not be wrong. I didn't listen to my closest friends and advisers who told me to just let the Ed Squire situation go. But pride is a spiteful, vindictive thing, as I'm sure your experience in this very room will have told you over the years,' he agreed.

'An interesting theory, but one I fear, from your point of view, is almost impossible to prove,' commented Cross.

'Then let me put something else to you, DS Cross. A few weeks ago I came into some information, from Ed himself, about the identity and whereabouts of the original seller of the stolen Columbus letters.'

'We are aware of this,' said Cross.

'Then you will know they were in Italy, which was where I was the first time you tried to see me. In Naples.'

'And what happened?' asked Ottey.

'After lengthy negotiations,' he said, with a knowing smile, 'an arrangement was made, and the monies returned.'

'Don't tell me. You made him an offer he couldn't refuse,' suggested Ottey.

'To be honest it was little more venal and direct than that,' he replied coldly, without going into any further detail. The smile no longer there.

'Can you prove you were paid back in full?' asked Cross.

'Sadly, not.' He laughed. 'My finances are quite complex, as was the source of the returned two million. I can't just get my current account up on an app and show you. It simply doesn't work like that.'

'It was paid in cash,' Cross suggested. Dimitriev paused briefly.

'Indeed,' he said. 'But what you have to ask yourselves is – why would I kill him, when I now had my money? The issue had been resolved.'

'We only have your word for that,' observed Cross.

'True.'

'And he was killed before you went to Naples,' Ottey reminded him.

'Also true, but I had the relevant information before he was killed.'

'You couldn't have known it would be resolved to your satisfaction, though,' Ottey pointed out.

Dimitriev said nothing. Silence filled the room. Cross just stared at him. The Russian blinked first.

'What are you thinking, Sergeant? That it makes a modicum of logical sense, which is irritating for you?'

'Not at all. I was thinking, your English is excellent,' Cross replied.

'Thank you.'

'But I have something for you. The justice system in this country is good, compared to many others. But it isn't infallible. A jury-based justice system rarely is. It all comes down to twelve people's opinion of the evidence laid out in front of them in court. They are supposed to be open-minded and without prejudice. But if I were you I wouldn't be too confident in your chances of acquittal when the evidence we have is presented in front of an English jury. People in this country, like many people all over the world, have a very ambivalent attitude when it comes to extremely wealthy people. They don't like them. They think that people like that feel the rules don't apply to them as they do to ordinary people. People like those on the jury. They see a classic yacht, stately homes, jets, helicopters and art, the ability to buy a two-million-pound, fifteenth-century manuscript on a whim, and they don't like it. Why does he need all that when there's so much poverty around? Maybe one or two of the jurors have to rely on food banks to feed their family. You're a Russian oligarch, used to getting his own way, the prosecutor might say. You've admitted threatening to kill Ed unless Torquil Squire released cash from the Berkeley Square building to pay his son's debt. You've had men, your thugs, he'll probably describe them as, hounding the bookshop and the square. Ed is now dead. I really wouldn't be as confident, as your current attitude would suggest you are, that with the facts, such as they are, an English jury won't find you guilty and have you sent away – this, despite the most expensive lawyers money can buy – to a prison where without question the Russian state, if they were so inclined, could get a shank plunged through your heart without going to too much trouble.'

Dimitriev said nothing. Then, to crown it all, Cross said, 'And there's one other thing which might sway a jury away from finding in your favour. You bear an uncanny resemblance to Vladimir Putin.'

Ottey was so shocked she actually had to stop herself from laughing out loud. Had he really just said that?

46

To Cross there was no denying the logic of what Dimitriev had said. It made him question, with the little or no evidence they had, that he'd been involved in the killing of Ed Squire. The jury scenario he'd suggested to the Russian was simply a way of maintaining a little doubt in his mind. Carson was ruminating over the idea of state involvement. Had Dimitriev really been set up by the Kremlin? It seemed a stretch, but it was enough to cool his desire to charge. For Cross, Dimitriev's claim he was in possession of information relating to the Italian seller had already been corroborated by Nigel Simpson. As he'd argued, why wouldn't he have waited to see how that played out before carrying out his threat to kill Ed? Why would he have killed him if there was the remotest possibility of getting his money back in Naples?

'We need to see if we can find any evidence of other people surveilling the shop,' said Cross.

'What other people?' asked Ottey.

'The FSB, of course,' said Carson grandly. 'We could be on the verge of smashing a Russian spy cell. Should we inform the security services?'

Both Cross and Ottey were so taken aback by this delusional, fantastical idea that they said nothing and simply left the DCI's office.

Dimitriev's two henchmen appeared voluntarily and handed themselves in for questioning at the MCU. They hadn't been summoned. This was presumably at Jeremy Perrin's instruction, Cross thought. But they had said one thing that he wanted to check out. They claimed to have stopped harassing Ed Squire – something they freely admitted to doing, in some detail – from the moment he told their boss about the Italian. This was a full three weeks before Squire's murder. Cross cycled over to the bookshop to confirm this. Persephone wasn't there, she had left promptly for the day, so he spoke with Sam Taylor and told him about the Russian's arrest.

'You've arrested Oleg Dimitriev?' he asked.

Cross always found this odd. He'd just told Sam this. Why was he then immediately asking him if he had?

'Arrested, not charged,' he clarified.

'I thought it might be him,' Sam said, knowingly.

'Why was that?' asked Cross.

'Nothing else made sense. Except, having said that, Dimitriev having him killed doesn't really make any sense either, does it? With Ed dead, how was he ever going to get his money back?' he asked.

'Well, he could've got it from Torquil,' Cross pointed out.

'Really?'

'From the sale of the freehold,' Cross explained.

'I see.'

'Mr Taylor, I need you to think very carefully about my next question. The Russians who sought to intimidate Ed and Torquil by visiting the shop and sitting outside in their car. Did they continue to do this right up until the day of Ed's death?' asked Cross.

'I think so, yes. It's not really something I've ever given thought to.'

'Well, please give it some thought now,' Cross said.

Sam sat there for a few moments, casting his mind back.

'No, they didn't,' he finally said.

'I see. Can you remember when this stopped?' Cross pushed.

'I'm not sure. Maybe a few weeks before Ed's death?' Sam suggested.

'That's right,' said Torquil, who had appeared at the door. 'I remember, because I commented on it to Ed.'

'What was his response?' asked Cross.

'He said there'd been a development and that he hoped we'd seen the last of them,' Torquil went on.

'Did he say what the development was?' asked Cross.

'No. Because I didn't believe him and tragically it turned out I was right. They killed him,' he said. Cross just nodded slowly. 'Am I sensing doubt in you, Sergeant?'

'You are.'

'Why?'

'Because the evidence we now have suggests he had no need to kill your son,' Cross told him.

'Why?'

'The development Ed alluded to was that he'd furnished Dimitriev with the identity of the Italian seller of the Columbus letters. Dimitriev then followed this up and got his money back a couple of weeks ago.'

'But that's after he'd killed Ed,' Torquil protested.

'Why would he kill Ed after your son had given him that information?'

'Why does any psychopath kill people, Sergeant? Maybe he

just wanted to teach him a lesson for causing him trouble. Who knows?' the old man suggested.

'I think that bringing himself to the attention of the authorities here in England for the sake of teaching someone a lesson is the last thing Oleg Dimitriev would want. He has allies in this country and is settled. Why jeopardise all that for a piece of empty revenge?' Cross asked.

The front door buzzed downstairs.

'I'll just go and answer that,' said Sam, getting up and leaving the room.

It was Thursday and so when George had finished at Squire's he headed to Stephen's parish church for his regular organ practice. As he cycled through the late spring evening he became aware of the season's imminent change. Summer was lurking round the corner, ready to make a welcome appearance. There were a lot more people on the streets; sitting outside cafés and pubs, smoking and vaping. The evening smelled different too. It wasn't just the blossom on the trees, but cooking smells wafting onto the street from the open doors of restaurant kitchens and takeaways. It was like cycling through clouds of geographically varied cuisines. Charcoal-cooked meats from Greek and Turkish establishments as well as the odd domestic barbecue, lemongrass and ginger from Chinese and Asian restaurants, the tang of cardamom and garam masala from Indian kitchens, spilt beer from pub gardens. People had dispensed with overcoats some weeks before. Every year Cross appreciated the arrival of British Summer Time in March, with that precious extra hour of daylight which inevitably lifted people's spirits. Cross was one of those who felt the burden of short days had been lifted. It had a profound effect on his mood. To such an extent that he had often wondered if he suffered from SAD. Raymond definitely thought he did and with that thought in mind had constructed a home-made light box for him to have in his flat. But it was so ridiculously bright it made his sitting room feel like a fluorescently lit waiting room of a driving test centre.

It wasn't until he reached into his pocket for the key to the church that a thought descended on him with such force and weight that his knees almost buckled. It hadn't occurred to him when he'd arrived at Squire's Rare Books to ask why Sam had answered the door personally and not used the remote release next to Ed's desk. Sam had then left the desk again to answer the door before Cross left. He immediately relocked the church door and got back on his bike.

'DS Cross,' Sam said as he opened the door, surprised by the police officer's sudden reappearance at the bookshop.

'Why have you opened the door?' asked Cross.

'Um, because you rang the bell?' suggested a puzzled Sam.

Cross walked past him and up the stairs. He strode into the first-floor room and over to Ed Squire's desk. He pressed the door release that was mounted on the wall.

'What are you doing?' asked Sam.

'The door release. How long has it not been working?' Cross asked.

'I'm not sure. A few weeks, maybe. We thought it was the battery, but it looks like we have to replace the unit,' said Sam.

'Was it working the night of Ed's murder?' asked Cross.

'No,' he replied. 'Definitely not.'

47

'We need to release Dimitriev,' Cross told his boss the next morning, just as Carson was preparing his media statement having decided, during the night, to charge the Russian.

'What? Why?' he asked.

'Because the door release by Ed Squire's desk isn't functional,' Cross informed him as Ottey joined them.

'You've lost me now, George,' said Carson.

'Persephone Hartwell said she heard Ed release the door to let someone in. But that can't have happened,' he told him.

'So maybe Ed went downstairs and let whoever it was in,' suggested Ottey.

'Exactly,' said Carson with a protective look at the typewritten statement looking up at him expectantly from his desk.

'So why wasn't he killed at the door?' asked Cross.

'Because the killer hadn't come round with the intention of killing him. We all agreed it was an impulsive act. We've said he knew the killer,' Carson went on.

'Are you suggesting that if it was Dimitriev, or rather one of his men, he let them in? Someone who had been harassing and threatening him for weeks?' asked Cross. 'It doesn't seem very likely.'

Carson had no answer for this.

'It also doesn't accord with Persephone's statement. She said, specifically, that she heard the door release being activated, then someone walking up the stairs with shouting following shortly afterwards. She'd thought it was Torquil and so got out the third cup for coffee. Why didn't she say she heard Ed go down the stairs and let the man in? She'd've heard them talking at the front door and two sets of footsteps coming up the stairs,' Cross pointed out.

'You're just talking details, George,' Carson replied.

Cross looked at him, confused by this statement.

'People will always attempt to be fastidiously detailed when asked about events leading up to a murder,' Cross replied. 'They are minutely specific because we tell them that any detail, however small or trivial to them, might be of significance to us. We need to let Oleg Dimitriev go.'

'You'll have to give me more than that,' said Carson.

'As I've already said. Why would Ed let Dimitriev or any of his men into the building?' asked Cross.

'It's a good point, boss,' said Ottey.

'Maybe he didn't have a choice? Maybe he was forced to?' replied Carson with a conviction that seemed to increase as he came to the end of the sentence.

'Then there would've been raised voices and possibly a struggle. Both of which Persephone would've heard.'

Carson sighed and looked down at his prepared statement, as if he was letting it down in some way. Cross turned and left the room.

'Where are you going, George?' Carson asked after him.

'I'm going to arrest Persephone Hartwell,' came the receding reply.

Before they left to make the arrest, Cross called into his office the WPC who had been at the Berkeley Square Hotel with the family on the night of the murder.

'You drove Persephone Hartwell home the night of Ed Squire's murder, after she decided not to go back with her aunt. Is that right?' Cross asked.

'Yes,' she answered cagily – she knew George Cross. 'Why? Is everything all right?'

'We'll be needing to take a more detailed statement from you later, but I have a question for you. Did you take her straight from the hotel lounge to your car?' Cross went on.

'No,' she replied.

'What happened?' asked Cross.

'She needed to get her handbag from the bookshop. It had the keys to her flat in it. She wouldn't've been able to get in otherwise,' she said.

'Did you accompany her?' Cross asked.

'Well, obviously. It was a crime scene. She couldn't go in on her own,' she pointed out.

'Quite so. Where was her handbag?' Cross went on.

'It was in a cupboard on the ground floor where she worked,' the WPC replied.

'How big was this handbag?'

'Normal size,' she replied.

Cross nodded.

'But she also had a small holdall. A leather one, which she took home with her.'

Persephone's behaviour when they made the arrest at the bookshop struck Ottey immediately as odd. This wasn't just because she was wearing a black net tutu over her leggings, with a ballerina's thick Alice band holding back her hair. She was also wearing stark white, Kabuki-like make-up. She looked quite mad. It turned out this was an attempt to promote a newly published romantic novel, set in the world of dance, she was stocking. She offered up her wrists to be cuffed in an overtly dramatic gesture, without them having actually asked her to do so. She sighed with an inevitable, knowing, resignation at her arrest, which could have come straight from one of the pages of the thousands of books that surrounded her. She was like a leading actress from the silent movies with over-the-top facial expressions of emotion.

'What on earth are you doing?' asked Torquil, aghast at the sight of his great-niece in police-issue steel bracelets.

'They're arresting me, Pa,' she said in a distant, lost voice.

'What for?'

'Murder,' she replied, dramatically.

'Percy, why are you talking in that weird way?' asked Sam, who was also obviously alarmed.

'Please get hold of my lawyer and tell them what's happened,' she continued, as Cross led her out of the shop.

'Why is she talking like that?' asked Sam. 'She doesn't have a lawyer. I mean, why would she?'

'DI Ottey, this has to be a terrible mistake. I thought you were charging Oleg Dimitriev for this?' pleaded Torquil Squire.

'He's been released,' she told him as she left.

'What?' Torquil asked.

'I'll get hold of Vicky,' said Sam.

After they placed Persephone in the car, Ottey said to Cross over the roof, 'That was strange. Do you think she's putting on an act in prep for a plea of insanity?'

'That would certainly make some sense of it,' he replied.

48

After Persephone was processed, they obtained her house keys and went to exercise the search warrant they had for her flat. When Swift arrived and walked into the pink paradise that was her sitting room and surveyed the extensive menagerie of stuffed toys, he turned to Cross and Ottey and said, 'Have you arrested a twelve-year-old?'

'I know. Right?' commented Ottey.

They proceeded to search the flat and it wasn't long before they found a leather holdall in a cupboard. Then Swift's voice called them from inside the bedroom. As they walked in they saw he was standing next to a bedside cabinet holding up a six-inch, or thereabouts, brass letter opener. It was covered in dried blood.

'You'd think she'd've got rid of it,' he said.

'It's a souvenir,' replied Ottey.

'Persephone, are you aware of why you've been arrested?' asked Cross in the MCU interview room. She was sitting next to her solicitor.

'Yes,' she replied quietly.

'Did you kill Ed Squire on the twenty-fourth of April this year?'

'No comment.'

'You told us that you heard Ed let someone into the building that night. Is that correct?' Cross continued.

'No comment.'

'No one came in that night, did they?' suggested Ottey.

'No comment.'

'You killed Ed Squire, in a frenzied attack, then hid the weapon as well as maybe some clothing in a holdall in the cupboard next to your desk. Which you retrieved before you went home. Isn't that true?' asked Ottey.

'No comment.'

'Persephone, we found the letter opener used to kill Ed Squire in the bedside table in your bedroom. Why did you have it?' asked Cross.

'No comment.'

'Why keep it?' asked Ottey. 'Were you so confident you wouldn't be found out? That it was so unlikely the police would look at the victim's own niece? Someone most people would adjudge owed him so much?'

Cross saw that Persephone reacted ever so slightly to this. A small, involuntary, twitch.

'Who'd taken you in as a troubled adolescent. Dealt with an unwanted teenage pregnancy. Then years later, when you lost your job, gave you employment,' Ottey continued.

'No comment.'

'Did you kill him, Persephone?' asked Cross.

'No comment.'

'We not only found the murder weapon in your flat, but there are also traces of blood in the holdall. It's being tested as we speak. I'm fairly certain it will come back as Ed Squire's. The evidence really is stacking up against you. Why don't you just tell us exactly what happened?' asked Cross.

'No comment.'

'Did something happen that made you do it? I think there must be a reason. If you did it. Did you have a good reason to kill your uncle, Persephone?' asked Cross. She looked up at him. Was she deciding whether to answer? Cross wondered. 'You'd been working for him for almost four years. Why now? Why at all?'

'No comment.'

'You told us you were grateful for the opportunity. You called it a lifeline. So, what happened?' Cross persisted.

'No comment.'

'Did you think that without Ed in the picture and his children showing no interest in continuing the business, that he would simply hand it over to you?' asked Ottey.

'What would be so strange about that?' asked Persephone, speaking for the first time.

'Miss Hartwell,' her lawyer cautioned her.

'Did he ever tell you it was his intention to let you run the business?' Cross asked.

'He didn't have to. It was obviously the plan,' she said.

'Miss Hartwell,' the lawyer said again. 'I need a moment with my client.'

Cross went back into his emails and looked at the information Mackenzie had sent him after their impromptu dinner together. Despite the development with Persephone in the interview room, the timing of her mother's recent scene at the house struck him as odd. He wasn't sure he believed Sarah when she said it was an argument with her ex, Ian. It had to be material in some way. He wasn't even sure if Hartwell was in the country on the day in question. He then checked and found that he was in fact in Spain at the time of the alleged argument. He was annoyed with himself that it hadn't occurred to him to check this earlier. But if Persephone was the culprit, if she had killed Ed through some misguided notion she would get control of the business, why now? The timing didn't make any sense to him. Had Ed let her down? Made her some promise he'd later reneged on? Or was she just deluded? She was certainly an idiosyncratic young woman, as Ottey had observed right from the start of the investigation. This reminded him of something else Ottey had said then. He got up and went over to her desk.

'You remarked on something Victoria Squire told you at your first encounter with her at the Berkeley Square Hotel. You said it struck you as odd,' he told her.

'I did?'

'You said she described Persephone as a niece "by marriage". Which you found strange.'

'Yes, that's right,' she replied as she remembered. 'Oh my god.'

He turned to a WPC sitting at a desk nearby.

'Could you get Persephone Hartwell back up from her cell for another interview?'

'What was your relationship with Ed like? Recently. Had anything changed?' Cross asked.

'No comment.'

'Can we go back to the events of 2014?' he asked. This was the first time it'd been brought up. She blanched a little and looked over at her solicitor. Was this an appeal for some sort of help, or was it an indication that she wasn't happy about such personal information being shared in front of a stranger? 'You fell pregnant. Is that correct?'

'Yes,' she replied quietly.

'And you had a termination which was organised for you by your aunt and uncle. Is that also correct?' Cross asked.

'Yes.'

'How did you feel about that?' asked Cross.

'I don't know. Relieved? Guilty, maybe? I thought it was the right thing to do,' she said.

'Why was that?'

'I was too young to have a child. I was only just sixteen. The pregnancy was a mistake,' she said.

'So you felt they made the right decision at the time?' Cross asked.

'Yes.'

'Do you still feel that way about it?' he went on.

She paused for a moment before answering. 'Yes.'

'How did the father of the child feel about the decision to terminate?' Cross asked.

'The father?' she asked, looking a little confused.

'Yes. Did you discuss it with him at all?' Cross went on.

This seemed to throw her. She shook her head in confusion as if to shake the question out of it. She muttered something inaudible.

'Did you know who the father was?' asked Cross.

'Yes!' she replied indignantly. 'What are you trying to say?'

'Did the father even know about the pregnancy? Maybe you didn't even tell him you were expecting,' Cross suggested.

'Um, yes,' she replied.

'You'd told him,' Cross clarified.

'Yes.'

'Who was it?' he asked.

'What?'

'The father. Who was it? Are you still in touch with him?' asked Cross.

'No.'

'You don't speak with him anymore?' Cross continued.

'No.'

'Is that because he's dead?' asked Cross.

'What?'

'Is that because the father of your unborn child is himself dead? Because the father was your uncle, Ed Squire. Your uncle by marriage?' he suggested.

She looked completely stunned by this, as indeed did her solicitor.

'I think we should have a break,' the lawyer suggested.

49

It was hard to tell who was more shocked and why, as Victoria Squire and her father-in-law sat opposite Cross and Ottey in the VA suite. For her, she was still coming to terms with her niece's arrest. For him, there was the added revelation of her teenage pregnancy which he had been unaware of, till now. And there was more to come for the poor, beleaguered man.

'Yes,' Victoria said quietly. 'Ed was the father.'

'What?' proclaimed Torquil, not believing what he'd just heard.

'When did you find out? Had you known all along?' asked Cross.

'No! Of course not. Do you really think… I found out when Sarah came to the house a few weeks ago.'

'Presumably she had only herself become aware recently?' asked Cross.

'Yes. Percy told her while they were on holiday this year,' she replied.

'Why tell her now?' asked Ottey.

'You'd have to ask her that. I think it was one of those clearing-the-air moments in a fractious, not entirely successful mother–daughter relationship,' she said with a hint of bitterness.

'I was curious as to why she would attack him about the termination so many years later,' Cross began. 'But of course, if she was only recently aware of the fact that her brother-in-law, your husband, had groomed and seduced her daughter, when she was a teenager, then it would make more sense.'

'He didn't groom her,' she bristled. 'You make him sound like a...' She couldn't bring herself to say the word.

'A paedophile,' Cross said for her.

'She was sixteen,' Victoria retorted.

'Just,' replied Cross. 'The grooming must have started when she was fifteen. Why don't we just settle for sexual predator?'

She made no reply.

'Why were you still with him?' asked Ottey.

'I was in the throes of working out what to do when he was killed. But you should know that Percy is a complex young woman who played her part in all of that,' Victoria began.

'Oh my god,' said Ottey, who couldn't help herself. 'Are you really going to go down the path of victim blaming?'

'What I'm trying to say is she came across a lot older than she actually was.'

'She was your niece. Ed knew exactly how old she was. That's an excuse sex offenders use when they don't actually know the victim. But this victim was known to you both. She was family,' said Ottey. Victoria made no reply. Cross decided to let Ottey continue, as her maternal instincts and outrage came to the fore. 'A young woman, seeking refuge and comfort in the sanctuary of your home, only to discover her protector, her guardian, would abuse her.'

'Ed said it wasn't like that. She was a culpable, willing participant. He didn't seduce her. She seduced him,' Victoria retorted.

'Is that what your husband told you? And you went along with it? She was a vulnerable young woman. A child, coming from a broken home, looking for some stability in yours,' Ottey pointed out. Victoria said nothing. There was an uncomfortable silence in the room. Almost as if everyone was digesting what had just been said. Then Cross spoke up.

'What happened the first time Persephone went up to Oxford?' asked Cross neutrally.

'She couldn't cope. She wasn't ready. Too young,' she began.

'This is the same young woman you just said came across much older than she looked?' asked Cross.

'In terms of maturity, she was young and didn't deal with the pressure well,' she replied.

'Oh, will you stop beating about the bush and mincing your words,' Torquil suddenly said angrily. 'She tried to kill herself. That's what happened. And after what you've just said, it's no surprise, and yet you sit there defending him? How can you? I can't believe you're speaking like this. What a bloody awful situation. I can't believe he did this. My son, it's inconceivable.'

'I'm not defending him. I'd decided to leave him before all this happened. What he did was indefensible,' said Victoria.

'She attempted suicide?' Cross clarified.

'Yes.'

'How did the family deal with that?' asked Cross.

'She went to a residential psychiatric unit. Which we paid for. Then she went back to Sarah. They travelled for a few months. She went back up to Oxford and it was fine,' she said. Cross thought she was quite muted now, as if she just wanted to get through this so that she could leave.

'What was the reason for the attempt?' asked Cross.

'I'm not really sure,' she replied.

'Really?' asked Torquil, his disbelief growing sentence by sentence. 'You're not sure? Ed impregnated her. God knows how he seduced the poor girl. What did he promise or lead her to believe would happen? Or did he force her? It doesn't bear thinking about. Then you both make her have a termination.'

'I didn't know it was his!' Victoria protested.

'Who was that for? Him or her?' Torquil continued.

'I didn't know!' Victoria almost shouted. 'I'm as appalled as you about all of this. I'm still trying to get my head around it.'

'But you didn't even tell the girl's mother? How can you excuse that? I can't listen to any more of this. Sergeant, will you call me if you need anything more from me?'

'I will,' said Cross. Ottey opened the door for the old man.

'I'll come back in if you need. Is Percy happy with her lawyer? Can you let me know if she isn't?' he asked as he left.

'We will come to you, Mr Squire, if we need to. No need for you to come back here,' said Ottey as she showed him out. The broken, aged, gentle man left without so much as a backward glance at his daughter-in-law. Ottey returned a few minutes later. Cross had been happy to sit in silence. Victoria Squire maybe less so.

'Do you really think Percy did this?' she asked them.

'It's certainly a possibility,' replied Cross.

'But why?' she asked.

'If we knew that I'd be able to answer your first question more authoritatively,' Cross replied.

He paused for a moment, wanting to phrase the next question as unprovocatively as possible.

'Mrs Squire, I need you to be completely honest. Did the sexual relationship between your husband and your niece continue after the termination?' asked Cross. He used the word 'niece' intentionally.

'Of course not,' she replied.

319

'What about recently? Is it possible the sexual relationship between your husband and your niece recommenced after she started working at the bookshop?' Cross asked. This floored the recently widowed woman for a moment. Maybe she'd thought things had reached rock bottom with the murder of her husband and couldn't possibly get any worse. But now he'd presented her with a scenario that did just that.

'I don't think so, no,' she replied with as much conviction as was available to her.

'But you don't actually know?' Cross asked.

'Of course I don't know. How could I have known? Why would that even have crossed my mind when I didn't know what had happened before? Thinking about it, though, I'm not sure how it could've, with everything that had been going on with Ed recently. Ed was in such a desperate place,' she said, thinking out loud.

'People do strange things when in desperate places,' said Cross.

'How were things at home?' asked Ottey.

'Strained. Because of all the pressure at work,' she said, then looked up at them desperately, as the very real possibility of a more recent affair hit home.

50

'He was the father of her unborn child?' exclaimed Carson, the relatively new father, in thinly disguised disgust. 'So what happened, do you think? She demanded he leave his wife? He refused and she killed him? Classic woman scorned stuff?' he went on without waiting for an answer, with a growing recognition that he might well have succeeded in cracking the case in that very moment.

'It's possible. A little Mills and Boon, perhaps,' offered Ottey.

'A little simplistic, perhaps, but possible,' added Cross, doubtfully.

'We should charge her. We have the murder weapon, found in her possession, blood traces in the holdall. I'll get onto the CPS,' said Carson enthusiastically. Then he saw an all too familiar look on Cross's face. 'What is it, George?' he sighed.

'I was just reflecting on the fact that you had the identical urgency for charging Oleg Dimitriev for the same crime, less than twenty-four hours ago,' Cross replied.

'I beg your pardon?' came the indignant reply.

'Am I wrong in that conclusion? As you know, I sometimes have difficulty in reading people's attitudes,' Cross informed him.

'Why shouldn't we charge?' asked Carson.

'I just think it would be wise to wait till we have the results of all the tests,' Cross told him.

'Fine. We'll wait till they're back, then we'll charge. I think it's an unnecessary delay but I'll leave it to your better judgement,' he replied and turned towards the door.

'But there remains the question of the three cups,' said Cross, stopping the DCI in his tracks.

'The suspect said she got one out because she thought Torquil had returned,' Carson said.

Cross and Ottey said nothing, giving him time to realise his mistake.

'Except, of course, if she did kill him, there was no one to let in.'

'Exactly. So why were there three cups out in the kitchen upstairs?' asked Cross.

'No comment,' was Persephone's response to that same question when put to her in the interview room.

'Was there someone else there?' Cross went on.

'No comment.'

'You were making coffee for Ed. Someone arrived, you got out a third cup. That's what you've told us.'

She said nothing.

'You said you thought it was Torquil. But that's not true, is it?' Cross went on.

'No comment.'

'We know Ed didn't let anyone in, because the door release isn't functional. No, someone had to go down the stairs to the ground floor and open the door. What's your job at the bookshop, Persephone?' Cross asked patiently.

'I run the new books department,' she replied.

'And what duties does that entail?' he asked.

'I answer the phones,' she replied.

'You answer the phones. All the calls come through you and your receptionist's phone on your desk,' he went on.

'I'm not a receptionist,' she snapped.

'No, you're much more than that. I know. But you're also responsible for answering the front door, are you not? On account of your proximity to it. Being located, as you are, on the ground floor, with everyone else on the floors above you. But that's part of your job. To answer the door. Your door release isn't currently working either, is it? Part of the same problem. So you open the door in person. What I'm trying to get at here is that Ed didn't open the door, as a general rule. Because he knew someone else would. Namely you. And that's what you did on the night of his death, did you not? You went up to make coffee when you heard the front door buzz, and you went down to open it. Isn't that correct?' Cross asked.

'No comment.'

'Who did you let in, Persephone?'

'Who said I let anyone in? Just a minute ago you were saying I didn't and had killed Ed. Make up your mind,' she retorted.

Cross made out that he was admitting defeat as he organised his files and seemed to be about to leave. Then he looked back up at her.

'Here's another thing I don't understand. Another thing maybe you can help me with. Why were you there so late that night?' he asked.

'No comment.'

'What are your normal working hours?'

'No comment.'

'Well, I can answer that for you. I already know from Sam that you work a strict ten to six day. Stricter, it has to be said, in observance of your finishing time rather than your starting time, according to Sam,' Cross said. She couldn't help but sigh at the source of this information. 'So why did you stay on so late that night?'

'No comment.'

'Were you helping Ed with something, perhaps? Helping him with some work? Not just simply providing him with some refreshment? Was that it?' Cross asked.

'No comment.'

'But, then again, he was only there at that time because he was waiting for his father's return from London,' Cross mused. 'So why was it?'

'No comment.'

'Was it because you knew someone was coming to meet Ed and you wanted to be there?'

'No comment.'

'Someone you'd arranged to come over. Someone Ed himself wasn't expecting. Someone you'd called earlier in the day to tell them to come over later?' asked Cross.

'No comment.'

51

'Who are you thinking?' asked Carson.

'I'm not thinking anyone,' replied Cross.

'We're looking at her phone records for the afternoon of the murder and the day before,' said Ottey.

'It has to be the mother, given their history and the recent, second assault,' Carson insisted.

'It doesn't have to be anyone,' said Ottey. 'The girl could be lying. Maybe she didn't let anyone in because she killed him herself.'

'But the three cups,' Carson pointed out, unable to resist the temptation to look in Cross's direction for some sort of approval.

'If it was premeditated, that could be part of a ruse to distract us,' Ottey pointed out.

'Are you bringing the mother in?' asked Carson.

'Not currently, no,' replied Cross, whose mind was somewhere else completely, demonstrated by his leaving his office to seek the shelter of the back staircase to make a phone call in peace.

Swift was working a few cases, which took up his time as he waited for the results from the holdall and the letter opener. His eyes always lit up when he saw Cross's name as the caller on his phone.

'DS Cross!' he answered with his usual alacrity. Almost. His enthusiasm was tempered by the fact that he was still in the throes of guilt-ridden angst about the door release. He felt he'd let Cross down with his failure to try it on his initial investigation at the crime scene. Cross had surprised him by disagreeing and informing him that his job was to process the scene, not question it. That was the job of the detectives, not the forensic investigators. Cross himself was the one at fault. He'd concluded this, with some annoyance, the very moment he discovered it was non-functional.

'Torquil Squire is still living at his daughter-in-law's house. For how much longer, I'm not at all sure. But it occurs to me, in the light of the current circumstances, with Persephone's arrest, that it's worth conducting a forensic examination of the bathroom I found her in. If she killed the victim it could be that she washed the blood off in the sink,' Cross suggested.

'What about clothing?' asked Swift. Cross thought for a moment.

'That's possible. If she got blood on her clothes, she might have put them in the holdall along with the letter opener. There could be traces, but I would imagine the clothes have either been destroyed or washed by now,' he said.

'Except that she did keep the weapon. Might she not have kept clothing as well?' Swift suggested.

'No suspicious clothing was found in the search of her flat, though,' Cross pointed out.

'True.'

'It's a long shot, but if she washed her hands, or anything covered in blood for that matter, in the sink I think it's worth a look,' said Cross.

'On it.'

★

It was at the base of one of the sink taps, around a disintegrating rubber washer, that Swift found a minuscule trace of blood. The sink had been rinsed down, but the point at which the tap joined the porcelain had been missed. He duly swabbed it. There was nothing else to be found in there. When he got back to the office, he found the results from the letter opener and holdall awaited him. He studied them for a moment then went straight over to the MCU.

Swift's appearance in the MCU always interested Cross as he knew it meant that he had something he considered important enough to deliver in person. That and the possibility of getting any approbation of his skills first-hand.

'So, the blood from the holdall is a match for the victim,' Swift began.

This elicited an over-sibilant 'Yes!' from a fist-clenching Carson, who had appeared in the door to Cross's office.

'It's most likely a transfer from the weapon,' he went on.

'Where else could it be from?' asked Ottey.

'Well, if she was wearing any clothes she'd then changed out of,' he suggested.

'Why would she have a change of clothes at work?' Ottey continued.

'A perfectly valid question,' said Cross.

'If she intended killing him, she might well have taken spare clothing with her,' Swift pointed out.

'A perfectly valid suggestion,' replied Cross.

'DS Cross asked me to go back to the crime scene and examine the bathroom where he found Persephone. It was a long shot, but it hasn't been cleaned since the murder. I found a trace of blood at the base of one of the taps,' Swift went on.

'Perfect, I'll call the CPS,' said Carson, turning to leave.

'Before you do that. There is something else. There were two traces of DNA on the murder weapon. The victim's and a third party. We've done a comparison between Persephone's DNA and the third-party DNA and it's a match,' said Swift.

'Excellent,' said Carson.

'But not an exact match. It's a familial match. It's not her DNA but someone she's related to,' he told them.

'So Persephone isn't the killer?' asked Ottey.

'He didn't say that,' said Cross. 'Simply that the DNA is a familial match.'

'The mother,' announced Carson. 'Excellent work, Dr Swift. Josie, bring her in.'

'Before you do that—' Swift cautioned.

'We have her DNA on file from the 2014 arrest,' interjected Cross.

'We do. I've cross-referenced it. It's not her blood. What's more – she's not even a familial match to the blood on the knife,' he told them. There was a moment's silence.

'Ian Hartwell,' said Cross, quietly.

'Who?' asked Carson.

'Persephone's father. But he was in Spain the night of the murder,' said Ottey.

'We don't know that,' Cross pointed out. 'All we know is that he arrived at the Squires' house in Henleaze the next morning, claiming to have just flown in from Spain.'

52

Sarah Hartwell came into the MCU willingly, just before lunch. She was shocked to learn that her daughter had been arrested. This struck Cross as interesting. Torquil had told Victoria of the arrest the moment it happened and yet she hadn't then informed Sarah? The news knocked the woman back so much that they left her alone for a while. When Cross and Ottey finally went into the interview room, she looked up and said, 'I think I need a lawyer.'

'Why is that?' asked Cross.

'Because I want to make a confession,' she told them calmly.

'To what?' asked Cross.

'Are you trying to be funny? I killed Ed Squire,' she said.

'It must be hard for you to see your daughter arrested on suspicion of murder. A daughter you feel, by your own admission, you've let down badly over her lifetime. Quite the gesture, to confess to something of such magnitude as murder just to make things better. Confess to something you didn't actually do,' observed Cross.

'She didn't do it. Don't listen to her. I did it. I swear,' the desperate woman protested.

'She didn't do it, no,' said Ottey. 'But then again, neither did you.'

'She didn't?'

'No.'

'But it said on the news that you'd released that man. That Russian,' she said.

'Because he, like you, didn't kill Ed either,' said Cross.

She sat there for a moment, trying to process this information.

'We found the murder weapon in your daughter's flat,' Ottey said.

'No,' she muttered in disbelief.

'It was covered in the victim's blood,' Ottey told her.

'You went on holiday recently. With your daughter,' Cross went on.

'Yes. Mykonos.'

'And she told you something there. Something she hadn't told you before which you found truly shocking,' said Cross.

'Yes,' she replied quietly.

'That Ed was responsible for her pregnancy in her teens. That he was the father,' Cross said.

'Yes.'

'Then you went to his house to confront him. Confront them, and the police were called to the property again. You were furious. How could he have done that? To your daughter who was suffering in the wake of your divorce. Vulnerable. How could Victoria have let it happen? Why didn't she protect her? Why had she stayed with Ed for all this time?' suggested Cross. 'What was their response?'

'Victoria seemed closed off. Almost completely. Like it wasn't happening. She obviously didn't know. Which was a relief, oddly,' she said.

'And Ed Squire?' asked Cross.

'He tried to deny it at first and it was like she knew in that moment, from the look on his face, that it was true. She challenged him. He became dismissive. Abusive. To both of us. It had all happened so long ago, he said. Everyone had moved on. Persephone herself was over it. He claimed me bringing it up now was only going to set her back. She was settled. Had a job. Was happy. Why did I want to do this? Was I trying to break up his marriage because my own had failed so badly? Or was I just trying to be the mother after all these years? He was so insulting. And to use her mental well-being against me? It was disgusting, frankly,' she said, getting more animated as she recalled what had been said that day.

'What happened then?' asked Cross. But she just continued with her train of thought and ignored him.

'You've met her. I love her to bits, but it's like Percy's emotional maturity just stopped at sixteen. As if she stopped growing up when her father left us. She still behaves like a teenager. An immature teenager, at that. She lives in her own world, as if that in some way protects her from the real world. She's never had a boyfriend. Not even at Oxford. And Oxford. The suicide attempt. That looked so different, knowing Ed was responsible for the pregnancy. That made me so much angrier. And confused. How could they have kept it from me, when they had to know it had to have had something to do with that? Surely it did. I said to him, if she's over it why has she chosen to tell me about it now? But he was so patronising. Almost implying I was making something out of nothing,' she said, shaking her head as if she couldn't believe the situation she was describing and the injustice of it all.

'That must've been so frustrating,' said Ottey.

'Well as you know, I flew at him. I wanted to kill the bastard. But he didn't press charges,' she said. 'I mean, how could he? All of this would've come out.'

'How did you leave it with them?' asked Ottey.

'Well, what could I do? I felt so helpless,' she explained.

'Mrs Hartwell, have you spoken to your ex-husband recently?' asked Cross.

Her face froze as the implication of this question hit her. She didn't answer.

'Did you call him after you confronted Ed Squire at his house?' asked Cross.

She still didn't answer. Then it was as if she realised there was no point in lying.

'There was no one else. I suppose I just wanted to vent. No, that's a lie,' she said and stopped for a moment. 'I called him to blame him. That's the truth. Tell him it was all his fault. We'd both failed as parents, but he'd really excelled as the shit, absent father.'

'What was his reaction?' asked Cross.

'Well, defensive at first. Saying it wasn't his fault. But then as the reality of what I was saying hit him, he just lost it completely. To be honest, he and Ed had never really got on. I often felt maybe Ian was jealous of him. I don't know why. But there was always something of an edge to their relationship. He saw it as another way in which he'd let Percy down. That he let this happen. That if he'd still been around maybe she wouldn't've gone to live with them and none of this would ever have happened.' She stopped for a moment, then looked back up at them both. 'Oh my god. Is this all my fault?' she said.

'Was that the last time you spoke to him, before Ed was killed?' Cross asked.

'Yes. There was nothing left to talk about after that. Can I see her? Does she know it was him? What has she said?' she asked.

'Nothing. She's gone no comment,' said Ottey.

'She saw him. She said she saw him, didn't she? She said she saw the killer but didn't say it was him. Has she said it was him?' she asked. They said nothing. 'Can I talk to her? I might be able to persuade her to talk. I might be able to get through to her.'

He turned to Ottey. 'You're the senior officer, ma'am,' he reminded her. She bristled at this but thought for a moment. It was possible she could get the young woman to open up.

Sarah Hartwell was with her daughter for just under an hour. Cross and Ottey watched on the monitor. But it was mostly the woman comforting her daughter. They'd asked her not to give away any of the forensic information they'd told her. Percy didn't tell her mother what happened as Sarah told her to save it for an interview. She also told her that the police knew she hadn't killed Ed. Finally the young woman conceded tearfully and asked for her lawyer.

53

'I think she wanted to protect her dad, either out of misguided loyalty or the age-old problem,' Sarah told them afterwards.

'Which is what, exactly?' asked Ottey.

'An attempt to get his attention,' she sighed. 'Trying to gain his approval, by saying look at what I'm willing to do for you. It's always been the same. Since he had the boys, his new family, she's felt like second-class offspring. He treats her like she's a grown-up and so doesn't need a father anymore. But weirdly in the last few years she's needed him more than ever. But right now, it's all about the boys. Even when she goes over to Spain, I think she feels tolerated rather than loved.'

'So she'll speak with us now?' asked Cross.

'I think so. I told her you think it's her father and not her. That now she has to find a way of lessening the trouble she's managed to get herself into. That sounds judgemental. It wasn't meant to. This is all our bloody fault. Both me and Ian,' she said.

'Thank you for talking to her,' said Ottey.

'Are you kidding? She's my little girl. What will happen with her now?' she asked.

'It depends on what she's charged with. It might help if her father surrendered himself. Without him the judge might look on her less leniently. It's hard to say,' said Ottey.

'I'm not sure there's much chance of him doing that,' she replied.

Persephone seemed a little more reflective when she returned to the interview room. There was a little less melodrama about her, Ottey thought.

'I didn't know he was going to kill Ed, honest. He just said he wanted to see him while he was over. I didn't even know Mum had told him about the pregnancy. That was stupid. Why did she do that?' she asked as if she hoped they might have an answer.

'Because she's your mother and she was angry. Because he's your father,' suggested Ottey.

'My father!' Persephone spat. 'So where was he when I was sixteen? What did he do when this all happened? Nothing. Because he was too busy with his own life to worry about mine. His daughter! He was nowhere to be seen. And now this is what he does? This is his solution? To kill the man who has been more a father to me than he ever was. Despite what happened. To kill the man who'd given me a job and a future after all the problems I've had. What was the point? To make him feel better, that's what. But what about me? What about me?'

The detectives made no comment as she wept quietly. Cross decided the best thing was to go to his prepared script for the interview.

'Let me tell you what we know,' he began. 'We know that your father flew in from Spain on the morning of April the twenty-fourth. Not the following day, as he claimed. We know this from Border Force. We know from your phone records that you spoke with him that afternoon, after he'd landed. We know the mast the call connected with was in Bristol. Which confirms he was here. What was that call about?'

'He told me he was in England,' she said.

'Did he tell you why?' asked Cross.

'He wanted to see Ed,' she said quietly.

'Why did he want to speak with Ed?' asked Cross.

'Like I've said, I don't know. Well, I didn't. I do now, obviously. He just asked me what time the shop closed and when Ed left. I told him that Torquil had gone up to London and Ed was going to wait till he got back,' she replied.

'So what happened that evening?' Cross asked.

'He called me around six,' she said. Cross checked the call log and saw this was right. 'He told me he was on his way. When he arrived, I let him in, then went to make us all coffee.'

'How did he seem?'

She thought about this for a moment. 'Looking back on it, nervous, maybe.'

'So, you went up to make coffee,' Cross prompted her.

'I boiled the kettle, got out the cafetière, put coffee in it, took out three cups, got the milk from the fridge. Then I heard shouting. Both of them yelling at each other. Then there was a loud kind of gasp, followed by nothing,' she said.

'You said previously it was a scream,' Cross pointed out.

'It wasn't. It was quieter than that. I heard Dad shouting. Like he was frightened or something. I went to the top of the stairs, and he ran out of the room onto the landing.'

'Did he see you?'

'Yes. He stopped and looked up,' she replied.

'Did he say anything?' asked Cross.

'No. He just looked terrified. Like he'd just seen something awful. Then he turned away and ran down the stairs,' she said.

'What did you do?' asked Cross.

'I went down to the first floor.' She started to weep. 'Ed was lying there, so pale.'

'Was he alive?' asked Cross.

'There was blood on his chest, seeping out. I thought he was dead at first. Then he looked at me.' A fresh cascade of tears prevented her from speaking for a moment. 'He smiled,' she said in disbelief. 'He smiled and said, "I'm so sorry." Then he died. He just stopped breathing with this awful, final, gentle sigh. I couldn't believe it. I didn't know what to do. I had no idea Dad was going to do that. I mean, he was obviously so angry. Maybe Ed attacked him and it was self-defence?' she suggested desperately. 'Then I saw the letter opener.'

'Where was it?' asked Ottey.

Persephone paused for a moment, as if coming to terms with the reality of what she was about to tell them.

'It was in his chest,' she said. Ottey looked at Cross. But he was still focused on the young woman. 'It all happened so quickly. I wanted to protect my dad, I think. I pulled it out. It made this awful sticky, gloopy kind of sound. I keep having nightmares about it. I put it in my holdall downstairs, then ran upstairs and locked myself in the bathroom.'

'Leaving Torquil to discover his dead son on his return,' Cross pointed out.

'I know. How terrible is that? But I wasn't thinking about that. I was only thinking about my dad,' she replied. 'Why? I have no idea. Maybe it was just a reflex.'

'You told us you heard Russian accents,' said Cross.

'I know. I'm sorry.'

'That the man was wearing a black bomber jacker, similar to ones worn by club bouncers,' he continued.

'Why did you cover up for him?' asked Ottey.

'I wasn't thinking straight. It was wrong, I know. But he's my dad and Ed was gone. Why did he do that? Why didn't he talk to me? I could've explained. Ed had given me a job. Everything was good. It just feels…'

'It just feels, what?' asked Ottey gently.

'A bit late to start behaving like my dad, to be honest. Like he cared all of a sudden. Ed has been so much more of a father than him, despite everything. Is this all my fault?' she then asked desperately.

'Of course it isn't,' replied Ottey, reflecting that the young woman's thinking was so confused. She'd had a sexual relationship with this man, after all. A therapist would have a field day with her.

'It's such a bloody mess,' said Persephone. 'I'm not sure I'll ever get over this.'

'It'll take time. But you will,' Ottey assured her.

'You seem quite conflicted about your father. You didn't want him to get into trouble for killing your uncle, so you protected him,' commented Cross. 'And yet here you are. On your own, without his protection or help. He's nowhere to be seen and by doing what you did for him, you now find yourself in a great deal of trouble. Something to think about going forward, perhaps.'

'Bloody coward,' Ottey said to Cross as they walked back to their office. 'Leaving his daughter with her dying uncle. Someone he's just killed. What kind of man does that?'

'It would seem as though it goes to form with him,' Cross replied.

54

The jury took just ten hours to return a verdict on Robert Warner. They came to their conclusion at the end of a day and so delivery was delayed until first thing the next morning. Alice wondered whether this was a discreet way of the judge giving all interested parties a chance to get to Bristol Crown Court in time. She and Swift were there ridiculously early, she thought. Only to discover so was everyone else. The two women who'd been raped by Warner were there and sent an encouraging smile over in Alice's direction. None of the victims concerned in the case seemed inclined to speak with each other. Maybe it was a case of not wanting to tempt fate. Cross, Ottey and Carson were there, so she went over to them.

'Hello, Alice,' Carson began. 'How are things going at Portishead?'

'Great. I'm enjoying it,' she replied.

'I'm sure you're doing fantastically well,' he said.

'How are you feeling?' asked Ottey. 'About all of this?'

'Um, I don't know. I hope for the sake of those two women,' she said, looking over at them, 'that he's sent down for a long time. My part in it all seems a little unimportant,' she said.

'Bullshit. What he did to you was appalling. It's not unimportant and you mustn't think of it as anything less than it is. An attack on you by a sexual predator, who needs taking off the streets,' Ottey chided her gently.

'So, great result with the bookseller,' Alice said, trying to change the subject. Then as she saw the expression on Cross's face she modified this statement. 'I didn't mean it like that. Nothing great about a murder case, obviously. Has an arrest been made yet?'

'No,' replied Cross. 'I think he'll be arrested in Spain relatively soon, but extradition could take months.'

They were called into court. Everyone took their seats in silence. There wasn't even the faintest murmur of whispered, anticipatory conversation.

Warner was brought up from the cells. His suit looked a little baggier on him. He'd lost even more weight. His shirt collar was at least an inch too big for him now, the gap between it and his neck conveying an almost pitiful vulnerability. This time he averted his eyes from the public gallery where his victims and some of their family sat. Instead, he concentrated his gaze on the jury. Maybe he thought this might have an effect on them. One last attempt to sway them in his favour. If that was the case, he was deluding himself. It was way too late for that. The decision had been made and was held in the foreperson's hand.

Alice noticed one or two of the jurors were looking intently at Warner. Something they hadn't done on her day in court. Was this because they knew his fate? she wondered. Because they'd found him guilty and could now look him in the face? Or was it just the opposite? That they were setting him free, and their looks were apologetic, for what he'd been through? The air was filled with similar, silent speculation going on inside everyone's minds. A courtroom has a strange, heightened sense of tension when a verdict has been reached and is about to be delivered; a fevered sense of expectation. Preparation for disappointment, anticipation of victory, then the checking of any optimism in case it doesn't go the right way. Different scenarios were playing out in the minds of everyone in court. Alice hoped her relatively firm faith in the British justice system would be endorsed with a guilty verdict. But juries were idiosyncratic organisms.

The judge appeared and asked for the verdicts. Verdicts had been reached on all of the counts, including the attempted rape of Alice. What was more, they were all unanimous.

Guilty.

Warner seemed momentarily stunned by this and bowed his head, shaking it slowly. Whether this was from a sense of disbelief or horror at what lay in store for him in the future, it was difficult to tell. Alice knew that a life in prison was a grim prospect for him as he was not just a convicted rapist and sex offender, a universally despised breed inside, but also an ex-policeman. She watched as beaded sweat broke out across his forehead. He started breathing heavily and then suddenly collapsed in the dock. It was quite a dramatic moment. The judge gave the guards time to attend to Warner, asking if he needed medical assistance. A doctor was called, and the judge cleared the court.

They were back an hour later. Warner took his place in the dock. He looked pale, but calm. The judge reappeared. He was going to sentence straight away. While this wasn't unusual, it wasn't common. He addressed Warner directly and talked about the abhorrent violation of his role as a police officer. He'd abused that position, not just at his place of work, but as a police officer dealing with victims of crime. He had preyed on their vulnerability and trust. He was a figure the public had a right to trust, and his behaviour had driven an incontrovertible wedge through that trust. The public's faith in the police had been increasingly tested by the behaviour of officers like Warner and Sarah Everard's killer, Wayne

Couzens. The judge commented that Warner's preoccupation with incessantly intimidating his victims was truly shocking.

He therefore had no option, in the light of the seriousness and multiple nature of his offences, but to impose a life sentence with a minimum term of fifteen years. For the first time there was another sound in the courtroom other than the judge's voice. It was a collective sigh, maybe of relief, or gratitude, that the right thing had actually been done. Alice, though, felt nothing. Absolutely nothing at all. No elation. No sense of victory. Not even a modicum of relief. Just an acknowledgement that it was all over now, and she wouldn't have to, or rather shouldn't, waste any more emotional energy on it.

As they walked into the hallway outside the court the two rape victims came over and wrapped Alice in a group embrace. She was slightly embarrassed by this, but smiled.

'We're going to make a statement to the press. We've checked it with the chief, who's also making a statement outside HQ. Would you like to stand with us?' one of them asked. Her obvious hesitation prompted Ottey to speak.

'You should,' she said. 'Be a united force.'

The statements were made. A question was asked in the House of Commons later that day, relating to the case. But it wasn't till the evening, when a bunch of people involved in the case, together with Ottey and Jacky Collins from the Kent force, met at a wine bar to celebrate, that Alice put her thumb on what had been troubling her all day. Something she perhaps hadn't wanted to confront before, or admit to. Warner had been found guilty. Had been sent away for fifteen years. But the truth was, she was still frightened. Not of him, obviously. But generally. It was a constant with her. Would it ever go away, or had the bastard damaged her irrevocably?

55

I t had been a stressful few weeks for George Cross. Investigating every case was stressful for him, because of the pressure he always put on himself to get a result. And not just any result, the correct one. He often couldn't settle when working a case because he felt he had to dedicate every waking hour to solve it. He'd been more stressed during this case and felt, on reflection, that it was a culmination of things. His father's stroke during surgery and subsequent rehabilitation was obviously at the top of the list of leading contributors. Warner's trial had also been in the back of his mind and it was only today, when the verdict came in, that he understood why. It was his concern for Alice. She'd behaved with remarkable composure when she'd been attacked. Her determination to pursue Warner in the courts was brave and had encouraged others to come forward. So, he was pleased that she had been vindicated by the verdict and sentence today. But he was troubled by the lasting effect he suspected it might have on her.

The third factor, obviously, was the case of Ed Squire's murder. Although they had reached the right conclusion in the end, the fact was that the killer was still at large somewhere in Spain. When an Interpol warrant had finally been sanctioned, he'd fled the family home. All in all, it was an unsatisfactory outcome for Cross that could take months to resolve, if they ever managed to find him. But he knew there was nothing he could do but put his case together for the prosecution for when Hartwell was hopefully brought before a court. It was something he enjoyed and took great pride in. The situation also made him realise that, despite never even acknowledging it to himself, let alone his colleagues, he took a great deal of satisfaction out of coming to a successful conclusion in an investigation. He hadn't really known this about himself before. Or if he had, paid it much thought. He was puzzled by Ian Hartwell that he could have left his daughter in such a situation with her dying uncle and, even worse, knowing now that she was in custody, had not surrendered himself to the authorities. He'd made a mess of his family with Sarah, had now, for different reasons, done the same thing with his Spanish family, and literally destroyed his sister's. He wondered what kind of a man, what kind of a father, could do that. People could be so surprising, he learned constantly through his work. He couldn't imagine Raymond ever treating him with anything but consideration and kindness. He would never have abandoned his child in the way Hartwell had with Persephone. This then made him think about his mother and how she had abandoned him and the assumptions he'd made about that, which turned out to be wrong. He had been under the impression all of his life that she had left because of his behaviour as a child. But it was far from the truth. A truth that was in itself complex and possibly a product of its time. Having said that, despite her maternal bonds, she had left him, her child.

On top of all of this there was the little matter of his partner's recent promotion. Something they hadn't had time to discuss. Or perhaps it was something they'd avoided. But it would have implications for the future. Would he need a new partner? If so, who would it be and would it work out? Another subliminal source of stress for Cross.

He packed up his things for the day to go and see his father and do their daily speech therapy. He'd been invited to the wine bar, of course, and, of course, wouldn't be going. As he was clearing up Ottey appeared. She was holding the envelope containing his resignation letter.

'Carson asked me to give you this and find out whether you'd changed your mind,' she said.

Cross took it and looked at it for a moment.

'I have,' he replied, putting it in his desk drawer.

'Then why are you keeping it?' she asked.

'In case it comes in useful in the future,' he replied.

'Have you told Raymond?'

'I have.'

'How did he take it?

'He was happy, I think.'

The truth was he had been as shocked at his father's unrestrained joy in receiving this news as he had been by his upset reaction when he first told him.

'I'm sure he was. What made you change your mind?' she asked.

'It clearly wasn't something he wanted,' he said.

'He's extremely proud of you and what you do.'

'So my mother told me,' he said.

'Did you need telling?' she asked. He thought for a moment.

'No. It's something I have been aware of all my life. He makes a point of informing me of it on an almost weekly basis,' he replied.

'I love Raymond,' she said.

Cross didn't know how to respond to this.

'For what it's worth,' she said, 'I think you've made the right decision.'

'Surprisingly that is worth more to me than I expected,' he said.

'This place wouldn't be the same without you,' she commented.

'No, it wouldn't,' he agreed. She smiled. He was impossible at times but also impossible not to love.

56

Cross and Ottey waited patiently in the arrivals hall of Bristol airport for the flight from Malaga. After six months of red tape, Ian Hartwell was finally being extradited to England. He had tried to evade arrest in Spain but only managed this for a couple of weeks. A couple of DCs were accompanying him on the flight back to where he belonged, in Cross's opinion – in their custody. He looked tired, his tan a little faded from months in a Spanish prison cell. He said nothing to them as they took him to their car and nothing on the way back to the MCU. Was it resignation, or arrogance? Cross wondered.

'Why didn't you surrender yourself to the Spanish authorities?' asked Cross in the interview room. 'And why fight extradition?' Cross was genuinely baffled and wanted to know. 'I ask because you knew we had your daughter in custody. Sarah told you. And yes, we know you were in touch with her. Did you not feel as Persephone's father the need to come back and get her out of trouble? You knew she was an eyewitness. Obviously, you didn't know what she might or might not have told us, or whether she'd told us anything at all. Maybe she was still blinded by her need to impress her father, to get his attention. Something she'd craved but been denied for so many years?'

Hartwell said nothing.

'We have an eyewitness, Mr Hartwell. Your own daughter. We know you arrived in Bristol the day of the murder and not the day after as you claimed. We know you called her saying you wanted to talk to her uncle, Ed Squire, that night. We know she let you in. We know she saw you on the stairs after your altercation with Ed and that she discovered him in a pool of blood in his office. We have your DNA on the letter opener you used to kill your brother-in-law. All we're lacking is the why,' said Cross, almost conversationally. Hartwell looked up after a moment.

'I didn't mean to kill him,' he said.

'But you did,' Cross affirmed.

'What happened?' asked Ottey.

'I just wanted to let him know that I knew,' he replied.

'About what?' asked Ottey.

'That he was responsible for my daughter's pregnancy,' he said, as if it should be obvious.

'You flew all the way from Spain just to tell him you knew?' asked Cross.

'Yes.'

'Why?'

'Because I wanted him to know we all knew and it wasn't okay.'

'Was that the only reason you came to the UK?' asked Cross.

'Yes.'

'Or was it to kill him?' Cross went on.

'No,' came the urgent reply.

'Your ex-wife, Sarah Hartwell—' began Cross.

'I know who my ex-wife is,' interrupted Hartwell.

'—told us she informed you of Ed's being responsible for your daughter's pregnancy the day before,' Cross went on.

'That's right.'

'How would you describe your reaction to this news?' asked Cross.

'I was angry. Obviously. Who wouldn't be?'

'Which is why you got on a plane the next day to confront him,' Cross suggested.

'Yes.'

'Were you still angry?'

'Well, yes. I'd calmed down a bit though.'

'But you were still angry,' commented Cross.

'Not angry enough to kill him,' he said. The detectives said nothing, their silence implying their doubt. 'Look, I'm her father. What would you expect me to do?'

'Any assumptions about what a father might or might not do are slightly clouded in your case, wouldn't you agree?' asked Cross.

'Yes, fine. I know I may not have been the best of fathers,' Hartwell began.

'That's one way of putting it,' Ottey chimed in.

'All right. Point taken. I was a shit father. But things had recently got better with Percy,' he said.

'So much so that when you heard she was in custody, you absquatulated,' said Cross.

'What?' Hartwell asked.

'You fled,' Ottey translated.

'I know, not one of my finer moments as a dad,' he acknowledged.

'Do you have any?' asked Ottey.

'We were back in regular contact. She came out to Spain, met the boys, her new family. It was great,' he recalled.

'This was before Oxford,' asked Cross. Hartwell paused as he processed how much they obviously knew.

'Yeah. I came back more often after that,' he said quietly.

'After what?' Cross asked. Hartwell looked at him. Cross looked straight back. Yes, he wanted him to say it. Out loud.

'Her suicide attempt. I felt I had to be part of the problem. A big part, according to Sarah. I wanted to take responsibility and help,' he said.

'How did you feel about her working at the bookshop?' asked Ottey.

'I was pleased.'

'Were you grateful to Ed?' asked Cross. Hartwell paused while he thought about this.

'Yes, I was actually.'

'How would you describe your relationship with him?' asked Cross.

'I don't know. Normal brother-in-law stuff, I guess.'

'I don't know what that is,' replied Cross.

'We weren't the best of mates. I always thought he patronised me a bit, if I'm honest. Always condescending about my work, particularly when I moved to Spain. As if inheriting a bookshop from your dad made you somehow superior,' he answered.

'How did you feel about Persephone moving in with your sister and Ed when she was a teenager?' asked Cross.

'I was grateful. Relieved, to be honest. Sarah was a mess. It was something I didn't need to worry about for a while.'

'Well, that's certainly something you took to heart,' said Ottey. He sighed and had no response.

'Why did you stab him?' asked Cross.

'He was just so outrageous when I told him I knew. It was unbelievable. Said I was a shit father, which obviously I wasn't going to take issue with. But then he tried to say that her getting pregnant was in some way my fault. That I'd put them in that position. Can you believe that? I was to blame for him sleeping with my teenage daughter? He was supposed to be an interim parent, as it were,' he said, shaking his head in disbelief.

'What else?' asked Cross.

'He said she was obviously looking for a father figure in her life as I wasn't there and she turned to him. The lines got blurred. She was fifteen, for Chrissake! He was supposed to be caring for her.'

'But how did it build up to your killing him?' pushed Cross.

'Because he said that. That it was my fault. Came right out and said it. Took no responsibility for it. He raped my girl and he has the nerve to say that. I couldn't believe what I was hearing. I don't think I've ever been so outraged or angry in my life. I didn't mean to kill him. You have to believe me. I just wanted to hurt him. It was like the only thing I had in my power. To hurt him like he'd hurt Percy. But it just went straight in. He looked at me, so shocked. I just stared at it sticking out of his chest and ran,' he said.

'Leaving your daughter alone with her dying uncle,' said Cross.

'I know. Yet again the dreadful father. But I panicked. I left her completely in the lurch. I felt so guilty.'

'Not guilty enough, apparently, to come forward when you knew she was in custody,' Ottey pointed out.

'I have a young family,' he said weakly.

'I was under the impression she *was* family,' said Ottey. 'I suppose you've just got used to not thinking of her as such, which I'm sure goes to the heart of her problems with you.'

He said nothing. It was as if he didn't have the emotional energy to challenge something which was so obviously true.

'What had you said to her when we saw you at her flat?' asked Cross.

'I told her I was sorry. She was distraught, obviously. I mean, for better or worse, even after what happened when she was young, she loved him,' he said.

'Like a father, perhaps?' suggested Ottey who was in no mood to go easy on this man.

'She was all over the place. Then when you arrived, she was like a different person. It was amazing really. We'd agreed that I should go back to Spain and see if it all blew over.'

'Murders don't tend to just blow over,' said Cross.

'It was odd,' continued Hartwell, almost as if he was thinking out loud and consoling himself in some peculiar way. 'She was angry with me. So angry and, like I said, distraught. But in a way it felt like it made us closer. What's going to happen to her now?' he asked.

'A bit late to concern yourself with that, don't you think?' asked Cross.

Epilogue

A year later

'Ian Hartwell was... today... found guilty of the murder of... Ed Squire, a Bristol... bookseller. In another... sterling piece of... investigative work by... the incomp... arable Detective Sergeant... George Cross...'

'It doesn't say that,' protested George as his father did his daily reading exercise with him from the *Bristol Evening Post*.

'It doesn't... but it should,' replied Raymond, whose speech was improving week on week.

'Hear, hear,' said George's mother as she walked into the room with a tray of tea and home-made biscuits.

'Are those...?' began George.

'Chocolate chip, yes,' she replied. 'What do you think he'll get?'

The judge was sentencing Hartwell in a few weeks' time.

'I'm not sure,' he said, snatching a biscuit from the passing tray, like a greedy child forgetting his manners. 'Life with a minimum term, probably. The defence will try and argue mitigating circumstances, as the victim had impregnated his daughter when she was an underage teenager,' said Cross, thinking out loud.

'Isn't that...' Raymond began, searching for the right word. 'Oh, help me out,' he pleaded.

'No!' they replied in unison.

'INCEST!' he finally bellowed in triumph.

'She was his niece by marriage. So, technically not, no,' Cross informed him.

'But nevertheless, it was a terrible abuse of his position,' commented Christine.

'It was indeed,' concurred George.

'What happened to her? The girl. I didn't read anything in the papers,' Christine went on.

'She was given a suspended sentence for concealing the knife and obstructing the police,' he replied.

'Poor girl. That family must be in tatters,' she said.

He imagined it was. Victoria and her children had been in court every day. Torquil hadn't appeared once. He was in the process, apparently, of selling the business and the freehold to Nigel Simpson, who had found a mystery investor to back the new venture. He was based in Somerset, apparently, and didn't want to be named. Rumour had it he was Russian. The new business was to be called Berkeley Square Books and Sam Taylor was made the shop manager, much to his undoubted delight. Torquil Squire and Denholm Simpson, now speaking again, finding their disagreement was much diminished by the intervening decades and comfort they found in each other's company, were made emeritus chairmen. The plan for the Park Street store was to convert it into a small independent bookshop, selling new books. A young woman called Aimee Gilbert, who had worked in Waterstones previously, was going to run it. Her enthusiasm for the new venture was boundless. She had a real love of books and had a clear view of the direction the shop should take. Persephone had, charitably, George thought, been offered a job there. But it seemed recent events had taken their toll on her emotionally and she couldn't face it. She was assured there would always be a job for her there if she changed her mind.

Christine had sold her house in Gloucester and was in the process of looking for somewhere to buy in Bristol, ideally close to Raymond. There had been one or two near misses but as yet, nothing had been found. George had observed over the months how devoted she'd been to his father's rehabilitation. But it was more than that. He noticed how his father was significantly happier. He looked healthier. Maybe that was down to her cooking. His appearance and personal hygiene were on a new level altogether. That wasn't to say he had ever been filthy, or smelly, just that there had been occasional lapses before her reappearance on the scene. He also realised that he'd been worrying about his father less of late. He knew this was because he was secure in the knowledge not only that he was being looked after, but also that he wasn't on his own. He had company. They had formed a routine together, Christine and Raymond. Did the morning crossword after breakfast – 'He's quite competitive you know,' Christine had told George one day, not that he needed telling – and listened to their favourite programmes on Radio 4 together. They went for short walks to the corner shop. With all this in mind, George had come to a decision which had surprised even himself. He was in truth very pleased with himself and wanted to inform them of it as soon as possible.

'How is the flat hunting going?' he asked her.

'Quite well,' Christine replied. 'But Bristol is a lot more expensive than where I was in Gloucester. I have another viewing on Saturday morning which we're quite hopeful about, aren't we, Raymond?' He nodded in agreement.

'Cancel it,' George instructed her.

'Why?'

'Because it seems to me to be a pointless exercise in which

you will only lose money to estate agents, lawyers and stamp duty,' he informed her.

'Well, that's just the way it is, George,' Christine protested.

Raymond said nothing. Partly because of the effort of joining in. When a break in conversation came up, he often found that by the time he'd thought of the word he was searching for, the conversation had started again or, frequently, moved on to another subject altogether.

'The point is, you both seem to enjoy each other's company,' George began.

'Well of course we do. We were married once,' Christine pointed out.

'And... had a child,' added Raymond.

'Yes,' laughed Christine. 'And brought you into the world.'

'I think you should spend that money on doing things together that give you pleasure. I understand people of your age enjoy going on cruises, for example,' he continued.

'But where am I supposed to live?' asked Christine.

'Well, here of course. Where else? Continue to live with Dad, but on a permanent basis. It makes complete sense,' he said.

There was a stunned silence from both his parents. This was a huge turnabout for George who had been so wary of his mother's reintroduction into their lives. They were speechless.

'Well, I wasn't expecting that, George,' Christine finally said.

'Thank you... George,' Raymond said. George said nothing. He just nodded in acknowledgement. The situation was in danger of getting emotional and therefore uncomfortable for him. 'I'm so glad... you said this.'

'It's very considerate of you, George, to suggest this,' his mother said. She looked a bit teary at this juncture. Her face reddened. His father was also gazing at him intently with his lopsided smile. Cross suddenly felt bathed in a pool of keenly felt parental gratitude which made him even more uncomfortable.

'Excellent, then there's nothing more to be said,' replied George, who got up speedily, nodded to them both and left before they got the idea that this new arrangement should be celebrated with a group hug or some other unwelcome gesture of emotional manifestation.

As he watched him leave, Raymond couldn't remember being more proud of his son.

His parents' living arrangements hadn't been the only things on George Cross's mind recently. He'd had ample opportunity to reflect on his proposed resignation from the Avon and Somerset Police a year earlier. What had surprised him was that the prospect of life outside of the police had been a far less frightening one than he might have otherwise imagined. There were plenty of things to occupy his time in a meaningful way. The idea of a life not preoccupied with murder and death suddenly seemed welcome. Did this mean his appetite for his work as a murder detective was perhaps waning?

Acknowledgements

IT'S HARD to believe this is already the seventh outing for George Cross and his team. I still love writing his character and thank you all for taking him into your hearts so generously.

I couldn't do it without the encouragement and support of my own team and there are several to thank. As ever, my editor, Bethan Jones, for her patience and constant positivity about GC and most importantly her belief in my writing ability and my detective. Lucy Ridout for her concise and constructive notes, as well as her understanding of George, all of which go to make the books so much better. Liz Hatherell for her eagle-eyed copy edit. The team at Head of Zeus, Peyton Stableford, Andrew Knowles, Polly Grice, Matt Bray, Emily Champion, Nikky Ward, Karen Dobbs, Jo Liddiard and Daniel Groenewald for all their hard work in getting George out into the world. My social media duo, Sarah Oldman and Lily Hill, for their tireless creativity. My agent, Sarah Hornsley, for her sage advice, encouragement and guidance. Angela McMahon, my PR, who works so hard to get me and the work wider recognition not only with the reading public but the crime writing community.

Thanks to the many booksellers I spoke to when researching this novel. Your advice and knowledge were invaluable. Particularly David Headley for his pertinent and entertaining insights into the world of modern bookselling and Bernard

Shapero for pointing me in the direction of the Columbus letters. Also to Sheila Markham for her advice and giving me her two volumes of Interviews with Booksellers, which were brilliantly insightful. To booksellers as a whole, my thanks. I'm sorry I bumped one of your number off. I do hope you forgive me. Booksellers are the lifeblood of all writers the world over. A special shout out to all the independent booksellers for your dedication to the written word. There's nothing like visiting an indie bookshop. It is such an individual experience with their knowledge shared with joyful abandon. I love the curated experience of a local bookshop, being introduced to authors they think you will like that you've never come across before.

To all the bloggers out there who have taken the time not only to read my work but also write encouragingly about it, thank you so much. Lastly, to you the reader, I still can't believe you exist and am so grateful you do. Thanks for taking the time to read and also for getting in touch. It is always so rewarding to hear from you and without you reading, well what would be the point of all this...

About the Author

Tim Sullivan is a crime writer, screenwriter and director, whose film credits include *Shrek, Flushed Away, Where Angels Fear to Tread* and *Jack and Sarah*. His crime series featuring the brilliantly persistent DS George Cross has topped the book charts and been widely acclaimed. Tim lives in North London with his wife Rachel, the Emmy Award-winning producer of *The Barefoot Contessa* and *Pioneer Woman*.

To find out more about the author,
please visit www.timsullivan.co.uk.